Table of Contents

YEAR REED
ONE

by
J.S. Dux

*Edited
and Cover Design
by James Van Treese*

Northwest Publishing Inc.
5949 South 350 West
Salt Lake City, Utah 84107
801–266–5900

ISBN #1–56901–109–5

Printed in the United States of America.

Acknowledgements

Thanks to…
Billy, Lucille,
Adreanna Michelle,
Cheryl, Juliette
and the guiding spirit of
Chimalma and Quetzacoatl.

1
The Stowaway

Santiago De Cuba, February fifth, 1519. Tehan willed his eyes to pierce the swirling grey mist in an attempt to spot his comrades lying in wait. In the town below him, early morning cooking fires started to glow while sleepy cocks began their crows for supremacy. The gradual lightening of the eastern sky soon sharpened into distinct forms and Tehan was able to spot his friend Kon. Laying a few feet away, Kon had pulled leaves and ferns around his bare skinned torso for camouflage and warmth against the early morning spring chill.

Tehan pulled his wool cloak closer around him. The brown garment was Tehan's pride and joy, taken from a Spanish soldier in a raid two months ago. For Tehan it represented a small victory against the "hairfaces" who had managed to ruin his people's lives in the few short years since they'd arrived on the island of Cuba.

Tehan let his eyes roam over the increasingly visible lines of the small town. This was where the Spanish had settled in the greatest numbers since they'd first come crashing through the peaceful Cubino jungles, looking for land to steal and the yellow rocks they called gold. High white walls and red tiled roofs marked the places the invaders called their homes. Claiming vast tracks of land, they had forced his people to toil over their domains, many of them dying from the labor and brutality. They even subjected them to life in tight little hovels packed together unnaturally. The cruelty and severe living conditions coursed his blood hot with anger and now he and several of his friends walked the trail of vengeance. Raiding the Spanish haciendas, they would nip and bite, take what they could, then withdraw to the jungles, hoping perhaps the Spanish

1

would go back to where they came from.

A signal from their leader sent the men scurrying across the road. Tehan almost tripped and fell on a low vine as they ran down the wooded incline that led into the Indian quarter of town. He raised a finger of silence to his lips as he passed the first hovel. A young woman sat in the doorway, her infant child suckling contentedly from her breast. The group of men moved silently around the huts, heading for the docks. Their prize goal was the stocks of foodstuffs they had seen being unloaded from the hacienda wagons, being provisions for the fleet of giant floating house canoes anchored in the harbor. It would feed their families for weeks.

Suddenly, one of the village dogs began barking, and soon a dozen more joined in. Just ahead of him he saw Kon fit a slender arrow to his bow as his pace picked up to a run. Then Spanish voices rose in alarm as the first raider was spotted. Tehan pushed a young girl of about nine back into her hut for safety as he passed by. With the nearby roar of musket fire, Tehan felt the hand of fear clench around his gut. His uncle had been killed by a "firestick" two years ago. He'd taken a basket of grain to feed his family, and a Spanish patrol had run him into the jungle, not content until he was dead. This happened at the other Spanish stronghold to the west, the one they called Havana.

Tehan now realized that without the element of surprise, they would never make it to the docks. All they could do was aggravate and run. He and Kon ducked into a doorway just as fire rang out again. They watched helplessly as Kon's cousin crumpled into a lifeless heap. Stepping out of the doorway, Kon let fly an arrow that found its mark in the unprotected throat of his cousin's assassin. The Spaniard fell, clutching the retaliatory shaft.

"For Spain!" echoed the call through the air, as suddenly the area was overrun with mounted riders. Retreating down a high-walled street, they looked back to see if any of the Spanish had spotted them. Tehan tripped over a slat-ribbed dog, sending it yipping ahead of them, its yelp lost in the din of the battle behind them.

The sound of women and children screaming marked the battle's progress into the Indian section as the conquistadors pursued the raiders. Undetected, Tehan and Kon soon found themselves deep in the Spanish section. Kon slumped against a wall in anger and pain at his cousin's death. Many of their friends had been cut down this morning. Tonight their women would cry and more of their children would go to bed with empty bellies.

Tehan put out a hand to soothe his friend and encourage him to hurry. Such a look of hatred came over his friend's face that Tehan stood back instead. "I'll kill them, I'll kill them all," Kon rasped. Tehan stood in the center of the alley, eyeing the nearby fields and his avenue of escape. He looked back at Kon's retreating form moving deeper into the Spanish section. Making his decision, he followed his incensed friend, praying the gods would grant them a successful coup.

Tehan grabbed Kon's arm, wrestling him into a doorway as a group of Spanish riders rounded the corner. "Brother, it's better to kill our enemies with the stealth of a spotted cat of the jungle than to allow the "smelly ones" to run you down like a feeble hare. Control your anger, that it may serve you." Slowly the wild look left Kon's eyes, but an angry glint remained.

To their surprise, the heavy wood door they crouched against opened, revealing a small courtyard. The men grinned at each other; maybe the gods would smile upon them this day. The smell of roasting meat, a slapping sound, and an angry voice permeated the air. They worked their way across the courtyard to an open kitchen door where huge chunks of meat roasted on a spit over an open fire.

Grabbing their attention was a fleshy man, his heavy black beard grizzled with gray. He was shouting and lashing out at the frail form of an Indian boy no more than ten years of age.

Curled in a ball, the boy was attempting to protect his head and face from the heavy leather strap. A deep, red liquid rolled across the floor from a nearby broken wine cask; it was too heavy for such a small boy to be carrying.

Anger was soon replaced by a look of surprise on the Spaniard's face as the two nearly naked men sprang through his kitchen door. The offending strap fell from his upraised hand as Kon's arrow plunged into his chest. He slit the still thrashing Spaniard's throat while Tehan pulled the dazed boy to a sitting position. Soothing the frightened boy, they sent him on his way with some meat for his family. Liberating the rest of the roasting meat and a good sized sack of corn meal for themselves, they stole from the kitchen. As they fled the hacienda grounds, Tehan scooped up a tan, wool cloak off a wooden railing. He threw it to Kon; their victory was complete.

As they ran they came upon a solitary rider. The chestnut mare reared in the air at the whooping onslaught of the two warriors. The red-cloaked, hooded figure struggled to control its mount. Kon lunged, pulling the rider from its perch. A feminine scream pierced the air. "A woman!" He shouted in triumph, "Now we do to their women as they have done to ours."

Just then Kon's face was stung by the bite of a riding crop and Tehan groaned, a well placed kick connecting with his body. Then the woman was up and running, her hood falling back and a mass of red-gold curls dancing in the early morning sun. Kon caught the molten colored hair, yanking her backwards and tripping her in a pile of voluminous skirts.

Their eyes widened at the appearance of their captive. She had a heart shaped face covered by skin so pale and translucent, it resembled the precious alabaster that occasionally made its way to Cuba from the mainland. Sooty lashes framed eyes as green as the lush plants of the jungle. Full, red lips covered perfect white teeth, and a delicately upturned nose finished the remarkable profile.

No old crone was this, nor even a stout matron, but one young and ripe. The warriors forgot their original plan of leaving her sprawled in the street with a slit throat. Eyeing the gold cross resting in the hollow of her throat and the rich fabrics of her bodice, they knew this one was too valuable. They would take her into the jungle as a hostage. The Spanish would surely want her back, making her worth much grain to their tribe. Besides, thought Tehan as he rubbed his bruised groin, she would serve other purposes as well.

They wrestled to carry her out of town as she kicked and screamed. It was like trying to carry a hornets' nest. Kon winced as she bit the hand he placed over her mouth. She managed to get out one more scream before Tehan's fist knocked her into oblivion.

They were so intent on their struggle, they didn't hear or see the horsemen until they were upon them.

Manuel Ortez, a tall, good-looking man with black hair and a mustache was the first to see the two natives in loincloths and wool cloaks carrying a woman in Spanish dress. Spotting the patrol, they dropped the woman and ran. An arquebus roared and one of the Indians grabbed his thigh, but ran on. "Damn!" Manuel swore as they rounded the corner and got away. The native quarter was right there and beyond that were the woods. Two horsemen followed, but Manuel doubted that they would catch the agile little devils. He reigned in his horse at the fallen form of the Spanish woman. Turning her over gently, he caught his breath. It was Maria! What was she doing out here alone at this hour?

The short, round figure hurried down the halls of the Ortez Hacienda. "I always knew that child would get in big trouble someday," Itza confirmed to herself. She knew Maria had gone riding alone that morning. Their hosts, the Ortez's, had thought she took an escort but Itza knew there was no way that fat, old Alfonso could keep up with Maria. It was even probable that Maria would gallop away from Alfonso on purpose. That headstrong girl had kept Itza on her toes since that day six months ago when she had come to work for her uncle, the Cuban governor, Diego De Velaquez.

Itza knew that because she was Indian, the governor hadn't wanted her as maid for his niece. Maria had picked her and would have no other. Since then Maria had treated her as a friend and not as a servant. She'd discovered that Maria filled that place in her heart she thought dead and buried. But now Itza's heart was heavy. After this morning's escapade, her uncle would surely demand Maria's return to Havana and he would most likely send Maria back to her parents in Spain.

Itza had heard the talk in many places that it was time for Maria to marry. Fondly she remembered back to the time her father had given her in marriage to the tall, young man with an easy laugh. The happy years they spent together were clouded with only one black memory. Itza shooed the dark spot from her mind as she pushed open the heavy, studded door marking Maria's chambers.

Entering the airy, white plastered chamber with terra cotta tile floors, she removed her black knitted shawl with small, work worn hands. It was the shawl she had worn in mourning for that young man of long ago. He had died a beaten man, his back broken from being worked into the ground by his Spanish taskmasters. Because he believed in the good of every man, he had even accepted their long suffering Christ upon his instrument of torture. He'd coaxed Itza to learn their ugly Spanish tongue, a skill she now begrudgingly thanked her husband for. It kept her from being just another old, Indian widow wandering the streets looking for handouts.

Noting the empty bed, Itza's heart jumped. Where was Maria now? Searching the chambers with her quick, roving eyes, she settled her gaze on Maria's white clad figure standing on the tiny half moon verandah. The young woman's figure, with just the last traces of childlike plumpness, was clearly silhouetted through the thin chemise she wore. She was nervously toying with her rosary. A closer look and Itza guessed that Maria was again questioning what other women just accepted...her future.

Itza hoped the girl wasn't thinking about that strange place again, that place the Spanish called a convent. She knew Maria had been schooled in a convent back in Spain, but to enter one to stay forever was unnatural. Women locked up together, all denying their purpose in life made no sense to her! Besides, wasn't the one they called Blessed Mary a mother and wife? Itza would never understand these people. Shaking her head, she silently turned to tidy up the chamber.

The late morning sun glimmered on the gentle swells of the bay. Scores of rowboats heavily laden with provisions paddled back and forth between the docks and the cluster of corracks, brigantines and caravels that waited hungrily in the center of the harbor. An inquisitive sparrow alighted on a branch of the tree nearest Maria's balcony. Then almost in bemusement, it hopped to the railing edge to study the girl. Maria stared straight ahead unnoticing, as her mind seethed and reeled and her fingers mindlessly tied her rosary into knots.

They had no right to interfere, she thought to herself. It was her life and who was to say she wouldn't be happy in a convent here in Cuba. Yesterday, she had gone to visit the Mother Superior in hopes of staying and had almost been pushed out the door. Her uncle must have paid the Mother handsomely to try and convince her not to wear a habit, but to return to Spain instead. She looked down at the crumpled sheets of paper by her feet and picked up the letter, smoothing it out. Hoping she'd missed a clue, she read it again for the sixth time:

Castile, Spain
December 14, 1518

My dearest Maria,
 It is the eve of the Grand Duke's Winter Ball, and as I prepare for the festivities, my mind reaches out to you so far away during this Christmas season. My dear, you should be here. Just last week Don Diego De Orion, the younger brother of the Viscount, asked about you and showed interest in speaking to your father on your behalf. He's very well received at court and is a fine figure of a young man.

"Fine figure of a man," she said out loud. "He looks like a toad."

 Really my dear, with so many suitors asking for you, you should be in Castile. I think it's high time for your return. Please, Maria, show more discretion when you write your friend Dona Cecillia. Her mother has been spreading rumors all over Castile that it's your desire to enter the convent. Darling, we know this isn't the truth, now is it? How can one expect to attract a proper suitor with absurd rumors like that? Everyone knows she's only spreading these tales to make her unfortunately plain daughter more attractive.
 Oh, I'm sorry my dear, I know Dona Cecillia is your friend, but it's just that it makes it hard for your father and I, when so much transpires and you're not here for proper presentation. After all, Maria, you are now sixteen and this is the year you can make your best impressions. You shouldn't be wasting it in Cuba. Before you know it, you will be eighteen and too old. People will think there's

something wrong with you.

Just last month at the festival honoring the holy expulsion of the Moors and Jews from our divinely favored country, Don Gaspar requested as to your whereabouts. He'd heard a rumor that you had contracted a disfiguring disease and almost accused us of hiding you. Can you imagine such a thing? Now do you see why it's imperative you return immediately?

Do you want to be an old maid, a girl with your looks and breeding? Maria, we've given you every opportunity to be seen in the right circles and have worked hard on preserving your good name, which hasn't been easy after some of your younger pranks and exploits. We've assured everyone that you've become quite a sensible young lady, and that the years spent in the convent school with the good sisters has straightened you out and prepared you to become a upstanding dutiful wife."

Maria sighed as she thought of her older cousin Amilia, who had married three years ago. Always laughing and happy as a child, she was now married to a duke three times her age. Maria shuddered as she remembered watching Amilia grow more and more somber and colorless, until she resembled the gray walls of the ancient castle she resided in, living only for her babies. Returning to the letter she read on.

Enough of that, perhaps you would like to hear some family news. Do you remember your second cousin Don Francisco, the one who became a priest? Well, he's taken a wife. A woman from the small village his parish was in. He's joined an order of the church that still allows that sort of thing. We've heard the Holy Father will outlaw marriage soon in all orders, and I wonder what your cousin will do then. Well, that side of the family was never quite proper.

The harvests are still bad and market prices are horrendous. One cannot even entertain properly. Some say it's because of the Moors and Jews having been expelled, but

I believe it's those heathen Medicis. Their greed is destroying all the decency in Europe.

Well, daughter, I now need to go prepare for tomorrow's ball. And don't worry, we'll keep your name in all the right ears. My dear, if you truly wish to become one of the holy sisters, of course we would not oppose your devotion to the Blessed Mother. But before you make such a decision, please come home first so we can properly present you at court.

Court no longer has the pious elegance we experienced during the reign of their most Catholic Majesties Ferdinand and beloved Isabella. King Don Carlos shows none of the responsibility of his uncle Ferdinand. He's outraging all of Castile with his flagrant spending of our money. His Majesty is at least a devoted Catholic, but it's sad that an Austrian upstart sits on the throne of Spain.

In spite of its shortcomings, court would still serve you well. Maria, with your pious beauty you could even, dare I say, marry a grand duke.

Daughter, we send our love and urge your immediate return.

Your mother,
Dona Nina De Velaquez

"I'll make my own decisions!" Maria cried out as she balled up the letter, casting it as far as her frustration would carry.

The dining room doors of the Ortez Hacienda were flung wide open, emitting a heavy odor of garlic and frying pork sausage. A thin, male Cubino Indian was lighting the tallow candles atop the five feet tall wrought iron candelabra. Manuel and Juanita Ortez sat themselves at the heavy wooden table and waited Maria's arrival.

A slight scowl darkened Manuel's face. A tall, handsome man, Manuel had been a captain with Velaquez in his conquest of Cuba eight years earlier. He was brooding on the latest string of Indian raids. There were only a few rebels left in the heart of the jungle; perhaps they'd have to go in there and clean the savages out.

In desperation, the Indians had grown bolder. This morning they'd struck at the center of the largest Spanish town on the island. He knew their target was the provisions on the docks.

They had almost gotten his house guest, Governor Velaquez's niece. He didn't want to think about what the governor would have done had they been successful.

What had she been doing alone on the streets at that time of morning? When he had brought her unconscious body back to the hacienda, he had been so angry he didn't trust himself to be civil—he'd immediately gone to the fields.

"Damn lazy Indians!" he said to his wife. "I had to whip five of them today."

"That's nice dear," she said, unconcerned.

Poor Juanita he thought, she's unhappy here so far away from Spain. Only nineteen and she has already lost all her woman-fire. He watched her smooth back a strand of mud brown hair. Perhaps he'd married too soon, anxious to get back to his holdings in Cuba. Even when they made love she stared lifelessly at the ceiling, waiting for him to finish.

He thought of the young Indian girl who earlier had brushed his arm with her firm young breast as she served him a simple empanada for lunch in the field. She had offered him more with the wiggle of her round hips and dark inviting eyes. Manuel flinched from his thoughts, glancing at his wife as the pretty, young senorita entered the room.

Maria hurried in, begging pardon for being late and quickly slipping into her chair. Manuel studied his guest a moment. "I trust you have quite recovered from your misadventure this morning." Maria steeled herself for what she feared was coming.

"To make sure there are no more mishaps, Alfonso has been relieved as your escort. From now on, if you wish to ride you will inform myself or the horse steward." Maria's mouth flew open to reply but Manuel cut her off. "To assure this, your saddle and bridle have been put in the stronghouse. I have decided not to inform your uncle as to what happened."

Maria knew she shouldn't speak up and was secretly grateful that her uncle wouldn't find out. That would have curtailed the small amount of freedom she had garnered here in Santiago. She would have to be more careful.

Manuel's deep voice led them in prayer and then a servant appeared with a steaming tureen of garlic soup.

"Senorita Maria," began Juanita, "how was your visit to the convent yesterday?"

Maria remained silent; her uncle's interference still rankled her. Not sure she could answer with grace, she changed the subject. "I've received a letter from Spain. My mother says the harvests are still bad."

"What does your mother think of your desire to become a holy sister," she tried again.

"It doesn't sit well with her," Maria said. "She has arranged many suitors for me to consider."

"That's a shame," she said, dwelling on the seeming unjustness between Maria's prospects of the future and her own. "Certainly she would never forbid you to enter the church, if that is what you choose."

"Maria," Manuel spoke up, cutting off Juanita. "You know my wife has planned a ball in your honor. I'm sure you'll be pleased to make acquaintance with the Gentry of Santiago De Cuba." In truth, he knew Juanita had staged it to assure her own prestige among the other ladies of Santiago.

Maria was silent. She was sure it would be tedious, everyone being polite to her on her uncle's behalf...just as it had been in Havana.

As the first course was cleared, a hot vegetable dish of rice, spicy yellow squash and boiled onion appeared. The talk turned to the ships in the harbor and the commerce they had brought to town. Maria learned that the ships were commissioned for a trade expedition to the new lands where a small Indian city had been discovered a few years ago. On this previous voyage usurps of gold had been obtained for next to nothing. Maria already knew about the discovery since her cousin Grijalva had headed the expedition. She hadn't known a second expedition was being launched, nor did she think her cousin was ready to go again.

"Who is to command this expedition?" she asked, feeling

confused. "Why only Hernan Cortez himself my dear," quipped Juanita. He's been sent an invitation to attend your ball and I think it would be a shame if he missed it...certainly his loss," she added smugly.

Maria's blood chilled at the mention of Cortez' name. She thought she had heard her uncle speak of him; she had even perhaps been introduced but she couldn't remember for sure.

"Tell me of him," Maria said.

"Oh my," cooed Juanita. "He's very well known on the island. I'm surprised you haven't heard of his sordid affairs." Manuel shifted uncomfortably in his large oak chair and attempted to deter his wife. "Senor Cortez has been treasurer for your uncle for many years. He's proven his leadership abilities time and again. Cortez has a way of getting men to put their trust in him and has garnered quite a following of loyal comrades. Your uncle is the one who commissioned him on this voyage. In fact, the governor even put up thirty percent towards outfitting it."

Tasting her boiled onion, she turned back to Juanita and asked, "What were the sordid affairs you spoke of?"

"Well, not too many years back a Senor Suarez arrived on the island with his three beautiful, unmarried sisters. The three women caused quite a stir among the bachelor population on Cuba. As you know, we women are outnumbered by the men on the island and I assure you, today is far better than it was then. One of the pretty young girls was just your age, Maria."

Juanita paused to take a bite of her slowly cooling meal. "Her name was Senorita Catalina. Senor Cortez developed quite a fondness for her. Some say he took the courtship past the stage of propriety." Manuel began shifting uncomfortably at the other end of the table, as she continued. "When Catalina's brother and eldest sister got wind of this, they insisted that the young girl's name be upheld and that a marriage make it consummate."

"Catalina's sister had the ear of your uncle at the time." Juanita smiled wickedly, suggesting an unspoken, illicit liaison. "When your uncle and Catalina's brother went to Cortez and demanded he do the honorable thing by the girl, he refused. This so angered your uncle that he threw him in jail until he changed his mind."

Maria was happy to be distracted from her own troubles and prodded Juanita to go on.

"Senor Cortez found a way to trick and overcome his jailer and escaped. He appeared late that night at the governor's palace in a rage and threatened your uncle with a weapon."

"Then what happened?" whispered Maria.

"No one quite knows, my dear."

"Instead of having him executed like everyone expected," Manuel spoke up, "the governor sent him on a mission, where he put down a local uprising and became even more popular."

"Oh, and Senor Cortez did end up marrying the Senorita Catalina. She resides here at his Santiago Hacienda and seems quite content."

Maria had been so engrossed with the story, she now realized she'd finished the third course. It was a plate of crispy pork in a cumin sauce with a whole round of bread and she'd hardly noticed.

Maria was reaching for the heavy, pewter water mug when it happened. She found herself staring at a vibrating, feathered shaft imbedded in the white plastered wall near her head. All at once the room seemed to erupt in chaos. Chairs overturned as a shouting Manuel pushed the women under the table and ordered the servants to fetch weapons. A sound issued forth from Juanita that reminded Maria of hog killing season.

From under the table, Maria watched groups of torch-bearing men race through the garden. The slightest trace of a smile spread across her face. This was an adventure; this is what she'd come to Cuba for.

❖

The Ortez Hacienda held the rich glow of candlelight in every window. The ballroom was ablaze with color and sound, as rows of dancers weaved to and fro to the spell of musicians who were tucked in a corner playing their instruments.

A small figure in a gold trimmed, black velvet dress moved from group to group. In spite of herself, Maria was having a good time. The snatches of conversation she was picking up around her seemed to focus on Cortez and her uncle. But she also heard about savages, gold, witchcraft and even of women warriors...real amazons located on an island off the coast of the new world.

The gentry of Santiago was the elite of the conquering forces of Cuba. Their talk reeked of Spanish might, adventure and the intrigue of an outpost society; all the things her parents had always kept her ears shielded from. It was no wonder her uncle had kept her locked away in the small hamlet of Havana. It held no excitement.

Maria worked her way over to the group surrounding her hostess. Juanita's hair had been woven in tiny intricate braids and she wore a new gown of three skirts posing as one. She had it patterned from one of Maria's and was letting the fashion hungry women study it.

She had launched into a description of how she was almost killed at her dinner table two nights ago; it was all because her husband had hung a native chief in the riots that morning. Maria had heard Juanita tell the story at least a dozen times. Each time was more dramatic than the last.

Shaking her head, Maria slipped away and over to a long table set with a tempting array of tapas. Choosing a small, spicy fish pie, she sat down to delicately nibble on it. That's when she noticed the tall, young man standing by her side.

Alfredo De Samano, son of the Regidor of Santiago, had big, kind eyes...the type that made him look rather like a startled fawn. Maria accepted his invitation to dance.

She was counting her steps to the Sardana, a dance she could never get quite right, when a tremor of anticipation passed through the crowd. Glancing to the entrance of the ballroom, she saw where the excitement had come from. The arrival of the three latest guests sent a chill down Maria's spine.

A tall, noble-faced, titan haired man was conversing with a pretty young woman in the center of the trio. The woman was dressed in the most daring fashion of a low-cut bodice and sheer underblouse. Her hand rested on the arm of the man that seemed to cause the excitement of the crowd.

He was an imposing figure, of medium height with quite an arrogance about him. His heavy-lidded eyes, sharp features and somewhat dark coloring hinted at more than a drop of Moorish blood. He wore black doublets and jerkin, and a scarlet-lined cape was flipped over one shoulder. Stepping into the room, he moved with a warrior's grace. Maria excused herself, timing her arrival at her hostess's side with that of the trio. Juanita took Maria's elbow and with self-importance, presented her to them.

"This is Dona Maria De Velaquez, the niece of our governor," looking straight at Cortez she added with a devious smile, "whom we all love and respect. The señorita is our house guest."

Somewhat irritated with her introduction, Maria held out her hand, each man taking it to press their lips against it. "And this," she said with a sweep of her hand to the intense looking man, "is the commander of the fleet of ships in the harbor Senor Don Hernan De Cortez, and his lovely wife Dona Catalina De Cortez." Then Juanita nodded politely to the tall red-bearded man, "And this is Gonzalo De Sandoval, his first in command."

"Yes, I believe we met in Havana when you first arrived on the island," Cortez spoke up. Maria couldn't really remember and only drew a hazy picture of their first meeting. "I hope your stay in Cuba has been pleasant," he added coldly. He then took his wife's arm and moved on.

Maria gazed after them, agitated and insulted, yet somehow intrigued. Not long after she returned to Alfredo, she saw Cortez stop halfway through a dance, take his wife's arm and escort her through the room and out the door.

The room erupted in a roar of conversation, everyone gathering in small clusters and the dancing all but forgotten. Maria spotted Juanita deep in gossip with a few of the regidors and hurried to join them.

"What's happening?"

"Oh Maria, you haven't heard? Your uncle has ordered Cortez to abandon his mission and return to Havana immediately! He must be there four days from now and some say there will be a duel! Cortez won't be giving up this expedition too easily, I suspect."

"What would happen if Senor Cortez didn't go back to Havana?"

"Oh, he has to," Juanita said. "The governor could confiscate all his property and brand him an outlaw."

Juanita pushed into the center of the crowd with a tray of

wristbells, announcing it was time for the Marishka. The Marishka was Maria's favorite dance. She ran forward with the other young men and women, donning the tinkling bells. Soon the room became a whirl of rapidly moving circles and laughing young people shaking their wrists in time with the music.

The cool, night air brushed across Maria's face as she leaned out over the veranda. Her nightshirt glowed in the luminescence of the full moon as it cast its chalky, lunar images across all it touched. Alone in the quiet of the night, she pondered long. It was as if by looking hard enough she could extract the answer she needed from the sea itself.

She hated to admit it, but Juanita's Ball seemed to have said something to her soul and she found herself choosing to return to Spain and marry! She couldn't believe she was thinking these thoughts. It was as if someone else had stepped into her body and thought them for her. How weird, she thought. She'd heard of such things; perhaps it was the Holy Spirit.

Wrapping her shawl closer, she checked the candle flickering behind her. The flames dancing on the edge of the rim told her the night was almost over. Her attention drifted to the ships anchored out in the harbor. The moon danced across the water with thousands of tiny crystal specks, as the ships rocked gently to and fro. She spotted a few small boats on the silvery water, sneaking their way out to the sea vessels.

Again she felt like someone was inside her speaking her mind, and she rejoiced as a warm flush of excitement raced from head to toe. Suddenly, she knew what to do. Cortez would be leaving Santiago two days hence and so would she! That night the excitement kept her from her dreams.

The two, dark clad figures moved in silence from pillar to pillar as they worked their way through the sleeping hacienda. In the predawn grayness, Maria and Itza shuffled their way into the private garden. Itza motioned the girl to stand guard as she headed down the long rows of vegetables.

Producing a large basket from underneath her garments, she

began to snap, cut and toss vegetables of all kinds into its round, wicker interior. Itza then headed for the opposite end of the garden and began snapping melons from their vines to top off the basket. She knew the melons would be their ticket to get on board.

Maria's hands itched. She wanted to scratch at the egg white and dirt that Itza had applied to make her skin look wrinkled, but she stopped herself, not wanting to ruin the disguise. She had to admit, the effect was surprising. She looked up at the figure hurrying from row to row and her heart opened in gratitude. She recalled the look of relief that had melted into horror on Itza's face yesterday. She had told her she wasn't going to become a nun, and had decided to return to Spain and marry, but that stowing away on board Cortez' ship back to her uncle's hacienda in Havana would afford her a last minute adventure; one she'd not get to experience in the future.

Acting against her own better judgment, Itza had refused to let Maria go alone. Somehow, Itza procured two black dresses and veils, the kind Spanish women wore in heavy mourning. Maria knew that some Indian women had taken up this custom, but heaven only knew where Itza had found these.

Maria didn't want to wear the big, shapeless dress and restrictive veil. She would have rather put her hair up under a hat and dress like a boy. But Itza wouldn't have it.

"What, you crazy? Too many know your face, you have big dance. Besides, where you hide breasts? Boys have no breasts." She had handed Maria the dress and said, "You wear this, no one question old lady with dead one's veil over face." Maria had reluctantly succumbed to Itza's persistence. Shivering in the early morning chill, she had a strange feeling that destiny stretched out before her like a road, and she had just stepped on that road.

It was Itza pushing her out of the garden that brought her back to her senses. Heading for the outer walls of the hacienda, they clambered over a waist high, stone barrier that marked the Ortez boundaries. They then halted long enough for Itza to take some melons from her basket and place them in Maria's, covering the neatly folded personal items on the bottom.

The eastern sky was turning pink as they scurried down the cobblestone street, heading for the wharf. Their movements awakened a dog who yawned, stretched, then barked at them. They hushed him back to silence and pressed on. Signs of life were just stirring through the sleepy streets, with cooking fires being lit in cubino hovels. Here and there a cock crowed, breaking the morning silence.

When they reached the wharf, it was already busy with local inhabitants determined to peddle their produce to the flotilla of ships preparing to leave. They spotted a rowboat and canoe not in use. Maria made a quick sign of the cross, thanking the Holy Mother for having an upper hand in keeping a few slave merchants in their bed that morning. She was heading for the rowboat when Itza grabbed her arm and said, "No little one, use canoe! In rowboat we catch everyone's eye; we no stand out in canoe."

Itza put the baskets in the bottom and steadied the small craft, urging Maria to get in. In her delight, she hastily jumped into the canoe, sending it rocking to and fro; with a startled screech, she was knocked flat on her behind. Itza, having used a dugout canoe all her life, deftly stepped in, sat down and pushed off, all in one swift motion.

As Itza paddled out into the gentle swells, Maria was oblivious to the older woman's emotions. Itza knew only too well that this act of disobedience would probably mean her life. Passing other small groups of paddling Indians, she eased her apprehension by calling out morning greetings in her native tongue.

Maria, thoroughly enjoying herself now, was paddling along merrily when she heard, "Ho little one, stop. Do you mean to drown me?" Turning around, Maria saw water run down Itza's veil and splashed across her dress. With a sheepish grin she apologized, realizing her proud paddling had left something to be desired. Itza explained that holding the top of the paddle with one hand made it possible to push down into the water, then sweep back, thus making them go faster and keeping the person in back dry.

A short time later, they found themselves at the side of the huge corracks. Maria wondered how they would tell which one was Cortez'. Itza headed straight for the one with the word "Catalonia" painted across its bow and flying the banner of Castile.

"That ship belong Senor Cortez," she said.

"How do you know," asked Maria?

"I ask!" she answered simply.

Stopping under the dangling rope ladder, Itza called out to the shouting voices above. "Two widows have best melons for sale. Catholic widows have juicy melons fit for king." Maria marveled at Itza's clever ploy and soon a bearded face appeared over the side.

"Show me!" the man yelled down at them.

"The best! Fit for king," she said, holding out the produce for him to examine. He hesitated, then waved them up.

Itza told Maria to go first while she held steady the canoe. She went to grab her basket and Itza said, "No. You leave, I bring!" Maria wondered how Itza would manage both baskets, but the woman had shown such ingenuity thus far, she decided not to worry. As soon as she stood up, she again sent the tiny craft rocking. Remembering that she didn't know how to swim, she froze with fear. Collapsing back into the canoe, bile rushed to her throat.

Itza moved to her side, pushing the ladder into her hand and encouraging quietly, "Use it, pull self up slow." Then Maria's pride stepped in and she began climbing the swinging rope, stepping on her garments all the way. At the top, Maria put out her hand, expecting the man to help her in, but she was shocked by his callous denial. His rude behavior brought home to her what it must feel like to be an Indian.

Itza scurried up the ladder with one basket balanced on her head and the other over her arm. Once on board, the man motioned them over to a group of Indians with their produce, all haggling with the cargo master. As they joined the group, Maria spotted a door ajar near the back of the ship, in the aftcastle. Remembering her trip from Spain, she knew this part of the ship held private cabins and storage rooms.

The Indians began to disperse and the sailors were running about preparing for departure, so she knew they would need to act fast. Maria motioned Itza to the door. Preparing for retreat if necessary, she casually strolled up to it. Peaking through the door, she found that the stairway leading down to the ship's quarters was empty.

Her heart beating furiously at the thought of being discovered, she slid through the door and down the stairs with Itza hot on her heels. Ahead to her right, she saw a door and hoped it would be a storage room. Not knowing what she'd find on the other side, she held her breath and threw open the door.

The small room was filled with chests and crates. Letting out a sigh, she rushed in and plopped herself down in relief. Looking around, she realized that this was a private storage room and was probably off limits to the crew, reducing their chances of being discovered. Itza shut the door, took a deep breath and then busied herself pulling out their provisions.

The deck overhead erupted in a crescendo of movement and a quick jerk forward told them they were underway. Maria settled down and went over the necessities she'd brought. She didn't need much for just two days, she thought. She had many things at her uncle's; she didn't need to worry.

Little did she know she would never see her things, her uncle, or Spain ever again.

2
Storm at Sea

The wind howled its fury and the steel gray sea rushed forward in assault. A crashing wave came rolling over the already drenched deck, then retreated back in a surge of white foam. Red capped sailors struggled with the slippery bunt lines furling up the sails. Men rushed up the rigging, intent on securing the flapping canvas before the escalating storm hit in its full rage. The storm's din all but drowned out the terse orders of the ship's officers.

A figure holding the railing of the quarterdeck surveyed the looming darkness growing around him, leaning out over the rail to get a better view of how the ship to his left was fairing. Its rigging looked like an agitated spider's web as men wrestled with the tangled tacklines, trying to subdue a wildly flapping foresail.

Damn! How did this storm come upon us so fast? His thoughts were broken by the spray of another wave crashing on the mid-deck and the urgent tugging at his elbow by the ship's boy.

"Senor Cortez," he said, "the boatswain urges you not to lean over the rail if you are not secured to deck, sir; one of the waves could take you overboard."

Cortez nodded to the boy to reassure him, stepped back and made his way across the rolling deck to consult his pilot on the advisability of dropping anchor to ride out the storm.

Below in their storage room, Maria and Itza were trying to secure themselves to one spot. As the ship moaned and pitched, crates and lockers slid from one end of the small room to the other. With its securing straps broken, the locker nearest the wall would slap against it, and the others would come crashing up behind. It was all Maria could do to keep herself from being crushed by their unpredictable movements.

Itza was bent over in the corner releasing that morning's breakfast of cazabi corn bread and melon, when the next lunge of the boat came. She tried grabbing hold of something solid, while the spray of her bile went careening down her dress and showered the locker just in front of her. Thankful that some of the nausea had subsided, she contented herself with her fear.

Maria had seen some storms on the way from Spain but she hadn't been locked in a small, dark room fighting off crates. She didn't dare light a candle in the storm, so their hideaway remained deep in darkness. They could hear the frightened neighing and bleating of the horses and goats in the hold below them, and Maria felt sorry for them in their limited understanding.

Earlier they had discovered that the storage room contained very little to entertain them, just chests of personal belongings and crates of officer's private foodstuffs. When she had seen this, she worried, thinking the ship's steward would come in for some provisions and discover them. So she had stacked up chests in the corner and hid her own belongings behind them. She then slipped a small wedge of wood she had found into the side of the door. They would have to push hard to get the door open, which would give her and Itza enough time to hide, she thought.

Suddenly, Maria's things began rolling and clattering about and she danced and lunged to retrieve them while managing to stay clear of the larger, heavier crates coming at her. The groans of the tossing ship were now getting so loud that Itza was covering her ears, convinced that she'd done the wrong thing and the gods were angry. "We die, little one," she shouted over the din.

"It's only a bad storm," Maria said, "It will pass." Her emotions jumped about, and her body shook with fear and excitement; she too was afraid, but she wouldn't let Itza know it!

At last she managed to stabilize the moving cargo by tying the securing-straps together and jamming the wooden wedge under one of the crates. She wrapped Itza in a blanket and sat down beside her to comfort the terrified woman. Had she made a mistake, she wondered? No, this was excitement! Thrill and fear played with her as the hours slipped past. Then at last, the groans of the wooden ship died down and the pitching slowed as the storm completed its anger.

Maria looked over at Itza. The poor woman, exhausted by her ordeal, had fallen asleep. She pulled the blanket up around her to make her more comfortable, and recalled stowing away yesterday. Almost as soon as they had settled, she had watched Itza leap up and begin dashing around the small room, muttering in her native tongue and flailing about with the basket as if it was a club. Intent on seeing what the commotion was about, she'd climbed over a chest and witnessed the fat, furry haunches of a mouse disappearing into its hole. Maria had been surprised that the usually stoic Itza would react so strongly to a mouse. When Maria gleefully questioned her she had retreated into her inscrutable Indian face, hunting the poor rodent mercilessly every time he poked into the room; lucky for the mouse, Itza was too fat and slow to catch him.

Glancing at the chest in front of her, she thought of her own chest of belongings left back at the Ortez Hacienda, imagining Juanita's surprise as she found the note of her departure. Pleased with her prank and with an exhausted sigh, she drifted off to sleep, woken suddenly when Itza bolted upright with a fearful cry; the storm had entered Itza's dreams.

Maria used the wedge of wood to slowly work out the nail that held the crate shut. The storeroom was stifling; perspiration rolled off her forehead as she concentrated on her efforts. The nail was putting up a fight, and Maria longed to give it a good swift jerk, but she feared it would cause too much noise and perhaps give them away. There seemed to be a lot of coming and going in the hall outside their door and Itza stood by, prepared to jam the wedge in the door if someone should try to enter.

Finally, the nail was free and they were able to push open the lid. She pulled out several oranges and passed them to Itza. At last, she thought, they would eat. They hadn't eaten since yesterday morning and the hunger pangs were growing acute.

Maria was confused; they should have been in Havana two days ago. Even if the storm had blown them off course, they still would have been there by yesterday. When their food had run out it seemed like only a minor inconvenience, since she'd been sure that they would arrive shortly. The day was more than half gone and the ship was showing no sign of arriving in port.

Early that morning, Maria had checked the hallway and slipped out of the storeroom. She sneaked to the stairs to see if she could hear anything about nearing port, but the snatches of conversation she had been able to pick up gave no hint of anything but being far out to sea.

Now hunger had forced her to break open the officer's food crate. Something was wrong, and the anxiety didn't set well with the citrus fruit on her stomach. She saw worry in Itza's face, and knew she herself was of like concern.

Their silence was broken by numerous footfalls passing their doorway and muffled voices that seemed to trail into the cabin next to them. Her mind flashed to the door she had found two days ago when, during the storm, a sliding chest had knocked open a hidden compartment of about two feet in width. She had dismissed it at the time with the storm taking precedence. Remembering the cracks of light that had shone through, she realized she might be able to see into the cabin. Perhaps she could discover what was happening.

Intent on locating the door again, she made her way to the corner of the storeroom. After much prodding and coaxing she found the right spot and the door swung open. Maria marveled at how close the fit was; this door was obviously meant to be kept secret. There was just enough room to climb in, which she was preparing to do when Itza grabbed her arm and whirled her around.

"Where you go?" she demanded, "No go there, danger!"

"I have to, this compartment is next to the cabin everyone is in, and I think I can find out what is happening. We've been out here way too long. Something's wrong!" she added desperately.

"No, danger!" Itza insisted, pointing to the rodent hole in the wall as Maria was preparing to enter.

"Itza, it's only a mouse; it's not going to hurt me. If I see a rat, I will come right back, but I need to find out what's going on." Maria wiggled her arm free of the woman's grasp, irritated at Itza's irrational behavior. She then gathered her garments close around her for more maneuverability.

Itza sat, rocking back and forth and muttering in her own

tongue. With remorse, Maria put her hand on Itza's arm, promising to be careful, and the woman clung pathetically to it for a long time before letting go.

The compartment was narrow and rough; a wooden splinter lodged itself fast into her palm and she stopped to wince at the pain. Tugging at the offending splinter, she sucked on the welling blood, then continued on through, finding a vertical sliver of light marking the tiny gap in the wall.

"My good captains, let us pay respect to our Most Benevolent Lord Jesus Christ, and our Truly Sanctified Catholic Majesty, the Emperor and King, Don Carlos." In the stifling heat of the small room, they allowed a still silence to pass through them.

At first, when Cortez had reacted with anger and spite and set sail, only Sandoval knew they would not be reaching Havana. He had not looked forward to this moment, since a few of his ships' captains were faithful to Velaquez, but since his vision, there was no doubt in his mind and he spoke with fire in his heart.

The small cabin was packed and there was hardly room to move. Eleven sea captains and six commanding conquistadors were present, and all focused on Hernan Cortez. Cortez, well known for his oratory skills, cleared his throat to sign his intent of commencement. Looking each man quickly in the eyes and with bold confidence, he began.

"You all know we've been out to sea longer than needed to arrive safely in Havana; my good men, we will not be reaching Havana!"

The room erupted with loud, hearty approval, but he noticed a few of the men remained silent.

"I've had a vision," he continued, "We are to be entirely victorious on this voyage. I have seen the riches to be won upon this undertaking, with enduring honor for Spain. Heaven has fated us for glory! We will go on to the New Coast as originally planned!" The men began to cheer as Cortez turned on his charm.

"And you, my fine God fearing men, are on this voyage by destiny. There is no mistake that each one of you are here, and not some other man in your stead. You are here because God wants you here! It is our destiny to bring wealth and glory home to Spain!"

Sandoval spoke up in support, "Let us offer salutations to our guaranteed success and seal it with a glass of wine."

The captains all applauded in verbal agreement, and when Cortez' wine had gone around, Sandoval continued. "To Spain, God, and glory!" A cheer went up as they downed the wine. Then quickly Sandoval added, "And to the wisdom and honor of Commander Hernan Cortez. May our Lord Jesus Christ guide this mission through his decisions and actions." Again the captains rallied praise and exultation in his direction.

To keep the strength of their morale, Cortez finished with, "Return to your ships and instruct your pilots on the affirmed course. Then announce to your crews that we're heading for the New Coast. Alert your stewards that every man is to have an extra ration of salted meat and water this night."

Pleased with these instructions and the new course of action, they all left the cabin, morals high. He had successfully diverted their focus from Havana and Velaquez without even mentioning the governors name, he thought arrogantly.

Pouring himself a generous glass of wine, he eased back into a chair and put his black booted feet up on the table in front of him, content with a job well done.

Only Sandoval remained, joining Cortez in a second glass of wine. Suddenly, the wall erupted in a series of thuds and a bump. Cortez sprang to his feet, "Someone's in the secret compartment. God damn it, one of Velaquez's spies," he yelled and surged for his cabin door.

Panic seized Maria with the realness of her blunder and she lunged toward the opening of the compartment and back to her hiding place. A protruding nail caught a large tuft of her dress, pulling her back to the wall with a thud. She heard a rip as she yanked her garment loose, then continued noisily, forgetting the need for stealth. She was worming her way out of the compartment when the door of the storage room burst open; she heard Itza give a startled gasp, then looked up to find herself face to face with a furious Cortez.

Shocked by the implications of having the governor's niece on board, Cortez was at first too stunned to speak. He grabbed Maria's upper arm, checked the hallway, and with a forward shove ushered her into his cabin with Sandoval and Itza following.

"Alright!" shouted Cortez, "What in God's name are you doing on board?"

"I…I…I…thought it would be fun," she stuttered, beginning to cry tears of a confused and alone sixteen year old.

Cortez stood impatiently with hands on hips, while Maria tried to explain how she came to be there, but her tearful blubbering was more incoherent than rational. Sandoval poured her a glass of wine, then dried her eyes and gently asked her to explain everything, starting from the beginning. As she talked, Cortez relaxed a bit, realizing that no one else knew she was there. Then he began to pace, not at all pleased with the implications of this extra responsibility. He knew he could out-parlay the governor's orders and bureaucracy with gold for the King, but with Velaquez's niece on board, the governor's revenge would run far deeper.

"Well my God, what am I going to do with her?" he said, thinking aloud as if she wasn't there.

"We could send her back on the caravel; we know Captain Montejo is faithful to Velaquez and would be willing to return," Sandoval replied.

Cortez stopped pacing for a moment and said, "No, we can't; we're still too close to Cuba. She will have to continue on with us for now, and we'll send her back to her uncle on the first return ship."

Maria, sensing she was safe and realizing that this twist of events was an added surprise to her adventure, whined, "I've been suffocating, I want to go on deck."

Cortez whirled around and said, "Oh no you don't, young lady, I'll not have you parading around in front of my men and flirting with them. I can't have your uncle's men starting an uprising because of your presence. You'll stay down here the whole time; you're going to cause me enough problems as it is. Do I make myself clear?"

"I could wear my veil," stated Maria, but Cortez ignored her. Then Sandoval spoke up, "It wouldn't be good for her to remain below deck the whole time. It would be much wiser to return a healthy niece back to the governor. And she can't stay here; too much transpires around these quarters. She can stay in my cabin and I'll share the pilot's quarters." Turning to Maria, "I have lots of books I'm sure you'll enjoy," he added, in hopes of keeping Maria out of Cortez' way and preventing any future tension between them.

So it was decided; Maria and Itza would remain veiled, still posing as two old women. Cortez would explain that they were family friends in mourning, and the crew was to leave them alone. But just before he left the cabin, Cortez threatened, "If you tell anyone who you are or hint at anything other than the masquerade we have created here, I will lock you both in a cabin and you'll not be let out at all. Understand?"

"And you," he turned towards the Indian woman, "I will hold you responsible for her behavior!"

Itza, relieved in knowing she would not be strung up, stammered her thanks and agreement as he stormed out the door.

The day was gentle and warm and the sailors were in good spirits from the previous day's news from Cortez. Maria was rubbing a little more earth over the egg white Cortez had provided her with. He told her she was never to go on deck without disguising her hands first. Of course she could wear her gloves, but the disguise was more fun, and she had been practicing a stooped walk and a cracked voice to go along with them.

When Maria finally went on deck, the men looked at her with mild curiosity, showing her the deference paid to the elderly. Maria was delighted. Clutching her back in imaginary stiffness, she climbed the stairs to the quarterdeck. Having heard that the pilot had actually sailed with Columbus on his third voyage, and Columbus being a national hero in Spain, she was enthused to find out all about it. Antonio De Alaminos was returning the binnacle cover after adjusting the magnetic needle, when he noticed the veiled figure standing at his side.

"What is that?" she inquired, pointing to the stone he was carefully wrapping in a soft, white cloth. Returning it to the special pouch he wore around his neck, he said, "It's a lodestone; it magnetizes the compass needle." Now that she had his attention, she drilled him about his voyage with Columbus and the previous trip he had made to the New Coast. The trip had been made with her distant cousin, Grijalva, and she wanted to know all about the stone city where they had found gold.

Maria's attention shifted a moment. From where she stood, she could see clear down to the galley where the boatswain quenched the cook fire, and then started for the quarterdeck where she and the pilot stood. When he reached them, he acknowledged her curiously, then reached for the hourglass, turning it. Out of nowhere it seemed, she heard the voice of the ship's boy ring out in a sing-song chant…"One glass is done and now the second floweth; more shall run down if my God willeth; to my God let's pray to give us good voyage, and through His Blessed Mother, our Advocate on High, protect us from the waterspout and send no tempest nigh."

Cortez, hearing the song of the ship's boy, came on deck to observe the crew shift. Glancing to the quarterdeck, he saw Maria in conversation with the pilot; good mood abated, his face turned to anger. His orders to her had been for minimal conversation, and there she was, going at it with the pilot. With her haughtiness, it wasn't going to be easy keeping her identity concealed, he thought.

Maria caught Cortez' face and guessed his thoughts. Her youthful arrogance rushed forward. No one was going to keep her from just talking, she thought. She wasn't doing anything wrong and she wasn't giving her disguise away! So just to spite him, she engaged the pilot in further conversation. When he approached them, she lifted her chin high, pranced past the scowling Cortez, and left the deck.

The looming black clouds were upon them almost as soon as they'd been spotted. In no time at all the fierce winds were howling all about, giving the crew little time to furl the sails. A man on each side of the mainmast scurried up the ratlines, swaying on the ropes and holding on for life while the storm blew them about. Once the canvas sails had been furled, it was all they could do to lower the yard and lash it to the mast so it wouldn't be broken by the fury of the winds. The mizzensail had already been ripped from four of its grommets, as the tackle and bowlines hadn't been relieved in time.

Abruptly the rain began and the sky was now dark as night, with vision almost non-existent. Antonio De Aliminos knew this would be a storm to remember; he sent for Cortez. The runner turned to leave the quarterdeck but his detail was already complete, as Cortez loomed up behind them. The pilot shouted to Cortez, his voice barely heard, "This will not be an easy one, I recommend you order the lashing of the ships. From the looks of the sky, this could last for days."

Cortez trusted his competent pilot under any condition, and would have done precisely that by his recommendation alone. Furthermore, he had come to tell Antonio of his own command to lash the ships. Knowing they were of like mind left him confident of his own judgment. He took this as a good sign; maybe God would guide their safe passage through this wrathful storm. As he turned to head down the quarterdeck, a monster wave rolled up its side and crashed onto the galley. Water ran everywhere, before retreating angrily back to sea.

Cortez found a drenched, fourteen year old ship's boy and ordered him to relay to the boatswain a command to signal the other captains that a lashing of the ships would take effect immediately. All vessels were to be lashed together in two's; with eleven ships, all would have a pair. He would go solo, his craft being the largest and most stable of the fleet. That done, he leaned into the wind and rain, making his way across the pitching deck to where Sandoval was assisting a seaman to secure belaying lines. "Come with me," he said.

The cabin rocked to and fro, sending small items clattering every which way. Maria was trying to read and act unconcerned, as if this storm was like the one of two days ago. Finally, she had to admit to herself that she was frightened. This was worse! Suddenly, a huge wave pitched the ship at such a severe angle, it seemed as if the cabin would turn upside down. Then just as sudden it righted, as the crest of the wave rode itself out. She heard the swoops of water as it propelled itself at the cabin door, and another small rivulet slid under the door to join the widening pool of water on the cabin floor. She thought to herself, what if the ship were to sink and I drown? She wondered if she would suffer a long time before the water turned her lungs to fire—before blackness overcame her in its mercy. She had swallowed a mouthful of saltwater when she was a child; she'd been romping in the surf while visiting her cousin. They were playing dare devil, rushing into the surf farther and farther each time, when a big wave broke over her head, sending her tumbling headlong over and over into the surf. It had so disoriented her that it seemed forever before she'd been able to crawl to shore, her cousin pulling her gasping from the water. The incident had left its mark, and now her thoughts recalled the full horror of it.

Itza let out another moan. She was tucked in a small ball, curled up against the bed and had been howling even louder than the earlier wind, howling that they were going to die and calling on all her Gods, then Jesus and Mary, then all the Old Ones again. She now had retreated to somewhere inside herself and her face was a set mask of terror with vacant eyes. Again the ship lurched violently, setting the cabin almost on its side. It sent Itza back into a long wail, and a panicked Maria sprung down to huddle by her side. The two women clung to each other for any small comfort as the barriers of age, culture and rank dissolved in their fear.

The cabin door flew open and two soaked figures stood at the threshold. Sandoval entered, quickly dressing the two women in long, heavy overcoats and tucking their veils close around them. Cortez explained in haste that they were taking them up on deck, where they would be lashed to the galley windwall.

Maria couldn't think in all the din and she meekly obeyed, following Cortez to the stairs. Looking up, she watched a huge wave wash over the deck, run down the stairs, assault her body and then pool around her feet. She halted where she was, planting her feet and gripping her hands on the stair railing. "Oh no," she thought, "I'm not going any further; I'll stay in the cabin where it's dry."

"I'm not going up there!" she demanded.

"I haven't got time for this," he barked back at her, whirling around to grab her upper arm and painfully force her up the stairs. As they reached the top step, the boat lunged, knocking her against the door frame.

Her left shoulder connected with the unyielding woodwork, wrenching it from its socket, and red waves of pain shot down her arm and across her vision as she went weak with nausea. Cortez still dragged her on, past the two laboring seamen attempting to repair the aftcastle door that had torn from its hinges. Across the slippery, bucking deck they went; he then tied her to the narrow wall in front of the now cold cooking fire. The alcove formed by the windwalls on the galley was the only place on deck that was somewhat protected. Cortez stormed off while Sandoval wrapped the length of rope around their waists, securing it to the rail by the fire pit.

Maria wailed in tears of pain, fear and despair. "I hate him; that's why he brought me out here, so I'll drown," she sobbed, "I hate him! He wants me to die!"

"If the ship capsized, you would have been trapped below deck in the cabin," Sandoval yelled against the din, "At least here you'll stand a chance." Then he, too, was gone.

Maria and Itza huddled in the corner, trying to keep off their faces the water which plastered the veils to their skin, making it difficult to breathe. Itza was sick again and spewed bile over both of them. Repelled, Maria stood, trying to shake some of the mucous and food from her soggy skirt, when the next pitch of the ship forced her to lunge for the corner. The pitch was followed by such a huge wave that it washed a sailor overboard as it crashed on deck and then rolled back to sea. The others ran to haul the battered, half-drowned man back on board by the rope secured to his waist.

This was too much for Itza. She buried herself between Maria and the wall and wailed. While the storm raged, Maria's thoughts became a mass of murmuring fears, and her insistent shoulder throbbed mercilessly. Resting her feverish head on Itza's huddled body, she went unconscious.

Standing on the poop deck, Cortez watched as swaying lanterns flashed signals from vessel to vessel. A final signal came their way and the boatswain flashed back in completion. Turning towards Cortez he said, "Sir, one of the ships is missing." Juan Sanchez, young for his position and rank, looked at Cortez feebly as he awaited instructions from his Commander in Chief. They read each other's thoughts as they both considered the lives of all the men aboard the missing brigantine.

Cortez again made his way to the quarterdeck to confer with his pilot. Reaching Antonio's station, he shouted over the fury of the storm, giving news of the missing vessel.

From behind him, the ship's boy appeared; he was cold, wet and terrified. Cortez saw the boy was scared half to death, but showed courage. Pedro was small for his age but fierce at heart, and reminded Cortez of himself at that age. He empathized with the boy and realized that he weighed so little, one wave could take him to his watery grave. He brought the boy down to the main deck and tied a rope around his middle, giving him a run of 15 feet. While he tied him up, the boy reported his news.

"Sir, the boatswain said you should know immediately; the Santa Lucia has lost her rudder and is listing badly."

Finished with the boy, Cortez pressed through the wind and rain back to the quarterdeck and ordered the pilot and boatswain into action.

"Do what you must," he said, "but turn this ship around. We must guide ourselves alongside the Santa Lucia, right her and lash her to our hull side. It's the only way she'll make it." He thought deeply, then said, "It's her only chance."

Maria moaned and pushed against the dream boulder pinning down her shoulder. Her eyes fluttered open to a grey blur, which soon became the grey beard and hair of the old, kind-eyed ship's surgeon. When she started to sit up, her throbbing, bandaged arm forced her to lay back down, a groan escaping her lips. A sudden recall of the storm brought panic.

"The storm!" she cried. Itza placed a wet cloth on her brow as the doctor gently pushed her back down.

"There, there," soothed the kindly weathered man, "the storm's over."

"How can that be? It's so fierce still," mumbled Maria, her head still foggy.

The doctor motioned Itza over, gave her instructions for Maria's care and then left the cabin. Itza sat at Maria's side. Maria was again mumbling incoherently in her feverishness; tears welled up in Itza's eyes, seeing her lying there so white and frail with her shoulder wrapped in swathing.

"The storm," she said again.

"Rest little one. The storm is over," she cooed, shivering at her own recollection of the three day ordeal. She had forgotten her own fear when she'd realized that Maria was sick and injured. Maria's arm had swollen to twice its normal size, and her face had gone dead white except for bright patches of red when the fever would return; she had lain senseless as they were hit by storm after storm. That first night, when Sandoval had carried Maria to the cabin after the worst of it was over, he'd pulled off her veil and was alarmed by her appearance. Reporting to Cortez on her condition, he summoned the ship's surgeon, whom he had known would be discreet concerning her identity. Itza's body felt bruised and hollow, and dark circles were etched under her eyes, but she had refused to give up her vigil. Now she sat calm and relieved at Maria's bedside, thankful for the girl's deliverance.

The sky was turquoise blue and the breeze was gentle. Mother Nature was on her best behavior since her three day bout of fury. With her arm still wrapped tight at the shoulder and resting in a linen sling, Maria was helped on deck. The calm, salt air breeze quickly revived her from the stiff, achy sensations that had been plaguing her mind and body in the dankness of the cabin. Taking a deep, full breath she sighed with relief. She was still alive she thought to herself—a little stiff, but nonetheless alive.

"Where are the others?" she said, looking around in the calm waters and seeing only one vessel directly behind them. Then she noticed the hemp lines and tackle over her head leading straight back behind the Catalina and rigged to the Santa Lucia.

"We're towing her," answered Sandoval coming up behind her. He had seen her look up, then follow the lines back to the Lucia. "She broke her rudder in the storm," he continued, "and the other ships went on ahead with the good winds."

"Are we near shore?" she asked, suddenly desiring firm ground again.

"The crow's nest overhead suddenly erupted in the cry, 'Land ho'!"

3
Cozumel

The noonday sun was intense. Swimming waves of heat caused the captain's vision to blur and rivulets of sweat rolled down his back, adding to the discomfort he found himself in. Cortez was furious with the stupidity of the act committed prior to his arrival in this Mayan village. He had seriously considered making an example of the man; he couldn't have any of his forces, especially his captains, pillaging without his authorization. He needed his captain's support, not his revenge. The guilty captain trudged two paces behind a fuming Cortez, uncomfortable with thoughts of possible retribution.

As they neared the town, Cortez halted his column of men and met the returning scouts. His lead scout stepped forward.

"Sir, the village is deserted; we saw only a few fugitives. We believe they're regrouping in the jungle for attack." I was afraid of this, Cortez thought to himself; that imbecile strips a temple of its paltry pieces of gold just when we need these peoples' goodwill. Cortez nodded to the scout, feigning approval and then continuing onward.

The village was a peculiar combination of primitive yet advanced architecture, with traces of having once been cultured but gone the way of time. This was evident in the stone houses, with elegant, high vaulted arches and well dressed limestone walls married with crude, thatched roofs.

Their approach scared a small spider monkey, who scurried from an open door and screeched his way across their path.

They'd advanced a few more paces, when suddenly an arrow whizzed from the open door, passing a few inches in front of Cortez' nose. The column burst into readiness, some looking for cover, some in pursuit of the assailant. Knowing the village held more surprises for them, he ordered his men to "keep sharp".

While rounding a large stone structure, they encountered a few native women attempting to flee town hurriedly and unnoticed. They were gathered up and brought back to Cortez. The central figure was a short, fat, bejeweled woman who was followed by her servants. Through sign language it was ascertained that she was the wife of a cacique, a chieftain, and she'd come back for her jewels. Expecting the worst, her eyes read fear, but she held her chin high in defiance.

Cortez was delighted. He saw in his captive a way out of his dilemma. He had her led into a house and made comfortable. Thinking fast, he sent for several items from his ship; he then turned on his charm. He signed as best he could, regretting that one of their temples had been rifled by his men. He conveyed to the woman his desire for friendship and a willingness to right his wrong.

When his men returned from the ship he gifted her with sewing needles and several glass beads, then let her and her servants go. Seeing this, her eyes lit up, and Cortez knew he'd acted wisely. He ordered his men to stay together and avoid engaging any more natives.

Before long a band of Mayans approached, warriors leading the way in readiness if any danger should present itself; they were followed by several caciques and more village men, with a few young boys and a couple of yipping dogs bringing up the rear. Their wary approach informed Cortez they didn't trust him, but were willing to listen. He went with them to the temple and returned the golden objects, then gifted them all with glass beads. Thinking these beads were jewels, they succumbed to Cortez' charm. He then sent the men responsible for the misunderstanding back to their ships, ordering them to remain on board until the fleet left Cozumel.

Village life soon returned to its lazy, normal pace and Cortez was quick to procure fresh water and provisions for his ships. Feeling guilty for her injury, he allowed Maria and Itza to roam the little town to their hearts desire…"As long as you remain veiled!" he said. Maria was delighted; she wanted to see as much as she could of these peculiar people. To move about again, she thought happily, would be a joy. Her body had grown stiff from being confined on board so long. Itza seemed pleased, and thought the island held something exciting in store for her too.

The red dirt streets were filled with peculiar sights and sounds. The day was starting to cool as late afternoon activities replaced the noon rest. A small, brown and mangy dog barked with a high, squeaky rasp before sniffing their ankles. Satisfied, he returned to his place on a thatched doormat. Two women with earthen pots of water balanced atop their heads stopped to scrutinize Maria and Itza curiously. Maria realized how strange they must look in their dark, bulky drapements. These women wore only loose, white dresses reaching just to their knees. The Holy Sisters would call them shameless and immodest creatures. Maria suddenly felt weighted and bulky; it went beyond wearing a veil. She remembered the freedom of the short shifts she had worn in the summer as a young girl. Feeling self-conscious, she walked on. A small child played in the dirt by her feet. Several men dressed only in loincloths passed by them with the bounty of their field strapped to bare-skinned backs. Not used to seeing the male body so openly displayed, Maria turned away in embarrassment, but her eyes lingered in curiosity.

When they reached the central plaza her senses were assaulted all at once. The plaza was full of women, many drawing water and gossiping around the communal well. Small, brown children were laughing and romping with their small, brown, chubby dogs and the pungent aroma of roasting chilies seemed everywhere. It all felt oddly familiar. This is what she'd come to Cuba to see, she thought, remembering how disappointed she had been when she saw the Indians—they had become almost like the Spanish.

Maria's attention was drawn back to the well and a statue figure adjacent to it. The figure was of a man laying back, with bent knees jutting skyward. The length of his abdomen was exaggerated, making it sort of an offering table on which someone had placed flowers. Each woman touched the statue, then pressed the hand to their lips as if a transference of power were taking place. Each then drew water.

"What are they doing?" she asked. "Go see what they're doing,

Itza." Maria grabbed the woman by her chubby arms and pushed her forward. With her short stocky legs, Itza strode forward obligingly. When she was among the women she began making sounds and using hand signals, and then pointing to the statue.

Like a beehive erupting, they were swarmed on all sides by chattering women signaling with excitement. They behaved as if they had just been waiting for the strangers' approach to satisfy their curiosity. Much to Maria's astonishment, Itza actually seemed to be able to communicate with them. Just for a moment, Itza lifted her veil, exposing her face to the chattering women. The familiar brown skin and features of her face sent a warm and renewed sense of excitement through them. A young, smiling girl of about thirteen— her long, shinny black hair in braids with red ribbons wrapped at both ends—playfully tried to lift Maria's veil. Itza rushed to her side, pushing Maria backward and pulling the veil back in place. She kept repeating a sound to the curious girl, who finally shrugged and let go. The inquisitive child still tried to peer through the fabric of her veil as Itza led Maria out of the commotion to a stone bench. One of the women handed Itza two small, wrapped bundles. They sat and watched the women finish their work at the well and then hurry off to their homes to prepare the family meal.

Maria couldn't stand Itza's stalling, and exploded with a rash of questions. "Itza, are these your people? Is this your home? You can understand them, can't you?"

"Ho little one, slow down."

"Is there anyone here you know?" She hardly slowed for a breath, "Oh Itza, is this how you once lived?"

"Not my people," Itza pushed back the girl's intoxication. "Understand only small words, but we know this people from heart," she put her hand on her chest.

"How?"

"These people," Itza said full of pride, "be the Great Ones, the Maya."

"Great Ones?" Maria asked, looking around at the small plaza. She was confused; it was a pleasant little town but hardly the citadel of Great Ones. Maria was disappointed. Somehow she had expected something else, and felt inside there had to be something else.

"This doesn't look so grandiose to me."

"Just last remains of Maya village," laughed Itza. Then in her broken Spanish she wove a beautiful tale of ancient cities far in the jungle, great lords holding sway over vast tracts of land and of magic and mysterious sciences, all in a time long past. Maria was fascinated, drawn in by ancient gods and peoples. Itza ended with "…and that is the great Mayan God, Chac Mool," as she pointed to the statue by the well, "the one who brings rain and makes the water good."

"But Itza, how do you know these things if they are not your people?"

"My grandmother was a Mayan," Itza said solemnly.

"But how? You said they lived far away!"

Itza went on to explain that when her grandmother had been a young girl she was out fishing with her father and brother off the coast, near the island sacred to women. A huge storm had hit, forcing them to lay down their canoe and ride the wind and waves out in the small craft. For several days they pushed hopelessly about on the water, praying for their survival. When the storm's fury had spent itself, they washed ashore on the land called Cuba. Having lost their sense of direction, they knew they'd never find their homeland again. Her father died of a broken heart within three years, and Itza's grandmother and her brother were left to grow up with their adoptive tribe, but she never forgot her heritage. "When Itza little girl, Itza's grandmother tell stories of Mayan people, and teach some words of Mayan. She also say her family come from city called Tulum, but long before that, before birth, her family live in a great city called Chichen Itza."

She told Maria her grandmother had named her Itza after this city and the ancient Itza lineage. As a child, when Itza questioned her grandmother as to why the Mayan people had left the Great City, her grandmother's face would tighten and she'd not say, but would hint at sorcery and war. Itza closed her eyes to rest, bathed in her thoughts and feelings.

Unwrapping the little gifts they had received earlier, Itza stated "Tamale", and handed over one of the corn treats to Maria. It was hard to eat while wearing a veil. She had to tear off small bits and bring it up to her mouth, her hand disappearing behind the black material. As she finished the tiny meal her eyes met with an astonishing sight. A young mother was entering the plaza with a tiny infant, its head strapped in an apparatus of two boards, one on the back of his head and one in front of his forehead. Maria's stomach knotted and she felt sorry for the child, believing perhaps it was afflicted.

Seeing Maria's horror, Itza exclaimed, "No, no…custom!" The woman explained that they did this on purpose; the boards were placed on infants' heads for just a few days to reshape the skull. That way they wouldn't offend the wind by forcing it to bounce off their forehead. Instead it would stream smoothly by.

"How queer," said Maria.

"Look there, little one." Itza pointed to another child. A boy of two, maybe three had a bead dangling in front of his eyes. His mother kept drawing attention to it, hoping it would keep his focus. "Maya think if eyes crossed, you look inside," she touched her heart and head, "as much as outside."

Looking around, she realized they all seemed to have odd shaped heads coming to a point, and a number of them were indeed very cross eyed! In her youthful arrogance, Maria quickly revised her opinion of Mayan customs.

Blue green water rolled in on the tawny sand, then rolled back out again carrying a crown of white sea foam. Maria was walking in the wet, shiny sand with the hem of her garments pulled up to her knees. This was as much freedom as she'd been able to obtain since she arrived in Cuba. The beach was deserted but for her and Itza, who was hurrying along the shore ahead.

Itza's short, strong legs propelled her along at such a pace that even with her long legs Maria had to work to keep up.

"Itza, slow down, I want to walk in the surf."

"No you come, we go special place," she replied over her shoulder.

"But I like it here," Maria said.

"This place no stop, better place you like."

"But where are we going?" she began again, just as they

rounded a wall of huge boulders. Two sand bars had created a protected cove with huge cliffs behind the beach. Cascading from the top, a small stream plummeted over the cliff face, then rushed out to join the sea. Maria ran forward in delight, stopping at the edge of the waterfall and allowing the gentle spray to envelop her.

"Now take off clothes. Too dirty, I wash," Itza said, pulling off Maria's veil.

"But what if someone comes?" Maria said, suddenly shy.

"No one come, this is women's bath place. No man come here."

"But the women might!" Maria bargained.

"No one come. I make sure," Itza said.

Maria put her hands on her hips and said, "How can you make sure?"

"I tell them you make vow and not show face. Maya honor vows. That's why girl at well not pull up veil."

"That reminds me," said Maria, "what was it that you kept saying to her?"

"Sacred!" Itza said. "To Mayas, break vow make gods angry."

"But I didn't make a vow to God," said Maria, somewhat piqued.

"But Maya know when you make vow to God, God be your care. Now you make vow to Cortez, he be your care," explained Itza.

Maria was confused now and tried to decide if Itza spoke heresy, but let it go. It would be nice to have clean clothes, she thought. She'd been in the same clothes for weeks now.

She stripped off her garments, leaving on only her chemise. It felt good to take off that scratchy shawl that Itza constantly wrapped around her middle; she had said it would hide the curves of her waist, giving the blocky look of an old woman's body.

She unfastened her hair, letting it fall and allowing the warm, gentle breeze to blow through it. She was sitting on the sand, eyes closed and face turned into the sun, when Itza came from behind and began pulling the laces of her chemise, saying "This dirty too, wash hair, wash skin."

Scandalized at the thought, Maria scrambled to her feet and haughtily informed Itza she had no intention of taking off her chemise. "That is sinful! And no God fearing woman would do such a thing," Maria scolded.

"God fearing?" Itza looked puzzled. "God make you, then God know what body look like! Why hide?"

"Shameful!" Maria exclaimed, mimicking the ominous tone of the Mother Superior.

"Shame?" repeated Itza, not sure of what the word meant.

"The body is shameful," explained Maria, full of false pride. She sensed her argument had no effect on Itza's opinion.

"Maria's body prit'tee, Itza's body good too," Itza said. Maria winced as she found all the teachings of her convent education rushing through her mind. She tried to find the perfect retort for Itza's illusions, but found none. Raising her eyebrows and shaking her head, Itza said "suit yourself" and before Maria's astonished eyes, removed every stitch of clothing from her short, stout, brown body. She let down her graying, black hair as she ran to the water, allowing the waves to wash over her. Diving into the gentle surf, she swam out into the inlet. The blue green water supported her body weight and gave her the fluidity and grace of a playful otter. All of Itza's tribe had loved to swim and cavort in the sea and Itza was no exception.

As Maria dropped down into the sand and watched Itza playing in the water, resentment began to rise, acknowledging Itza's natural sense of freedom. Part of her wanted to run out and join the woman even though she couldn't swim a stroke; another part made her sit there on the beach and wallow in her self-satisfied righteousness.

Itza swam to shore, running past Maria to her clothes; grabbing the small pouch she had brought, she pulled out a handful of herbs and returned to the surf. She scooped up handfuls of sand, working the sand and herbs into her scalp. Diving back in, she allowed the waves to wash her clean.

Returning to the water's edge, with hands on hips framing her round, ample belly and pendulous breasts, she motioned to Maria, "You come wash, you no smell good!"

I stink? thought Maria indignantly. That was all she needed to propel her to the water's edge. She allowed Itza to give her the same herb and sand treatment, working on her hair and arms, then everywhere her skin was exposed. The coarse sand tickled and revived her skin, bringing a flush of blood to the surface.

The same euphoric feeling which overtook her on the verandah in Santiago crept up on her—again the expanded sensation, as if someone was thinking in her mind. Pulling the chemise over her head and tossing it skyward, she joyfully allowed Itza to cleanse every part of her body.

Feeling clean like an innocent child, she laid at the water's edge, letting gentle waves wash over her. Itza busied herself washing their garments in the surf; taking them to the waterfall, she rinsed out the salt and laid them flat on the sand to dry.

Maria felt the warmth of the high noon sun bathe across her wet and exposed skin, reveling in her tactile senses coming alive, as if awakening from a dormant sleep. The tickling sand beneath her limbs and the warm, refreshing salt water across her firm body were causing her to lose her senses and become dizzy. Picking up a handful of sand, she let it fall over her wet body, leaving a trail from her bosom to her groin.

Unconsciously she turned her body feet first into the lapping waves, spreading her legs to a warm rush of water as it filled her openness. She moaned as the pleasure sent rivers of heat through the rest of her body. Her hands came to rest on young, full breasts, tracing the nipples with her fingertips. Then she pressed her caressing hands down the long, smooth contours of her torso and hips.

"Come! We braid hair now. Dress almost dry," Itza's voice broke the trance. Realizing what she was doing, she scrambled to her feet. Covering her nakedness and red faced in shame, she ran for her clothes. Her hands shook from embarrassment and frustration and she fumbled again and again to tie the still damp laces of her undergarments. Watching the scene, Itza shook her head and calmly walked over to help.

Fully dressed, she sat still while Itza finished braiding her hair. Her mind in turmoil, she could clearly hear the Mother Superior's voice calling her a shameful hussy, bound for hell on the road of sin. Yet part of her acknowledged how good it felt; somehow, she thought, in the elements of nature it seemed innocent and holy.

Female voices called out from the other side of the rocks. Itza answered, donning her veil and motioning for Maria to do likewise. A group of laughing women waved happily to them as they rounded the rocks. Then just as Itza had done, in their unabashed freedom, they peeled off their dresses and ran for the surf. Maria was still embarrassed and tried not to stare, but she couldn't help observing that these women all had identical bodies. They were short, round and stocky, with almost no breasts or hips to speak of...like barrels, she thought in bemusement. Even more unusual, they like Itza had virtually no pubic hair.

As a young girl of about eleven ran by her, carrying a gourd of fresh water from the falls, Maria saw a dark spot about the size of a coin at the base of her spine. Then she noticed that all the girls, and even some of the younger women, had a similar spot in varying sizes and colors. Calmly she became conscious of her own body again. Allowing intrigue and curiosity to sweep over her, she noted the differences between her own long limbed frame and the short, stout structure of the Mayans. Her large breasts, lean waist and bright bush of pubic hair stood out in obvious contrast. This was the first time she'd looked subjectively at her own body since puberty had touched her. She had grown much thinner since they left Cuba and all her pudginess was gone. Feeling light and more supple was rather to her liking.

As she walked back from the beach, her veils felt oppressive in the damp heat. They passed open fields where farmers were setting fires to burn the vegetation; sowing season was approaching. Upon arrival in the village, they noticed a small crowd gathering at the plaza. Coming close, they watched. At the center, an old woman holding an infant of maybe five months, lit a candle and spoke a few words to the group. She placed a tiny spear in the child's hand, followed in succession by more tiny implements. Finally, she set the baby on her hip and proudly circled the group.

"This is the first step from infanthood to babyhood; now baby's big spirit can come in," Itza whispered.

"Oh baptism!" said Maria.

Itza walked on ahead while Maria, curious as to how the Maya lived, paused at the door of a house. Inside, a young child lay napping in a swaying hammock and hooks for many more hammocks dotted the walls. Two open doors opposite one another created constant circulation and through the back door she spotted a smaller hut where a woman tended a cooking fire. She ran on to catch up with Itza.

The two headed out of the village, making their way down to where the ships were anchored. Reaching the clearing, they saw what looked like hundreds of men gathered in rows. Horses stood in harness on long lead lines attached to tackle blocks and pulleys. Hearing a cry of "Heave ho!", the men all began to strain, grunt and pull. Two cables ran out over the water, fastened to each side of the Santa Lucia's hull, and a third went to her capstan. The ship pulsed landward, and before long the Lucia was beached.

Awed by the sight, she ran ahead to find Sandoval. He'll tell me what's happening, she thought. Staying clear of Cortez, who was overseeing the operation, she scanned the crowded beach to find the tall, good-looking man. At last she spotted him up with the horses, calming them from their labors.

"What by King Carlos' name is going on?" she said, with the demeanor of an adult. She had begun to find Sandoval to her liking and sought him out when she needed pertinent information she knew wouldn't come from Cortez. His gentle manner pleased her.

"The Santa Lucia has been beached so we can fix her rudder," he said.

"All this for a rudder?"

"She's been beached for leaks, too, and now the repairs will be made," Sandoval explained. "Those must be done while the vessel is beached. They're preparing now to careen her."

"What does that mean?"

"You see the men working with the tackle to the ship's right?"

"Yes," she said, following his pointing finger as Itza came waddling up to listen quietly.

"They're reattaching the tackle and blocks to the capstan, and when they're ready, she'll be careened over to one side, allowing the caulkers to do their work."

"How long will it take?"

"All the rest of the day." Noticing her interest, he continued, "They'll paint the underside of the hull with tar, so as to prevent worm rot; then when she's dry, we right her, she's floated for a time, then careened again so the opposite side can be tarred."

"What next?" she asked, too impatient to witness what she suspected would be a long and arduous process.

"You'll have to follow me if you want to know more. I'm supervising other operations."

She scampered after him with Itza following. As he headed for the Lucia, the boat began its careen, moaning as it went. Maria was amazed at how large it looked from the underside.

"They've been pumping the bilge water for two days now, so the caulkers can seal that as well."

"What's the bilge and what do they seal it with?"

"Inquisitive, aren't you?"

She shrugged innocently, thinking to herself that it's better to know more than less...never can tell when you'll need it.

"The bilge is at the bottom of the hull. A certain amount of water, along with large stones, must be kept in the bilge to keep the ship stabilized during storms. Having water on both sides of the hull is also why it must be kept sealed to prevent rot and leaks."

"Oh," was her only reply.

"The caulker makes a mixture of oakum and tallow which he fills the leaks with. Then they paint the hull inside and out with tar and tallow, as I described earlier."

Feeling hungry, she thanked him and set off for the Catalonia. Once she quieted her stomach, she thought, she could return and watch the men at their labor until the sun set.

It had been two weeks since they had landed and Cortez was now standing on the forecastle of the Catalonia observing the loading of fresh fruit and water. He eyed the two veiled figures and watched their progression toward the ships after their final visit to the village. He felt irritable; he'd been hoping to return Maria to Cuba by now. A passing ship from Hispanola would have suited his needs. The thought had passed his mind to send a ship back with her on it, but he couldn't see wasting the ship or its men. She would have to stay on until a later date.

He turned for his cabin as he remembered to tally and log the total amount of beads and trade stuffs he'd used in buying off the Mayans' goodwill. He was descending the forecastle steps when a small canoe came into view. The occupant paddled furiously, shouting and waving as he rounded the bend. Pulling up on shore, he started running for the ship. Cortez was intrigued. Sensing the man's urgency, he veered instead for the gangplank.

The man stopped directly in front of Cortez and bent down, touching the earth first with his hand and then with his head in native fashion. Standing up he introduced himself as Geronimo De Aguilar, a shipwrecked Spaniard, and begged Cortez' help.

Cortez heartily welcomed him and placed his cloak around De Aguilar's shoulders, considering the simple native attire unsuitable for a Spaniard.

"Get this man some britches," he ordered the boatswain. "And now my good man, you must be needing a rest from your journey. The boatswain will see you to suitable quarters. It would be my pleasure if you'd sup with us tonight and tell us your story. Until then, rest well."

Maria managed to skirt into the cabin just as the door was being closed, gambling that Cortez wouldn't order her out with this newcomer, Sandoval, and the doctor all being present. She didn't like eating with the veil, but a little bread was all she wanted anyway, and as long as she sat back in the corner remaining veiled and quiet, she'd be fine, she thought. They dined on olives, cheese, salted meat and bread, washing it down with wine.

When De Aguilar would eat no more, he asked, "What day is it?"

"March 4th, 1519," Cortez answered.

"Fifteen nineteen. My God eight years," he said to himself. "I'd been studying for the priesthood and was visiting the Spanish outposts, when on our return voyage from Hispanola to Cuba we were hit by a storm that ravaged the ship. Many of us drifted for several days in the small yawl that was aboard the ship. I prayed constantly it seemed, and by God's holy grace we washed ashore just north of here, I believe. Upon landing we were met by heathen cannibals." He drew his breath in disgust, "and before we knew it, eight of our number had been dismembered, cut open and eaten."

Maria was repulsed at the grisly thought, as were the others as they all became restless, and Cortez called the boy for more wine.

"My heart was sickened; my stomach and legs were weak from the horrid experience, but by God's blessed presence, I and a comrade managed to escape before our fated lot." He stopped for a mouthful of the pungent wine, as if to relinquish the flesh eaters to his past.

"We retreated into the jungle, where we found a village of Mayans. The cacique kept us as slaves, but treated us with kindness…again God's grace."

Maria thought of Itza, and for a moment put herself in Itza's place. She shook it off as he continued.

"My comrade took to the life and soon found a young woman. Her father bought his freedom, and he's now fully native at heart, with children by her. My cacique encouraged me to marry into their custom as well; he constantly tempted my manhood with many young girls."

Maria shifted about, not sure where his story was leading.

"He would send the women to me on a constant basis and one day even sent a young boy. With that I was outraged and went to him, demanding he stop. At last he was convinced, and by the strength in my abstinence for the sake of the priesthood, he entrusted me to safeguard his women, in which position I learnt much from and kept almost until this day. Before the last rainy season began, we received word of a Spanish explorer who had sent beads in exchange for our release. How he heard of us, I don't know. My cacique didn't want my release, for he had grown to like me. Finally, he relented, but to my misfortune, it was too late; the explorer had set sail before my arrival. I spent another full year with the cacique and his people before word again came that Spanish explorers were near. I reminded my cacique that my freedom had been previously bought and it would be a dishonor to the gods if I could not return to my homeland. He agreed, and none too soon! Thank you Holy Father for my deliverance!" He touched his heart, and allowed gentle tears to express thankfulness to Cortez.

All remained quiet. At last Cortez came out of deep thought and leaned forward on the small captain's table and asked, "In these eight years you have learned the language of these people and their customs?"

"Well, yes of course."

"Of course," repeated Cortez, "then you will be the expedition's interpreter."

❖

The cluster of ships drifted slowly up the coast. They were in the area that De Aguilar believed he first came ashore. Cortez held a spyglass to his eye, searching the dense underbrush for signs of the village De Aguilar had described. He wasn't sure what his intentions would be if he found the village, but the idea of savages eating his countrymen rankled his soul. Finding no traces of the village, they sailed on.

Later that day they found themselves at a small island the earlier expedition had named Island of the Women; they had named it so, because the deserted temples all had statues of goddesses in them, and only goddesses. Itza leaned over the gunwale with the excitement of a small child. For her, the island marked the vicinity where her grandmother's journey began. Because the island was uninhabited, the two women were allowed off ship while the men obtained fresh water.

The sanctuary felt cool after the blazing noonday sun. Itza was explaining that pregnant Mayan women used to come to this island to ask for a safe, healthy birth. If they were blessed, they would return for the birth itself.

"No men allowed on island," she said firmly. "Them paddle women to island, then leave. Return next day, maybe longer." Itza went on and on, overwhelmed at seeing the place her grandmother had so animately described to her long ago.

Maria wondered how long the temples had been deserted. It couldn't have been long, she thought. The walls were still neatly white-washed and the bright colored paint on the geometric figures on doorways still held, although humidity had caused them to peel. Even the small outer buildings had traces of thatching left on them.

She had discovered a broken urn with intricate geometric glyphs on it and was busy trying her imagination for its original use, when she noticed Itza. The woman had lifted her veil, knelt in front of an altar, placed a cake upon it and remained in stillness.

She's praying to her gods again, thought Maria. Every time Itza began reverting to her heathen ways, Maria became distraught.

Maria felt it her duty to convert her friend to the Light of the True Lord, Jesus Christ! She couldn't help thinking that she was failing by not giving more direction to Itza's soul. She stood back to watch, torn by her feelings and her morals.

Itza looked so happy when she lifted her veil to pray. The Divine Mother will surely understand, Maria thought, trying to rationalize her feelings.

It looked as though the prayer had lifted the burden. She was compelled to ask Itza what she'd prayed for. At first, Itza remained in quiet contemplation. Then while rising, her eyes fell to the cake on the altar, and she lit up with a gust of renewed devotion. Thanking the deity profusely, she turned toward Maria, face full of joy, and explained that she'd prayed for the soul of her daughter.

"Goddess say, Itza's daughter with her. And look," she said triumphantly, "proof!" She picked up the cake, which now had a piece missing from it and showed it to Maria—a piece that looked just like a bite.

Maria was stunned. Things like this don't happen, she thought, rushing forward to find the piece that must have broken off. It was nowhere to be found. Maria's mind was overwhelmed. How could that be? "There is only one God," she said, picking up the cake and pointing to the statue. "How can a hollow stone create miracles?"

"Little one," Itza laughed, "You pray to Divine Mother, why this be different?"

"That's, well, I don't know. It's just different," she struggled. "She's the mother of our Lord Jesus Christ!"

"This be Mother, too."

Not knowing what to believe now, Maria grew quiet. Each in their own world, they headed back towards the yawl in silence.

The sun's white brilliance was almost painful to the eyes, and the small scrubby trees offered little protection. A huge rat scampered from a temple and across the path, breaking their reverie. Maria gasped at its breadth, stopping in her tracks. She expected Itza to go into her usual panic and attack, but she simply stepped back, pushing Maria behind her as if for protection. Itza's calm reaction so contrasted her earlier behavior with the rodent on board, that Maria insisted on an explanation.

Itza looked at her like she was a simpleton, saying, "It's Okay, she safe now," like that explained everything.

"What's okay, who's safe?"

Itza took Maria's hand, sat her down, and shared of the love she had with her daughter. The images flashed in Maria's mind: a happy, wide eyed child running through the surf as fast as her short, plump legs would carry her; her first basket woven of sweet smelling grasses; limbs grown coltish and her young face smiling with pride as she emerged into a shy, giggling young girl with the first signs of budding womanhood; a horrible rat bite, her body growing feverishly sick and eyes clouding over and closing for the last time.

The images caused Maria to shake as Itza continued: two anguished parents in tears of pain and sorrow from their loss; the devastated face of a young Itza, injured in a fall, never to bear children again. "Itza never forgive self, but Mother Goddess of temple give grace, and Itza okay now. Rat okay now too," she finished.

Now Maria understood. Reaching over, she kissed Itza's cheek through her veil. Itza flung her arms around Maria and they sat holding one another, gently rocking, until they heard the cries of the men from the last yawl departing, calling them back.

The water was turquoise blue with a crystalline quality and the bottom appeared just inches away. Maria, absorbed in all that had transpired on the island, entertained herself by spotting swerving fish that dodged the boat in the warm Caribbean water as they rowed back to the fleet of ships.

The men, in good spirits, were splashing one another as they rowed. One stood up, removed his shirt and boots and dove from the yawl to their right. They all stopped rowing for awhile to enjoy the beautiful day. Maria longed to remove her gloves and allow her fingers to trail in the water. She watched the man strike out in powerful strokes, then dive beneath the waves, emerging a moment later with a pink lipped shell taken from the sandy bottom.

"Shark!" a shrill voice rang out in alarm.

Behind them, a grey fin sliced the water's surface, heading straight for the swimmer.

A deathly chill ran through Maria, stirring goosebumps to her skin; she jerked herself back from the gunnel to the center of the yawl and watched in helpless horror.

The boats erupted in a frenzy. The men splashed the water with their oars to draw attention away from the frantically swimming man and yelled encouragement to swim to the nearest yawl waiting to pluck him from the water. The shark veered and passed within inches of the helpless man. Someone threw a boat hook, just missing the swiftly passing fin. As he finally reached the boat, numerous hands reached out, pulling in the panicked swimmer just as the yawl was rocked by the shark's angry attack. At almost the same moment, a shot rang out. Maria jolted in surprise, turning toward the gunner who held a smoking arquebus aimed at the water. A widening pool of red blood spewed in all directions as the shark splashed out his death throws with a lead ball lodged in his head. While the boats exploded in cheers, the gunner was slapped on his back for a good shot. The shark floated quiet on the water's surface as someone deposited a boat hook in the once menacing fin to tow the sea prize back to the ships.

They sailed for four days with good winds before another storm hit. The fury was just strong enough to force the fleet to hug the coast, obliging them to enter a small inlet and wait the storm out during the night. The morning of March 9th dawned clear and calm, and what they thought to be an inlet revealed itself as a broad bay with sandy, white beaches. Anchored at the opposite end of the bay, was by heavens grace, the ship they had thought lost. Cortez called his men together on shore and had his chaplain conduct mass. They thanked heaven for this omen, the divine intervention which led the lost brigantine to safety, and them to the lost ship.

They found a small shrine on the beach, but it appeared to have been abandoned long ago. There seemed to be no inhabitants about, which surprised them considering the beauty of the bay and the presence of fresh, running water.

The lost crew had not been idle, having already beached their vessel and made repairs. They had been preparing to set sail, and their morning details had been fresh water replenishment from a nearby stream and a foraging journey into the dense jungle before departure. Cortez adopted their plan to forage the jungle. He was curious of its resources and wanted to see if there was anything of use.

Maria was in Cortez' cabin, begging to be allowed on the expedition and getting on his nerves. Her arm was totally healed now, and he no longer felt the guilt which had made it possible for Maria to experience the freedom she had in Cozumel.

"No!" he animately refused. "I'm responsible for your safety until we can return you to Cuba, and the jungle is no place for a spoiled little girl." Emphasizing 'spoiled little girl', he brushed by her and stood by the cabin door, hand extended, ushering her exit and signaling the end of the discussion.

Maria was furious as she left the cabin in a huff; spoiled little girl, how dare he, she thought. She was a grown woman and she would prove it. She would arrange her own expedition into the jungle, just a little way, to prove she could. She'd wait until Cortez was gone and Itza took her siesta. Then there would be no one to stop her.

The sun filtering through the dense canopy of trees gave everything the illusion of being underwater in fluid, green motion. The humid air smelled of rotted vegetation and the stifling damp-ness caused her garments to stick to her skin, making her even hotter. Soon though, excitement was racing through her and she forgot her discomfort.

A brightly colored parrot cawed over her head. She looked up, lifting her veil to get a better view. Then gingerly she stepped over a massive jungle root protruding through the ground. She played a fantasy, imagining herself a tragic heroine lost in the jungle. The air became more and more oppressive. The humidity made it hard to breathe and she began to feel dizzy. From out in the jungle came the groan of an animal. A bit frightened, she lingered in her tracks. She hadn't stopped to think if there'd be big, dangerous beasts here. But a second groan, closer now, made that possibility real.

Panic welled up within her as Maria looked around. She'd been so lost in her game of fantasy that she hadn't paid attention to her direction. Now she couldn't remember how to get back. All directions looked the same—she was lost! Maria tried unsuccessfully to calm her pounding heart. She hadn't been in the jungle long, had she? She couldn't have gone far! She stood still, holding her breath and straining for any sound of the surf to indicate her direction; all she could hear was the cawing of birds and the incessant hum of insects. A rustling behind her sent Maria headlong into flight. As she stumbled over roots and tripped on her garments, mindless panic overcame her as she ran deeper and deeper into the jungle. Finally, her burning lungs forced her to stop. Raising her veil, she gasped in mouthfuls of wet, rancid air, but swarms of stinging insects compelled her to drop her veil again.

Maria reached up and grabbed a hanging vine to hold her balance while she rubbed her burning ankles that she'd twisted from running. The vine developed scales and moved in her hand, and Maria found herself holding on to a snake as big around as her leg. She screamed from the depths of her soul, stumbling backwards in stricken fear. Turning from the huge, slithering reptile, she ran blindly for all she was worth.

From somewhere, she heard the familiar sound of dogs barking and she steered herself in their direction. Bursting into a small clearing, she recognized the faces of the Spanish foraging party grouped there at a small riverbank. Suddenly, a monstrous creature, all teeth and long, crusted body, appeared from the water in a quick blur of motion. Its jaws closed on the legs of the nearest yapping greyhound, and before anyone could act, it drug the hapless canine to its watery grave. A black curtain flew across Maria's eyes as the ground rushed up to meet her.

4

Battle of Tabasco

The mouth of the river played host to several small boats, each armed with a long pole. They'd row a few feet, push the pole to the bottom of the channel, wiggle it around to test the depth, then pull it up and move to the next spot. Maria was leaning over the railing, ardently watching the progress. She'd heard this river led to the city where her cousin Grijalva had bartered for gold last year. It's not that Maria cared all that much for gold, but her experiences with the Mayans left her hungry for more. She was sure these people would be fascinating too. She'd overheard De Aguilar tell Cortez that these people called themselves Tabascans, and he believed they understood Mayan.

She stood tiptoe to get a better view. It wasn't the best vantage point, as that was on the other side of the ship, but Cortez was there and she was giving him a wide berth. It had been three days since her foray into the jungle and he was still furious with her for disobeying his orders. She knew he didn't believe her when she had said that she only meant to walk to the edge, and then somehow had gotten lost. She was feeling guilty for lying and wanted to go tell him the truth, that she'd done it for spite, to anger him. Well she achieved that, but she wasn't so sure she liked the outcome. Maria vowed from now on that she would take responsibility for her actions. No more lies, she thought, they left entirely too nasty a feeling in one's stomach.

The returning launches broke her thoughts as Juan Sanchez climbed up over the edge with the report and Maria moved within earshot.

"Sir, the river bottom is clogged with silt and sand. I suspect they've had a lot of run off from feed streams recently, but nearly everywhere we tested proved too shallow for the ships to pass."

Cortez turned to Antonio, and inquired as to the distance upriver to the city. Then, knowing the distance to be short, he ordered launches from all ships to be readied. Before he left, he placed Maria in the doctor's care, and informed her she was not to go ashore exploring under any circumstance!

The riverbanks were heavily shaded by vegetation, with huge interlacing mangrove roots blocking any clear view of what lay beyond. The cluster of small vessels was making its way steadily upstream, when dark figures hiding behind the mangrove roots were spotted. Cortez hailed them amiably, but they answered with menacing gestures. This surprised Cortez, since he'd expected the same welcome Grijalva had received. He called his men to alert. Shortly they arrived at a large, open landing which marked the edge of a town. The landing was filled with groups of angry natives shouting and waving their weapons. Stopping in the middle of the river, he instructed De Aguilar to inform them that the Spanish came in peace, and all Cortez wanted was provisions for his men. De Aguilar translated their reply, "There's no food here, or anything else for the Spanish, go away!" Any further attempts at contact were met with jeers and hostility.

Having spotted a large island in the middle of the river he retreated for the night, knowing discretion was the better part of valor. He would enter the town in the morning and make those heathens trade their gold, Cortez thought. His reputation, and yes, his very neck depended on his returning with booty!

He sought Antonio for conference, since he knew the lay of the town from his previous expedition. They had passed a road earlier which entered the town from the rear. He would send Avila downstream with a detachment of one hundred men, letting them march up the road and come in from behind, guaranteeing submission.

Morning broke with the painted faces of hundreds of angry warriors covering the riverbanks everywhere. Rousing with speed, Cortez moved the majority of his forces to the center of the river. Again, De Aguilar hailed the angry natives for a peaceful parlay, and again they were met with loud whooping jeers, followed by a showering of arrows.

"Very well," declared Cortez, "let it be known, if there's any bloodshed, it will be on your heads." Drawing his battle sword from its sheath, he hailed, "In the name of His Sacred Majesty, King Don Carlos, and for the glory of Spain, may The Holy Catholic Church and our Blessed Lord Jesus Christ be with us now." With a downward swipe of his sword, the troops surged.

The warriors held their ground until the Spanish launches came within range near the banks of the river. With grace and speed they swept into the river in their dugout canoes. With the jostling and ramming, nearly all the crafts were capsized, leaving both the Spanish and Tabascans waist deep in water. The fighting moved to the riverbanks as the lightly clad Indian warriors leapt to dry ground, leaving the thickly armored and heavy booted Spanish struggling to get a foothold in the loose, slippery mud of the riverbanks.

The Tabascan warriors sported macaw feathers in their hair, with red, black and white mineral oil based war paint, smeared across their faces and limbs. They wielded wooden war clubs, studded with black obsidian points that lined the full circumference of the weapon. The clubs were deadly and the warriors attacked with ferocity, but when they clashed with the swords of the Spanish, the razor sharp tempering and strength of the blades sliced them through like soft clay.

Cortez had made his way to firm ground with much difficulty, when De Aguilar appeared at his side.

"Stay alert Commander, the Indians have sighted you as our leader and are shouting among their numbers to steer the assault towards you."

Surrounded on three sides by painted, screaming savages, they moved slowly forward; Toledo steel slashed and carved a human path, allowing the rest of the Spanish to gain solid ground. Cortez noted, the captain responsible for the Cozumel misunderstanding had moved into position directly in front of himself, acting as a shield. At least with the fighting this close, one needn't worry about arrows, thought Cortez.

The captain of artillery expertly worked his men to the front of the battle and the swordsmen gave them cover while they loaded their arquebuses. A slow match passed from one to the other as the "thundersticks" roared into the fray. A number of savages were propelled backwards, arms flailing skyward and collapsing, too stunned by pain to utter a cry. A chief among them lay sprawled on the ground, clutching his reddening chest. The painted faces of the Tabascans registered surprise at this sorcery, as the roars came again and again. Now retreating, more warriors fell, shot in the back running for cover in the dense forest.

Suddenly, Avila and his detachment of one hundred men swarmed in from the backroad. More belching thundersticks and the reflection of the sun on the men's cock-crested helmets, sent a panic rippling through the Tabascan warriors. Their nerve broken now and rapidly being surrounded by the demon-like Spanish, the Tabascans abandoned their city and fled in all directions into the rain forest.

Cortez marched to the plaza center and solemnly proclaimed, "I, Hernan Cortez, claim the City of Tabasco for Spain in the name of His Most Catholic Majesty, King Don Carlos."

As the sun began its descent, Cortez had the town searched for gold, positioned guards for the upcoming night, and established his headquarters in the large temple.

Settling down with the early evening sounds from the jungle, Cortez withdrew his logbook and quill, dating the entry March 14th, 1519. He then began to scrawl:

> *Engaged the natives of Tabasco today. We first offered the royal call for peace and requested safe passage, but this was denied, forcing action to protect Spanish lives.*
> *In ramming the Indians' canoes, the launches capsized and...*

"Sir!"

He was interrupted by a young aid who was still rattled at his first taste of battle. Cortez turned and studied the seventeen year old lad. He noted the bloodstained bandage wrapped around his forearm, and wondered if this one would gain enough experience, in time to ever see Spain again.

"Sir! They have a captive, and Sir, they believe he came back to spy on our encampment."

"Good!" said Cortez, thanking the aid. He slid his writing quill back in its slot in the leather writing case. Pulling on his jerkin, he followed the aid to the doors of the temple and into the now cooling evening air to interrogate the Tabascan.

Tabasco was still blanketed in the deep grey of night, but shadowy figures moved through the town in readiness. As the eastern sky graduated to early tones of pink, Cortez gave last minute instructions to the two squadrons of men.

"Keep a sharp lookout! Our scouts have reported there are warriors nearby. Find out where they're camped if you can, and absorb the lay of the land as much as possible; I'll not have us caught here like sitting ducks. Be gone, and Godspeed."

The first detachment was well down the road, when they were surrounded on all sides by native warriors and were forced to seek refuge in a small, stone building nearby. The Indians, sensing an opportunity for victory, attacked with vengeance. Their loud cries brought the second detachment, led by Alvarado, to the stranded unit's side. Alvarado slashed his way in and cleared a path for Lujo's men to escape.

The two detachments retreated down the road with a new, much larger number of native warriors hot on their heels. As they neared the small city, they were met by Cortez leading his main forces out to assist the two detachments. Hearing the firing arquebuses sent the natives running; they were not ready to face the firesticks again. Cortez then led his forces back to the city to plan his next move.

While coming to his units aid that morning, he noticed that some of the natives they had encountered were wearing different war paint and clothing, proving there was now more than one group present. This matched what the captive had told him last night. All the countryside was in arms and rushing to help the Tabascans. He'd have to act fast, as the numbers of his enemies were growing hourly.

❖

Maria was exhausted. Ever since the injured had arrived, she'd worked alongside the kindly old surgeon, tearing bandages, cleaning wounds and comforting the men in their pain with cool, wet towels on their foreheads. At first, she had only done it because she was bored and had nothing to do. Besides, she liked the doctor. He'd tell her stories of the early days in Spanish exploration. But soon, she realized that helping out made her feel good. She could really be of service, and not just a nuisance, which was how Cortez made her feel. This heartfelt feeling of accomplishment kept her by the doctor's side well into the night.

There were two more doctors on the expedition, but they were upriver with Cortez, treating the wounded who could still fight. The seriously injured were sent back to the ships.

The doctor was grateful for Maria's help, in spite of her youth. She had stood by, flinching only a little, when he poured alcohol onto the flesh of a gaping wound, then hold the man's arm still while he carefully sewed it shut with a needle and wax thread. He explained to her that the wax made it easier to remove the stitching when it was healed, and offered protection to the wound as well.

Early morning found them walking on the deck together. The doctor sucked on his pipe and they watched the smoke curl away in the cool sea breeze. Maria took long gulps of the fresh, salty air, cleaning her lungs of the night's work below deck. Soon, the doctor insisted she get some sleep, and she found herself thankful for her bunk.

The day was now half gone, and Maria felt she hadn't slept a wink. Her dreams were intruded upon by images of bloody limbs and feverish faces, and she couldn't seem to shake the excitement of the previous day. Were they going to fight again today? Were they fighting now? When she thought of the actual battle itself — men trying to kill each other—she got a queasy feeling in the pit of her stomach. Finally, she left her bunk and went on deck, thinking the air would do her good.

Maria was leaning over the boat's side, peering into the woods. Yesterday the ships had been moved back from the river's mouth; natives had been spotted in the clearings and the boatswain didn't want any trying to sneak on board. She'd heard they painted their faces, and hoped to catch sight of them.

Her attention was captured by a launch appearing at the river's outlet and heading for the Catalonia. She maneuvered herself near the boatswain's side to hear the news when he received Cortez' orders.

"Unload six of the heavy canons, and ready the horses. Tell the doctor to pack his things; he'll be needed. We're to prepare for a major battle."

The ship soon bustled with the activity of cannons and shot being loaded into the yawls and launches. The holds' trap doors were opened, and a intricate system of pulleys and tackle were set up. All sixteen horses were hoisted up and out of the ships bowels, then lowered over the sides. Shortly, the small yawl boats herded the swimming horses to shore, where men waited to rub their stiff, quivering legs.

Maria went below deck to where the doctor was packing his supplies.

"I want to go," she said firmly.

"No chance, young lady! You're not to leave the boat and you know it."

"But I'm under your charge, and besides, I'm your assistant now," she quipped.

"Nice try," he laughed, "but it'll never happen."

She watched him leave. Feeling left out, Maria went on deck to watch the boats depart. After the first had pushed off the sides of the Catalonia, she remembered that she had left her gloves down below. Returning to the doctor's cabin to fetch them, she noticed he had left the pouch with the waxed thread in it. Divine providence, she thought...it was her duty to deliver it to him.

Arriving on deck just as the last launch was being loaded with shot, she talked her way on the craft. The head sailor, not sure of what to do but knowing she'd helped the doctor last night, allowed her to board. Maria settled down in the launch, anxious to get underway before the boatswain saw her. After what seemed to take forever, they finally cast off.

Maria saw Itza appear at the side of the ship just as her launch disappeared around the lip of the rivermouth. She felt a little guilty about leaving without telling Itza, but she knew the dear old woman would have protested. Besides, she reasoned, how could she stay on board knowing so much was happening elsewhere.

She kept peering through the trees as the launch worked its way upstream, but was disappointed by the lack of painted faces to stare back at her. When they reached the landing two hours later, it was filled with the Spanish artillery preparing the canons and the cavalry exercising their horses. This made Maria a bit nervous, but her thirst for excitement propelled her onward with her mission.

She made her way to the town and was inquiring as to the whereabouts of the doctor, when she found herself face to face with Cortez.

"Now what's your excuse?" he yelled at her.

Maria found herself calmly saying, "I was helping the doctor on board the ship and I can help here as well." She showed him the pouch, "See, I have his surgical supplies with me."

Then something surprising happened. Cortez, distracted by his pressing duties, simply said, "Oh". Pointing over to a building at his left, he said, "He's set up over there." Then he turned on his heels and left. Maria was a bit overwhelmed at how easy the encounter had been, and joyfully ran off to find the doctor.

The Spanish encountered little resistance on the road entering the plane of Curtla, but found the Tabascans waiting for them across the broad plain in long lines of battle formation. Alvarado had barely filtered his men onto the plain, when thousands of screaming Indians charged the dwarfed ranks. The cannons, loaded with scrap metal shot, exploded into the dense middle of the Tabascan forces, ripping arms from torsos and shattering skulls. Hundreds of Indians lay dying and broken in the tufts of scattered sod. Shocked and surprised from the thunderous metal rain, they slowed their charge and covered the bodies with leaves, hoping to confuse the Spanish with the amount of their dead.

The Tabascans were up and running again when the second round of cannon shot tore through the front ranks of the Indians. This time large, sharp rocks had been added, and hundreds more bodies were thrown backwards, with heads ripped from shoulders, gaping holes in chests, and blood splattering everywhere.

Again they stopped to cover their dead, and again hundreds

more soon lay scattered and dead. At last, they stopped no more to cover the dead, and the frenzied screams of their chiefs led them rushing into the ranks of the Spanish. The vast numbers of Indians attacking seemed like a great human wall coming in around them, but Alvarado pressed on, moving the men forward into the heart of the fray.

The Spanish cuera armor protected them from the worst of the arrows and the crashing obsidian lined hatchets, while their own steel swords cut right through the wooden handles of the Indian clubs. The sharp points slashed through the cotton padding the Tabacans wore, then cut skin, tendon and bone to the marrow.

Still the Indians pressed forward, threatening to overwhelm the Spanish by sheer volume. The Spanish were now tiring from holding their ground, while each new layer of attacking Indians came on with fresh strength.

Alvarado stepped back for a moment to wipe his dripping brow with the cuff of his sleeve. His arm and shoulder throbbed from the constant wielding of his sword. A painted face flashed by him and a war club came crashing down, shiny obsidian teeth ripping open the flesh of his arm. Flinching just in time, he sliced his sword down the Indian's wrist, and the war club fell to the ground with the hand still gripping its handle. Pointing his sword at the warrior's throat he thrust it through, slicing the jugular vein. As he withdrew it, sticky, red blood spewed back at him and all down his front.

"Where the hell is the cavalry!" he screamed, holding his blood drenched arm.

Like an answered prayer, there came thundering hoofs and someone crying, "For Spain and San Jago!" St. James had long been considered the patron saint of Spain, and his aid was truly needed now. Cortez led the cavalry. His chestnut bay's legs carried him swiftly forward, and his voice rang out, "Viva San Pedro!" acknowledging his own patron saint and protector.

The Indians looked up in horror at the terrifying creatures riding down on them. They threw down their weapons and ran from the huge, four legged, half-man monstrosities...the horses had proved their weight in gold. Their courage broken from the Spanish "sorcery", the Tabascan Army fled the battlefield, abandoning their dead and dying.

A tired, thankful Spanish Army cheered as the Tabascans retreated from the plain. Cortez ordered the injured be taken captive and that a head count of the dead be done. Soon word came that two thousand native warriors were dead. Although seventy had been wounded, not one Spanish life was lost.

Cortez called his men together and said, "In the name of San Pedro, let us thank heaven and the Lord that we have victory." Turning to the two captive chieftains he said, "Submit now, or I will ride over the countryside and destroy everything I come across." The chieftains, trembling next to the horses, eyed the vast number of dead warriors. Spotting not one Spanish body among them, they were released with fear in their eyes to deliver Cortez' mandate.

Maria was working as fast as she could; the wounded, it seemed, were everywhere. Itza had arrived just in time to help her clean and bandage the slightly wounded, while the surgeons cleaned, lanced and sewed the more severe ones. So this is victory she thought, looking around at all the torn and battered bodies.

A soldier arrived carrying a screaming boy of about ten, his arm a lacerated mass of scrap metal shot, with blood running profusely along the arm and dripping from his side.

"Here," the man said, thrusting the child into the doctor's arms, "Sandoval said to bring this one here. He thinks his life can be saved." Eyeing the boys painted face, he said, "kinda young for a warrior, huh?"

"Oh my God!" gasped Maria, her stomach wrenched with nausea at the extent of the child's open wounds. His pain filled eyes were frantic and his little body trembled with fear. Itza brushed past them, took the child from the doctor and into her ample lap, then lifted her veil and cooed words of comfort to him. Upon seeing a motherly, native face amongst the alien, white bearded ones, he clung to Itza pathetically.

Maria held rags to the lacerations, trying to clot the blood as the doctor pulled pieces of metal shot from the boy's flesh. Each probe brought more sobbing wails from the small, terrified boy. At last the final piece was extracted, but gobs of bright-red blood continued to well from the ruptured vein. After compression and stanch rags failed, the doctor relented to the fire and withdrew a long, red hot metal rod, then thrust the stanching rod into the wound. The boy screamed, stiffened, then passed out.

Maria watched from a second floor window, hopping on one foot as she pulled on a sock. Her new black dress billowed about her. Cortez had given Itza fabric some time ago, and she'd just finished a set of new clothes for each of them. "More black!" said Maria, disappointed, "they look just like my other widow's weeds." Her old garments lay discarded on the floor and Itza bent to gather them up, wrinkling her nose at their blood stained appearance.

"I try to make clean, then we have two!" she said.

Maria didn't hear her, as she was in a rush to dress and get down to the plaza where something important, it seemed, was about to happen.

Cortez sat at a long table in the center of the square, surrounded by his officers. He looked every bit like a judge about to try the downcast native men standing across from him. Suppressed in their own city, the Tabascan leaders ordered their slaves to drop the bundles on their backs at the feet of Cortez. Upon opening, the sacks revealed the gold of Tabasco. The chiefs, through De Aguilar's translation, asked if this pleased Cortez.

He looked directly into the eyes of the Head Cacique who'd spoken and said, "Why did you make me fight you yesterday? Do you see how many of your people lay dead on that plain?" His voice grew hard, but with a note of pleading, "Why wouldn't you trade like you had before? All Spain wants is peaceful barter."

The Head cacique asked permission to squat on the ground. Then pulling his cloak around his knees he began, "We are a peaceful people; when the earlier one came we were happy to trade our gold for his beautiful jewels. But when he left, our neighbors called us old women and weak for trading with the Spanish one. Prior to this they had always respected our sovereignty. Then they began raiding our outlying villages and carrying off our food and women. They grew ever more bold. We've had constant skirmishes with them.

"When word came of more Spanish ships, we decided now was the time to show strength. We had to defy you; our honor was on the line. When we prepared to make war our former enemies rushed to our side, choosing to ally us when we crushed you. But the gods didn't smile on us." He touched the earth respectfully, "Your magic is too strong."

"That is because our magic is the only true God, our Lord Jesus Christ," Cortez said fervently. "If you threw down your powerless idols and accepted the true God, you too would know this."

"Perhaps," the sullen cacique responded. Cortez turned his attention to the gold. It was not near as much as he'd expected.

"Is this all your gold?" he asked.

"All," he replied, "we are not like the Aztecs. Our streets are not made of gold, and it doesn't flow like water as it does in the Aztec city."

"Tell me of these Aztecs," said Cortez, hiding his piqued interest.

"They live to the north, far inland. They are the most powerful people on earth."

"And that is all?"

"They are the center of much wealth and power. They are the center of the One World."

"I see," said Cortez, knowing he would get no more from the cacique. Complete with his questioning, he made an alliance with the Tabascan caciques and their neighbors, setting them free to return to their lives and to help him outfit his ships.

One day, the head Tabascan cacique arrived at Cortez' headquarters. Intent on pleasing him anyway he could, he gifted the commander with twenty strong, male slaves. "To do your labor," he said. Then he led in ten young, attractive women. "To cook for you, or take care of pressing needs," he hinted.

Cortez observed the eyes of the men around him, and knowingly ordered the slaves be sent out to the Catalonia. His eyes followed the swaying hips of the last woman out the door. "Great!" said Cortez, ten women for six hundred men. "Well, perhaps I can use them to gift anyone showing particular loyalty," he reasoned out loud for all to hear. Little did he know that one of these slaves would be the key to his conquest.

5
Kidnapped

They had been walking about an hour now, and Avila and his squadron were enjoying the peculiar wildlife that the jungle offered. He was thankful they hadn't run into any rebellious tribes as they had on their last surveying outing Cortez sent them on. Fearsome-looking but harmless, fat iguanas sat sunning themselves on the trail. Strange, round creatures that looked like tiny rhinoceros ran from their path. "Look," they shouted, "an armored one." So they called them armadillos. One of the huge black and white birds so highly prized by the natives flew overhead. They'd heard one of its feathers was worth as much as a healthy adult slave.

Screeching native war cries caught them off guard and a small band of Indians materialized, surrounding the squadron as if they'd been part of the foliage. An arrow whizzed through the air, hitting the unprotected neck of a seventeen-year-old aid. Clutching his neck he fell, gasping aloud. Quick to respond, they fired their arquebuses and chased the Indians into the dense growth. Avila returned to the retching lad, and gritting his teeth, yanked the arrow from his throat. They hoisted him in the air and hurried back to Tabasco.

The boy's face was ashen. His chest barely raised, then fell, sending a whistling sound through his punctured windpipe. The doctor, finally stanching the blood flow, stood shaking his head, "He probably won't make it, the wound's too deep." Appalled, Maria pleaded, "Surely you can sew it up, I've seen as deep or deeper."

"No Maria," he said, "I've seen many wounds, and this one's a killing wound if I've ever seen one." Maria sat by the young man's side and mopped his feverish brow, determined to pull him through by her sheer will. Several times his eyelids opened and he looked at her with unseeing eyes. The doctor kept passing, checking his pulse and shaking his head. Maria grew irritated at the doctor's denial of the boy's life. She sat helplessly by, watching the youth's face grow paler and his breath more shallow. Then his eyes opened, lit with the spark of knowing, "I'm dying."

"No!" she said desperately.

"I'm not afraid, Jesus is near, I can feel him." He focused half-empty eyes on Maria, "Thank you for being here grandmother."

"But I'm not your grandmother," she said, thinking he was delirious.

"But you're like her, I can tell. I love my grandmother," he rasped. She mopped his brow and he said, "Can I see your face before I die. Please, it would mean so much to me."

"I'm afraid I would disappoint you," she said gently.

"Please," he whispered. She hesitated, remembering Cortez' orders, then defiantly lifted the veil. He looked at her in puzzlement, then his mouth turned up in a smile, "an angel, thank you God, an angel." Then his eyes closed for the last time.

Maria watched the boy's face for any sign of life and disbelief confronted her. How could it be, she thought, how could he be talking one minute and a package of emptiness the next. He'd been young, just like her. She wondered what his unfulfilled dreams had been. She didn't know this young man, but his death touched her deeply. Where was he right now? Was there really heaven or did one just go to sleep forever. Maria was just sitting there an hour later, when the doctor pulled the blanket over the youth's face and led her gently away.

Maria was weeping, the salty tears rolling down her cheeks and dripping from her chin. Itza entered the cabin and was alarmed to find her crying, "Little one, what's wrong?" Maria had been withdrawn ever since the death of the young man, and Itza was concerned. She'd been finding her too often deep in thought with that faraway look in her eyes.

"Oh Itza, this book is so sad." Itza felt relieved and looked at the intricate scribbling on the binding of the book Maria had just set down. She only vaguely understood writing, not quite sure how one man could put down thoughts with funny looking black marks, and another person could come along, see these marks and understand them.

"Tell me about book?" Itza said.

"It's called La Celestina. It's been popular back home for ever so long, but my parents wouldn't let me read it. When I saw Sandoval had it, I just had to."

"Maybe shouldn't read, if parents say no!"

"Too late, I already finished it." Maria smiled, "it's a beautiful story, but so sad," she said, wiping the tears from her face.

"This boy Calixto wanders into a beautiful garden and he hears an angelic voice singing. He follows it to its owner who is sitting on a bench and finds the most beautiful girl he'd ever seen. Her name is Melibea. When they share conversation, he falls so in love that he tries touching Melibea where he's not suppose to, and she runs away heartbroken. He hires a celestina, a go-between, to deliver his feelings to the girl. He writes beautiful poetry to her and soon she succumbs. They are in her room making love when her father breaks down the door. Calixto tries to escape down a ladder, but falls and kills himself. Melibea runs to the turrets of the house and throws herself off to her death. It ends with her father heartbroken and crying in torment, knowing he was the cause of his daughter's death."

All that in this little book, an amazed Itza thought.

From the deck came the familiar call, "Boats in, friends out," signaling departure. Maria knew Cortez would work his way north, closer to the fabled golden city he'd heard about.

They were near shore again and the ship moved close to the mouth of the river and its fast flowing, sweet water. Maria leaned over the gunwale as she watched the launches push off that were carrying the huge water barrels. She and Cortez seemed on better terms since she'd helped with the wounded, and this gave her more freedom.

"You there, look sharp," Cortez roared. Several of the Indian maidens had come on deck, and crew members were so busy ogling them that one young sailor climbing the rigging lost his footing and almost fell. Cortez' voice brought them back to their tasks.

"Sandoval, find De Aguilar and inform him I want those girls kept off deck when we're underway. Also Sandoval," he said quietly, "if one of those young ladies catches your fancy, consider yourself welcome. Does one?" Sandoval studied the group for a moment, "the one with the red headband Sir."

Maria scrutinized the girl, feeling a bit jealous. She was a tall, slender girl about twenty four years old, with soft, doe eyes and a bright-red band wrapped around her head holding down her full, dark cloud of hair.

"Fine, she's yours," Cortez said.

Maria was still studying the girls. She noticed these didn't look quite like the women she'd seen in Cozumel; some did, but some, such as the one Sandoval chose, were taller and more slender with finer features, and none had the malformed heads or crossed eyes.

"Tell me Sandoval," she heard Cortez' voice again, "why her? She's the oldest girl in the group."

"That's why Sir. I prefer more mature women over ones just out of swaddling," he teased.

Maria felt resentment rising. So that's why he treats me like a child too, she fumed. She didn't want to admit it, but she was infatuated with the tall, handsome Sandoval. Her thoughts were interrupted by the muffled gunshots of arquebus fire. Cortez and Sandoval sprang into action, rounding up men and weapons, loading and lowering the launches and sending off the reinforcements, all in five minutes time.

Before too long the Spanish returned. Tied up in the bottom of the boats were several human bundles. These bundles, when hauled on board, proved to be the rudest savages Maria had seen yet. Their entire bodies were covered with tattoos and their long, twisted locks of uncombed hair were sticking out in all directions, reminding her of the creature Medusa from Greek mythology. Their lips and noses had large holes poked in them with pieces of bone sticking through the holes. Were these the cannibals De Aguilar had spoken of? She cringed, stepping back a couple of paces.

De Aguilar stepped forward speaking a few words; there

seemed to be much head cocking, with trial and error in communication. Then De Aguilar tried again, this time adding hand signals, which brought a rash of words and gestures and ended with the savages breaking into wide smiles and touching the deck in front of Cortez.

"Sir," De Aguilar reported, "they say they are a tribe of people living deep in the woods—good warriors for many generations. But now they must pay tribute and submission to the Aztecs. They say from here on, all are subject to the Aztec Empire.

"At first they thought we were connected to it. But Sir," he continued, "they hate the Aztecs and they want to join us as allies. They seem to think we were sent by the gods to destroy the Aztecs."

Cortez looked seaward...another small omen. Thank you Lord, he said to himself. After reloading the barrels of fresh water, they sailed on.

The men were rowing from the small island as if they were being chased by demons. Climbing up over the gunwale, the officer was white faced.

"Well?" asked an impatient Cortez.

"Sir, we didn't come across a soul on the island and there are no signs of life, just temples. But..." he stammered.

"Well, what is it? Out with it man!"

He began to shake. "Sir, in the temples there were vast pools of blood all over the alters and floors, and even splattered on the walls. They reeked with putridness.

"And Sir," he added, "it was recent. The blood was only a couple of days old. There were no bodies to be counted, but judging by the blood, many people were slaughtered." Dismissed, he wandered away muttering, "so much blood, so much blood."

"Damn heathens," said Cortez, turning his eyes toward the island. "What went on there?" he added softly. The incident hardened his resolve. He was sure this was why Spain had been chosen to fulfill this holy mission...to bring the Lord Jesus Christ and the Holy Catholic Church to these barbaric savages. They sailed on.

In early April they arrived at a large, regional native market where people had come from many miles around to sell their wares. The traders acted as if they were expecting the Spanish, and welcomed them as friends. The market was spread out in many directions. One section held row after row of produce: cocoa beans, melons and papayas from the Mayan lands; onions, avocados, and amaranth grains from the Aztec capitol; and an abundance of corn, limes, peppers and turkeys having come from all the surrounding areas. Another section was devoted to rows of dyes and materials, especially the cotton cloth woven into hupilis, or skirts for women. For the men, there were loincloths and large rectangular pieces to be tied on one shoulder as a mantle.

Maria was rushing up and down the rows in excitement. Castile has markets, but not like this, she thought. She examined an embroidered and feathered blouse, then spotted a patterned vase that sparkled in the sunlight. "There's so much," she squeaked in delight. Itza tried to stay in Maria's wake, keeping a close eye on her elated charge, but she was pretty overwhelmed herself. Maria looked up from a necklace of large, stone beads carved into different faces, trying to see how far she was from Cortez. He'd warned her she was to stay within sight and earshot. She noticed that a number of Spanish had gathered around Cortez, and a growing excitement held them. She pushed her way over to join them, stopping just long enough to admire two brightly colored parrots sitting on the shoulder of an old merchant. Then, working her way through the group, she came up behind Cortez.

Her eyes widened at the large, gold bowl with huge clusters of emeralds set into its finely etched sides. The merchant was offering it for the handful of beads Cortez held, but there seemed to be a hitch in the arrangement. The man kept pointing to the beads and holding up several fingers. Cortez would count out the beads and try to give them to him, but the merchant kept shaking his head.

"Try again De Aguilar," said an aggravated Cortez.

"It's no use," De Aguilar said, "he doesn't understand Mayan and I don't know what he's speaking. No one here seems to understand Mayan." Cortez was getting upset, and the piles of riches laid out before him only added to the frustration. "There's got to be a way out of this," he said.

Suddenly, Sandoval motioned him toward a young woman.

It was one of the slave girls the cacique had gifted him with. She was eighteen, with beautiful tawny skin and a voluptuous healthy body she carried with grace and dignity.

"Ah yes, I've noticed her before," Cortez said, feeling a stirring in his groin. She was bartering with one of the merchants, gesturing towards some flowers and obviously speaking their tongue. "By Jove, get that girl over here!" he commanded.

After a few Mayan words with De Aguilar she turned to Cortez, saying in broken Spanish mixed with a bit of Mayan, "My Lord, the merchant wants all green jewels."

"Thank you," he said graciously, while eyeing her splendid body.

With the girl's help, the trading progressed smoothly and Cortez soon reveled at the numerous, beautiful gold items he'd bought for so few beads. When he had his fill, he ordered his men to set up tents along the beach; they would stay for a short time. The trading was good and Easter would be upon them in three days.

Cortez was watching the ships' padres set up an altar for tomorrow's Good Friday Mass, and he bowed his head in reverence as the ship's statue of Madonna and Child passed him. He then sat down as De Aguilar arrived with the young Indian woman. Cortez asked her how she had learned so much Spanish in just a little over a week's time. She explained that she usually needed to hear a word only once to remember it.

"Oh," said Cortez, "this is how you understand the language here."

"No sir," she said, "this is Nahuatl, the tongue of the Aztecs, and I am Aztec."

Cortez sat forward with interest, wondering how an Aztec girl had come to live among the Tabascans. "My mother was a secondary wife to The Second Reverent Speaker, the Lord of Texcoco," she explained fervently. My mother was caught up in harem intrigue and was betrayed. She was innocent. They executed her by wrapping a tong around her neck and choking the life from her body. I was a child of seven and was forced to watch her death.

"Then they sold me into slavery," she said coldly, "and I was sent far away from my home and the capital. I speak many tongues because the gods have fated it."

"So," said Cortez, "you are an Aztec Princess. How would you feel about seeing the Aztec capitol again?"

"I hate the Aztecs. They ruined my life!" she said, as her lovely face screwed up with anger.

Cortez sat back at the girl's venomous reply, realizing how valuable she would prove to be.

"What's your name?"

"Mexitla."

"Have the good fathers baptized you yet?"

"Yes Sir, they have."

"What name did they give you?"

"Marina."

"From now on," he said commandingly, "you will be one of the expedition's interpreters. I shall call you Dona Marina." His grey eyes lit up as they met her dark luminous ones.

A small, dark, bird like man arrived and was standing outside Cortez' headquarters. On being shown in, he quickly prostrated himself on the ground and then stood up, blurting into rapid speech as if the information he carried was about to make him burst. When he was finished De Aguilar and Dona Marina turned to Cortez, and in a three way translation they informed him that the governor of the area, the Great Lord Tudilli, was on his way and would arrive the day after tomorrow.

Maria had a secret. She giggled and imagined herself a great queen, as she regally picked up the bottle in front of her and poured its contents into the pewter goblet on the table.

"Oops, missed," she said, as part of the rich liquid rolled down the side of the cup. She picked it up and licked its side, then let the pungent liquid roll down her throat. She pretended she was the fair Melibea and her secret lover Calixto had presented her with this rare wine from the farthest reaches of the world. To prove her love for him she must drink the whole thing down and let its magic essence of love flow through her whole body.

Maria had gone back into the private storage room looking for a small item she'd lost there, when she noticed that the steward had opened a huge crate of Cortez' private liquor stock. One small bottle would surely never be missed, she thought. Now, Maria had drunk watered wine her whole life, but only on rare occasion had she been allowed to drink the strong liquor, and only tiny amounts. But now she was a grown woman, right?

She gulped down more of her magic potion and imagined herself high in a tower with the noble Calixto, but his face kept changing to Sandoval's. "Damn! Oops, mustn't say that," she giggled, covering her mouth. The room seemed to be turning and her eyes kept getting fuzzy. She tried to get up but her legs wouldn't support her, so she sat back down. "Shame Maria, your drunk," she admonished herself, then hiccuped and giggled some more. She found herself fantasizing about what it would be like to kiss Sandoval. Would the kiss be soft or would he press hard? Would he try to stick his tongue in her mouth? She'd heard some men did that.

Maria was brought out of her musing by footsteps in the hall. It was a young girl giggling, and then Cortez' voice shushing her. "Ah ha!" thought Maria, Cortez has company. Maybe he's holding her hand, or even kissing her. No, no, he's married. Besides, he doesn't even like other girls; look how he treats me. "Maybe," she whispered to herself, "she's telling him secrets about the gold and the Aztecs. Yes, that's what it is; well I want to hear too!" She pulled herself up tall, as if standing in front of an imaginary commander, "Yes Sir! I, Royal Spy Maria De Velaquez, do take on the mission to find out the great Aztec secrets." Then with a tipsy salute, Maria stumbled from her cabin and headed back to the store room.

"Sssh, quiet," she told herself as she swayed back and forth, trying to get her fingers to work the secret latch, "it's here somewhere." She started giggling again and clamped her hand over her mouth so hard that it brought on a fit of hiccups. Finally, she opened the trap door, and reminding herself that spies must move with stealth, she tiptoed back into Cortez' secret compartment. Maria pulled her veil off so she could see better—spies need clear vision, she reminded herself. Looking into the room, she could see no one sitting at the table. Pooh, they left. Mission aborted, she thought. Then she heard a soft giggle in the corner of the room; she repositioned herself to get a better view.

Cortez' boots lay on the floor and his white shirt lay next to them. The young girl ran her fingers through the short, dark hairs on his chest and laughed. Then she playfully tugged at his goatee.

"I thought it would be that Aztec girl," breathed Maria, finding herself drawn in by the scene unfolding in front of her.

Cortez pulled the girl's loose, white dress up over her head and cupped his hand over her small breast. Toying with its dark nipple, he pressed his mouth to her lips and pushed her back onto the bed. Then lowering his mouth to her breast, he teased her nipples with his tongue while fumbling with the wrapped length of cloth covering her woman parts. Finally, freeing it, he pulled off his own pants. Maria was a little embarrassed at the sight of two completely naked bodies but couldn't tear her eyes away. Then Cortez pulled the tawny-skinned girl under him, and separating her legs, he thrusted downward. The bed creaked and jostled, their movements coming faster and faster until, with a cry, Cortez collapsed onto the heaving girl.

Maria, mostly sober now, sat on the bed back in her room. Itza lay quietly sleeping. Maria had pretended to be asleep so she wouldn't have to talk to Itza, and she didn't want to speak to anyone. The images of what she'd seen kept going through her head. She pulled her knees up and wrapped her arms around her legs, resting her chin on them.

Was that making love, she wondered? Was that all there was to it? Was there more, something she'd missed? The girl seemed to like it—would she like it? The Mother Superior had said sex was just for having children, and was simply the duty of a married woman, not something to be enjoyed. But that girl seemed to enjoy it, she thought wistfully. Looking down, she noticed her nipples pushed hard at her chemise. "Maria," she said, imitating the Mother Superior's voice, "you shameless hussy!" Then she turned over and went to sleep.

❖

The open square seemed to be overflowing; it looked as though every Indian from miles around was there to greet the governor. Everyone was in a holiday spirit. Young girls wore flowers behind their ears and looked shyly at young men, who pretended not to notice them, but strutted as they walked by. Cortez stood under a pavilion wearing a fine, lace-edged shirt with black doublets and tunic. A velvet cape hung down his back and an ornate sword, originally owned by his grandfather, was strapped at his side. The rest of the Spanish officers were dressed in similar, elegant fashion and Maria was surprised that such attire had been on board.

Dona Marina was standing by Cortez' side. Her white dress was heavily embroidered at the neck and hem, and she wore a bright red band around her head. She looked every inch the Aztec princess; gone was the slave girl. She held her presence as to make it obvious that she was the commander's woman, and likewise expected that respect.

The buzzing of the throng quieted, as the calling of conch shells sounded over the crowd. Then, with the measured beating of drums, row after row of warriors came through the crowd. Their costumes were designed to make them look like huge birds of prey or giant hunting cats. They carried clubs edged with rows of deadly sharp obsidian teeth, and each held a shield ornamented with rare feathers displayed in geometric patterns. Each group seemed to be more elaborate than the last, and still they came in long, ordered rows, till it reminded Maria of how it must have been in Imperial Rome.

After the warriors, came retainers or slaves, carrying huge baskets of food, cloth, feathers, golden vessels and what looked like spices. What must have been close to a hundred baskets were all laid out in even rows in front of Cortez.

Maria guessed there were thousands of people accompanying this governor, and she wondered what he'd be like. She didn't have long to find out. Another bellowing call from the conches and a huge litter carried by ten slaves appeared. The backrest arched high into the air and was covered by what appeared to be a canopy made of nothing but feathers. Maria gasped as the sun hit the iridescent ones, causing the canopy to glow like a stained glass window.

Then she saw him. She guessed him to be about forty years of age, with broad shoulders, a high arched Roman nose and firmly set lips that gave him a look of haughty regality. When the litter was set down, Lord Tudilli stood and walked over to Cortez. Maria could see he was a tall man, hovering over Cortez by several inches, and the height difference was made even more apparent by the tall, backward swooping, feathered headdress worn by the governor.

Easter Sunday was one of her favorite times. She wondered what the women in Castile would be wearing this spring. She had to admit, as much as she usually mocked the fashion conscious back in Spain, it would have been lovely to wear a new dress for Easter Mass. Something of the new trend, with the see-through blouse and one skirt posing as three would be nice…something with color, anything but this drab black. She thought of her parents, especially her mother. Celebrating Easter had been the first calm experience bearing resemblance to anything she'd left back in Spain, or Cuba for that matter.

The altar was alive with bundles of native flowers. The Madonna and Child looked ethereal with their forms bathed in clouds of incense. The padres passed through the crowd with censors swaying to make all present holy. The native population had gathered close; even Lord Tudilli was present and seemed impressed with the sacredness of the occasion.

With the Mass about to start, Maria's eyes fell on the statue of Mary and she thought of the Divine Mother's presence in her life. Her heart opened and tears began to form. Yes, she thought reverently, this is the way life should be observed. She vowed to herself and the Holy Mother that she'd never again do anything less than what the Holy Scriptures taught. From now on she would be a paragon of virtue.

Maria was furious. She clenched her fists so hard the knuckles drained of all blood and the egg white and earth plaster cracked. "How could he?" she fumed. A baffled Itza trailed in her wake, struggling to keep up. They had gone to the market to entertain themselves with the array of new merchandise that appeared almost hourly, as different merchants came and went. Maria spotted Sandoval. She smiled and hurried in his direction to ask if he knew when the Easter feast started. Suddenly, the Indian girl, the one he had chosen, walked up to his side. Maria watched them cavort, and then saw him purchase the most beautiful necklace for her, just like the one Maria wanted. She whirled on her heels and bumped into a display of pots, sending them rolling. Itza showed up in time to help her pick them up.

"What's wrong with you?" Itza asked, grabbing her arm.

"How could he?" she spat out, with hurt in her voice.

"Who he, Cortez? You fight Senor Cortez again?"

"No, Sandoval!" Maria cried.

"Sandoval? What Senor Sandoval do?"

"He bought that, that girl a present…the most beautiful necklace you've ever seen!"

"How do you know the most boo-ti-ful?" Itza asked, copying Maria's words. "And what girl?"

"That native girl Sandoval chose." She spit the words out, "and I know about the necklace because I saw it yesterday and I wanted it, and now she's got it!"

"Oh," said Itza, finally understanding, "you like Senor Sandoval."

"I don't like him!" she said rebelliously.

"If Maria like Senor Sandoval, why not you tell him?"

"I just said I don't like him. I'm not going to tell him anything, besides he's got her," she said vehemently.

"If you no like him, how come you jel-us?"

"I'm not jealous!" she said, as her voice rose above the crowd and several people looked their way. "I don't like him, I just wanted the necklace, okay?" She turned and fumed off.

"She bad jel-us," Itza said to herself and laughed, "She grow fast."

The hot sun was at last receding and the beach was near full. Cortez had prepared on this day to impress. Dressed as he had for Tudilli's arrival, he sat atop his war horse Colorado, and paraded forward to meet the Aztec Governor and the invited one hundred dignitaries. Stopping directly in front of Tudilli he drew his sword and pointed it skyward. Holding steady to command attention, he then sliced it downward through the humid air. Fourteen canons in succession sent their thunder into the air. The natives present began to run and the dignitaries behind Tudilli started shuffling about, talking among themselves and not sure what to make of the loud thunder noise.

Cortez reined Colorado until he was prancing backwards, his knees lifting high in ceremonial fashion; then they turned and galloped down the beach. As he reached the far end, he joined the ranks of the cavalry, and in uniform maneuvers, they made their way back up the sandy beach. Sixteen horses in total made up his cavalry, but to the Indians who'd never seen this type of animal before, these armored beasts looked horrific. The sixteen men atop their mounts were also in full armored regalia. They cantered up the sandy stretch of beach, Cortez at the head, with one man carrying the flag of Castile, and another to his left, the flag of Spain. Still another to his right was bearing the flag of the Church of Spain.

Cortez led the cavalry up and past Tudilli, and back again while the canons repeated their roar of thunder. Once Cortez led them through one traverse of the beach he veered off to join Tudilli, while the cavalry continued in this fashion for half the hourglass. Tudilli remained unimpressed, still and silent.

Maria was frustrated; she could either sit at the main table and eat with the accursed veil, or retire to a small tent off to the side and eat alone with Itza. If she ate with Itza, she could really enjoy the juicy roast pig that she'd been looking forward to all day, but she would miss most of the excitement at the main table. Finally, she decided on a compromise; she'd coax the Catalonia's cook to serve her first in the little tent. That way, she could take her veil off and enjoy every sumptuous bite, then hurry outside to sit with the rest of the crowd.

The ship's cook motioned to Maria to come into the tent, where he served them plates of her beloved crispy pork, squash baked in honey, a pumpkin soup fragrant with sage, fresh crusty bread and slices of juicy papaya—a fruit Maria had never eaten before. As Maria and Itza ate, they could hear the yelling and occasional gunfire, and she knew that the martial entertainment was still going on. Maria felt inside, that perhaps guns and wild horse antics were not appropriate entertainment for the Lord's resurrection day.

Voices outside the tent signaled the commencement of the feast. Maria licked the sweet, sticky fruit juice from her fingers and lowered her veil, hurrying outside so as to miss nothing.

Lord Tudilli noticed the small figure in the strange, black drapements hurry from a tent and scramble to a seat near the end of the table. What? Is she going to eat here with the men, he thought? Shocked and amazed by her courage, he observed her from the corner of his eye. Women are supposed to eat separately and only after they'd rightfully served the men. The governor noticed that Cortez kept a close eye on her and he wondered what their relationship was...a relative, or his mother perhaps. He had heard she was an old woman; maybe that's why she'd been allowed to sit at the table. But what about the other one, he thought, the short round one? Who was she? She'd remained behind but had poked her head out briefly, he remembered. Why were they dressed so strangely? Was this something religious? His thoughts shifted as Cortez stood to command silence for the prayer.

Maria ate small pieces of bread and aptly watched the governor and his men. Sometimes a veil was a good thing, she thought. You could observe someone to your heart's content and no one would be the wiser. She was curious about this haughty man; he was so alien with his swinging, gold earrings and strange mantle tied on one shoulder, trimmed at the edge with bright feathers. His face was so frozen and emotionless, he reminded her of her Great Uncle Juan. She'd heard that her uncle never smiled once in his whole life. Perhaps Lord Tudilli was the same way.

"To His Most Catholic Majesty, King Don Carlos. The greatest prince in the world!" Cortez said, raising his glass in salute at the close of the meal. Dona Marina, sitting just back of the table, was translating for Lord Tudilli.

"Tell me," asked Tudilli, "who is this King Don Carlos?"

"Only the greatest monarch in the world," Cortez said. "His Majesty maintains vast holding of land, and his power stretches even across the 'great sea'. His grace was given to him from heaven, as the arm of Catholicism. He is my King!"

"He must be as the Great One, My Lord Montezuma, Ruler of all the World, and Sovereign of all you see here," said Tudilli, "But I'd never heard of another so great until now."

"Tell me," asked Cortez, "is he the ruler of the city further inland we've heard so much about?"

"Yes, my Lord Montezuma's city, Tenochtitlan, is the greatest city in the One World."

"Well then," said Cortez, thinking fast. "I am the emissary of the Great Lord Don Carlos, and it's my duty as his representative to visit this Montezuma in his magnificent city with my king's greetings. When can we leave?"

"I will send word to my Lord," said Tudilli carefully, "and ask his permission."

"Do so then, and how long will the message take?" he asked, trying to gauge the distance.

"My runners will be at the capital within a day and a half."

"So the capital is very close!" exclaimed Cortez.

"No sir," said Dona Marina, after conferring with De Aguilar for the correct distance terms. "It's seventy leagues."

"How on earth can anyone run seventy leagues in a day and a half? Impossible, you must be mistaken on the distance," Cortez said.

"Oh no sir," she said, "not one runner but many; each run a certain distance, then pass the message to the next. They train their whole life, these runners. It's a much sought after and respected position."

Tudilli watched the interaction between Cortez and the Aztec woman and guessed its substance. Looking Cortez in the eyes, he bluntly said, "What do you want? Why have you come here?"

"Gold!" said Cortez. "I suffer from a disease of the heart and gold is the only thing able to relieve it."

Tudilli sat back and interlaced his gold laden fingers in front of him. He'd never heard of a disease cured by gold but nothing of these strange people would surprise him. Somehow he didn't believe Cortez. He had the forces to easily destroy these pesky Spanish intruders, but he would seek his lord's council first. He would send the message and its request for gold, but he'd also send his own message…a message of distrust.

The camp was buzzing and everyone seemed to be discussing Montezuma and the city. Maria had heard the walls and streets were covered with gold, everyone ate off gold plates, and that the gold was so plentiful, it laid around the city until someone needed it. While walking by a campfire, she had heard one pockmarked veteran tell his companions that the gold was just laying there to be scooped up by anyone who had a mind to do so, and the dumb Aztecs didn't even know its worth. All they had to do was enter the city and take what they wanted. The stupid Indians wouldn't even be aware of what they were doing until it was too late.

Maria entered the small tent Cortez had set up for her and Itza; it was a relief not having to sleep on the cramped ship, even if it was only for a little while. Itza was setting up the bedding and humming to herself.

"Itza, what do you think about the Aztec city and king?" she asked.

"Think? What you mean think?" she said as she kept working.

"Do you believe the stories about all the gold?"

"Me think gold stories go to man's head so they no longer think right, and me think Aztecs much love their gold, like Spanish do. Itza hear stories about Aztecs too. Me not want to go to Aztec city. They cut out heart, Itza want to keep heart."

"Who told you that?" Maria said.

"Itza hear in camp, from Mayan girls we bring from Tabasco. Senor Cortez best not go to Aztec city. Death maybe wait there."

Maria felt a sense of foreboding and a chill ran through her.

She was walking along a road that led to a golden city looming in the distance. The sun reflected off the streets and rooftops, almost blinding her. A man appeared on the road, draped in gold garments from head to toe. When Maria looked into his dark eyes she felt gladness rush from her heart. She had found him; she always knew she would. He reached down and took her hand, leading her towards the city. Maria's eyes flew open as the morning sun heated her face through the tent wall. A feeling of half-forgotten yearning warmed her, but for what, she couldn't remember.

❖

The word spread through the market like wildfire; the king's message was here. A group of runners moved through the camp, packs on their backs and thump lines tied across their heads. Beads of perspiration rolled off their foreheads and down their hairless chests. Their long, sinewy leg muscles were cramped from carrying the unaccustomed burdens. Lord Tudilli escorted them right to Cortez' tent. The commander came out pulling down his jerkin and smoothing back his hair as a disheveled Dona Marina appeared at his side. Maria pushed through the crowd to hear what the Aztec King had said.

Tudilli had the runners drop their packs in front of the commander and reveal their contents. Gold!! Inside were gold cups, bracelets and bowls, gold earrings and necklaces, hundreds of tiny gold hatchets and quills full of gold dust. All were pure gold…some of the most exquisite items they'd yet come across on their journey.

"This," Tudilli indicated, "is gold for your heart, a gift from my lord."

"Thank you!" Cortez replied in awe.

Then, taking a piece of bark paper he gently unfolded like an accordion, Tudilli began to read:

I, Montezuma, Chief Reverent Speaker, Ruler of the One World, send my greetings to King Don Carlos and his emissary, Hernan Cortez. I regret that as of late, I've been unwell and therefore am unable to visit you at the coast bordering my lands. Due to my many enemies between the Big Water and my capital, I could not ask you to take such a long and dangerous journey. So I regret that a meeting at this time would not be possible. I ask you to send my greetings to your king and have sent along an emerald shaped as an egg, without flaws, with several other small tokens for his pleasure. The gold is for your heart disease. I hope it brings you relief.

> *First Reverent Speaker,*
> *Montezuma.*

Tudilli extracted a bag from the first parcel, which he handed over to Cortez. It produced an emerald as big as a man's fist, and a necklace of finger length carvings of lustrous jade. Dona Marina gasped and then whispered to Cortez, "This is most valuable, Sir. Jade is considered most precious thing to Aztecs." Tudilli produced several more pieces of jewelry set with gems, and finally a necklace of dark green jade beads and perfect pearls. Cortez all but ignored these things.

"Tell your Lord thank you for the gifts," he said to Tudilli, "but I have been two thousand leagues on this journey, and seventy more is no hardship at all; so he need not concern himself with my safety. Therefore, I'm ready to leave for the capital at once."

"So be it," said Tudilli as he turned and walked from the camp.

While they waited for Montezuma's next reply, Maria overheard Cortez tell Sandoval, "one had to be firm with these people." He was sure Montezuma wouldn't refuse him a second time; after all, if he ruled a vast empire, Montezuma must realize that it would be better to have Spain as an ally rather than an enemy. Maria found herself hoping this was so. She too, wanted to visit the city.

This adventure was shaping into something beyond her wildest imaginings. She could just see the expression on Dona Cecelia's face. When she told her all about it, she probably wouldn't believe her, so she'd have to save some Mayan and Aztec trinkets as proof. Just then she heard the servants running through the market, making way for the governor. Maria finished dressing and rushed off to Cortez' headquarters to hear the news, but Tudilli had already got there. She arrived in time only to hear the tale end of it…"so I must make it clear, it's not at all possible for you to visit the capital at this or any time in the immediate future…First Reverent Speaker, Montezuma."

Cortez' face went pink, then red and finally purple. Maria stepped back into the crowd, not wanting to be in range of his anger. "What?" Cortez exploded, "this is an outrage to Spain, to King Don Carlos, and to myself. I'll not stand here and except this insult; no one will keep me from the capital. Let them try and stop me!" Dona Marina was trying to translate as fast as she could, while Cortez raged on.

Lord Tudilli's face remained in its usual, impassive expression all throughout Cortez' tirade. Before Dona Marina had even finished translating, he turned and left without a word. He honored his King Montezuma, but he wouldn't stand and listen to this for anyone's sake. These people have as much control as undisciplined children, thought Tudilli. He'd follow Montezuma's orders as it would be dishonorable to do anything else; but he still thought it would be better to destroy these erratic children before they became any stronger.

Maria stayed away from Cortez; his anger scared her. The whole camp was in an uproar, with each man swearing at the imagined insult to country and king. Maria noticed the Indian servants were slipping out of camp; all that remained were the slaves given to them at Tabasco. The market seemed to be dwindling by the minute. She reasoned that it was the Spanish wrath, which seemed to roll from all directions; so she didn't blame them.

As twilight fell, Maria, seeking to escape the oppression of the camp grabbed Itza's hand urging her to walk through the now abandoned market plaza. A slight breeze ruffled their veils, bringing a cooling relief after the day's disturbance. The fast-darkening sky showed the first glimmer of starlight. Maria felt the tension of the day start to lift, and she interlaced her hand through Itza's fat fingers.

Suddenly, strong, forceful hands grabbed her from behind, pinning her arms to her sides and clamping her mouth shut. This can't be happening, thought Maria as she struggled to get free. Out of the corner of her eye she saw Itza break free from her abductor, and like an incensed mother bear sensing danger to her cub, she charged. Her assailant raised a war club in the air and brought it down on Itza's head. She dropped to the ground in a motionless heap. A scream rose from Maria's soul as she struggled to free herself. A sharp blow to the back of her head and stars flashed before her eyes, sending her into darkness as she thought...my god, they've murdered Itza!

6
The Journey

Blood was everywhere. It was splattered on the floors and across the walls and it dripped down the sides of the altar, forming thick, sticky pools around its base. The air was dense with the buzzing of flies that had come to feast on the blood. They flew around the heads of the men standing in the doorway, their sunburnt faces gone pale and their stomachs clenched with nausea.

"It's the same here too, Sir," spoke up one of Cortez' officers. Cortez turned from the door of the temple to survey the deserted village. The wind caught a broken wicker basket and sent it rolling across the dirt street.

This was the fourth village they'd visited that morning and they were all the same—deserted, everyone gone. The natives had fled during the night and even though they'd left most of their belongings, Cortez had ordered his men to confiscate nothing but food.

Where were they, Cortez wondered? Were they preparing for war? He'd sent back orders to strike camp, moving most of his men back to the ships. They wouldn't be sitting ducks, if that's what the natives intended. It appeared every one of the small, stone temples in the surrounding villages held the same macabre scene, with fresh blood everywhere.

Even though the temples had been made mute witnesses to sacrifice all night, not one body was found. This disturbed Cortez, especially since Maria was missing! Early yesterday evening he had noticed their unoccupied tent, and around ten o'clock he'd sent Alvarado out to find them, thinking Maria was on another one of her pranks. He began to worry, when two hours later the search had widened and they still hadn't been found. When Itza's basket was discovered at the other end of the plaza, he became sure they'd been taken.

Did one of these temples contain Maria's blood? With no bodies it was impossible to tell, he thought. Cortez kept looking in every village for signs of either of them, and every dark piece of fabric caught his attention. If she's not dead, he kept thinking, then where is she, or who was with her? Was it Tudilli, a local chieftain, or Montezuma? Who? He didn't like the idea of her being snatched from right under his nose. She was a pest, but he still didn't want to think of her dying on a heathen altar somewhere. God, he couldn't even give her body a Christian burial! What would Velaquez do if he should somehow get wind of this? Dead or alive, he had to find her!

Her hands and feet were numb. They were tied tight, cutting off all blood flow, and her shoulder throbbed incessantly from the pressure of lying on it. She tried to turn over, hoping to relieve some of the pain, but her head exploded in a white hot ball of agony from the slightest move. With the pain stopping her from moving, all she could think of was to keep breathing deeply to prevent nausea from overtaking her.

She seemed to be in a hut, but she couldn't be sure. The room was dim, and seeing through the veil was a bit hard at the moment. Hearing a groan from behind her, she pushed through the pain and rolled over to find another body lying there. Her heart rose in joy, "Itza, you're alive!"

"No little one. To feel like this, one must be dead!"

"Oh Itza, I was so worried about you. I thought they'd killed you for sure!"

"Me too, little one. Head feel like tree fall on it," Itza moaned. "Me too."

Just then, two men entered the hut and pulled them both to a sitting position. Itza let out a long groan from the manhandling. Maria's head swam, but began to clear as they untied her hands and feet. She had just begun rubbing her ankles to try and coax some life back into them, when she spotted a dark stain in the dirt where Itza's head had lain. "Itza you're bleeding," she said.

Before Itza could answer, they were jerked to their feet. Itza collapsed in a heap, and another man entered to help carry her to one of the waiting sedan chairs. Maria managed to stumble to the other one, leaning back to rest her throbbing head against the backrest. An old woman approached and placed a bag in her lap, and then put another one in Itza's. The chairs were hoisted in the air, and for the first time Maria didn't care about native villages. All she wanted to do was close her eyes and hide.

When Maria opened her eyes, she saw that they'd arrived in a center busy with women carrying baskets on their heads and quacking ducks being herded across the courtyard. Then she noticed the big, white building at the end of the courtyard. A large, stern man came to stand by the chairs, his legs wide apart and arms crossed over his bare chest; his message was clear...no one was to come near and they were to remain in their chairs.

She looked over at an unmoving Itza. Either she was unconscious again, or asleep. Maria watched Itza closely; reassured with the slight rise and fall of her chest, Maria turned her attention to the building.

Its whitewashed walls rose two stories in the air and the facade was a riot of color. A huge mural of an eagle sitting on a cactus with a writhing snake in its beak stretched itself across the front. Just then a familiar face emerged from the doorway. He was bareheaded without his plumed headdress, but the same, set features and unusual height gave him away. Lord Tudilli! So he's the one responsible for this! How dare he, Maria thought. She wanted to give him a piece of her mind—language barrier or no language barrier. He couldn't treat her like this, even if he was a governor. After all, her uncle was a governor too. She was just about to get up out of the chair when another familiar figure appeared. She couldn't remember where she'd seen him before, but she certainly recognized him. He was tall and slim, with well muscled legs like those of a runner. The Governor motioned to the two chairs and handed a letter to the youth, sending him on his way.

Now she remembered. Several times back at the camp, out of curiosity for the Aztecs, she'd wandered near the Governor's pavilion. Twice she'd seen the same young man slip out of Tudilli's headquarters, tucking something into the pouch worn bandoleer style across his chest. Suddenly, it dawned on her that this man was a messenger. Tudilli had been keeping private correspondence with Montezuma all along! A chill ran down her back. Had Montezuma been giving secret orders, she wondered? Why would she be part of his orders? She hadn't caused anyone harm. Perhaps all of them were in danger now. New men were assigned to the chairs, and without Tudilli even acknowledging them, they were whisked swiftly from the courtyard.

The sun had already slipped below the horizon when they arrived at the small traveler's hut. Maria and a now awake Itza were escorted inside, and their chairs disappeared with the bearers into the gathering dusk. A small fire greeted them as they entered the hut, and a wrinkled old Indian woman with a friendly face helped Itza to a straw pallet. Then she motioned to the table, which held two simple wooden bowls of steaming soup. Lastly she held up a wide-mouthed jar, indicating that this should be used to relieve themselves with; she then slipped out of the hut. Maria followed her to the door but was stopped by a tall, broad-shouldered man wrapped in a blanket, who had settled himself at their door for the night.

So! They were prisoners, she thought. She hurried over to assist Itza, who was trying to peel off the veil that had been caked to her scalp by hardened blood. Gently pulling it free, Maria leaned close to inspect the wound. A dark gash ran across the top of Itza's head. She found a jar of fresh water, and using Itza's veil she carefully cleaned away the clotted blood; it was a long gash, but fortunately not deep. She fetched one of the bowls of soup from the table and placed it in Itza's hands, and then busied herself washing the blood from Itza's veil. Their roles were reversed, she chuckled to herself; she was taking care of Itza now.

Then she spotted another jar. Carefully working the sealed clay lid loose, she took a whiff of a pungent herbal balm. Her instincts told her this was good, and was healing. Hanging Itza's veil by the fire to dry, she carried the jar to Itza's bed and spread the cooling salve into her scalp. Having laid the exhausted Itza down, she turned towards her supper of corn porridge. It was filling and tasted faintly of anise. She put a few more twigs on the fire and lowered her veil for sleep. Funny, she thought, now she felt safer with the veil on.

The day dawned bright and clear. Maria felt much better now that her pounding headache had lifted, and she was only a little stiff from the struggle. She could tell Itza felt better too, even though she kept grumbling about being too old for this sort of thing. It was the kind Indian woman who had given them the healing salve, and upon seeing Itza's cut she supplied them with a second jar, insinuating Itza should drink from it.

The morning's sunlight revealed that they'd spent the night on a hilltop surrounded by a pine forest. An immense valley stretched out before them and in the distance loomed a purple-hued mountain range. As they departed, they passed small children gathering berries, their lips stained bright-red from popping as many in their mouths as they put into their baskets. The forest trail was littered with pine cones, and Maria spotted a grey squirrel scampering up a tree. They stopped at a swiftly running stream, and one of the bearers gathered a cupful of cool, refreshing water for her to drink. Some women were chattering as they beat their wash on the rocks and playfully slapped the bare fannies of their laughing children. The children ran along the river's edge splashing water everywhere, with their small yipping companions close on their heels.

Watching the charming scene in front of her, Maria felt strangely at home and familiar.

A small man of about thirty trotted up to Maria's litter, and in native fashion he touched the ground and then his head in greeting. He broke into a wide smile and then started chattering away. His endearing demeanor reminded Maria of a little monkey eager to please.

Itza shifted and then turned in her chair, calling the man over to her. He cocked his head and looked from chair to chair, then trotted over to Itza and started his chattering again. Itza motioned for him to slow down. After exchanging a few slow words, she turned back to Maria.

"His name Kalti," she said. "Him come from Tudilli. Him speak Mayan; him come with us."

"Good, I like him," said Maria.

As they continued their journey, Kalti ran alongside and pointed out the vistas. Maria was amazed at his stamina. He, like the bearers, was able to keep a fast pace hour after hour. However, chair attendants were changed three times a day, usually at large villages such as the one they were just entering.

Kalti commented on numerous village scenes as they passed, and Maria was particularly intrigued by a woman who was coiling clay on a large stone slab. She was touched by the simplicity of the woman's craft, watching her squat in front of her hut, dip her hand in the adjacent jar of water, and then smooth the pot.

Soon they arrived in the courtyard of what appeared to be an inn. They were led inside to a large room on the second floor with a sleeping chamber.

"Why have we stopped so soon? The sun is still well in the sky." said Maria. Itza turned to Kalti, who looked embarrassed. He blurted out something and Itza laughed. She tried some more slow words with him and he nodded, then scurried from the room.

"Him say, this only place with public inn," Itza said.

"So why aren't we staying in a hut like we did last night?"

"Him say, they have bath here. Chair bearers say we stink."

"Well!" Maria said, insulted.

"Kalti check bath, so we be only ones there, then get clean clothes for Maria and Itza."

The bathroom had benches to sit on, and the stone floor sloped just enough to channel the water into a trough that ran down the center of the room and through a small tunnel leading outside. Maria felt chilled and exposed; Itza had insisted she remove all her garments in the little changing room, and only the comment of her smelling bad kept her from rebelling. She realized that the longer she was separated from her own people, the quicker her old ideals seemed to be falling away. She'd noticed today that all these people smelled good, and in fact all her own people really stank! She wondered, why was it that her people never bathed? Funny, she'd never noticed that before.

Itza, still sore from the abduction, showed Maria how to pour wooden ladles of soapy water over herself and scrub down her body with a bristle brush. Then, feeling tingly all over, Maria busied herself with rubbing the healing herbal salve into Itza's scalp. She was pleased at how fast it was working. The wound, already closed and turning pink, showed no sign of infection. She wondered what was in the salve, as it seemed better than what the Spanish doctors used.

When they returned to the changing room their filthy garments had been replaced by two flowing, full-length, white robes and a length of white fabric to be used as veils. The soft cotton felt good against Maria's skin, but she felt bare with no undergarments on. She pulled the veil over her newly braided hair, the soft drapes making her feel like a Greek princess. Even her gloves had been taken to be cleaned, so she had to keep her hands inside the voluminous sleeves.

Returning to their room they met Kalti, who'd gotten them something to eat. Dinner consisted of those little corn treats Itza called tamales.

"Kalti," said Maria, with Itza attempting translation, "are you Aztec?"

"I am both Mayan and Aztec," he said proudly.

"Oh, please speak to me in Aztec," she begged him.

"The Aztec language is called Nahuatl," he said obligingly. She entertained herself the rest of the evening by pointing to objects and asking for their Nahuatl translation. She found it strange that every word seemed familiar; she only had to hear the word once and it seemed implanted in her brain. Once or twice she knew the word even before Kalti spoke it. This had Maria spinning with excitement. She had been required to learn Latin in convent school and every phrase had been an ordeal, so she had assumed her ear was not meant for languages. This had disturbed her, for she'd fantasized learning French and English and then seeing the world. But now with this Nahuatl, it was as if she was just being reminded. As they retired for the night Maria kept reflecting on her newfound skill, until a tired Itza begged for mercy.

Maria felt hot and sticky. Her familiar black garments, now clean, felt particularly stifling after the cool, white cloth she'd worn last night. They'd traveled across the hot, arid plain all day, accompanied by extra bearers laden with supplies. As their traveling came to a close each evening, the bearers went into action and erected a small tent, placing sleeping blankets in it. They then started cooking fires for dinner.

Maria was bored. She'd longed to quiz Kalti on the names of things they had passed, but most of the day he had been busy. At least Itza felt better. She wasn't drinking much of the medicine anymore, so the pain must have subsided; but it seemed that she'd withdrawn into her own world. Maria felt guilty...Itza was obviously wishing she'd never come with her.

Even though they'd been keeping a close eye on her, she attempted to walk a few paces from the camp. No one tried to stop her, probably because there was no place to go. Now she really was tired of her veil. A couple of days ago it had seemed like a safe harbor, but now it was just a hot, oppressive thing. She kicked a small pebble, sending it clattering and raising a small dust cloud. Leaning against a boulder, she watched the men preparing dinner. Simple loincloths with mantles tied over one shoulder was all they wore, and they looked cool and free.

Maria began to reflect on her situation. She seemed to be a prisoner but they treated her well. Were they taking her to the Aztec capital, she wondered? Kalti couldn't or wouldn't tell them anything of their fate. It seemed clear that they were probably hostages for ransom. She wondered if Cortez had already received a ransom note, with demands for her safe return. Would he honor it? Well, Cortez wasn't here now. Why didn't she just take off this stifling veil and at least be comfortable? She headed back to the tent, intending to tell Itza that it was time they ended this masquerade.

Tears were welling in Itza's eyes. "What's wrong?" asked Maria.

"We go to Aztec capital," she said.

"Well, maybe not," responded Maria.

"Yes, we go there. Aztec people cut out hearts."

"Itza, don't say that," Maria pleaded.

"Itza old woman, maybe they no want me. Maybe give Aztec gods sour stomach. But Maria be young and prit-tee, they much like that. Itza's soul break, like wound on head. Bad pain, to see Maria's prit-tee heart cut out." She began to cry, "You leave on veil, they think Maria be ugly old woman."

"Itza, sooner or later they'll find out. I don't think they kidnapped us and brought us so far just to be sacrificed," she said, holding the woman close. "They've treated us well. I think we're hostages. Maybe they'll make Cortez return the gold to get us back."

"Senor Cortez pay to get you back, but he no want old Itza," she sobbed gently.

"Well, I wouldn't go anywhere without you."

"No matter. Itza old, have long life. Maria no have long life yet. No have man, no babies yet. Itza want to see Maria do these things."

"Well, something tells me everything's going to be all right," Maria said, trying to reassure her. "This city feels good to me. I want to see it and I don't think they are going to cut out our hearts; but I do think we should keep quizzing Kalti to learn more of his Aztec language and culture. That way we might find out what's going to happen to us."

"Aztec people cut out hearts, that be Aztec culture," Itza said stubbornly.

"We've been with them for three days now and I haven't seen one heart cut out," she said assuringly. She reached for the tent flap, intent on searching for Kalti.

"We no reach big city yet. Big city scare Itza." Placing her hands over her heart, she said with quiet intensity, "Me feel this city hold Itza's death." Maria froze as goose bumps rose on her arms. She collected herself and said, "You're just scared Itza. Everything will work out fine, you'll see." She hurried out.

Maria was walking on the hills overlooking her parents' country estate. Kiltos, her favorite fox terrier, came bounding up the hill to greet her with his little tail wagging ecstatically. Maria picked up a stick and gave it a toss for Kiltos to chase. A strange, soft light suddenly appeared, growing larger and brighter until a beautiful lady took form. She was dressed all in white, and rays of blue and white light shaped as a cross radiated from the center of her heart.

"Divine Mother," Maria spoke softly as she fell to her knees in awe and reverence, "I always felt someday I would see you." The Mother Mary looked at Maria with deep love and tenderness, raising her hand in greeting. Then other soft lights appeared and slowly took form around her. An angel floating in a beautiful, green light with pink rays emanating from her heart smiled at Maria, and then merged into The Virgin.

A loving, powerful woman with long, beautiful, coal black hair manifested. A silver crescent crowned her, and her perfect form radiated through her full length, pleated, white dress. She too, seemed to briefly pause before Maria, gazing knowingly at her with exotically painted eyes, before she became one with The Divine Mother. She was followed by a tall, regal woman with hair the color of wheat, who carried a sickle tied to her side. She gave way to still another and another; each had a beautiful countenance and each gave Maria a feeling of The Mother.

Lastly came a golden brown one, with sleek, black hair falling to her knees and crowned with a mass of swooping white feathers. Scenes of nature girdled her strapless gown and she carried a golden broom. She gently touched Maria's forehead, and then she too merged into The Mother Mary. Then, like soft music, Mary spoke, "You see my child, all this is The Mother and all this I AM." Then she disappeared.

With tears in her eyes Maria cried out, "Divine Mother, don't leave!" Her heart raced as she suddenly found herself in darkness. Slowly she laid back down and remembered she was in a tent and out on an open plain, far away from the green hills of Spain. She wiped away the tears and cried softly, "Please don't leave."

A sprawling, white city lay before her. The center plaza was clearly visible from the bluffs where they stood, and its streets were busy with inhabitants scurrying to and fro. Maria held her breath. Was this it, she wondered with excitement? She turned to find Kalti but his eyes were fixed skyward. Following his line of vision, she saw an amber-colored eagle swoop by them majestically with a writhing serpent dangling from its beak. Suddenly, the bird gave a great cry, dropping the snake and then following the same crashing course to the ground.

The Indians around her all cried out in dismay, and a group of women carrying produce for market let out shrill wails and covered their heads. Even Kalti, who was always so jovial, looked stricken.

"What's going on?" cried Maria, mixing Spanish with her newfound Nahuatl.

"The worst of signs," said Kalti.

"Well, could it be the eagle was old?" Maria reasoned. "Perhaps that's why he fell."

Kalti drew a deep breath to calm himself, then spoke slowly in a combination of Mayan and Nahuatl, so Maria and Itza lost nothing. "The eagle and the serpent are symbols of the Aztec people, symbols given by the gods themselves. When the Aztec people first arrived in the valley called Mexico, a good omen greeted them, of an eagle perched in a tree with a writhing snake in its beak. In spite of it being marshlands, they knew by the sign that this was to be their home." He was still shook up as he said, "There was a prophecy of an evil omen that an eagle carrying a snake should die midair."

"Oh," said Maria.

Looking around her, she saw that most of the people had gotten to their feet. Some were in huddled groups talking fearfully, while others were hurrying away as if the very spot was cursed.

She turned her gaze back to the city and asked, "So do the Aztecs think something bad will happen?"

Kalti pulled himself from his thoughts to answer her, "These people not Aztecs, these people Tlaxcalans. But Aztecs and Tlaxcalans like brothers. What is good for one also good for other."

"Then this city is not the capital?" asked Maria, disappointed.

"No," laughed Kalti, "this is the city of Cholan."

As they continued, they passed by the city. This disappointed Maria. It was the largest city she had seen yet and she wanted to experience it up close. Reading her thoughts, Kalti said, "We will be there tomorrow."

"Do you mean Tenochtitlan?" she asked hopefully.

"Yes," he said.

All the rest of that day Maria entertained herself with the wonderful stories she'd heard of the great city.

❖

Maria held her breath. Dumbfounded, she climbed out of her chair and walked to the crest of the hill. The valley stretched out before her. A patchwork maze of green cultivation surrounded a silver blue lake, enfolding a white city whose beauty took their breath away. Stretching in all directions, shimmering canals of water wove through the vast city and surrounding land like a bloodstream, and a cluster of pyramids marked the city's heart. But what really caught Maria's eye were the huge, brightly colored banners wafting in the wind above each tall building. They reminded her of angels hovering protectively above the rooftops.

Behind her and off to the side, a huge stone aqueduct ran down the mountain, slashing through the city. The distant mountain peaks caught her eye as the sun reflected off their snowcapped summits. To Maria it looked like a magic city out of a fairy tale.

Kalti called her back to her chair as many men passed by on the road, loaded with huge packs in the Aztec fashion of thump lines across their foreheads. Right behind them two men in sedan chairs whisked by, trailed by a flock of small, yapping dogs on long lines.

"Pochteca," said Kalti in Nahuatl, "merchants off to bring Aztec goods to our neighbors in the south."

"But why do they have so many dogs with them?"

"Food," said Kalti. "Good, yes? This way food carry self!"

"You mean they're going to eat them?" asked Maria, revolted.

"Yes, this kind of dog good. Aztecs much like them," he smiled.

Maria watched the merchants' caravan disappear around the bend, feeling sorry for the small waddling forms, blissfully unaware as they brought up the rear.

The road they traveled wove back and forth down the mountain, then erupted onto a wide thoroughfare passing through lush, green fields. They began to pass farmers and Maria watched as they poked a stick in the ground, dropped in a seed and then covered it over with their foot. The road soon became thick with traffic. In the beginning it was mostly farmers, their backs loaded with produce, but soon it seemed like a festival. There were groups of children, some carrying ducks and melons. Women with hair crossed over their heads in braids called out to the laughing children. Some had sleeping babies kept close to their bodies in a sling that left their hands free for the net satchels they carried.

The people respectfully stepped aside, as a group of warriors adorned in spotted skins and feathers passed. The children peered wide eyed with curiosity at Maria and Itza's veils. More farmers were working on what appeared to be plots of turf roped together and floating on the lake surface. Kalti told her that the white caking at the lake's edge was from the brackish water.

Passing over a wide bridge that appeared to be removable, they left the outer lands behind and entered the city limits. The bridge rose about ten feet above the water's surface, and a small fishing craft passed underneath with its nets trailing behind. Nearly every building in the city was white, some rising three or four stories in the air.

Passing by one of the many courtyards, Maria peered in at a young girl about her own age who was stirring a huge pot over a small fire. She had a faraway look on her face, and Maria wondered if she was thinking of the attractive young men she'd seen on the streets. Looking around, Maria had to admit these men were handsome. Taller than any group she'd seen so far, most of them wore their shiny, black hair at shoulder length, framing clean, sculpted features. Yes, these people were attractive, she thought to herself.

They passed over a walkway that crossed a canal. Small craft floated up and down it, using the waterway as a road. The houses were larger now and some of them had colorful murals slashed across their walls. Looking up, Maria caught her breath as one of the beautiful banners floated directly overhead. It must have been twelve feet long and she could now see it was constructed entirely of feathers, their bright colors creating patterns on a background of white. How beautiful she thought, as the slight breeze stirred them to float and drift.

Maria watched an endless feast of new sights as the city seemed to sprawl on forever. Finally, as they rounded a large street Maria caught sight of the market. She couldn't believe her eyes. It far surpassed anything she'd seen in Spain. "Holy Mother," she giggled, "one could be at market for days and not finish."

Presently they arrived at the immense plaza, bordered on every side by huge pyramids that reached skyward, smoke drifting from their apexes. Maria wondered why the bearers stopped and took off their shoes. She spotted a man with sandals in hand making his way across the plaza and she figured it must be out of reverence. Then she saw a man in a hurry who hadn't removed his sandals. He slipped and fell almost immediately. Kalti laughed and said, "It's so smooth that one can slip and fall from its polish if one hasn't learned."

As they crossed the plaza, Maria could see it was constructed of pure, white marble and its brilliance was almost blinding in the noonday sun.

Suddenly, everyone stopped and bowed as a sedan chair appeared from a side street. It was covered in gold and its feathered standard rose high in the air; a green snake was embossed on its surface. A small, elderly, bird-like man wearing a mantle edged in bright red and yellow feathers reclined in the chair. He stopped the litter and peered curiously at Maria. Itza was terrified and got out of her chair to bow. Maria, not sure what to do, dropped her head and the man went on his way.

"Snake woman," Kalti whispered. "He's very powerful."

"Snake woman?" exclaimed Maria. "But he's a man!"

At the far end of the plaza a young man carrying a staff appeared and demanded Tudilli's official letter. Bowing low, Kalti obliged. The official glanced first at the letter, then at Maria and Itza, motioning for them to follow. The bearers deposited the chairs outside a gate guarded by two warriors feathered in blue and gold garb. They exchanged words and the gate was opened. Maria felt a knot of fear rise in her throat as the man commanded her to leave the chair and follow him. As she passed through the gate she sensed her life was about to change forever.

7
Montezuma

It was cool here, water trickled over the rock causeway to form a shallow pool. Lilies floated on the surface and gave cover to darting silverfish. The hanging branches of a willow tree dangled in the pond and shaded its surface. Montezuma removed his sandals and waded into the refreshing water. He spotted a hovering attendant and sent him away with an irritated wave of his hand. He wanted to be alone in his private sanctuary in the palace gardens. He needed to think, and forget about courtiers, taxes and a battling harem, even about the strange pale ones on his coast.

He laid back on the soft grass and threw one arm across his face to shield his eyes. He hadn't wanted to be First Reverent Speaker; he would have been happier to have followed a calling as a priest. He had spent many nights fasting and praying in his private chapel, but when the time came, his father passed over several of his older brothers to choose him as successor.

Montezuma's early reign had been one of constant war. His ailing father had been too lenient with the outer provinces and they'd become insolent, forcing the young Montezuma to take up his war club. As he marched against them, it had seemed each new peace treaty brought him another woman, until his harem was near bursting. They constantly bickered amongst themselves with one intrigue or another.

His life just kept getting more complicated. His courtiers constantly buzzed around him like peacocks, each one trying to outdo the others. He'd ordered them to dress in simple white and come unadorned into his presence at court, and he knew they considered him vain for still dressing richly; he only did it to get them to respect the crown. He hadn't wanted it, but by the gods, he would make them respect it.

Montezuma was brought from his thoughts by the palace messenger hurrying across the garden. The youth prostrated himself and then handed the letter to Montezuma, explaining it was the latest from Lord Tudilli on the pale ones at the coast. Montezuma read the letter, then suddenly leapt to his feet. His warrior's body instantly responded, and he was halfway across the garden before the youth had even gotten up.

The chamber was cool, the early evening breeze drifting in through small windows. A brazier burned in the middle of the room, giving off a little warmth. Montezuma shifted in his seat, pulling his fur lined mantle close around him. He'd called a private council for the three Reverent Speakers of the Aztec triad cities. Even though Montezuma, as First Reverent Speaker, had the final say, he highly valued the word of Nezahualpili, The Second Reverent Speaker and Lord of Texcoco, who'd been a friend of his father's and who was as wise as his years.

Nezahualpili leaned close to the brazier to read the letter, then sat back and said in his usual reserved fashion, "So you think one of these men may be Quetzalcoatl?"

"I don't know," answered Montezuma. "They are unlike any men we've yet encountered. They have shells that protect them better than any of our quilted cotton armor and they have weapons that steal the thunder of the heavens. Huge beasts do their bidding and carry them faster than the wind...and, there is one among them who is tall and has hair like the sunset." With this last remark the young, Third Reverent Speaker gasped at the implications.

"But this one," Montezuma continued, "by Tudilli's report, is not the one giving orders. I know the idea sounds strange, but who knows the mind of gods! Perhaps this tall one who appears to be Quetzalcoatl allows the other, the one called Cortez, to act in his stead. After all it is the Year Reed One, the year Quetzalcoatl promised to return. There have been so many signs as of late."

"I know, I know," the older man said, irritated, "but they don't behave as gods; they don't even understand our tongue. If

Quetzalcoatl is supposed to be able to look in a man's heart and know him, then he would know his tongue as well. Also, this ailment that needs gold for its cure, could a god not cure himself? I know," he said calmly, "all seems such a mystery. I've heard their behavior can be vicious. Is that the way of a god?"

"Maybe they seek to punish us," said The Third Reverent Speaker. "Perhaps this is Quetzalcoatl's revenge. Do not the stories say he was driven to the Eastern Sea?"

"This is so," said Nezahualpili. "This report bothers me. This Aztec woman who is helping them, who is she?" There was a strained silence as the other two men looked at each other.

"I believe she is your daughter," Montezuma said dryly, "the one that was banished long ago through harem intrigue."

The Lord of Texcoco went pale. "So this is how the nasty incident chooses to come back and haunt me," he said, pushing back into his chair with a distant look in his eye.

"These two older women that Tudilli sent you, what will you do with them?" asked The Third Reverent Speaker.

"I don't know," said Montezuma. "I'm displeased he took it upon himself to do this without my consent."

"Lord Tudilli is a loyal Aztec and a good governor," interjected Nezahualpili.

"That I am not disputing; but these women, we don't even know their relationship to this man called Cortez, or the tall one," said Montezuma.

"Have you questioned them yet?" asked Nezahualpili. "This report implies Tudilli thinks one of them could be Cortez' mother."

"Yes, I know what Tudilli thinks," said Montezuma, irritated that these women hostages were becoming such a thorn in his side.

"You could offer them as sacrifices. That would appease the gods and break the powers of the pale ones," suggested The Third Reverent Speaker.

"The rashness of youth," quipped The Second Reverent Speaker. "I don't think it wise to offer them for the flowery death. Judging by the pale ones' heedless behavior so far, the women may need to be used as a bargaining key."

The Third Reverent Speaker glowered at the remark about his

youth. "Well, I don't think offering them is a bad idea," he said, then added with anger, "If it pleased the gods, they would destroy the pale ones!"

Nezahualpili turned to the youth and said, "At your father's death, he told you to listen and learn at these councils. I did not remark on your youth to dispute your abilities. You are a fine warrior and you have a good mind. Your father made the right choice with you but some things are best learned by experience. I have held this office forty years. Montezuma has been First Reverent Speaker fifteen years. You have held the responsibility barely a year…please listen."

Nezahualpili's wisdom and humility cooled the young lord's arrogance.

"Now, it's time that an old man such as I was to bed." He winked at the youth then left the room with a strength that denied his frail appearance.

Montezuma lay awake, sleep refusing to come. Turning over, he pulled the rabbit fur blanket up over his shoulders and caught a whiff of the girl's perfume. She was young and had been in his harem only a short time. He'd been attracted to her soft, doe like eyes but her childish ways were still prevalent, as she'd become angry when he'd sent her back to the harem. He didn't like anyone sleeping in his bed all night; often not sleeping well, he preferred to sprawl his ample limbs.

Climbing from the bed, he grabbed and wrapped the fur throw around him while walking towards his terrace. The tiles tingled cold against his bare feet as he stepped out onto the terrace. The bright moon cast a silver glow on the garden below, and he heard a soft tinkle from the fountain just under his balcony.

Still, his mind was in turmoil. Something told him not to let these strange men come to his city. But what if they were gods? To deny them would be blasphemy. Tudilli had wanted a surprise attack to crush them. He wondered if he had made a mistake by forbidding it. Could this really be Quetzalcoatl? There had been so many signs over the years and he just knew something was going to happen. A night bird stirred in the shrubs, startling Montezuma as it took flight.

What of these two women, he thought. He would need to find out more about them, but how would he know if what they spoke was the truth? He felt a slight heat in his loins as he thought of the lovely Chimalma. Yes of course, he thought, the High Priestess. She could discern the truth. He would send for her in the morning.

The smoke drifted to the ceiling, veiling in a haze the frescoes painted on the walls. The High Priestess closed her eyes and cleared her mind. "Mother, please show me, help me," she pleaded; but no matter how she tried, all she saw was blackness. For some reason, The Goddess had veiled her vision. There must be something she was not permitted to know. "So be it," she said, pulling herself up to her full, stately height. She placed another piece of copal on the fire and tried to reason through this new information.

Several days ago an eagle carrying a snake had died in midair, and the people of Cholan still huddled in fear at this dreadful omen. There were so many omens now. She felt a coldness in the pit of her stomach as she remembered the incidents of two years ago. The temple atop the Great Pyramid had burst into flames for no apparent reason. Even though it was made of stone, it had burned all day and all night and nothing would put it out.

Just prior to that, Lake Texcoco had erupted. Even though there had been no earthquakes and the smoking peaks were quiet, the lake still jumped its banks and ran through the city in raging torrents, destroying everything in its path. Many people were washed away and met their deaths that day.

Chimalma wished the old priestess was still alive. She remembered being brought to her as a small child; the dear, wrinkled, old face was practically ancient. The old one had looked deep into her eyes, as if she could see to the very root of her soul. Announcing that she was the one she had been waiting for, the dear one promptly took her under her wing.

She'd been very young when dedicated to the temple, and the old priestess had worked her twice as hard as anyone else. She remembered crying one night at the seeming unjustness of it, when looking up she saw the old one standing over her. Her heart had leaped in terror as the priestess wrapped her arms around her. She soothed her tears, saying that it was an honor to be the next representative of The Mother but she must continue to work hard. It was because The Goddess really needed her that she was driven harder than the others.

A new light dawned in her, and from that point on she worked with zeal. Her inner vision unfolded rapidly, and the old priestess introduced her to whole other worlds most mortals didn't even know existed. Her soul had been tried by fire and she had won. She remembered the joy on the old one's face when she'd passed initiation and become a priestess in her own right. She had been deeply saddened when the old dear one passed on; but then she had been named High Priestess. She was only nineteen, the youngest one ever.

That was six years ago, and even though Chimalma could still speak with her in the spirit realms she missed the old priestess on occasions, and one of those times was now. As of late, even her spirit voice had grown dim. This reinforced her feeling that something was amiss, something The Goddess wouldn't let her see. Sighing, she pushed back a strand of ebony hair and swept from the room. The King had ordered her presence.

The hall was immense. Red jasper pillars ran down the length of each side and the space was filled with courtiers, all there to beg the King for their cause. Montezuma had sat in audience all morning and the line of petitioners had seemed endless. He shuffled uncomfortably in his seat; the hand carved, golden throne was designed to impress, not to be comfortable. Where was she, he wondered? Then he heard the strong voice of the throne attendant announce, "Chimalma, High Priestess of the Goddess Coatique." Montezuma found a knot forming in his throat as she gracefully entered the room and prostrated herself before him, then rose to her feet to await instructions. Montezuma couldn't help but notice the difference between her and the courtiers present in the hall; the priestess looked at him clear eyed, while the rest wouldn't even meet his eyes.

He motioned her forward. The knot in his throat grew as he watched her progress. She had fawn colored skin, almond eyes, a full, sensuous mouth and a proud chin. The shiny, black hair falling past her hips added to her height. She was as tall as most men, but there was nothing masculine about the lush curves of her body.

The gods have a cruel sense of humor, he thought. She was the most beautiful woman in Tenochtitlan, and she belonged to the one Goddess that demanded celibacy of her priestesses. He had always been impressed with the way she spoke the truth, clear and unafraid. What he wouldn't give to have a woman such as her.

"My Lord, you sent for me," her deep, throaty voice rang out.

"Yes. You've heard of the pale ones on the coast?" he questioned.

"Yes my Lord."

"I have two old women of these pale ones. I need to know who they are. I believe one is the mother of the one called Cortez. Do you know who this Cortez is?"

"Yes my Lord, word travels quickly to the temple. May I ask how you came by these women?"

He waited a moment, but then knowing she would hold her council he said, "They were sent to me to be possible hostages."

"And are they hostages?" she tried further.

"Yes, I want you to find out as much as you can about them and report back to me today," he said, trying to steer his attention away from her beauty.

"May I have several days with them? My days are full and I can only spend short periods with them. I wish to be thorough and clear, and since they are important hostages to you their fate may rest on my findings."

"You may have three days," he said, knowing that only she would dare dictate her own conditions.

"Thank you my Lord," she said, then exited the audience hall through the tall, gold-studded, cedar doors.

Maria and Itza had been locked and guarded in a small suite of rooms for several days now. Their rooms were magnificent with beautiful, high, carved wood ceilings, and the bed was the most comfortable she'd ever slept in. Each bed had layers of soft, fluffy, feather quilts. She could climb in wherever she pleased, positioning herself for either more padding under her, or for more warmth, on top. The bath had a marble tub with a wonderful device called a spigot. You pulled it out and in rushed all the water you could want. The attendant had poured in a huge jar of steaming water, showing her how to operate the spigot to obtain the exact temperature she desired. The toilet had a similar spigot on it, and it flushed clean with the lifting of a lever.

At first these marvels kept her enchanted, but they wore thin fast as the reality of their situation became clear. The guard was rough with them and the attendants wouldn't speak at all; no matter how much she plied them with questions they just brought their meals and departed, making it bleakly apparent that their adventure had gone sour. Being three stories off the ground, they were entrusted with a small balcony off one of the rooms and she sat for hours upon hours looking down into the gardens. She sorely longed for her mother and fear seemed to be creeping into her thoughts every-where. She was in a strange land with heathen people, and suddenly she was all alone and very homesick. She spent hours repeating Hail Marys and crying softly to herself.

After two days of this, she began to sense that she had no choice but to try and accept her predicament. She would try to accept the newness all around her, even if she was locked up and might never see her parents again.

On the third day she was feeling better. She was sitting on the balcony watching the men below her play a dice game with brown beans, when a knock came on the door. Up until now no one had knocked, but had just entered at their own will. Maria hurried from the balcony to the main room, and there standing in the doorway, was the most beautiful woman she'd ever seen.

"I am Chimalma, High Priestess," she said.

"Oh, one of the heart cutters!" wailed Itza.

"Shhh," said Maria. She then asked Chimalma, "What do you want?"

The priestess didn't answer, but stood looking from Maria to Itza. Gliding to Itza she put her hand on Itza's veil to lift it, then stopped. Turning, she changed her mind and went for Maria instead, unhesitatingly grabbing the veil and lifting it.

❖

It was early the next morning and the sun fell across Maria's neatly braided hair, while the discarded veil lay in a heap on the floor. Without the veil, she felt freer than she had in months. She still wore the black gown, but its shapeless bulk was now pulled in by a scrap of red cloth belted around Maria's waist. Itza, also unveiled, sat wringing her hands.

"Oh Itza, it's all right. There's no reason to wear the veil. Now they know. Besides, I was so sick of it. It's wonderful to see clearly again," she beamed happily.

A sudden crash turned their attention to the door. The attendant had stopped to pick up the splattered contents of the breakfast trays, his eyes wide and staring at the flames of Maria's red hair. The attendant cleared the mess and stumbled from the room, while even the guard stood with his eyes affixed to Maria's shocking features. No sooner had the door closed, when it reopened and in walked the High Priestess.

"Kalti!" Maria cried to the man behind Chimalma. The guard gave him a small shove into the room and shut the door. Kalti stood there, mouth gaping at Maria.

"I brought your interpreter in case you don't understand some of the questions I will ask," said the priestess.

"I thought you were an old woman," croaked Kalti.

Maria threw back her head and laughed at his newfound shyness.

"Sit down Kalti," ordered the priestess. "Ma-ree-a, is that how you say your name?"

"Yes," answered Maria.

"From our short conversation yesterday, I gather you're no relation to this man Cortez. But you are related to the one who sent him?"

"Yes, my uncle is the Governor of Cuba."

"Yes I see, so you would be valuable to Cortez as such," the priestess said matter of factly.

"I think my uncle would have his head if he came home without me," Maria giggled.

"Good," Chimalma said. "How did you learn to speak the language so fast, it's true that you couldn't speak it until just over a week ago?"

"Yes, for some reason it just comes to me. I hear a word once and remember it. And sometimes I know what the word means without even being told. Isn't that strange?" she wrinkled up her face in delight.

The priestess studied Maria intently as she spoke. She liked the girl. There was a special quality about her, something that reminded Chimalma of herself when she was Maria's age. "Do you know what Cortez intends to do?"

Maria found she had to answer such a direct question with the truth, "He wants to come here, but whether he can or will, I don't know."

"If you are no relation to Cortez how is it you came to be with him?" she asked, her steely gaze seeming to pierce through Maria.

Maria explained how they'd stowed away aboard the Catalonia, and how when Cortez found them he demanded they wear veils to pose as old women.

"Yes, I can see why he might do that," the priestess said.

As they were speaking, the attendant returned with a new tray of food and Chimalma noticed that the man never took his eyes off Maria. Kalti had been the same, and when the attendant left she also excused Kaliti, as it appeared she didn't need him anyway.

"May I ask some questions?" Maria tested politely. The High Priestess nodded in agreement.

"Where do you live?" she asked.

Rather surprised by the simplicity of the question, Chimalma replied, "I live in the temple with the other priestesses and young girls under the guidance of The Goddess Mother."

"Can I come live with you? I'm so lonely locked up here," pleaded Maria.

"Why?" asked a startled Chimalma.

"I like you, I want to be where you are," Maria said innocently.

The priestess got up to leave, "I will see." She stopped at the door and asked, "Were you Cortez' lover?"

The very idea of the question brought Maria to a bright-red blush, "No, we didn't get along well."

"Were you the lover of anyone else with him?"

Maria now was a bit upset and her convent education came

rushing to the surface. "I've never been married and I'm not the kind of girl that would bed a man that wasn't my husband," she stammered, blushing brightly.

"So you are untouched?"

"Untouched," mused Maria, "you mean a virgin? Yes I'm a virgin."

"Vir-gin," the priestess said, rolling the Spanish word off her tongue.

That night Chimalma walked alone in the temple gardens. Tomorrow was the third day and she would have to report to Montezuma. What would she say about this young girl posing as an old woman, she wondered? Montezuma had quite a different dilemma than he'd suspected. The priestess was sure that Cortez would still want her back; she was obviously more valuable to him than an old woman would be. Strangely, she could not seem to think of Maria as just a hostage, a nonentity. She liked the girl.

She thought of Maria's request. It was true the temple would be as good a safekeeping as the palace. No one could get in or out of the priestesses' quarters without permission. As a hostage, she would be more valuable if she remained in the same condition she was taken in.

Chimalma didn't know these Spanish ones, but what she'd gathered from Maria's words is that they placed as high a value on virginity as did her own people. Judging by how the men stared at Maria today, she probably would remain safer in the temple. She didn't blame the men; Maria was beautiful by anyone's standards. Yes, she thought as she sat for meditation, she would give that recommendation.

Montezuma was in a foul mood and his attendants kept their distance. The very air around him bristled as he walked the palace gardens. He lifted his head at the approach of the High Priestess; today his mood wouldn't even let him respond to her. He took a hard, deep breath and sat himself on a marble bench, motioning for the priestess to sit beside him.

"Well, what did you find out?" he asked.

"My Lord, there is more to these hostages than what they first appeared." Chimalma explained all about Maria and her masquerade, ending with Maria's request to stay in the temple.

"By the Gods! This is just what I need, another young girl in my house," he complained.

That morning there had been a battle in his harem with some of the younger girls, including his newest who'd been in his bed the last couple of nights. There had been name calling which escalated into a battle that left broken furniture, cracked pots, bruises, scratches and missing tufts of hair. But even worse, one girl was left with a cracked skull, and another who was carrying his child had been pushed down some stairs and was bleeding. His first wife had responded swiftly by having the perpetrators whipped, this being her duty as head of the harem; but that didn't right the damage done.

"No," he said, "I don't want to hear anymore about difficult young girls this morning. She may make a good hostage, this Maria as you call her, but she brings trouble with her. She'll probably be the catalyst that lures these Spanish ones right to Tenochtitlan." He stood to signal the end of discussion and said, "You say she wants to stay in the temple. Fine, take her. I'll feel better knowing she's not under my roof!"

"Gather your things, we are leaving for the temple," said The High Priestess.

"They cut out hearts now," gasped Itza, beginning to wail.

Embarrassed, Maria tried to quiet her but it did no good. She wailed and wailed, past hearing and reason. Chimalma walked over and soundly slapped Itza across the face, cutting her off mid-wail.

"You are going to the temple to live," she said. "Your station in this society is that of hostage, not sacrifice. The flowery death is an honor not given lightly and you aren't one of the candidates at this point. So now hush your wailing and get your things."

Surprisingly, Itza shut right up and gathered their meager belongings together.

At the door the priestess took Maria's veil from Itza's hands and dropped it over Maria's head, explaining that they could get to the temple with less disturbances this way. Then she led them down the long maze of blue-tiled stairways and out to the waiting sedan chairs in the smoothly paved courtyard.

8
The Temple

Maria pulled the plain, white dress over her head while Itza folded their nightclothes and returned them to a simple wicker chest. Then Maria fluffed the blankets and pillows on their cots, scanning the small, cell like room and looking for anything else needing to be straightened. Itza grabbed her and made her sit so she could braid her hair into two simple plaits down each side of her head. Since the girls here weren't married, none of them wore a braid cornice over the top of their head like matrons did; simple braids or just loose were the mark of a maiden.

They'd been in the temple a week now and Maria was overjoyed. The priestesses hadn't let her do much yet, so she just walked in the gardens and helped when she could. She'd been somewhat frightened the first day, not sure how the other girls would receive her; but after the girls got over the shock of her bright red hair and pale skin, they accepted her as one of them.

The girls in the temple seemed divided into two groups—the girls sent by the better Tzin families who were here to learn the womanly arts, after which they would return to their families and most likely be married off; then there were those who were dedicated to the temple by virtue of innate skill or desire to be a priestess. These were expected to stay on, learning each grade of priestesshood.

The priestesses themselves conducted the ceremonies, ran the temple and tutored the girls in temple life. Maria seemed to be a part of the first group, but fortunately there was an easy camaraderie among all the girls.

Maria jumped up, smoothing an imaginary wrinkle from her dress. Who would have thought she'd get used to wearing just a loose dress that only hung to her knees and a simple loincloth-like undergarment. She was taking special pains with her appearance today; she wanted to look just right. The High Priestess had informed her she would start temple training, and that as long as she was here she would be just like the other girls. Maria was of course, delighted.

After breakfast she was given a broom and told to sweep out the private chapel that was used exclusively by the priestesses. This wasn't quite what she'd had in mind when she heard it was time for training, but she still put all her being into it. The Aztecs were so clean; everything was straightened and swept every day. She was told it was a great honor to be allowed to sweep out the temples and at the Great Festivals women competed for the task.

She was bending down to lift the collected dust from a corner, when she noticed that the door to the inner sanctuary was ajar. She knew she wasn't allowed to enter, as it was for the priestesses only, but she couldn't resist a slight peak. Maria swept her way to the door and was just about to take a quick look inside, when the penetrating voice of the High Priestess stopped her in her tracks, "Maria don't, it's not allowed." Embarrassed, Maria turned to apologize, but the priestess had already moved on. She was amazed; The Mother Superior would have beaten her hands until her knuckles bled.

She had finished sweeping and was about to leave when the High Priestess reentered. She was carrying a bowl carved of the purest white alabaster, so delicate that light glowed through its shape. Handing the bowl to Maria, she requested the girl's assistance. The priestess went to the altar and placed some fodder in its center brazier. Lighting it and holding her hands straight out in front of her, she invoked The Goddess Mother. Maria stood quietly, as physical sensations of discomfort crept over her. Once again the voice of The Mother Superior took a most inopportune time to ring through her mind, as Maria heard her cursing the heathens that worship false gods. The palms of her hands began to sweat. What had she been doing, she thought, damning her soul forever?

She noticed the priestess had been observing her reactions to the ceremony. Suddenly, Maria remembered the dream of The Virgin Mary on the hill, with all the other images merging into her. In her mind she heard the words, "All of these are me, and all of these I AM."

"Can The Goddess Mother take other forms?" Maria asked Chimalma.

"One Mother is many Mothers," answered The High Priestess, as she took the chunks of pungent retsin copal from Maria's bowl and laid them into the fire to purify the chapel. This was all Maria needed to hear. She sank to her knees beside the altar and reverently bowed her head.

❖

"Oh no, embroidery!" Maria said with chagrin, as she looked first at *lection* of brightly colored threads, then at the plain, white blouse whose neck and sleeves she'd been instructed to decorate. She had always gone to great lengths to avoid any kind of needlework, first at home in Spain, then with Juanita in Cuba. Maria seemed to sprout eight more thumbs every time she picked up a needle. She didn't even consider herself capable of sewing on a button. Somehow it always seemed to end up leagues away from the buttonhole.

Dismay began to well in her as she watched the other girls expertly weave their needles in and out of the fabric, creating beautiful patterns almost like magic. She knew that among the Aztecs and in Spain as well, beautiful embroidery stitch was a sign of womanhood. Maria wondered what line she'd been standing in when they were passing out needlework abilities.

She took a deep breath and picked up the copper needle; it wasn't too different from the ones her mother had. Taking up a strand of bright green she threaded the needle, then tried to waste time by pretending to study the faint pattern the priestess had drawn on her blouse; it had been embarrassing enough to have to ask for that. The girls Maria's age were working on clean white cloths, creating the patterns as they went. It was only some of the younger ones who needed patterns.

She noticed that the square reed hoop held the fabric as taunt as the metal ones in Spain. She laid the fabric across her lap and began with resolve. She jabbed the fabric and heard a pop; the bottom half of the broken needle fell to the ground and rolled away. All right, so they weren't as strong; that was one way copper needles differed from her mother's steel ones. Sheepishly she picked out another needle and threaded it. Itza, sitting across from her and knowing full well Maria's sewing abilities, had a bemused expression on her face. Well I'll show her, thought Maria as she squared her shoulders and began again. Four precarious stitches later she pricked her finger, let out a yelp and sucked away the welling blood. Then she noticed that even little Taxca was working away. Taxca was three years younger than she, and such a klutz that she wasn't even allowed to carry the food to the dinner table. Maria couldn't see one flaw in her work; that sent her back into the work with a fury.

The next hour seemed to be a maze of slipped stitches and tangled threads, but at last some of the pattern was filled in by a little color. Then she realized that she had made what was supposed to be a red flower, all green. Maria threw down her embroidery and rubbed her tired eyes, then started to peek at the other girls' work. Holy Mother of God she thought, her work looked like it had been done by a two year old. That does it. I just wasn't meant to do this, she fussed as she stood up. I'm going to the toilet, get a drink of water, anything! But as she stood, the embroidery hoop came with her. She had embroidered her skirt into her work!

It started as a titter and then swelled into hysterical laughter. Some of the girls were laughing so hard that a couple of them rolled over. Maria stood red faced with anger and embarrassment. Then a clear picture of what she must look like jumped into her head and she too began to laugh. She laughed until she could no longer stand, and had to sit.

Finally, Shera, the attending priestess, gently encouraged the girls back to their work. The priestess took a small knife and carefully freed Maria from her creation. Shera was one of the younger priestesses. She had a gentle manner about her which endeared her to all. She helped Maria undo her work, then made her close her eyes and keep a clear picture in her mind of what she wanted to stitch.

"…then simply follow that picture. Think of each thread as you put it in," she said. "See it become part of the whole pattern. Keep the complete picture in your mind all the while and don't worry so much about the individual thread. Just let it become part of the whole."

Maria sensed the priestess was talking about more than just embroidery. It seemed the laughter had healed something in her; a resistance was gone. All of a sudden she saw what the priestess had been talking about. She could think her threads into the pattern as she went along and somehow the threads obeyed, well, most of the time anyway.

Then Taka, a tall, quiet girl said, "Shera, tell us the story of The Goddess. Maria hasn't heard it yet and I think we'd all like to hear it again." She was joined by a chorus of "oh, please."

Maria was all ears as Shera smiled and relented. "Coatique was a little bored with what was happening in Flower World," she began. Maria knew that 'flower world' was the Aztec name for heaven. Shera continued:

"She'd been watching the Earth and decided to come down for a short visit. So she dressed as an old woman and appeared at one of the temples. They took pity on what appeared to be an old woman alone in the world, and said they would give her food and shelter in exchange for her sweeping. She enjoyed being among her Earth children and her life was simple and pure. At night she would walk in the woods and all the creatures of the forest would follow her, happy to be in the presence of such a being.

One day when she was sweeping the temple a beautiful, pure-white feather drifted down from above. It was the most beautiful feather she'd ever seen. She picked it up and tucked it in the waistband of her skirt, that she may look upon it later.

After her sweeping was finished she couldn't find the feather. It had disappeared, and she felt the stirring of new life in her womb.

Soon she returned to Flower World. When it became obvious that she was going to bear a child, her celestial children (her sons the stars and her daughter the moon) grew angry with her, demanding to know who the father was. She lovingly responded that no one was the father, and in their blindness they grew ever more hateful and full of vengefulness. Then deep from within her womb, she heard a voice, 'Mother, I will protect you'.

One day, her ungrateful sons and daughter confronted her and demanded her life as payment for the shame she had put them through. From her womb popped Huitzilopochtli, full grown. He was the Sun. His face was pure radiance, his hair the color of gold."

Maria felt some of the girls eyeing her hair. "Well, don't look at me," she laughed, and they all giggled and turned back to Shera.

Huitzilopochtli demanded, 'by what right do you threaten our mother?' His brothers, the stars, rushed him and he cast them far into the heavens where they could do no damage. Then his sister, the moon, tried to lay her hands on Coatique. He grabbed her and cast her to Earth where she broke into many pieces. Then he took his place in the heavens as the Sun, Lifegiver.

Coatique, The Mother Goddess, looked down and took pity on the broken body of her daughter the moon, and repaired her. But because of her arrogance she could never hold her body together, and that is why the moon goes from full to pieces and back again.

Shera finished as the girls all clapped with delight. Maria fell deep into thought. Here was another immaculate birth with no physical father, and a son that gives life! This put it all together, and now she knew her heart would no longer be torn.

"Where are we going?" asked Maria.

"Shhh, just follow us." Maria allowed herself to be pulled along by the other girls. They worked their way along the tall, thick, mud and wattle wall marking the boundaries of The Goddess' temple. After pushing back the branches of a small tree and making their way around the huge leaves of a springy rubber plant, Maria saw a hole poked in the wall.

One of the girls stooped down to peer through the hole. She giggled and said, "Perfect, come look." With her curiosity aroused, Maria knelt down and fitted her eye against the opening. The peephole view looked out over a broad playing field covered with lush, green grass. A few buildings, much like the ones the priestesses lived in, were adjacent to the playing field. The field was full of young men with their black hair caught up in ponytails, running all over the field chasing a small ball and bouncing it off their shoulders, knees, heads and scantily clad buttocks.

"Come on Maria, let us look too," nudged one of the girls. She stood up and dusted off her knees while each of the giggling girls took a turn.

"What is that place?" she asked.

"The Temple of Huitzilopochtli," said Taka. "The boys go to study there just like we come here."

"Just on the other side of the wall?" questioned Maria.

"Yes," she said, "the mother and the sons' temples stand side by side."

"Oh I see," said Maria. "Did you make this hole in the wall?"

"No silly, the boys did. They wanted to look in our courtyard but it backfired," chuckled Taka. "The bushes were in the way. They can't see us but we can see them."

"Awwwh! They have their clothes on," said one short, plump girl that reminded Maria of a chubby puppy.

"Sometimes when they are wrestling, they have no clothes on!" exclaimed Taka.

"You mean they're naked?" asked Maria, wide eyed.

"Yes," she said, "I think it's so there's no clothing for their opponents to grab hold of."

Laughter arose as a girl poked a finger straight out from between her legs, "But there's still one thing left."

"Yes, but I think they get disqualified if they hold on to that," said another, and soon all the girls were in fits of giggles.

"Shhh," said Taka, "the priestesses will hear us. Here Maria, do you want to look again? It's almost time for dance practice."

Taking a last peek, Maria felt a tingly rush in spite of herself. The boys were very handsome—all long legs and perspiration glistening on young muscles. She noticed that some of the boys wore red browbands and some wore blue.

"What are they playing?" she asked, without turning from the peephole.

"Tlachlli," someone said, just as the voice of a priestess calling them to dance sent them scurrying from the shrubs.

❖

"Now, Maria, pay attention," said Taka. The girl had become Maria's friend, quietly teaching her how to do the things the other girls already knew. Maria was grateful; the friendship had saved her a lot of teasing. Taka ladled corn kernels out of a pot where they had been first soaked overnight, then boiled with white lime. This treatment caused the kernels to swell to three times their size.

"This is called a quern," she explained, spreading it on a flat stone with an indentation in the center. She then used a mona, a hand held stone, to grind the kernels into a coarse meal. Adding a little water she made a dough, slapping it between her hands to form little cakes.

Maria had been feeding the small fire in the three stoned hearth. She shivered a little, the sun not yet up; everything was still deep in shadow and the air still brisk. Taka took the flat, clay griddle and placed it on the stones to heat as she handed Maria the grinding stone. "Lets see you do it," she said. It had looked so easy but when Maria tried it, it seemed to go everywhere. "No, don't just push. Roll the stone so you don't knock all the maize out," Taka gestured. When it was Maria's turn to form the cakes they kept tearing, and some of them were any shape but round.

Each morning, two of the girls were chosen to make all the tortillas needed to feed everyone living at the temple. Most girls learned this skill as a child; even the ones from the upper classes knew how. Maize was the staff of life among the Aztecs, and making the daily tortillas was considered a sacred trust.

Maria's ears pricked up at the distant sound of drums and conch shells; the morning ceremonies were about to begin. Every morning the priests and priestesses climbed to the top of the city's pyramids to start the day by welcoming the sun. Maria was not allowed to participate in these ceremonies yet. In fact, she hadn't even been allowed out of the temple.

Noises drew Maria's attention to the back of the courtyard, where she saw Itza disappear into a doorway with other temple attendants, all carrying armloads of clothing. This was the happiest she'd seen Itza since she'd gone to work for her uncle. One of the other temple servants was a Mayan, and she and Itza chattered by the hour. Maria could see that Itza's Nahuatl hadn't gotten much better, but her Mayan sure had.

Taka flipped the cakes onto the grill, turning them with a small, wooden paddle. Then Maria placed them in a small, clay oven to keep them warm.

Later that morning Chimalma motioned for Maria to come to her and said, "Today I'm going to teach you to meditate."

"What's that?" asked Maria.

"It's how you go inside yourself to find the truth that is locked within you. Come! Sit on this bench," she guided. "Put your feet flat on the ground and clasp your hands together on your lap. Now close your eyes and relax; let your mind begin to follow your breath, in and out of your body."

For several days Maria practiced this technique until the priestess gave her a new one to use; she was to repeat her name to herself over and over again. Soon strange things began to happen. Long forgotten scenes from her childhood were surfacing, especially the blue light. She remembered how as a child when she closed her eyes, often a blue light would appear in the middle of her forehead. Now here it was again, and the longer she meditated, the more the blue light seemed to become a flame.

Maria grew fascinated by these things happening in her, and was now looking forward to her meditation sessions. One day the priestess said, "Now you're going to learn to contact The Goddess. Close your eyes and repeat her name over and over while creating a picture of her in your mind. She looks like…"

"She looks a bit like you, Chimalma," Maria cut her off, "with feathers in her hair, and her dress has scenes of nature on it."

"Yes! How did you know? Did one of the girls tell you?" she asked.

"No, I saw her," Maria said.

"Where, in a dream? The energy in The Goddess' temple is strong. Sometimes this will happen."

"But it didn't happen in the temple; it happened on the way here, in the desert."

The priestess raised an eyebrow and said nothing, but Maria noticed that Chimalma kept a keener eye on her from that day on.

❖

"What's this?" the priestess asked, holding a sprig of white and yellow flowers.

"Chamomile!" shouted the girls.

"And what is it for?" she continued.

"To calm nerves," said one girl.

"To make one sleep," said another.

"It's good for headaches too," offered a third.

"And this?" The priestess held out a lump of thick resin.

"Pine tar," squeaked one of the girls after a quick sniff.

"What's it for?" the priestess asked.

"To get rid of things like little worms in the body. Also, it's good to chew. It makes your breath fresh."

Holding up a powder, the priestess said, "This is senna, what's it used for?"

"It makes one go to the toilet. Lots!" said one experienced young lady.

"When would you use it?" she asked.

"When someone ate something rotten," somebody spoke out.

"Also during a fever," added Taka.

"And why is that, Taka?" the priestess asked.

"To get the poison out of them," she smiled.

Maria hurried to her place among the girls, "What are we doing?"

"Sacred herbs," said Taka. "The Mother Goddess is custodian of the healing herbs, so all her priestesses are responsible for knowing how the herbs do their work. It's also helpful to know them if you get sick yourself," she added.

"What helps pain?" asked the priestess.

"Arnica," suggested Taka, who prided herself in her knowledge of the sacred herbs.

"Good," the priestess said, "what else?"

"The bark from Peru!" they all shouted.

"Where's Peru?" whispered Maria.

"Oh, it's far to the south of here," said Taka. "It takes many moons for a trader to get there, but sometimes we get trade goods from them just the same. Their people are called Incas. My uncle says that they have great cities but that they are a boring people. He says that even The Emperor dresses plainly, and things like that."

"Taka, Maria! Pay attention," said the priestess. "Now what else helps pain?"

"Cayenne and jimsonweed, but you have to be careful with the jimsonweed because it can make them sick," someone said.

"Also mother wart," added little Taxca.

"Good. Now girls, I'm going to be assigning you all to different healing priestesses over the next few days; listen carefully and learn."

The man shook and rocked. His skin was a sickly yellow and his tongue swollen. "What's wrong with him?" asked Maria as she backed away, the stories her parents had told of the plague running through her head.

Tansa, a large set, older priestess answered, "Help me hold him, you can't get it. It's called malaria, and it comes from the Mayan jungles. When a person is bitten by the flying bloodsuckers of their jungle they sometimes react this way, and it keeps coming back if not treated."

Tansa had Maria and Taka hold the man's head as she forced a clear liquid down his throat. Next, she refilled her clay cup with hot water from the brazier and opened a wooden box filled with a variety of dried herbs. Then she selected a pinch from two different types and added them to the cup. By the time the herbs had steeped, the man was already much calmer and he was able to drink down the tea on his own. Tansa told him to go home and rest, and to drink often from a flask she had prepared for him. The thankful man put his two, small, hatchet shaped, copper coins into the donation box and left.

"What did you give him?" asked Maria.

"The first thing he drank was a liquid made from the bark of Peru; that was also what was in the flask I sent him home with. It stops malaria. If someone has it they should drink a tea of the bark every so often. Then I gave him a tea of blue cohosh to bring on perspiration and vervain to bring down his fever. He will be better in a few days."

Their conversation was interrupted when four men carried in an older man clutching at his heart in pain, with his hands in uncontrollable spasms. The priestess moved swiftly into action; choosing a dull-white powder, she sprinkled some under his tongue, explaining it was foxglove. Then she ordered Taka to pour more water into a fresh cup, and to take a pinch of both tobacco and cayenne from the herb box to add to the water. This was poured down the man's throat and more foxglove was put under his tongue. Tansa noticed the four men staring at Maria and ordered them from the room. Then she took an herb that Maria recognized as arnica and knew to be for pain. Looking into his eyes and putting her ear to his heart to listen, she then selected one more herb and added all this to the man's cup. Soon, the much relieved man closed his eyes and slept.

Tansa planted her feet firmly on the ground to connect with the Earth current. Putting her hands over his heart, she closed her eyes and remained in silence for awhile. When she reopened them she said, "It's his heart, it has turned against him. The last herb I gave him was henbane to make him sleep. But I must monitor him by connecting to the Mother Earth current, and check his heart to see if it is strong enough to handle the herbs."

"But I thought nothing could be done for a heart attack," said Maria. "My uncle in Spain died of one when I was little, and I remember the doctor telling my mother they could do nothing."

"Pooh," said Tansa. "Sometimes the person does die, but foxglove calms the heart and usually saves the person."

After the attendants took the old man home, Maria began cleaning up the small chamber just outside the healing temple. She wandered over to the door and watched the slow progress of an old man leaning heavily on his staff, as he made his way down the street. He was talking to himself and swatting at the stray dogs who came up to sniff his ankles. He teetered, groped for the wall and fell on his rear end. Maria started out the door to help him, when the priestess placed a restraining hand on her.

"No, don't. He's drunk on octili," she said.

"But I thought it was illegal to be drunk in public," said Maria.

"It is for everyone else; just the old ones are allowed," she said.

Mumbling, the man picked himself up, brushed off his knees, straightened his dust covered mantle and stumbled on down the road.

"But why didn't you let me help him? Were you afraid I would run away? I wouldn't, you know," she said.

Knowing well enough that this was the first time that Maria had been out of the temple gates since arriving, she said, "No, little one. We aren't worried you would run away. Where would you go? And looking as you do, where would you hide? No, it's because it's against the code to be drunk. When the old ones do it we must appear not to notice. He would've been horrified had you run out to help him."

Suddenly, a group of angry people rushed in and dropped a writhing, young girl on the healing table. They said a few sharp words and left. As Tansa prepared and administered another dose of arnica, Maria noticed that Taka had a look of reproach on her face. Tansa had to snap at Taka to get her assistance. She also observed that after they had questioned the young girl, both Taka and Tansa became quite curt with her.

Tansa put her hands on the sobbing girl's stomach, gently pressed and massaged it and said, "Yes, it's gone. I'm preparing an herb. Shepherds purse, it'll stop the bleeding." Spreading a strong smelling salve on a wad of manguey fabric, she pulled the girl to the end of the table, hiked up her skirt and removed her undergarment.

Maria looked on, horrified. "What are you doing?" she cried.

"This girl is the daughter of a lord, and a very promiscuous daughter at that. She has aborted herself with a stick." The girl let out a shrill scream as the medicinal tampon met her lacerated tissues. "You leave this in today and I will make you one for tomorrow, so you don't get the killing disease from dirty sticks," she said, emphasizing her last words. A Tzin servant stood at the door to collect the girl; there seemed to be no kindness there either.

Maria's heart opened to the girl's trauma, and she was disturbed by the way everybody seemed to treat her. "Why is everyone so mean to her? She's obviously in a lot of pain!"

"Aztec girls are supposed to remain chaste until they are married," said Taka. "She's the Lord's only child; her father needs her to marry and produce children. But all the young lords won't have anything to do with her. She has brought dishonor upon herself and her whole house."

"Well, she's sorry. Maybe it won't happen again. Everyone will forget about it and she can marry. I've known girls in Spain that've done such things."

"You don't understand," said Taka. "This is the third time. She might as well become an auianime and give some dignity back to her family."

"What's an auianime?" asked Maria.

"It's a woman for use only by the warriors," said Tansa.

"Does everyone come here to be healed?" asked Maria, wanting to change the subject.

"No," said Tansa, "some go to the doctors in the market, but others only turn to The Goddess."

The shadows grew long as Tansa escorted the girls back through the temple gates.

Tansa handed the donation box to Maria. It held a handful of copper and silver hatchets, and one gold one, probably from the lord. Maria was intrigued. How peculiar she thought, to use tiny, metal hatchets as currency.

"Sometimes we get cocoa beans as well," said Taka. "They are highly valued and delicious too!"

Gathering around the High Priestess, the girls wrapped themselves in cloaks against the night's chill as the crickets chirped their evening song. "Tell us the stories of when our people arrived here in the Valley of Mexico," the girls shouted.

"Tell us about Chimalma," piped up Taxca the Clumsy, as she was affectionately called.

The High Priestess lifted her lovely, golden-brown face to study the stars a moment, and with a smile she began…

Long ago, there lived two tribes of the same people, far to the north of here. One of the tribes began to worship by using sacrifice. This displeased the other tribe and they were outcast, then banished. They became a homeless people, wandering through barren wasteland for several generations.

It sounds like the children of Israel, thought Maria.

They arrived at a lake's edge where they saw an eagle eating a snake, and by this good omen they knew this was where they were to live. They built their city and grew stronger than any of their neighbors. Even the last, great Toltecs living to the north became their allies, and taught the Aztecs the secrets of The Sacred Pyramid in Teotihuacan.

In the beginning our people had four leaders, three men and one woman. The three men were called Tlatoami, or Reverent Speakers, of which The Three Reverent Speakers now are all direct descendants. The woman who was called Chimalma was the first to face initiation in the Sacred Pyramid, and she became the first High Priestess of The Mother Goddess. From that point on, all The High Priestesses have taken the name of Chimalma in her honor."

"What's your real name then?" interrupted Maria.

"My real name is Chimalma; my given name was Petatzin," she replied.

"Petatzin! Then you were nobility." said Maria, knowing that Tzin was a suffix only the nobility were allowed to use.

"Yes, my father was a noble."

"And they put you in the temple?" she pushed.

Taka poked an elbow in Maria's ribs to quiet her. They considered it rude to question The High Priestess so forwardly.

"The Goddess desired it," she said with affection, dismissing the group for the night.

It was early June now and Maria had been in the temple six weeks. She'd grown so content in her temple cocoon, she'd almost forgotten that there was another world outside it. She lived, breathed and ate temple. Except for the time spent with The Healing Priestess, and the occasional impish peeks through the hole in the wall, she'd forgotten about the alien city she was in the middle of. Cortez, along with the rest of the Spanish, seemed far away in another world. Only once or twice did she worry about the anguish that her parents must be in. She wished she could send them a letter, stating she was all right and very happy.

Taka was teaching Maria a new embroidery stitch and the girls were laughing and gossiping, when The High Priestess passing by brought them all to a hush.

"The dress," they all whispered.

"What dress?" asked Maria.

"Shhh Maria, wait till she's gone," Taka said, with all the girls shushing her.

"She's been in council," they said after Chimalma had passed. "Council of the temples, that's why she's wearing the skull dress." Then Maria remembered noticing black skulls all over Chimalma's skirt.

"It's a bit morbid," said Maria, "but hardly worth all the fuss."

"You don't understand," said Taka. "The dress symbolizes the fact that she met death in The Great Pyramid to the north, and came back among us."

"How can anyone meet death and come back to life?" scoffed Maria.

"It's said that many who go for the great initiation don't come back, but die in the dreaded ordeal instead," someone said.

"Well, have all the priestesses gone through it?" asked Maria.

"Oh no," said Shana, a petite young beauty. "Very few do. You have to petition, it's special. Most priests and priestesses never attempt it. It's too dangerous!"

"But I've heard you are never the same after the experience. You return with powers," added Taka.

"Well, Chimalma certainly has powers," Shana said smugly.

Maria thought upon these words for many days, until the part of her that knew it to be true gave birth to something deep within her.

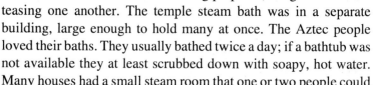

While the steam room was being prepared, the girls ran about teasing one another. The temple steam bath was in a separate building, large enough to hold many at once. The Aztec people loved their baths. They usually bathed twice a day; if a bathtub was not available they at least scrubbed down with soapy, hot water. Many houses had a small steam room that one or two people could fit in, but the temple steam was a whole stone building with benches and faucets. The room was purified with sage and then each girl was given a small willow branch to softly strike the skin, bringing the blood to the surface.

Maria had grown to like the wet baths, but hadn't mustered the courage to join the others in the steam ritual. Only after they teased her about how smelly and dirty her insides must be, did she finally relent. She showed up with a cloth wrapped around her while the others were all nude. It was just what she'd been afraid of. Each girl waited to be saged before entering. Maria was in line behind Taxca, when looking down she noticed the same dark patch of skin at the base of Taxca's spine that she'd seen on the Mayan girls.

"What's that?" she pointed and asked.

"Don't you have one?" Taka looked at her with surprise.

"No, I'd never seen one before I was in the Mayan villages," Maria said.

"We nearly all have one. It's on a baby girl at birth and stays with her until sometime after womanhood sets in; then it slowly fades away," Taka proudly explained.

"Oh," said Maria politely.

After she entered the steam room, she sat still wrapped in her cloth. Bathing was one thing she thought, but this nudity was something else. When she looked at the others, all tawny, golden-brown skinned and pretty faced, she felt pale, ugly and skinny. They were all perfectly hairless, just like the Mayans had been, with nothing on their legs, underarms or even their pubic region. She had a fine pale down on her legs and arms, but her pubic area was a bright red bush! While Maria sat thinking, Taxca came up and grabbed her protective cloth, running away laughing.

Several of the girls drew deep gasps. "Maria," said Taka, "you're beautiful!"

"No I'm not," she said, as she groped to cover herself.

"Yes you are," she said, "just look at yourself!"

Maria's face blushed a deep red. Sensing her denial, the girls all gathered round her, cooing to her with trust and support. Reluctantly, she opened her eyes to her body. Then she saw that in the last few months her breasts had grown full, her hips round, her waist slim and her legs long and sleek. She heard The Mother Superior's voice condemning her body and calling her a shameless hussy, but she pushed it away.

"I am pretty, aren't I?" she said, as tears began to well up.

"Oh yes, Maria. You're so beautiful!" they all said.

Suddenly, she was crying, and tears gave way to laughter as her shame and The Mother Superior's voice dissolved for the last time.

Itza was snoring and Maria couldn't sleep. The moon, almost

full now, shone through the small window that faced the courtyard, beckoning to her. Quietly she snuck out of her room and into the courtyard, making her way to the temple gardens. She knew she probably shouldn't be doing it, but something about this particular night felt safe. Besides, she couldn't sleep.

The moonlight cast eerie shadows off the garden's plants and trees, as she slipped up to a meditation bench and sat down. Life seems so different now, she thought. I'm changing so fast, I hardly recognize myself. I do love it here though. It feels so much like home, I don't care if I ever go back to Spain! Then she thought of her parents and knew they were probably terrified for her. If only I could get a message to them that I'm so happy here, she thought. Then she remembered Cortez. Well, if he really does make it here, perhaps I can send a message back with him, she reasoned.

Looking up into the sky, she spotted among the stars a comet trailing its way through the heavens. Remembering the stories that a comet can bring doom, she shivered and pulled her cloak closer.

The Goddess had awakened Chimalma and instructed her to go out into the night air. Her position of High Priestess afforded her a small suite of chambers on the second floor overlooking the temple gardens and courtyard. As she stood on her balcony, the low-hanging comet drew her focus skyward. Another one, she thought sadly. Even though I'm sure the court astronomers have noted it, I'll have to report it to the King.

Movement down below the balcony brought her attention into the garden. The sudden glow of moonlight on her hair gave Maria away. The priestess knew it was her, for no other girl had hair that would reflect light like that. Chimalma drew away from the balcony so Maria wouldn't notice her. She remembered the occurrence of The Mother Goddess appearing before Maria even before she'd reached the city. This young girl is indeed special and peculiar, Chimalma thought. Quietly from the shadows, she watched Maria leave the garden and return to her quarters.

It was a warm afternoon and Maria was between lessons. She'd gone back out into the garden and was doodling with a stick in the dirt, writing a few Spanish words and attempting to spell their

Nahuatl counterpart.

The High Priestess came up from behind and asked, "What are you doing?"

"Writing," answered Maria.

"Writing? But there aren't any figures," she said.

"We don't use pictures," said Maria. To show the priestess, she drew each letter of the alphabet and pronounced each one. Then she illustrated how the sounds and letters formed a word.

"Why haven't my people thought of this?" the amazed priestess wondered. "It looks quite practical, even if it is a bit ugly."

She took Maria to the temple scribe and showed her how picture writing was formed, how even the colors told a story. Somehow the talk turned to the skies, and Chimalma mentioned that she'd seen Maria in the garden the night before. Maria froze, not knowing if she'd be in trouble.

"Did you see the moving light?" she asked.

"Yes, in Spain it's called a comet and it's sometimes considered to be a harbinger of doom," she said.

"It is here, as well. It's the third one in a short period of time," Chimalma said, turning to leave.

"Do you think something bad might happen?" Maria asked. Her question brought the priestess to a standstill.

"Yes," she said. "But bad for who, I don't know. Bad for one can be good for another," and she left the room. Maria felt a chill run through her; somehow she was part of all this. Deep in her being she felt it to be so.

The sky turned a pale lavender and then a brilliant rose, as the sun prepared for its daily journey. Maria held her rattle with anticipation as the priestess lit the altar fire from high atop the pyramid. The priestesses began a steady drumming beat that was soon answered by the priests' conches over on the next pyramid. Maria shook her rattle in steady rhythm, her excitement building over her first chance to partake of this integral aspect of Aztec life. She felt as though this was her life, it always had been. Her earlier life among the Spanish had been a dream, and she had just awakened.

9
Royal Courtship

Tiny, yellow flowers peeked their heads up through the bordering mass of green leaves and a cooling spray misted the air. The heat of the day was still upon them, and Montezuma sat by a cool fountain watching a 'waterskater' as it skimmed across the top of the pond. The meeting of the council was about to commence; it was not something he looked forward to. Quite often it ended up an ego match with each of the Tzin lords. They'd all try to outdo each other, and would even employ warriors for security. The council chambers had begun to remind him of an armed camp. But tonight he had more distressing news to share—the Spanish had continued their approach.

Montezuma had hoped that by ordering all the villages in his path vacated, they would have no sustenance or jungle guides with which to travel. He thought that maybe they would return to where they came from, but they persisted in their advance. Even the message he'd sent, proclaiming that he held the Spanish girl and that they endangered her life by drawing closer, had seemed to do no real good. Tudilli sent word that they'd even started building a city and were calling it Vera Cruz. This disturbed Montezuma even more.

Again the feeling of uncertainty crossed his mind; were they gods or not? If they were, was he wrong by not giving them an escort right to the city, or should he return the girl in exchange for them leaving his shores at once? He started back through the courtyard with these questions on his mind, when he was greeted by a small boy running as fast as his short legs could carry him. The boy laughed at his victory over his nurse, who was in hot pursuit. Montezuma caught his three year old son in his arms and tossed him high into the air, bringing on a fit of delighted screams. He then held the tiny boy close, smoothing the tousled black hair before relinquishing him to the maid. The young boy's presence reminded Montezuma that he was going to plan a special outing for all of his children, a day that he could spend just with them. His life was so busy that he didn't get to see his children nearly as much as he'd like.

The nurse carried the prince over her shoulder as she walked just ahead of Montezuma. The boy was quiet now and was studying his father with an estranged look on his young bud of a face. It reminded Montezuma of his own youth, and of a father he had seen rarely and for only short periods of time. His father was a stranger to him until the day he died. Montezuma felt a constriction in his chest. He'd promised himself he wouldn't let that happen to his own children. He struck out for the council chamber with new resolve; his children would have their time with him. He would plan their outing and wouldn't allow anything to get in the way.

"You say that our tax paying enemies of the The One World are rushing to ally this man Cortez?" questioned old Lord Talisitzin. "How can that be? They wouldn't dare defy us."

"The man Cortez encourages it, and it's treason," sneered The Third Reverent Speaker.

"I think we should run these pale monsters into the sea," a young lord, cousin to The Third Reverent Speaker hotly offered.

"It's Year Reed One, it might be Quetzalcoatl. Would you run a god into the sea?" challenged Montezuma.

"Do you know yet, if it's Quetzalcoatl?" another lord addressed Montezuma.

"No."

"Well, if they were gods they would show themselves as such. These pales ones act very much like men, deranged men at that," said the hot headed young lord. "I don't believe they are gods! Besides, who ever heard of a disease of the heart that needed gold," he sneered.

"We don't know what a god needs," Montezuma said with distaste. The warning look in his eye quickly silenced the young man. He continued, "I have fasted and prayed for many days, looking for a sign telling me these are just ordinary men. If the sign comes, I will push them into the sea."

"Speaking of signs," said Montezuma's cousin, "there was another comet observed the other night." The thought that yet another omen brought doom to the Aztec people silenced the group.

"Tell us of the other news sent by Lord Tudilli," inquired Lord Talisitzin after a pause.

"The pale ones have burnt their huge floating houses they travel in," said Montezuma.

"Burnt them? And strand themselves on purpose? Why would they do that?" asked one puzzled lord.

"I can think of only three reasons," answered Snake Woman. Everyone turned in surprise to the powerful and usually quiet old man.

"Tell us," said Montezuma.

"First, they truly are gods and have no need for the water crafts. Second, they are waiting for others of their kind to arrive and are not stranded at all." Several men squirmed uneasily in their seats. "Third, they're crazy!" His final reason brought the relief of laughter.

"I think it's the third one," added a young man. This brought on more laughter and the closing of the council session.

The hand of the Third Reverent Speaker grasping his arm brought Montezuma up short.

"I have some business to conclude with you," he said.

"Speak," said Montezuma.

"Your daughters, the twins, are now fourteen. You promised them to me when they came of age. Now I'd like to claim them, as it is my right," he said. "I've held off taking any of my women as a wife, so that the twins would hold the honor of first wife jointly. This is only fitting, they being the first daughters of The First Reverent Speaker."

"Can't you wait a bit longer? They're only just fourteen, and still so young," Montezuma pleaded.

"At fourteen many girls are already mothers," said the young Reverent Speaker. "If you're worried," he continued to assure Montezuma, "I will use them gently, and they will have all that their station in life demands. But now I must insist you follow through on your agreement. They are the link of our alignment. Are you not pleased at the prospect of being a grandfather?"

"Very well. We will speak in the morning."

Montezuma came away from the conversation uneasy. He didn't want to think about his twin daughters already leaving his house. They'd been born during the early years of his reign when much of his time had been spent in battle. He'd been able to spend little time with them then, and now they were going. They still seemed as small children, and he wasn't ready to accept another man looking upon them with lust. Where do the years go, he thought. He was only thirty-five and he felt like an old man.

Looking up he saw The Second Reverent Speaker walking towards him, his arm wrapped around the shoulders of the petite and attractive Maliche, his daughter, and Montezuma's first wife.

"But father," she pleaded, "can't you remain until at least morning?"

"No, my daughter," he said gently. "I have remained in your city long enough. I must return home to Texcoco."

"Are you off?" inquired Montezuma, overhearing the conversation.

"Yes, I must be back," he said.

"Thank you for all your council. I will come to see you soon; I've heard you've done wondrous things with your gardens," Montezuma said.

He walked the old man down to the palace landing, where The Second Reverent Speaker boarded his craft. The oarsmen rapidly pushed off, leaving a strong wake slashing against the canal wall.

"Come wife," Montezuma said, gently taking her arm. He knew that the love she bore for her father made her heart heavy at his departure. While leading her back to the palace, he studied her profile. It was a shame he felt nothing for her but respect. She was the mother of his eldest son and ran his harem well; she never bothered him with unimportant details. In fact, weeks would pass that he wouldn't even see her. She hadn't shared his bed in years.

Montezuma couldn't possibly know the anguish that Maliche felt. Her father had raised his children very tenderly, and daughters had been given the same respect as sons. She'd been taught the womanly arts, as well as scribing, poetry and psychology along with her brothers. The Lord of Texcoco cherished her, and she knew that she was special and loved. It had shocked her when she was given in marriage to Montezuma and he didn't treat her the same way. Montezuma treated her like any other woman. Oh, she had the respect due her as his first wife, but she never felt the love, the cherishing. She had cried inside, but outwardly she was the model Aztec wife.

As the years passed and he quit sending for her, and as his harem grew ever larger, her heart had turned to stone. Now she occupied herself with her duties and their two children, both of whom were almost grown. Sometimes she befriended Montezuma's other wives but lately she didn't even do that much; it was too humiliating to keep seeing their bellies swell with children while she went on ignored.

His sister lay dead. Montezuma's heart cried out. She was his favorite sister, so young to succumb to the fever. She was to be married soon, and even though it was a match Montezuma had arranged, it was also a love match and she was happy. She was their father's youngest child, born when Montezuma was already grown. She hadn't known their father, who'd died right after her birth. Montezuma had taken her under his wing and she was like a daughter to him…and now this tragedy.

It was the third day and time to bury her, and he'd taken one last look at her still, pale, waxen features. Suddenly, her eyes flew open and a strange light lit them. People gasped and stood back.

Searching their faces until she spotted Montezuma, she sat up and pointed at him, "Beware brother, your empire is doomed!" Then she fell back into a lifeless heap. He looked out the window. His city was in flames.

His eyes flew open, his heart beating furiously. He lay in his own bed, the early morning light just dawning and the night's brazier gone cold. Montezuma forced himself to get up and splash cold water on his face from his alabaster basin. The nightmare, he said to himself, it had come again. This was the fifth time since the event's true occurrence a year ago. The priestess had told him that through the love his sister had for him, she'd chosen to deliver a message from the other world. Others had hinted at darker things such as witchcraft and sorcerer enemies of the state. One had said it wasn't his sister at all, but the voice of the comet which had passed a few weeks earlier. If that was so, what would the latest comet bring?

❖

Taka was teaching Maria how to play patcholli, the gambling bean game. Maria wasn't doing so well; Taka had won nearly all her beans. As she tossed again hoping for a better throw, their game was interrupted by the presence of The High Priestess. "Follow me, Maria," she said, then turned and hurried back towards the main temple building. With a puzzled look on her face, Maria hustled to keep up with the priestess and her long legs. Her mind worked furiously, trying to remember if she'd done anything wrong lately. The priestess seemed all business.

Chimalma led Maria into the room that served as her office. Maria hadn't been here before. It was filled with a bewildering array of codexes, charts, stones and crystals of all colors and sizes. A wall held pouches and jars of what looked like dozens of herbs, and the drums and rattles used for ceremony were stacked in the corner. Maria looked around in fascination, until the voice of the High Priestess brought her to attention.

"The First Reverent Speaker King Montezuma wants to see you," she said, as she picked up a white cloth from a long, wooden table.

"The Emperor!" gasped Maria.

"Yes, The Emperor," Chimalma said.

"But why? How?" Fear struck Maria.

"He wants to question you about the men on the coast," she said.

"But can't you just find out what he wants to know and tell me?" she pleaded.

"No, he wants to see you," Chimalma said firmly.

"Has Cortez done something bad?" she asked in a small voice.

The priestess stopped what she was doing to look at her, "What are you afraid of Maria?"

"Usually when a king wants to question someone, you are in

trouble," she said. "Will he hold me responsible for what Cortez does?"

"I do not know what exactly he wishes to question you on." She put her hands on the trembling girl's shoulders, "But he has ordered your presence, so you must go. But go proudly. Now you are a part of the temple; in a way you represent us."

Chimalma's last comment brought a squaring of Maria's shoulders.

"Montezuma is a logical man. He's not cruel so don't go in fear," she said, beginning to smooth Maria's tousled hair. "But be sure to answer all his questions in truth. When you enter the king's audience chambers, as soon as your name is called you are to walk to the foot of the throne and prostrate yourself on the ground. Make sure your forehead touches the floor, and remain there until you're told to rise."

"Prostrate myself!" cried Maria. "Can't I just curtsy?"

"What's a curtsy?" On seeing Maria's demonstration, Chimalma admitted that it was graceful but just wouldn't do. "You are lucky. Some of the earlier kings made their subjects crawl in and out on their knees," she said.

"How rude," said Maria.

"It's our way and you're among us now," she gently reminded Maria.

"Are you going with me?"

"I can't, I have just come from there and have pressing duties here."

"But I'll get lost or something," Maria reasoned.

"Everything has been taken care of." She unfolded the white cloth and said, "I want you to wear this over your head as a veil; the streets are busy today and I don't want you to be the focal point of attention."

"But won't they stare at me with this on?" she exclaimed, not wanting to wear anymore veils.

"Not as much as they would without it. The people know that the priestesses sometimes wear a white veil when they're in prayer or fasting periods, and must go out."

"Oh," Maria said with disappointment.

"Good grace, and report back to me as soon as you return from the palace." Guiding Maria through the gates, Chimalma put her in the waiting sedan chair and gave the bearers their orders.

Chimalma was right, the streets were very busy. It seemed as though all the city's inhabitants were out and about. The chair had a runner who cleared the way while warning people that they were on the King's business. They seemed to take mostly side streets, avoiding the main thoroughfares to speed along faster. Finally, they arrived at a gate of the palace that Maria hadn't seen before. A man stepped forward and motioned for her to follow him. They moved down a broad hallway with walls that were worked into fantastic pictures with thousands of tiny, colored pebbles. She was led to huge, ornately carved doors set with pieces of jasper. A tall, formal looking, middle aged man took her name and told her to wait. She couldn't see the throne or its occupant from where she was; too many people stood in the way. So she intently studied her surroundings, so as not to think of what might lay ahead. Her line of vision followed the bright red jasper columns to the ornate ceiling. She was engrossed in its intricately carved patterns, when she heard her named announced and felt the hand of the chamberlain pushing her forward.

She walked slowly, keeping her head down to guard against tripping and embarrassing herself. She felt the weight of all the curious eyes upon her and was glad for the veil. She was sure she was blushing madly. When her eyes were in line with the bottom step leading to the throne she fell to her knees, touching her forehead to the marble floor. Almost as soon as her forehead touched the cool, hard floor she heard his voice commanding her to arise.

Slowly rising, she first noticed the gilded gold and green sandals on his feet, and then the strength of his muscular body. He wore a cloak of green and blue feathers and held a green, stone scepter shaped like a snake. His hairless, sculpted chest half-covered by the cloak, was decorated by a necklace of gold and jade, also in the shape of a writhing serpent. He had broad shoulders outlined by the shimmering, feather mantle and was crowned with a gold, triangle diadem set with emeralds.

She drew in her breath as she focused on his face. His jet black hair fell to his shoulders and framed the strong features of his smooth skinned face. His luminous, dark eyes were accented by his strong jaw and strong, sensuous lips. Maria's heart stopped and she felt a familiar longing rise within her; she'd seen that face somewhere before, but where or how she wasn't sure.

"Are you the Spanish girl?" his voice jolted her back to attention.

"Yes," she answered nervously.

"Please remove your veil," he said, not wanting to speak to a piece of cloth. Montezuma assumed that the Spanish girl would either respond much the way his own women did in front of him, adoring and somewhat useless, or she would be deceitful to protect her own people. Either way, he would only ask her a few questions and then send her back to the temple for safekeeping. He was glad audience was nearly over. The day was growing hot and he'd planned to swim in his private pool to cool down, then retire to his chambers where he knew a pleasant diversion awaited him—one of the mountain girls, a cloudmaiden from the south. These women were famed for their beauty, and this one came as part of her region's tribute to him.

"Remove your veil," he repeated impatiently.

The skylight above the throne allowed shafts of sunlight to bathe its immediate vicinity, and as Maria removed the veil it caught her perfect, alabaster complexion, turning it into a translucent glow. Her unbraided hair became a torrent of red-gold lava and the simple, white dress glowed as it caressed and displayed her full, round breasts.

All present in the audience hall gasped and then went silent. The floor seemed to slip away under Montezuma's feet; the walls lost their shape, and he felt and heard his breath echoing in his mind. He was left dumbfounded and sweating. It must be true, he thought. No mortal being could look like this. They must be gods! His voice echoed through the vaulted hall as he heard himself proclaim the end of audience and command that Maria be placed in the palace wing reserved for visiting dignitaries.

Maria paced the luxurious chamber with her mind and heart in turmoil. Why was she here? Was she a prisoner again? Had she done something to offend Montezuma, and why did she have such a strange reaction to him? Even now, when she thought of the bold, handsome figure sitting on the throne she couldn't breathe properly; her palms became sweaty and her heart raced. It felt a bit like fear. Was that it? Was she afraid of him? She must have done something wrong or else she would be on her way back to the temple by now.

She stopped pacing and sat on a carved, wooden stool covered by a bright purple pillow with gold tassels decorating each of its corners. Is this it, she thought? Am I really going to be sacrificed? Are they going to cut out my heart and offer it to the sun? Her body shuddered at the thought of being stretched out on an altar. Then the door flew open and she saw the dear face of her Itza.

"Itza! How did you get here?" She jumped up to cling to the woman. "Did they get you too? Oh I'm so sorry. I must have done something terribly wrong."

"Make sense! What you talk about? Itza told you stay in palace awhile, you need me. So here is Itza," she smiled.

"You were told I'm staying here?" Maria asked softly. She walked to the door and opened it. No menacing guard stood there, just an old attendant who jumped to his feet and asked if she needed anything. She shut the door, relieved; she hadn't thought to look. Feeling sheepish, she explained her behavior to a bewildered Itza. Still, she wondered why she was here; Montezuma hadn't even questioned her yet. That must be it, she thought. He was tired and wished to question her later, then she could return to the temple.

A man stood waiting to be admitted. His arms cradled a huge, wicker chest. Following Itza into Maria's chamber he placed the chest on a black and white checkered table made of onyx and marble. "My Lord, The First Reverent Speaker Montezuma, requests you join him in a boat ride this afternoon so you may experience the City of Tenochtitlan." The bearer bowed his head, then exited.

Itza opened the chest and riffled through it. "Come look, little one," she exclaimed with delight. Maria got up from her breakfast of maize porridge sweetened with honey and a drink of cocoa nectar. The chest was full of embroidered blouses and skirts,

studded and embroidered belts, gilded sandals, carved stone bracelets and strands of stone beads. All were much more elaborate than
what she was used to wearing in the temple. The bottom held several
bottles of perfume, an obsidian mirror and a carved bone hairbrush.

"Him want Maria to look pretty," she said, giggling delightfully
and holding a skirt up to Maria.

"Itza, I can't accept these. A priestess doesn't dress like this."

"All fit, someone have good eye," Itza said, taking a pastel
blouse and measuring it up to Maria.

"Itza didn't you hear me? I can't wear this!"

"You must. King send them, him mad if you not wear."

"Well, if you think so. I'll only pick something to wear today,"
she reasoned. "Then when we go back to the temple I can send it all
back to the King with thanks. Perhaps he chose this boat ride to ask
me his questions. I could dress for that."

Then with feminine glee she dove into the basket, picking a
matching blouse and skirt that were densely embroidered in red and
purple flowers. After Maria chose a red belt and some sandals, Itza
added red jasper beads and bracelets, finally tucking a red blossom
in Maria's hair.

At the same time, Montezuma paced in his chambers; he
couldn't seem to settle his agitation. He hadn't slept at all last night,
just tossing and turning while the face of the Spanish girl kept
coming up to haunt him. Was this some kind of sorcery, he
wondered? Yesterday evening had been especially unsettling. When
he'd returned to his chambers the Cloud Maiden awaited him, and
she was as beautiful as the legends had predicted. But as he made
love to her he kept having visions of alabaster skin and flaming hair.
Would that hair feel different? Would it feel hotter to the touch, he
wondered? In the middle of making love to his prize, the Cloud
Maiden's moaning had brought his focus back to her; but the skin
he was touching, no matter how beautiful, wasn't alabaster and the
hair wasn't fire. His manhood went soft with disappointment. It
took him a few minutes before he was able to continue.

Still, she haunted him. He'd become irritated with himself. He
wasn't a teenage boy in the first throws of passion. He had nearly
one thousand women in his harem, all waiting to please him any way

he chose; he didn't need this pale one. Maybe the boat ride today will clear everything, he thought. She probably isn't as exquisite as she appeared yesterday; it was the light, or the surprise of such exotic coloring. After today it would be different. He would call back the Cloud Maiden tonight and give her the attention she deserved.

❖

Montezuma studied Maria's profile out of the corner of his eye. She had the most delicate nose he'd ever seen and her cheekbones were as high as his own. This ride had done nothing to dispel the image he held of her. He settled back under the canopy of his pleasure craft as they drifted up and down the canals that laced through the city.

Passing the plaza, they witnessed stately pyramids rising high into the sky, their pinnacles crowned with drifting plumes of smoke from burning altar fires. Colorful murals graced the canal walls in many places, painted for the pleasure of the water traffic passers-by. Maria's eyes widened at their intricate details. The city was more beautiful than she'd ever guessed, and in her excitement she forgot her nervousness toward the good-looking man sitting at her side and the funny, weak feeling in her legs that she got in his presence.

As they passed the landing that led to the great market, Maria leaned forward to catch a better view of the activity. Several boats were lined up at the quay, having brought merchandise from various outlying areas. One group was unloading wicker crates full of gobbling turkeys. An old woman was lifting clay pots that she had obviously made with her own hands. She handled each one as carefully as she would a child. The pots gleamed in the sun, their delicate glazes reflecting the care and love they were created with. A farmer stacked large pumpkins on a yoke and prepared to transport them to his stall, deep in the market.

She saw a young girl thread a blue and white flower blossom into her shiny, dark braid while pretending not to flirt with the young man helping his father unload huge baskets of bright red tomatoes. His eyes rested on the young girl's form and he tripped over a basket of the produce, sending the crimson orbs rolling all over the dock and earning a sharp kick from his father.

Beyond the landing, Maria could see the edge of the market. The air was full of voices raised in friendly competition as they hawked their wares. A waft of spicy, roasting meat enticed Maria's nostrils. Boar, thought Maria as she recognized her once favorite smell. She hadn't eaten flesh since entering the temple; the priestesses refused to consume anything but the fruits and vegetables of Mother Earth. Animals have souls with emotions, they had told her. She hadn't even missed its absence, but the smell of roasting pork triggered an old, built-in response and her stomach growled loudly. Embarrassed, she looked at Montezuma with a side glance, hoping he hadn't heard. He was reclining on the large, striped pillows under the canopy and intently studying Maria's backside. Fleeting rays of sunlight peeked in around the canopy and ignited sparks in Maria's hair. He couldn't tear his eyes from the thick braid that ended in delicate curls. It fascinated him; all his women had straight, sleek hair. He yearned to touch the mass of tiny swirls. Then, irritated with himself and his weakness, he sat upright. He hadn't even addressed the subject of why he'd called for her in the first place. He must purge himself of this adolescent infatuation. Resolutely he turned toward the alien creature-woman, prepared to ask the necessary questions and end this cruise, and his self-torture.

They passed a huge pool formed by the presence of an aqueduct gate which stood open. A small cascade of sparkling water rushed in to replenish the pool, and when it was full the attendant closed the gate. A throng of chattering women gathered around the pool, filling large pots with the life giving fluid.

"What's happening there?" Maria asked, her gentle, questioning voice melting Montezuma's resolve.

"This is where the water from the aqueduct is drained off," he softened.

"But I thought the water came from clay pipes that went right into the houses," said Maria. "I mean, that seems to be the case in the temple and the palace anyway."

"Through most of the city this is true, but these people live on the bordering farms and the public plumbing doesn't reach that far," Montezuma answered.

Maria already knew that all the city's drinking water came from the springs high on the hills of Chapultepec, and an aqueduct system fed the precious fluid to the city. The lake water was too salty and therefore unfit to drink.

Maria, fascinated by his melodious deep voice, turned to face him as he spoke.

Green eyes, he thought in astonishment. Her eyes had always been downcast, but now he could see that they were as green and bright as the emeralds that come from the south. He found himself falling into them like a green tunnel, into a space which threatened to claim his very soul.

Maria had been listening raptly to his explanation, unaware of her affect on him but noticing that he had the most beautiful, white teeth she had ever seen. Each one was perfect in shape and seemed to gleam as he spoke, adding still another facet to his astonishingly handsome and alluring face. Feeling uncomfortable with the sensations welling up from her body, she looked away hoping to break the spell she seemed to be in. Suddenly, she saw a barge loaded down with great limestone blocks appearing around the bend. It was too large for the canal and it carried an extra momentum of speed from the weight of its load. In that instant she realized a collision was inevitable. Stiffening, she dug her fingernails into the wooden column supporting the canopy. Their small pleasure craft rammed into the looming barge right at the point where the canal angled toward the lake, the only lane too narrow for both crafts to pass at once.

The scene seemed to unfold in slow motion, as she watched the oarsmen paddle frantically to get out of the way. Then the boat tilted into the air and they were thrown into the water. She saw a flutter of yellow feathers appear to take flight and then drop, as the water closed over Montezuma's head and his feathered cape followed him into the murky waters. Maria didn't even have time to scream, throwing her arms around the seeming comfort of the canopy pole. Then the water claimed her too and she was surrounded in cold curtains of watery darkness. Still clinging to the pole, she panicked for air as her tortured lungs screamed for release. She followed the pole to its end, hoping it would be near the surface but she hit her head on something hard. Feeling around, she realized in horror that the boat had tipped completely over and she was under it. Still in her panic, she wouldn't let go of the pole. It represented survival. She opened her mouth to scream and gushes of brine water rushed down her throat. A burn started to run through her lungs. Itza had been right; this city did hold their deaths. Suddenly, strong hands forced her to let go of the pole. She clung to the broad shoulders with the bright yellow mantle as darkness settled into her mind.

When Maria came to, she was lying at the side of the canal. Worried peasants had wrapped her in blankets and the palace attendant hovered above her. At first she wasn't sure where she was. A coughing spasm brought on expulsion of her body's hoard of brine water. Then she noticed the burning. Her lungs threatened to turn themselves inside out as she forced herself over onto her stomach and continued retching the painful water into the red earth. The sounds of angry, shouting voices filtered through Maria's mental replay of the near-death experience. The commotion stirred her upright as she pulled the soddened red blossom from her drenched hair.

The terrified barge captain had thrown himself at the feet of a furious Montezuma, begging his pardon. He'd tried to excuse himself by explaining that his employer was an impatient man and had ordered that the barge arrive at market by a certain time, regardless of safety. He'd been frightened of arriving late, and came through the safety lock faster than was lawful.

Maria looked beyond the wildly gesturing man to the water. The royal boat floated ignobly, bottom side up with cushions drifting on the water's surface everywhere. Soon a few of the oarsmen began swimming out to gather the floating debris. The crew of the barge cringed behind their captain, sure that their life was over. While barely keeping his fury under control Montezuma tore off his drenched cape, throwing it to the ground and ordering the barge crew to clean up the mess. He demanded that the captain and owner report to court the next day. Then he informed the palace guards, who'd just arrived, to impound the barge and its contents.

Maria, looking at the discarded yellow cape lying in the sun, remembered seeing yellow draped on the broad shoulders of her rescuer and realized the King himself had saved her. A shudder of gratitude rushed through her. When she looked up, Montezuma was standing over her. Taking her hand, he pulled her to her feet and asked if she was all right. He led her to one of the two waiting sedan chairs and had her whisked back to the palace.

Maria stood looking at the boat with apprehension. The pleasure craft was just like the one that had carried her to the mishap two days earlier. The last two nights had been full of nightmares of her caught in the watery arms of death and not able to get away. It had been made worse by the fact that she'd been sent back to the palace alone. She hadn't seen Montezuma in those two days, nor had she been allowed to return to the temple. She longed to speak to the priestess of all the things that were happening to her. She couldn't seem to keep Montezuma's eyes from her mind. Then this morning a message arrived; she was to join Montezuma for the games. Hoping that their talk would transpire today, she yearned to escape back to the temple. She'd assumed they would be attending the games by sedan chair but then the attendant had led her to the palace wharf, and now this boat.

She stood looking at the boat as it gently rocked. Having vowed never to enter a small watercraft again, her heart pounded with fear. Where was the King, she wondered? As if hearing her thoughts, the attendant announced that the King would be along shortly and suggested she board and make herself comfortable. Then she knew that she had to face her fear and board the craft with a steady foot, or she would be afraid the rest of her life. Suddenly, hearing the High Priestess's voice, she knew she could do it. Taking a deep breath, she steadied her footing and stepped on board. Just as her heart calmed, a distracted Montezuma arrived and they pushed off.

The journey to the ball court was taken in complete silence. Maria found herself again tongue tied in his presence. At first she was happy that he had brought a beautiful young girl with him, thinking that now she didn't need to cope with the King as a man. The young girl slid by Maria with grace, displaying her long limbs. Coyly, she pushed back a strand of hip length, jet black hair, glanced at Maria, then fixed her attention on her lord and lover of these last few days.

Montezuma sat back in the low chair, his mind occupied. He'd permanently confiscated the barge that had rammed him two days ago. When the reports came back that the owner was just a greedy man, caring for nothing but his profits and beating all those that labored for him, Montezuma had taken all that the man owned. He decided to make the man into an example to those who cared for nothing of other's safety or piece of mind. Sending his advisors to find out how many people the man had cheated in his climb to financial prominence, he determined that the confiscated property was to be sold to pay anyone he'd taken from.

The last two nights he'd called the Cloud Maiden to him, but his mind had been filled with visions of the Spanish one's struggle under the water. He'd been surprised that she couldn't swim. All his people swam, learning as small children. He had dove under the boat when he realized that Maria hadn't come to the surface. When he spotted her, her struggling form had struck terror in his heart. He'd pried her fingers loose of the canopy pole when he noticed that her eyes were closed. He feared that she'd gone limp from death, and it was only when he'd gotten her to land that he realized she'd only gone unconscious. His relief was so great, he was afraid he would make a fool of himself in front of his courtiers, and so he all but ignored her.

He'd invited the Spanish girl to the ball game as retribution for the fate she'd almost suffered on his boat. He thought he'd quenched the fires of his desire for the pale one, with the perfect body of the Cloud Maiden, but just in case, he'd brought her with him as a distraction from the red haired Maria. He purposefully fixed his attention on the graceful, black haired creature, running his eyes down her smooth legs and meeting the inviting look in her dark eyes.

Then he glanced at Maria. At that moment a ray of sunlight shot through her unbraided hair and the fire was rekindled; he couldn't tear his eyes away. She sat with her back braced against the canopy support, while her long, slender fingers idly traced a pattern on the bright green cushion. Why did she affect him like this, he thought to himself angrily. He forced his attention back to the Cloud Maiden and kept it there during the rest of the ride.

Maria studied the Cloud Maiden out of the corner of her eye. Her hair looked like a dark waterfall resting against her white blouse. She was taller than Maria and her tawny legs glowed golden against the boat cushions. She saw how Montezuma rested his eyes on the lovely creature and her heart constricted in spite of herself. She felt pale and ugly, curling her legs up close around her as if to disappear.

Finally, they arrived at the landing of the ball court and Maria saw a line of brightly colored pennants leading to a pavilion. The King stepped out first and then the beautiful girl, with Maria bringing up the rear. Maria was painfully self-conscious as the graceful girl glided ahead of her, while she seemed to be plodding along behind. She fell further and further back, not wanting to walk so close to the beauty; the comparison was too obvious, she thought.

Arriving at the pavilion, Montezuma sat on a leopard draped throne and the girls were directed to two low chairs on one side. The ball court stretched out before them, its sheer walls broken only by two vertical, stone goal loops built in at opposite ends of the court. The top of the walls were thronged by gaily dressed, laughing people and at the other end were stone benches occupied by nobility. Hawkers passed through the crowd peddling fruit and tamales. The whole scene held the feeling of a carnival. Soon Maria was thoroughly enjoying herself and her self-consciousness melted away.

A priest entered the court. The fragrance of copal drifted from the stone censer he carried, as he intoned a dedication and sensed the four directions. His exit signaled the entrance of the two teams. Their feathered headdresses reached high into the air, with one team predominately blue and the other red. Heavy leather aprons protected their groins and they wore leather pads on their elbows and knees. As they paraded around the ball court, their friendly chastisement with one another brought on cheers from the crowd. Maria noticed money changing hands everywhere throughout the crowd. It must be a special event, she thought, to be so heavily bet on. The termination of the parade brought the removal of headdresses and the start of the game. The players lined up in front of the pavilion. In another rush of self-consciousness she felt all eyes turn to where she and Montezuma were seated. He stood, took a small, rubber ball from a platter by his seat and threw it into the court.

The players scrambled into action, one of them knocking the ball high in the air with a flip of his knee. They ran all around the court, keeping the ball in constant motion by contact with their elbows, knees, heads and hips. It appeared they weren't allowed to touch it with their hands. The game moved so fast that the field was a constant blur of bodies in motion. Maria leaned over to ask the Cloud Maiden the name of the game.

"It's called tlachlli," she said as she stood up. Maria watched her glide over to a beckoning Montezuma, sink to a pillow by his feet and rest her head on his knee. Again feeling the constriction in her heart, Maria forced her attention back to the game.

One player knocked the ball high in the air while his teammates, blocking and grunting, held back the opposition. As the ball fell from the air, his well placed elbow sent the ball sailing through the loop in the wall. This triggered a mad rush in the crowd, with players in hot pursuit pulling off garments and grabbing jewelry from the spectators. Puzzled with this behavior, Maria questioned an attendant standing nearby.

"When the ball is sent through the loop the game is immediately won," he said. "But because this method of winning is so rare…"

"I would imagine," she cut him off, eyeing the tiny loop set high up in the wall.

"…the winning team is then able to chase down the spectators," he continued, "and take anything they are wearing for their own."

"Anything?"

"They're not allowed to take the clothing of a woman and leave her exposed," he said. "Other than that, anything else is fair game."

"Well, if this only happens rarely, how do they usually win?"

"You see the circles painted in the wall near the rings?" he pointed. Maria spotted the different colored circles radiating out from the ring. "Each circle represents different credit points," he said. "The players try to bounce the ball off the colored rings, and at the end of the game the team with the most points wins."

She thanked him and came to her feet as Montezuma signaled her for their departure.

❖

The animal displayed an elegant beauty, its black spots dancing over its tawny, white coat as it prowled back and forth. His strong, feline muscles rippled under the spotted coat and a low growl rumbled from his throat. His mate lazed on a high, stone shelf with her long tail draped over the edge as it curled from side to side. Stone bars kept them separated from their onlookers.

The next room held a family of chattering monkeys with bright blue faces that peered back at Maria with equal curiosity. The next, a brown creature held by a keeper. It had small, bulging, round eyes and a long tail. When the keeper put it down it slowly meandered its way to a tree and rested on one of the low-hanging branches.

"What's that?" she asked.

"A sloth, they're slow moving as you can see, and very gentle," answered Montezuma, who was standing at her side.

He had been showing her his private zoo, and Maria was overwhelmed by the beautiful array of animals. Each one was kept in its own habitat, with trees and ponds. They all looked clean and well cared for, even if she did feel sorry that they were locked behind bars. Soon they left the zoo buildings and entered part of his private gardens. The green, manicured lawns and bright flower beds did nothing to relax Montezuma's nerves. He had to get this conversation over with and get on with his duties. Yesterday he'd had every intention of speaking with her at the ball game, but his strong reaction to her, even after making love for hours with the Cloud Maiden, had so unsettled him that he had chosen not to speak to her at all. But today he was determined to go through with it.

They stopped at a bench by a small pool. A beautiful, blossoming tree overhead had cast many of its flowers adrift on the smooth, watery surface. No sooner had she sat down, than she was up again, peering over the edge of the pool and looking like an impetuous child. Still, there was nothing childlike about the curve of her hips as they protruded back toward the bench and Montezuma.

"How old are you, Maria?" he asked dizzily.

"Sixteen, my lord," she said, returning to the bench beside him.

Sixteen! It's me that feels like sixteen, he thought to himself. "Do you like my city?" he stalled.

"Oh yes, it's beautiful; and by the way, thank you for saving my life the other day," she said, turning her emerald eyes on him. As their eyes met, a heat flushed through his senses and he was lost in her world again, forgetting all about interrogating her. They passed the next hour in gentle innocence, talking of the city, the animals and flowers. Montezuma was enchanted. Maria spoke like The High Priestess, from the heart and honestly saying what she felt, so unlike his other women who could only muster intrigue and jealousy.

When she inquired about the owner of the barge that had hit them a few days previously, he was again amazed with her frankness, but found himself telling her about his decision and ruling anyway. This was something he refused to do normally; speaking of court matters with his women had always been out of the question. It didn't concern them and most of them were devious enough already. He was impressed with her sensitive wisdom when she said, "In a way I feel sorry for the barge owner. For someone to behave that way they must be in a lot of pain, or very frightened of something. The High Priestess says that all anger is a cover-up for some deep fear."

They sat in quiet contemplation for awhile. He realized that what she'd said was quite true, having seen it in his own life time and again.

Soon he realized it was time for him to visit his children. Excusing himself he headed for the nursery, deep in thought of his intrigue with this strange one. He was aware that the interrogation still hadn't happened, but Maria had left him in such a gentle state of wonderlust that he didn't really care.

Maria walked in the garden, the sun warming her back and shoulders. A bright blue and red bird landed on a bush to her right; he peered at her, cocked his head from side to side, then flew off. She was happy. Suddenly, Montezuma lay on the grass in front of her. She sat down next to him, rubbing her fingers on his cool forehead. He grabbed her wrist and gently pushed her onto her back. Laying his body on top of hers, he pulled her blouse up and placed his moist lips on her nipple.

Maria sat straight up, her heart pounding and a warm sensation lingering in her groin. Her nipples tingled, as if she could still feel his lips there.

She stole out of bed, and tiptoeing past the sleeping Itza, she slipped out onto the terrace. A crescent moon hung low in the sky and crickets chirped loudly from the garden below. What's wrong with me? she wondered; I'm a priestess of The Mother Goddess. Well, at least I feel like one, she reasoned. Dreams like this aren't appropriate, she thought; I've been away from the temple too long. Tomorrow I'll go to Montezuma and ask him what he wants from me. Then I can return to the temple. Good, she thought; having made the decision, she felt better. Suddenly, she remembered the dream she'd had back on the coast, and the furrow of her brow squinted in confusion. It was a dream with a man beckoning to her, a man with eyes like Montezuma's. She pondered the thought a moment, then chided herself. Maria, don't be silly. He doesn't want you; you're pale and ugly. He's got beautiful women with golden skin and hair like black waterfalls. Feeling confused and miserable, she returned to bed.

The sweat rolled from his back as he threw the small wooden shield on a green jasper table at the entrance of his chamber. A bath would feel good, he thought. Wiping his forehead, he called for his servants to fill his bath. He exercised with his warriors several times a week, not wanting his body to become soft. He may be First Reverent Speaker, but he was also a warrior and always would be. Sometimes he wondered what his life would have been like had he not been born a prince. It would have been much more simple, that was for sure. His mind wouldn't be filled with affairs of state. He could have been a full time warrior, or perhaps a priest. Life would've been less complicated.

"My lord," interrupted the attendant standing at the door, "it's the Spanish girl. She says she must speak with you."

"Send her in," he said, surprised by her boldness to come uninvited to his chambers.

She was dressed in the plain, white temple dress and strode forward with an air of purpose. Directing her to a seat, he asked, "What is it? Why have you come here uninvited?"

"I desire to know why I am here, Lord," she said with courage.

Montezuma took his own council, turning briefly toward the garden terrace before answering her. She watched the play of light on the sweat of his back, his muscles rippling as he moved. When he turned around, he perched himself on the edge of a leather stool and asked, "These men at the coast that you were with, are they gods... Quetzalcoatl in particular?"

At first, Maria was puzzled by his question. Then she laughed, "Why, do you think so?"

"Do you know who Quetzalcoatl is?" he asked her.

"The priestess mentioned him only a little," she said. "Something about him appearing, to teach the people plants, medicine, arts and such. Then when the people betrayed him he left, vowing to someday return."

"Yes," Montezuma said, "he vowed to return in Year Reed One. This is Year Reed One!"

Maria thought back over all she'd been taught about the Aztec calendar, a series of fifty-two years called a sheath. Year Reed One would only happen every fifty-two years, she remembered. As a sheath was completed they would celebrate the return of Year Reed One with a special ceremony, and everyone would be especially careful not to offend the gods. All fires throughout the city were extinguished for a certain length of time, and it was only when the sacred fires atop the pyramids were relit, that the people of Tenochtitlan were allowed to rekindle their own cooking fires.

"Why do you think Cortez has anything to do with Quetzalcoatl?" she asked.

"It's not actually Cortez," answered Montezuma, "but the tall one, the one with hair much like yours."

"Sandoval," breathed Maria.

"The legend says that Quetzalcoatl was tall, with hair the color of the sun," Montezuma continued. "His eyes, they say, were the color of the sky."

"Sandoval's a good man, but he's hardly a god."

"Are you sure?" said Montezuma, with pleading in his eyes.

"Of course I'm sure," smiled Maria. "I know him!"

"Would you allow them to visit your city as men, or gods?" he questioned, still unconvinced.

Suddenly, she saw his predicament and her heart leapt at the thought of Cortez coming to Tenochtitlan. Remembering Cortez' lust for gold, her eyes rested on Montezuma's bed; its headboard was a complete sheet of pounded gold. A vision flashed through her mind of Cortez turning his cannons on the city; the palace and the temple were a pile of ruble. She could see her new, young friends lying dead and bloodied. The vision so frightened her that she dropped to her knees in front of Montezuma and pleaded with him.

"Please my lord, don't let Cortez come here. He's not a good person and he's most definitely not a god!"

This was the answer he'd been looking for, yet somehow he couldn't accept it completely. Perhaps this girl hadn't gotten along with the Spanish men on the coast, or perhaps she was a goddess herself. That would explain his involuntary reactions to her. He found himself asking her to stay on in the palace a while longer, under the guise of political briefing. She agreed, seeing the need to keep the warning of Cortez fresh in the King's mind.

"But I don't want to go," Maria groaned.

"You must, the King say so!" Itza stood firm, hands on hips, "You no want to make King angry."

"But I don't need a jewel," she said, picking up the piece of bark paper stamped with Montezuma's seal. It had arrived this morning, with the request that Maria visit the great market and pick out a jewel with the King's compliments. Maria felt uncomfortable; this would leave her indebted to Montezuma. Again she studied the piece of paper that was to serve as a payment voucher to the merchant of her choice. The coat of arms depicted a tiger and an eagle in mortal combat. She'd heard that the eagle was really a griffin, not an eagle at all, and that in a nearby valley called Ahucatlan these griffins had once lived. Fingering the bright colored pattern, she looked into Itzas's determined face.

"Well all right," she said, "I would like to see the market place, perhaps a small jewel would be acceptable."

Again she wore a thin, white veil so she wouldn't be the center of attention. As the bearers turned the corner the market spread out before them and Maria caught her breath with awe. The great market was laid out in rows of streets, a row for each type of ware or specialty. Fragrant smoke curled in the air marking the spots of the food vendors. Her chair moved down the streets slowly so she could get a good view of the wares. To go any faster would have been impossible anyway; the streets were packed thick with people.

She spotted an old man who sat puffing on a stone pipe with his mantle wrapped close around his knees. A plethora of rolled up fiber mats, some plain, some dyed in exotic colors, were stacked around him. He looked like he could have been in Spain, or any other country for that matter. As they pressed on down the street, she noticed all the old wizened ones were calmly sitting in the sun while almost everyone else around them seemed to be anxiously running to and fro. Soon they turned onto the street displaying pottery of every shape, size and color. She smiled at a bright-eyed baby who amused himself by beating on a huge earthenware jar while his mother sold a small, glazed, black flask to a sour-faced matron.

On the next street, they found themselves passing rows of stalls of clothing and she perked up. Piles of white fabric stood under beautifully embroidered blouses and skirts that were tacked to the woven rush walls for display. She watched a young peasant woman try different lengths of manguey fiber against her growing son, proudly measuring him for a mantle. Mothers will always be the same no matter what country you're in, Maria thought to herself. They passed a stall displaying a strapless, deerskin dress bleached to a pure white. A row of blue and silver feathers drifted from its neckline and nuggets of turquoise hung from its hem. Maria stopped her chair for a moment to admire its exotic appearance, but at last moved on.

They passed a group of men gathered outside a stall selling weapons and discussing the condition of several spears. A boy of about seven fingered an obsidian lined war club while lost in a fantasy world of being a great warrior. They all moved aside to admit a haughty jaguar knight into the stall; the proprietor rushed to unwrap a small, black and white ceremonial shield for his inspection. "Move on," Maria ordered the chair bearers. "There's nothing I want with weapons," she said under her breath.

At the end of every row was a free for all of peddlers and food vendors. Leaving the stalls of weapons behind, they turned the corner where a group of wealthy pochtecas sat under a canopy and a young girl served them tamales fragrant with sage and cocoa. Maria salivated as the young girl dripped honey on their tamales. She heard them talking about the trade conditions and watched one of them pull out a rush chest full of bright colored feathers; the others oohed and aahed over the rare ones. Maria giggled as a small boy armed with a stick ran under her chair chasing a group of runaway ducks.

The next street was filled with the market doctors; it produced more new sights, smells and curiosities. Several stalls held herbs gathered in bundles and hanging to dry. Maria recognized several of them from her healing classes at the temple. Many of the herbalists were grinding herbs in stone mortar pestles for expectant customers as they passed by. She watched a young man digging his nails into the wooden bench he sat on, while a dentist prodded his open mouth with a thick set of pliers. A quick jerk, and the dentist proudly displayed the offending tooth to his apprentice who sat nearby wrapping a wad of cotton.

At last they came to the gems and jewelry. Silver and gold glittered everywhere. Many stalls were dedicated completely to one type of gem, like jade or jasper. Everywhere she looked there were piles of silver bracelets and gold rings. She spotted a string of perfectly matched pearls; they were an opulent, pinkish cream color. Her eyes opened wide when she saw an old gem merchant proudly displaying a huge emerald, cut like a flower. Maria stopped her chair, where a colorfully dressed merchant woman wearing earrings made of little rows of dangling turquoise and jade was holding up her best jewels. She held two huge, gold rings, one with a deep red garnet surrounded by jade so dark it almost looked black, the other had a profusion of tiny opals dancing around a huge, cream colored pearl. Maria couldn't decide. Itza had gotten down from her chair and was trying on a necklace of deep blue lapis beads.

Then she saw it! At a stall of what appeared to be antique jewelry, a tiny ring drew her in. It was a beautiful, milky white moonstone surrounded by chips of amethyst; she couldn't take her eyes from it. Asking to try the ring on, she found that it fit as though it were made for her.

In a flash vision she saw a desert scene. She felt thirsty; the sun beat down mercilessly. A tawny skinned woman wore the moonstone ring on her brown hand. It was Maria's hand!

"So," the merchant brought her from her vision. "it's very old, perhaps four or five sheaths of years."

What did he say, she thought? Four or five sheaths, that's close to three hundred years old. It was hers; she knew it. It always had been. She gave the man the promissory note from the palace, adding Itza's necklace to the tally, hoping Montezuma wouldn't mind. As she settled back in her sedan chair, her mind was so occupied with her familiarity with the ring, she scarcely noticed the market's splendor on the return trip.

The air still held the morning's chill; Maria pulled her shawl closer around her. Again she admired her new ring. Like her crucifix, it had become a part of her in just two days time. Montezuma had promised her a picnic at a very special place. The huge royal boat was decked out in flower garlands and purple pendants. She was delighted by the presence of Montezuma's children; today she felt like a child herself.

Itza had been allowed to come as well, and was happily chatting with some of the younger children's nurses. It felt like a holiday. The children ran about chasing each other and squealing with delight. Looking around, Maria realized that other than the nurse attendants, she was the only woman. It seemed this outing was only for the children, not the wives. She felt honored to be invited, even if it suggested that Montezuma only looked at her as a child, just as Cortez had. But she decided not to dwell on that.

A sharp pain in the back of Maria's head flinched her around. A small boy of about two had grabbed a fistful of her hair with his chubby, little hand and was curiously studying its bright color. Upon catching Maria's eye, his face broke into an impish grin. Laughing, Maria pulled the boy onto her lap. Delighted at the attention this remarkable looking person gave him, he settled in, still touching her face and hair. Acceptance of the little boy brought the rest of the small children crowding around Maria with curiosity and wonder in their faces. One small girl wearing a tiny jade bracelet stroked Maria's eyelashes and said, "Eyes pretty," then sweetly planted a kiss on Maria's cheek.

The arrival of Montezuma sent the nurse attendants scurrying to collect their small charges and return them to their assigned places. He took his place on a couch surrounded by many cushions. Along with him came several of his older children that he'd been walking with in the garden. Two of the girls sat down beside Maria as the signal was given to cast off. The two girls were also curious about Maria and they quickly struck up a conversation. Soon Maria had learned they were Montezuma's eldest daughters, twins, and they were soon to be married to the Third Reverent Speaker. They were quite amiable and the three became fast friends.

As the royal boat floated through the city Maria noticed the happy faces of the people as they watched their King's children pass by. As they reached the edge of the city, Maria stiffened involuntarily. A feeling of panic rushed over her as she recognized the spot where the boat had capsized one month earlier. The craft slowed, and maneuvered itself through the narrow, zig-zag opening. Finally, realizing there'd be no mishaps, she relaxed. Leaning over to one of the princesses, she asked why the opening was so narrow and jagged when the rest of the canals were so broad and straight.

"Father says that when the capitol was built we had many enemies. And so where the lake could've been used as an access to the city by an enemy, the people built these canal locks in this way so they could be guarded," explained Teja.

"And the canal locks have stone gates that can be fitted into place so no one can get through; plus all the bridges crossing over the canals leading into the city are removable, so no one can get in that way either," added Meja.

The princesses names were Tejatzin and Mejatzin, but they were affectionately called Teja and Meja. Maria turned to look back at the city as they moved into the lake. It looked like a huge, white fortress—a magic fortress. She noticed Montezuma was holding the little girl with the jade bracelet, the one who had kissed her. Montezuma was pointing out sights to his daughter; a happy smile sat easily on his face. Catching Maria looking at him, he smiled at her and was rewarded with a dazzling smile in return. Feeling happy and at ease, Maria turned back to her conversation with the princesses. Their talk turned to the girls' forthcoming marriage, and Maria thought of her own earlier brush with matrimony. It now seemed alien. It didn't matter though; she was going to become a priestess, or so she thought. They talked of life in the harem, which Maria thought she could do without. The girls felt like old friends now, each sharing their hopes and desires.

As they moved across the lake's surface the boat's many rowers kept time to a beating drum. They passed small fishing boats dragging nets and farmers' boats loaded with produce. Heavy barges lumbered along with thick slabs of limestone, or tree logs placed in long rows and tied together with hemp rope. As they reached the other side of the lake, their attention was caught by one old man as he spread tortilla crumbs onto the lake side. When the wild fowl drew near to taste the crumbs, he threw a light fowler's net over them and hailed his captured prey to shore.

Arriving at a set of stairs, the boat was pulled up to a wide, stone quay. Montezuma stepped from the boat, followed by a procession of children, nurses, palace servants, and Maria. The stairs led to the most enchanting gardens Maria's eyes had ever seen. A small river cut through its middle spanned by several small, wooden bridges, each one painted a different color. Artfully placed rocks produced manmade waterfalls that fed into a small lake surrounded by manicured grass, huge shade trees and brightly colored flower beds. Tiny, tame deer roamed throughout the garden, copper bells tinkling around their necks. The King led all to a huge, marble platform shaded by a large, purple canopy; on it were numerous tables covered with delicacies of all kinds. A kind faced, older man waited nearby and several of the children ran to him calling out, "Grandfather, Grandfather."

"Whose that?" asked Maria.

"The Second Reverent Speaker, Lord of Texcoco. That's who these gardens belong to," said Teja.

"Why do so many of the children call him grandfather?" she asked.

"He's the father of Montezuma's first wife, the lady Maliche.

But he likes all the children to call him grandfather," giggled Meja.

"He looks like a very nice man," Maria said softly.

"He is! Come with us!" The twins started to pull Maria over to the man whom they also called Grandfather.

He wrapped a fond arm around each of the girls and said, "I hear you two will be married soon." The girls giggled their acknowledgments, then presented Maria to the Lord of Texcoco. The old man smiled warmly at Maria, and as he took both her hands he welcomed her to Texcoco. "I hope you're comfortable here my dear," he said. A wonderful sensation of warmth and love flowed down from his arms and into hers. Suddenly, she was glowing with a lightness that left her feeling accepted, as if she really did belong. Then, telling her that it was time to eat, the twins happily tugged her away.

The array of food was overwhelming. And this is only a picnic, thought Maria in amazement. She chose whitefish in a tart cherry sauce, a honeyed squash and some bread made of the grain amaranth; then she settled down on the grass with her new friends. Soon they were sharing choice morsels with a young doe who'd wandered near for any handouts. After the meal, a jolly faced nurse attendant who reminded her of Itza, gathered the children up and announced that there were little treasures hidden in the garden and they were going to hunt for them.

"Lets go look!" shouted Teja and Meja.

"No, you go ahead without me; I'm too stuffed to move," Maria said. She watched them scamper off with the rest of the children as though this was the last of their childhood. Looking around for Itza, she spotted her over with the nurses, all happily embroidering clothing for their little ones. Someone slipped down beside her and she swiveled around to see who it was. She was surprised at how agile the Second Reverent Speaker was.

"My dear, are you lonely not being with your own people?" he asked gently.

Other than feeling the need to warn Montezuma about Cortez, she realized she no longer felt a connection with the Spanish, and she said, "Even though I've only been here a short time," she looked at the ground, not sure of how he would receive what she was about to say, "I feel like you are my own people." This was the first time she'd fully acknowledged these feelings. "Other than wishing I could get a message to my parents," tears began to form in her eyes, "to let them know I am fine, I think I don't care if I ever go back to Spain." She began to gently cry. "I want to stay here in the temple," she managed.

He took her in his arms and held her silently while she trembled. When she was calm and had taken a deep sigh of relief, he held her by the shoulders at arms length and smiled knowingly. "You're a brave, young lady," he said. The gods have you on quite an adventure, but I believe you shall grow strong from it. I'm sorry about your parents, but I think you are right; The Mother Goddess probably recognizes that you are Aztec in heart." Smoothing her forehead he smiled and excused himself, leaving her to reflect on their words together.

Feeling vulnerable and empty, she had finally dropped the burden she'd been carrying. Sadly she realized how much she loved and missed her parents, and that she'd probably never see them again.

The sound of squealing and splashing drew Maria down to the lake. Several of the children had removed their clothes and were splashing in the water, and some of the boys were diving from the last waterfall. At the shallow end, Montezuma, clad only in a loin cloth, guided a small child who was rapidly dog paddling along.

"Come Maria," he smiled at her, "come swim!"

"But I can't," she backed away.

"Then it's time you learned," he laughed.

"But I can't," she said again shyly.

"Yes you can," chorused the children, "it's easy!"

Then the twins arrived carrying tiny, turquoise eggs they'd found on the treasure hunt. "Come on," they laughed, pulling Maria to the water's edge.

"But I don't have anything to swim in," she pleaded.

"Just take off your sandals and jewelry," Teja smiled.

All the children looked at her expectantly.

"Oh all right," she said coyly. The children's voices squealed out in cheers as she removed her sandals and jewelry and stepped into the cool water.

Taking her by the hand, Montezuma led her out to the deeper water. Instructing her to lean back and relax, he supported her shoulders and hips, and soon she was floating. She closed her eyes. The water felt cool and the sun on her face so warm, she gradually let her body relax in his strong arms. Getting comfortable, she floated for several minutes; then he gently pushed her upright. Turning her on her stomach, he showed her how to kick and move her arms. A wave of panic surged through her as she thrashed against the water. Then she remembered that Montezuma still supported her. Her body relaxed, and suddenly she was doing it! Her legs and arms pushed through the water purposefully.

Montezuma moved his arms away and she was swimming, or more aptly, dog paddling with her head straining to stay above water. When she realized she was doing it, her concentration broke and the water closed in over her head. As she thrashed, his strong hands pulled her to the surface. She clung to his bare chest as she coughed. A smile of triumph broke out on her face. "I did it!" she beamed. The children laughed and cheered.

Montezuma held her close for a moment more. A warmth rushed through both their bodies. Then he let her go as the twins ran into the water. The girls splashed and played, each helping Maria with her dog paddle.

Montezuma retired to the shore where the Second Reverent Speaker stood smiling, having witnessed Maria's first swimming lesson. While the children played, they spoke of the Spanish, and he revealed to his father-in-law what he'd gathered from Maria. Soon a palace attendant arrived, arms full of thick towels for the swimming children. When the girls got out, Montezuma's eyes fell on Maria. Oblivious to his gaze, she emerged as her wet, thin blouse and skirt clung revealingly to her nakedness underneath.

❖

Their sandals slapped softly on the marble floor as they made their way down the hallway. Chimalma listened patiently as Maria babbled on about boat rides, picnics and an old ring from the market.

"Let me see that ring again Maria," the priestess said, as she bent over to get a better look at the ring on Maria's finger. At first a distant look, then one of disbelief crossed her face. Then she shook her head, saying softly, "It can't be, it must just look like it."

"Look like what?" asked Maria. But Chimalma said nothing, so Maria went back to describing the picnic. Suddenly, the priestess took Maria by the shoulders and said, "Do you love Montezuma?"

"Love him? How can I love him? I'm going to be a priestess," she blurted out before realizing what she'd said.

"A priestess?" questioned Chimalma raising an eyebrow.

"Well maybe," said Maria hopefully.

"Don't you want to go back to your own people?"

"It's funny," she said, "they don't seem like my people anymore," she hesitated, "I feel at home here among the Aztecs."

The priestess studied Maria with a thoughtful look, "The gods' ways are many; who can tell what they will bring."

"Right! See what I mean? A few months ago who would have thought I would end up here? My life has completely changed," she said as they entered the banquet hall.

Tall, stone braziers illuminated the ruby red veins of the magnificent jasper walls. The scent of cedar filled the air as resin danced on the fires. Many tiers holding long banquet tables were already full. The high, plumed headdresses of nobles and warriors reared everywhere; the scene reminded Maria of a flock of giant, exotic birds of prey. They stopped at the door and the attendant led them to some seats in the back reserved for women.

"I don't understand why men and women don't eat together," she wondered aloud.

"Shhh!" whispered Chimalma.

Maria's strapless gown followed each curve to the floor, where it ended in a blaze of colorful patterns. One of the princesses had lent her a headdress. Its gold and red band crossed her forehead and ended in a splendid display of pheasant feathers, while more red-tipped feathers sprouted out from the back of her head. The feathers danced and weaved as she walked, and at times she felt like she was being followed by a big bird as she caught their motion from the corner of her eye. Looking around at the other women present, she knew she was dressed correctly. But still she felt everyone was staring at her; how she wished she had black hair and copper skin. Sensing her discomfort as they sat down, the priestess placed her hand on Maria's arm reassuringly.

Montezuma's arrival signaled the start of the banquet. The King disappeared behind a tall, ornate, green screen.

Food began to disappear around its edge, only to reappear a moment later to be served to the crowd.

"Why does he sit back there?" Maria asked.

"The King always eats separately," Chimalma smiled.

"But why?"

"Because it has always been the way of the First Reverent Speaker."

"Doesn't anyone eat with him? That must get lonely," Maria shrugged.

"He has some of his wives serve him, but no one eats with him," the priestess explained.

After the main course was cleared away a group of girls gathered at one side of the room. They wore short, low-cut blouses exposing most of their breasts and the whole of their midriff, while their skirts rested low on their hips. Glancing toward the screen, Maria noticed Montezuma had come out from behind it and was sitting in a golden chair. He wore a red and gold mantle and collar set off by a heavy golden headdress. The girl that had attended the ball game with them sat by his feet feeding him cherries from a silver dish.

Music from a drum and flute drew the girls out to the center of the hall as they swayed to and fro. Bare bellies undulated and hips rotated alluringly. Holding hands, they looked like a writhing snake of sensuality. The priestess leaned over and explained to Maria that the girls were the auianime, the warriors' courtesans. So these were the auianime, she thought. They were the women that she'd heard so much about, that were for the exclusive use of the warriors. Studying them closer, she noticed all had their eyes heavily ringed with a sooty substance. Their lips and cheeks were dyed a deep red. She'd been told only queens, brides and auianime could wear cosmetics.

Looking back at Montezuma, she watched the Cloud Maiden lean heavily on him and seductively whisper something in his ear. Her heart constricted; he looked so handsome in the soft light of the banquet hall. Why was she feeling this way? What was happening to her? He couldn't possibly want her…not with that sleek, beautiful creature by his side. Besides, she wanted to be a priestess, she reminded herself.

Before she could tear her eyes back to the dancers, Montezuma caught Maria's glance and noted the look of pain on her face. Was she unhappy, he wondered? She looked so beautiful tonight; he could never grow tired of looking at her. He'd always thought the High Priestess was the most desirable woman in Tenochtitlan. Now seeing them sitting side by side, he wasn't so sure. Maria's beauty seemed to eclipse all the others in the room. The High Priestess keenly observed, and took note of the exchanging glances and constricted emotions of both her King and her young neophyte.

Another watched Maria that night as well. Cualpopoca was the elite of the warrior class. A tall, handsome, arrogant man—at twenty-five he was a captains' captain, bested by no one. As the dance ended, all the women turned his way hoping to be chosen. Motioning to one beauty, he pulled her full, round bottom next to him. The girl cooed and fed him cherries, yet his eyes remained on the foreign one.

He had always prided himself on disdaining anything that wasn't Aztec. The Aztecs were meant to rule the world. Yet as he gazed on this creature that definitely was not Aztec, his groin ached and throbbed. He had dreamt of her last night…her flame colored hair laying against the cushions of his bed, and her full mouth open as to suck in his soul through his manhood. His eyes flashed icy daggers at this outlandish creature that stirred his manhood with such unwanted force.

As she stopped by the red jasper garden bench, the late afternoon sun felt good while Maria wiggled her toes in the grass. Several ducks quacked their way across the pond behind her. Her red sandals lay on the grass; sighing, she slowly placed them back on her feet. There was another banquet tonight; this one was a celebration for the twins' marriage twenty days from today. It was necessary for her to go but this time the High Priestess wouldn't be present, so she would have to go alone. She hated being stared at, and that seemed to be happening a lot lately. Well, maybe she could sit with the princesses.

She thought of her walk with Montezuma and how he'd been surprised when she asked why men and women didn't eat together. She'd told him they did in Spain and it was quite pleasant. As usual, she'd gotten that funny, weak feeling in her knees when he looked into her eyes. She'd even almost fainted once when he touched her arm.

As she walked toward the banquet chamber a drift of copal reminded her of last night's dream. The Goddess had appeared to her. She was dressed the same as she was when she merged with the Mother Mary in her previous dream. She had beckoned to Maria; she pointed to a pyramid in the distance...a wide pyramid, larger than anything in the city and surrounded by ruins. Somehow she knew it was the sacred city to the north, the ancient Toltec city, Teotihuacan. The Goddess had said "Come"; she knew she was to take initiation and become a priestess after all. The dream had brought her joy, and she walked with new clarity.

She entered the banquet chamber and was disappointed to see that no seat remained by the princesses. She was led to a seat in the upper gallery and placed next to a wife of a wealthy pochteca. The woman bragged incessantly and clattered her gaudy golden bracelets around, as to draw attention to herself. Maria realized she'd been placed with a whole different class of people—the insecure, yet newly rich.

The arrival of the King again signaled the banquet's start. This time he stood on a platform, and was joined by his daughters. He presented them to the crowd and announced their forthcoming marriage to the Third Reverent Speaker, and that they would share the station of first wife. The annoying woman seated by Maria's side loudly remarked on how handsome the King was and how much his daughters looked like him. Maria chuckled at the woman's assessment; they were so far back, no one could've seen that clearly! During a ceremony when a priest sensed the twins and declared them brides-to-be, the woman looked at Maria, pointed a pudgy finger at her, and asked if she were an albino. Maria, wondering if the Goddess was testing her, smiled sweetly and replied, "No, this is how my people look."

The King scanned the crowd until he discovered Maria way in the back, by an obnoxious looking fat woman. What was she doing there, he thought? She shouldn't be sitting with the common people. Irritated, he disappeared behind his royal dining screen.

Maria was tasting a bowl of pumpkin soup that was fragrant with herbs; she didn't feel like eating much of anything else. The fat woman was going on and on about the success of her husband and the new house she was having built. A headache had begun to build, when a chamberlain appeared at Maria's elbow requesting that she follow him. As she got up to leave she heard the woman remark, "They'll probably throw the albino out; she obviously doesn't belong here."

She followed the man around the outskirts of the banquet hall, while wondering if perhaps she was being thrown out. She looked down at her white skirt and blouse embroidered with pink blossoms, and felt the pink flowers braided in her hair. Then she checked the beautifully studded pink belt wrapped around her waist. Maybe she had dressed too simply tonight; she wore no elaborate jewels or elegant feathers. She rather liked the effect, but perhaps she looked out of place.

Waking up to her senses, she realized the chamberlain was heading straight for Montezuma's pavilion. Standing by the royal screen, he ordered her to go in. She knew that every eye in the room was on her and she wasn't sure what to do; but the chamberlain impatiently motioned her in again. As she stepped around the screen, she was aware the whole room behind her buzzed over this most unusual occurrence. Montezuma sat behind a small table laid out with gold dishes. The chamberlain entered carrying a second chair for Maria. She stood not sure what to do until he asked her to take the seat.

"I've been thinking about what you said, about men and women eating together. I want to experience it for myself," Montezuma said as he smiled at her.

Four lovely women attended Montezuma, serving his food and supplying him with a constant line of clean white napkins before one was even dirty. One of the girls Maria recognized as the Cloud

Maiden from the ball game. She had attended Montezuma at almost every meal now, and was called nightly to his chamber. It was apparent to all that she was now the favorite, and she reveled in her new found position.

The Cloud Maiden recoiled venomously when Montezuma ordered her to pour warm scented water over Maria's hands and provide her with a napkin. Disdain rose in Montezuma as he watched the Cloud Maiden's reaction. How dare she be rude to my guest, he thought? Who does she think she is? Angrily he ordered her to serve Maria exclusively. Maria saw and felt the hatred in the girl's dark eyes as she served her the dinner of pheasant.

Maria walked back to her chambers with her mind in a whirl. Two palace attendants in yellow tunics stopped and stared at her while whispering to each other. Having been called behind Montezuma's screen had all the palace talking. She figured most of the people believed she'd been called to serve the King. Luckily, the screen had hidden what really transpired. She hoped the wives wouldn't tell that they'd had to serve her as well. She also hoped that everybody else didn't believe she was his woman now.

When Maria arrived at her chambers Itza came running out; she too had heard, and wanted to know all about it. For Itza this was a victory. She strutted about like a new mother hen making allegations about how good of a man he would be for her. Maria put up her hands and curtailed Itza's excitement by telling her about last night's dream of the Goddess and the pyramid. A subdued Itza prepared Maria for bed.

The brazier gave off a faint light. The doors to the terrace were open and the night sounds of the garden drifted through the room; a cricket chirped loudly nearby. Maria pulled the covers to her chin and readjusted her pillow. Suddenly, the door to her chamber opened and she sat up. There he was standing in the doorway, the light shining on his black hair. Shutting the door he moved quickly to Maria's bedside, leaned down and placed his lips softly on hers. He gently probed her lips open and his kiss seared her body. With one hand he swept back the covers exposing her unclad form. His eyes roamed hungrily over her body; his hands soon followed his eyes.

❖

Her eyes flew open. The brazier gave off a faint light. The doors to the terrace were open and the night sounds of the garden drifted through the room; a cricket chirped loudly nearby.

Her heart pounded. He's coming, she thought. She tore the covers back and jumped to the floor. Her skirt and blouse hung on the chair nearby; her panicked fingers fumbled to get them on. Searching the floor, she found her sandals and a large red shawl, then she ran to wake Itza. As she reached to rouse the sleeping woman, she remembered Itza's disappointment when she had told her of the dream; she knew Itza wouldn't want her to go back to the temple. She would send for her in the morning.

Peering out of her chambers to make sure the hall was clear she put on her sandals, wrapped the shawl around her, and pulling some of its length over her head, she slipped out.

She thought she could find her way to the temple from the palace. A guard remained at the temple gate all night; if they didn't admit her she would sit at the gate until morning. She figured the guards would never let her out, so she snuck down a flight of stairs leading to the garden. Having remembered seeing the gardeners use a small access door that led to the water from the garden, she hoped for the best.

The garden was cool. The night air was condensing into cold little droplets that clung to the grass and bushes, and tickled her feet and ankles. The door was open and she was able to slip through without incident. The walkway emptied out into a small alley that led down to the water, where several plants wrapped in dirt and manguey cloth awaited planting; she turned and went the other way. The alley ended at another unlocked wooden gate, and she breathed a sigh of relief at someone's lack of security. Deciding not to cross the pyramid plaza—there were always too many people about—she chose a side alley that she thought might connect her to the street she was looking for. She hugged the high, mud brick walls that protected the courtyards of the affluent from the rest of the city; her sandals made the only sound on the deserted street. From over a wall loud voices lifting in laughter rang out, marking the spot of a late night party. She frightened a small mongrel dog sleeping in a corner, that began yipping at her in its high, squeaky voice. Maria tried quieting him, then quickened her pace to avoid being discovered. The air of the early morning hours had turned cold; pulling her shawl close around her she pressed onward.

It seemed she'd been walking for too long now. Turning down another alley that seemed to be heading in the right direction, she moved on while saying a silent prayer to keep the fear away. It turned out to be a dead end, forcing her to retrace her steps. Where was that street? She was worried; she should've crossed it by now!

She thought she heard footfalls behind her, but when she turned there was no one there. A few more steps brought the same strange echo, as though she were being followed; but each time she turned around no one was there. Once she even thought she saw a shadow melt into the darkness. What was she doing out here alone, she thought as her fears crept in; something could happen to me and no one would even be the wiser. Her steps quickened and so did the echo. She broke into a run, tripping over a piece of broken pottery. The strap on her sandal snapped and she had to remove the flapping footwear. Tiny stones on the cold pavement dug into her exposed foot; still she ran on, stumbling at last onto the very street she knew would lead to the temple.

Two fishermen with nets slung over their shoulders passed by her on their way to the canal. They looked at Maria with casual interest, and she pulled the shawl closer around her face. She passed a late night song house, and a couple of men stumbled drunkenly onto the street thinking the night would cover their unlawful state. Maria stepped into the shadows of a doorway as they passed, slapping each other on the back and roaring about the serving girls pumpkin-sized breasts. A stone had cut Maria's big toe and she limped gingerly down the street. At last, she looked up at the huge golden gates of the temple, and sighed with relief.

10
A Priestess Is Born

Maria slipped back into temple life as though she hadn't been gone for over a month at all. If Chimalma was surprised with her return, she didn't say so; she simply assigned her duties for the day and sent a message off to the palace. The mid-morning produced a rather sullen Itza, angry that Maria would run out on her, and the King as well. But her usual good nature quickly returned and she was soon happily sweeping the courtyard with the other temple attendants.

As the day wore on Maria relaxed, realizing that no one from the palace was going to come and drag her off. She was safe at last. She wouldn't have to see Montezuma or feel those feelings; her mind could be at rest. As the evening drew near, Maria found her thoughts returning to the dream of the pyramid. She must speak with the High Priestess; she knew she was supposed to take initiation. She must request it.

Chimalma was sitting with the temple scribe by her side recording her directions for the forthcoming season, when Maria arrived and requested to speak with her. The priestess dismissed the scribe and closed the scroll she was studying.

"What is it Maria?" she said. Maria stood leaning on one foot, then the other, not sure how to start. Finally, taking a deep breath she blurted out, "I want to take initiation! I had a dream and I know I'm suppose to!"

Chimalma studied Maria for a long moment before she stood up and said, "That's impossible."

"But why?" pleaded Maria.

"Initiation can only be taken by an Aztec, that's how it's always been."

"Well maybe it's time for a change," Maria said, irritated.

"That's enough Maria, I won't argue with you; please return to your duties," Chimalma said, as she watched the girl turn on her heels and stalk from the room. Chimalma wondered if she had spoken too hastily, but she saw no reason to build the girl's hopes. The tradition would stand; she was sure of that. Nonetheless, something about the Spanish girl's request was appropriate. Maybe it was time to change.

❖

The sun hadn't yet crested the horizon, as Chimalma stood on her terrace watching the priestesses prepare for sunrise. Finally, drums in hand, they trooped from the courtyard. She had asked one of the other priestesses to take her place this morning. The implication of her dream last night had left her want of counsel. The face of her brother, High Priest of Quetzalcoatl, came to mind.

Within the hour she stood in front of the temple gate and the guard admitted her with a little bow. He led her past the young men just returning from the sunrise ceremony; they looked curiously at her. As she entered the reception room of Quetzalcoatl's temple she was greeted by a man as handsome as she was beautiful. He was a kind natured man, four years her elder. Chimalma was a tall woman but her brother towered over her by several inches. Their poor father had never gotten over the fact that the temples had claimed his two eldest children. Furthermore, they were both temples that demanded chastity of their priesthood, thereby guaranteeing there would be no grandchildren in his house from either of them.

After holding his sister close for sometime, he motioned her to a seat. He knew she would never come to his temple at so early an hour unless it was important. Chimalma told him all about the Spanish girl and her request for initiation. She then explained that The Goddess had come to her last night to say that Maria had been High Priestess to The Mother Goddess in the past, and she wished her to become a priestess again. She wished it to take place right after the corn festival.

"The corn festival!" her brother exclaimed, speaking for the first time. "That's only within the passing of one moon. How can she be trained in such a short time?"

"That's only part of it. I keep getting the sense that she is for Montezuma. I feel it. It's as if they are one…true mates. So how could The Goddess wish her to become a priestess?"

"The gods work in many ways; it's not our place to question their motives. We are only to translate their will to works. I feel the rightness of The Mother's decision. I'm only concerned for an untrained girl being subjected to the pyramid. But if it's as The Goddess told you, then perhaps her training lies locked deep within her soul and will surface in the time it's needed."

"But the tradition," Chimalma got up to pace, "what of the old laws?"

"Judging by what you have told me, the girl is Aztec in everything but skin. And remember my sister, we didn't build the pyramid; we just use it."

"But the other priesthoods will be furious if we do this."

"Let them, we must obey. When your young neophyte, Maria, starts her sacred journey, my priests will be there," he reassured her. "Now return to your temple and prepare her as best you can!"

Taka was helping Maria prepare the evening meal; sage was being ground into corn porridge. "What do you mean you're going to be initiated?" Taka frowned.

"Yes, The High Priestess told me today," Maria smiled.

"But Maria, that can be dangerous. Some people die during initiation. And I know some train for years before they attempt it," she spoke softly.

"I know Taka; but somehow it feels right. I know I can do it."

The girls were interrupted by Chimalma, "Maria, your training will begin after the evening meal. You'll be working with most all of the priestesses, but tonight you'll start with Shera."

"We live many times," instructed the priestess. "Each body is a vessel used to carry us through pre-destined experiences, then it's discarded to make way for the new." Maria and the soft-spoken Shera were sitting on the floor tying bundles of herbs. Her training had began.

"But how can that be?" asked a puzzled Maria. "If I've lived before, why can't I remember it?"

"By the gods' mercy, we forget and are not allowed to remember; this way we may concentrate on the lessons of our present life," she explained.

"Gods' mercy, how would that be merciful? If what you say is true, I would certainly want to remember," Maria laughed.

"If you had been a great and wealthy king in a past life and you could remember your success and leisure, do you think you'd ever be happy in a life as a common farmer?" Shera questioned her. "Would you ever be content?" She smiled, then said, "Each life we live is precious, but soon we would come to think that only the great lives were important and we'd refuse to participate in the simple ones, even though the lessons they offered could be far more beneficial."

"I think I understand, but do we ever get to remember?"

"Sometimes," Shera said. "Occasionally one of life's experiences can duplicate something we've done previously in another life; this can stir up a particular memory."

Maria shivered as she looked at her ring and remembered the vision she'd had when buying it. The dry land, the thirst and the brown finger—all in another time—she knew must have been hers. "I've had that happen," she said softly.

Shera reached over to grab another handful of yarrow by the roots and began to tie it into a bundle. "While you're training to become a priestess in the temple, there are certain techniques and ceremonies that can sometimes trigger a past-life memory or recall," she looked sidelong at Maria, "like initiation."

"Do you mean I'll remember at the pyramid?" Maria beamed.

"Perhaps," said Shera calmly, "every initiation is different."

"Do you remember any of your past lives Shera?" she questioned innocently.

"The Mother Goddess has revealed a few to me, but only those that will make me a better priestess and draw me closer to her," she said with conviction. They both paused, allowing Maria to absorb what had been said thus far.

Maria pushed a strand of hair from her face, reached for a bundle tie and said, "What about people who kill? Do they live more lives too? In Spain, the church teaches that when you do something bad you go to hell, and that we only live one life."

"What is hell?" asked Shera.

"I'm not really sure anymore," she looked downward, "with all that I'm learning now, I don't know what to believe."

"Don't worry Maria. You are learning the Aztec way now, and if your former gods taught you different than ours, there may be much that confuses you in the beginning. And as far as killing another is concerned, it is the law of the gods that what we do shall be done to us. This is why some suffer in their life, because they caused suffering to others in a previous life. And that is why, while we are here in the temple The Mother Goddess teaches us to observe our every thought, so we don't cause another harm and bring it back upon ourselves."

"What if we've wronged someone, and then are sorry?" Stealing from her cousin and lying to her mother came quickly to mind. "Are we still punished?"

"That's where the mercy of the gods comes in. If you're sorry, that means you've learned the lesson, and your scroll is wiped clean."

Blood rushed to Maria's face as she stood up over the bundled yarrow. With hands on hips, she said, "But why doesn't everyone know about this? I mean about having many bodies and how to avoid having bad things happen to you. I've been here many months and this is the first I've heard of it. I know you said these things are the secret teachings and I promised not to talk about them to anyone else, but they seem very useful for everyone to know."

"One day in the future everyone will know. But now it's the temple's duty to safeguard the old wisdom until the day when everyone is ready for this knowledge. All knowledge can be misused in the wrong hands, when someone is not ready for it."

Sweat dampened her temples as she awoke from a restless night. The week that had passed since her training begun had exhausted her, and it seemed that the work went right on even while she slept. She'd been meaning to ask one of the priestesses if what was happening to her at night was normal, but with so much to learn during the day, she always seemed to forget.

A bit more alert now, she remembered that this morning she would be working with Chimalma for the first time. Pulling herself up out of bed and mustering the enthusiasm needed to work with The High Priestess, herself, she dressed for morning duties. After her chores, the morning meal, and waiting for the other girls to go off to exercise, Maria waited patiently by Chimalma's door. When the priestess emerged she greeted Maria warmly, then led her out to the garden.

As they sat down together on one of the garden meditation benches, Chimalma pointed to a large, leafy plant and said, "Beautiful isn't it? Its leaves are going to be your teacher today." They both smiled and laughed. "Look around you Maria. Everything you can see, the gods have made, and it's all imbued with a life force. The life force is in everything…in the wind, in the air, in water and fire, in you and me, and in this beautiful plant. Within this life force is the spark of intelligence. Today we're going to contact it—first by feeling it, then by communicating with it."

"But how can I possibly do that?" Doubt rolled across her face.

"With faith and patience…watch me, then do the same." She briskly rubbed her hands together, then held them facing each other a few inches apart. "Do you feel the tingling heat? When you do, gently press your hands toward one another."

To Maria's amazement, she could actually feel the thick, invisible substance balling up between her palms.

"Now quickly, before it dissipates see if you can feel it along the length of your arm," Chimalma instructed.

"Hah!" Maria giggled as she felt the life force current and then a wisp of air pass between her hand and forearm.

"That's your energy sheath, see how easy it is," Chimalma grinned.

"I always thought that was just my body heat."

"The body's heat is only part of it; there's much more to it than what the eye can see. Now let's try the plant. Approach the leaf as if you wanted to touch it but it was too precious to do so. As soon as you feel the life force, stroke it the length of its leaf."

"Yes, I feel it," she beamed, "it's fainter and a bit cooler than my own arm but I definitely feel it!"

"Good! Let it linger there a bit longer and then stroke it again."

"Look what's happening," she said astonished and breathless, afraid even her breathing might destroy what she was seeing. "The leaf is following my hand!"

"It likes you!" laughed Chimalma.

"This is fun," she giggled, kissing the plant and settling back down.

"You learn easy, not everyone is quite so fortunate. Now let's try communicating with the plant."

"All right," Maria smiled, more assured now.

"Take a deep breath, close your eyes and relax. Go to your heart and ask The Mother Goddess to help you. Now take the leaf into your hands; think of it as a living thing you want to speak with. Hold its image inside of you and quiet your thoughts. Now let it speak to your mind," the priestess instructed.

Maria tried. At first nothing happened; she was distracted by the buzzing of bees and windblown strands of hair tickling her face. She kept trying, and then suddenly something changed. The plant became real in her mind; a scrambling of images started to form thoughts she knew weren't her own. Her eyes flew open in amazement! "It likes me to touch it," she said, "but it doesn't like the groundhog that's dug a hole near its roots; it wants it to move."

"Yes, well we'll have to contact the groundhog and give him those instructions," Chimalma laughed.

"Does this mean I can talk to any plant this way?" an amazed Maria asked.

"Any plant, animal, even the stars…two people can communicate the same way—mind to mind; even the stones can speak to you. Now let's try another exercise with your energy sheath. Come with me."

That night when Chimalma was alone, she reflected on the reports from the priestesses and the work she had done herself with Maria. Her brother had been right; the knowledge and instinct was buried in Maria and was coming to the surface quite easily. The Goddess was most certainly with her.

❖

A comatose child lay on the healing table with glazed-over, unseeing eyes. His mother stood by, ringing her hands and softly crying. "Please help me," she begged. "The market doctors don't know what to do with him. He just lies there not moving, getting weaker and weaker, and burning with a great fever."

Tansa, the old healing priestess, asked the mother to wait outside. She then scanned the child's life force by running her hands along the length of his body. "Maria, you've learned of the energy sheath. Close your eyes and run your hands over his body; tell me of this child."

After following Tansa's instructions Maria opened her eyes and stared softly, not sure if her impressions were accurate. "Well, he seems weak at his groin, heart and head. But that doesn't make sense; why would a small boy have anything wrong with his groin?"

"It's not his groin, but an energy center in the body that resides in that place; his whole physical structure is weakened by an unseen filth that has entered his body there. You're going to help me direct healing life currents back into his body. Position yourself at his feet and listen carefully. Imagine that you are a tree with roots growing deep into the earth, and see if you can feel the life force of the earth itself…just like you did with the plant. But don't be surprised, this will be much stronger."

"Tansa, it's moving through my body! What do I do?" she cried.

"Just relax, don't be frightened; that's quite normal. Let your mind direct the life force through your hands and into his feet."

It seemed to move right through her hands on its own accord. Soon she relaxed and was quite enjoying it.

"Now I'm going to place my hands on different spots on his body," she continued, "and I want you to do the same. But wait until the voice that you sometimes hear in your mind tells you where to go."

Before too long Maria felt an urge to move both of her hands to his knees, and then to his hips. How exciting! she thought; she could really feel something working.

"Now place one hand on his heart and the other on his groin," guided Tansa. "Begin to think of good, loving thoughts while you let a great and dazzling green light fill your heart. Are you still with me Maria?"

"Yes, I think so; it's a lot but I think I can manage."

"Good girl, you're doing very well," Tansa assured her.

"Now let the earth current mix with the loving thoughts and the green light at your heart, and send it all down your arms and into his body."

Maria felt a tremendous rush of the life current move through her, and she almost fainted. Still she kept her hands on the child until at last the surge of life force subsided. Then she said, "Please, I need to sit down now."

"Yes, you deserve a rest; you've done well and the healing current likes you." With a smile she said, "Chimalma will be very pleased with your work."

Maria seemed to regain her composure as she watched Tansa wipe the boy down and apply an herbal balm to his forehead. The child appeared to be in a healthy, healing sleep now and his fever had left him. Suddenly, Maria realized she had helped to heal the boy, and she felt flush with pride.

A palace messenger awaited her in the reception chamber. Maria walked slowly, afraid of what the message would bring. She wouldn't leave the temple she fussed...she couldn't. The face of Montezuma drifted through her mind but she pushed it aside. A young man wearing a sun-colored tunic paced the room as she entered. His staff of office leaned against the wall.

"The Princesses Mejatzin and Tejatzin request your presence at the"...started the young man. The High Priestess stopped at the doorway to listen. "They have requested you come to the palace two days hence and spend the eve of their wedding with them at the harem, and then be a member of their wedding party the following day."

"But why have they chosen me?" Maria asked.

"I don't know. My only orders were to deliver the message."

"Well I don't know either," she said, with heat flushing her face as she began to pace.

"Instruct the princesses that Maria would love to come," Chimalma's low voice answered. The man bowed, retrieved his staff and left.

"But Chimalma, I'm not sure I want to go," she said. "Why did you answer for me?"

"You told me these girls befriended you," Chimalma said. "To an Aztec girl this is the greatest time of her life; they've shown you a great honor. "Besides", the priestess' voice went stern, "it's fear that's keeping you from going. Fear in a priestess is not a good thing."

"But you don't understand!" Maria pursued Chimalma who was walking towards the gardens now; her fingers worked the ends of her braid nervously. "The King," she stammered, "I had many dreams of him, and he did things to me."

"He touched you against your will?" a surprised Chimalma asked, stopping to look at her.

"No nothing like that," Maria said embarrassed. "But whenever he did touch me, even the slightest bit, my knees turned weak and I got a funny sensation in the pit of my stomach."

"Those are normal feelings Maria; you must learn to deal with them. You can't run from yourself."

"But I want to be a priestess. And you heard yourself; the princesses want me to stay in the harem with them...his harem," she moaned.

"Maria, if you want to avoid the King, the harem would be the safest place for you to stay. Montezuma doesn't enter the harem except to visit the nursery; his women go to him, he doesn't go to them," she said calmly.

"But how do you know?"

"Because that's the way of the harem, it always has been," she smiled.

The guard ushered Maria through the carved cedar doors of the harem. The receiving chamber was floored with a pale pink marble; whitewashed walls held scenes of the goddesses; the ceiling was the same but carved in cedar. An older woman with hair wrapped in braids over her head came forward to welcome her.

"I am a guest of the princesses Teja and Meja," Maria said. The woman nodded and asked Maria to follow her.

A huge courtyard opened before Maria; a fountain splashed invitingly. Several young women sat in the sun braiding each other's hair. They all stopped to look at her curiously as she passed by. The old woman led her down a hallway with small doors on each side. She could hear the soft voices of women laughing, talking and singing everywhere; here and there she heard the wail of a baby. Three little girls chased each other around a corner, stopping short at Maria's appearance. She smiled at them as they giggled and ran on. The woman turned and led her down another corridor; these doors were much bigger and farther apart. One was open and the sound of young laughter echoed from it. The old woman left her at the door.

As she stepped inside, she saw dozens of opened wicker chests and clothing scattered everywhere. The princess Meja was sticking a flat implement into a sooty paste and attempting to paint her eyes.

"Maria! Come in," cried Teja, as she grabbed her wrist and pulled her into the room. "Look, we are choosing our wedding apparel," she said, pulling out a dress trimmed with blue and green iridescent feathers. "Aren't they beautiful! Our husband to be sent them just this morning," she gushed.

"Tell me about him," Maria said, as she smiled and pushed boxes of jewels to the side, so she could sit down.

"Well," said Teja, "he's the Third Reverent Speaker, and he's young, only twenty-one, and very handsome," she giggled.

"He waited for us and wouldn't take any other wives so we would be his mat wife," said Meja turning to face them. Her appearance brought on a fit of hysterics from Teja and Maria.

"Meja, you look like a raccoon," laughed Teja. The girl looked back into the mirror at the black rings around her eyes and began to wipe them from her face.

"Oh, I'm never going to get it right," she moaned.

"Here, let me try," said Maria, as she wiped the girl's face clean and then proceeded to paint two smooth, black lines around Meja's eyes. "What's a mat wife?" she asked as she worked.

"When an Aztec man marries his first wife, they are married on a special mat in front of a priest. Only the first wife is married in this way. It takes place in front of many people and a big party follows.

All other wives are married less formally," Teja explained.

"I see. Well what is it you'd like me to do?" asked Maria.

"Tomorrow morning our future husband's family will come to collect us and take us to the old palace where he is staying," she said. "You'll follow us over and help us get through the party; then you can help our mother prepare the bridal chamber."

"Oh, I'm a bridesmaid," Maria said with delight. "But why did you choose me?"

"You probably noticed that none of our younger sisters are old enough to do it," Meja giggled.

"And we like you!" added Teja.

"But I don't understand. You just met me and there are so many women here at the harem already," Maria said.

"Oh, we could never choose a concubine; they're below our station," Teja said bluntly.

"What's a concubine?" asked Maria, as she fingered one of the dresses.

"They're just all of father's women used for his pleasure. Only wives and princesses come from Tzin status; concubines are commoners," she explained politely.

"But I'm not a princess either," Maria said, lifting her eyebrows.

"But we were told that you were a daughter of nobility back in the country you came from," Teja said.

"Yes, that's good enough for us," her sister added brightly.

"All right," laughed Maria as she surrendered.

"The three girls laughed and talked through most of the afternoon, trying on their finery and becoming closer friends. Later in the evening, their mother, a tall, elegant, stately woman, came to check on her girls with last minute arrangements. Maria liked her immediately, but wanting to give them some privacy, she went for a walk.

Dusk set in and shadows deepened. A number of older women passed through the halls lighting braziers to chase away the evening chill. Maria stopped every so often to examine one of the frescoes on the whitewashed walls. Coming to a small, open courtyard she watched several young women tying long straps to their ankles. The straps had large dried seeds attached to them, and they rattled and tinkled like tiny bells when the girls walked. A dance mistress clapped her hands to get the girls' attention, and Maria watched as the women practiced several dance steps to the beat of a tall wooden drum. They must be rehearsing for Teja and Meja's wedding tomorrow, she thought.

She moved on through more courtyards and past numerous gardens and buildings. The harem seemed huge, a small city unto itself. The princesses had said, Maliche, the first wife, ruled the harem. What a task! she thought. She came upon a group of women playing with dice grids, betting small trinkets as the stone was tossed. When they spotted Maria, the game stopped and they whispered and pointed at her. Feeling self-conscious, she decided it was time to return to Teja and Meja's rooms.

Turning on her heels she found herself face to face with the Cloud Maiden. The lovely face snickered at Maria, then spat and swore at her. Maria knew she'd been called a whore.

"Why did you call me that?" she asked, as she heard the other girls snickering behind her.

"Because the King can have you and doesn't even officially claim you as his own; you're a whore." The air filled with tension.

"But the King hasn't even tried to claim me," shot back Maria.

"That's because you're a pale, hideous creature," the girl said venomously.

"If the King didn't have you, why did he demand you go behind his dining screen?" called out one of the other girls.

"He had me eat dinner with him. She knows," Maria pointed to the Cloud Maiden, "the King had her serve me!" The other girls turned to the Cloud Maiden with a start of confusion.

"Liar!" the girl shrieked.

"Oh yes?" The hair on the back of Maria's neck bristled with anger. "Shall we go to the King and have him verify the truth?"

"You whore!" she screamed, hurling herself clawing and scratching at Maria.

Suddenly, the girl had both her hands buried in Maria's hair, trying to yank it out by the roots. A surge of anger welled up in Maria. She remembered her cousin Juan telling her that if she were ever attacked, she shouldn't fight biting and scratching like a girl.

Maria curled her fist tight and struck the girl's midsection with all her strength. The Cloud Maiden doubled over, her raging shriek cut off midstream. Maria raised her knee catching the Cloud Maiden's chin, and the girl's hand flew open releasing Maria's hair as she fell backward. No sooner had she landed, she was up again and resuming her attack. Maria's fist doubled up again, and with all her might she connected with the Cloud Maiden's nose and eye socket.

"The girl lay screaming as the blood swelled from her nose. The other girls crowded around Maria, begged her forgiveness, smoothed her ruffled hair and torn blouse, and pleaded with her not to tell the King of the incident. If there was anything the Aztecs respected, it was a warrior. The Cloud Maiden limped off, ignored by the others.

When Maria arrived back at the princesses apartments, Teja cried out in surprise, "What happened to you?"

"I tripped and fell in the sticker bushes," she said, hating to lie; but she had promised the others. The girls' mother, guessing what might have happened said, "One must beware; some bushes carry a nasty prickle." Maria and the older woman looked at each other in perfect understanding.

The Third Reverent Speaker's family waited in the reception chamber as the small brides' procession worked its way through the harem. The twin brides wore dresses trimmed with numerous blue and green feathers that matched their tall, plumed headdresses. Maria followed the twins. She wore a wreath of pale blue blossoms that complimented her pale blue blouse and skirt; both her skirt and blouse were trimmed with red embroidered flowers at the neck and hem. She carried a small casket which held two elaborate gold bracelets set with dancing jade figurines—gifts from the princesses to their bridegroom.

The First Wife had appeared at the princesses' chambers to wish them well that morning. She was a quiet woman, and Maria wondered of the hurt she could see in Maliche's dark, fluid eyes. The other women gathered at different points throughout the harem, as they smiled and called out greetings. This was the first royal marriage of this stature in many years. The harem was in preparation for a huge feast to follow after the wedding. Gay garlands of flowers were starting to appear all throughout the harem; a large, beautiful string of white flowers had been draped over the princesses' door during the night.

As the procession appeared down the hallway, a quick movement ahead caught Maria's attention. The sleek form of the Cloud Maiden stopped just long enough to flash a look of hatred at Maria, before disappearing into the small cubical that served as her room. Maria noted that her eye was puffed almost shut and was the color of eggplant.

At the reception chamber several old women greeted the princesses and put them in two sedan chairs decked with long, bright colored streamers. The procession wound its way from the palace, up the street lined with throngs of citizens, all turned out to wish their King's eldest daughters well. Maria walked behind Teja and Meja's chair with their mother and two more daughters of nobility who were picked as brides attendants. She was really enjoying herself, even though she was uncomfortable with the curious scrutiny the Aztecs still gave her.

Soon they arrived outside the walls of a second palace. She'd been told this palace had belonged to Montezuma's father and was now the official residence of visiting dignitaries. It wasn't as large as Montezuma's, but still impressive inside its walls. High above the palace rooftops huge, feathered banners majestically drifted in the early afternoon air. Beautiful terra-cotta porches rose several stories high with black marble pillars standing guard at each level. The porches' backdrop was an intricate fresco that rose three stories high connecting each porch with its collective image. It was the plumed serpent Quetzalcoatl, rising high in the air guarding a recreation of the city. Depicted at the other end was The Sun God, Huitzilopochtli, who viewed the same city from a black and yellow mask.

The Third Reverent Speaker stood at the doorway of the private temple. He was slight in build with a young, handsome face. He wore an elaborate gold headdress with pieces of jade set in and around it and crowned with tall quetzal feathers. He held a dark green stone censer carved in the likeness of a dancing goddess. Her skirt was made of a row of plates curved upward to hold the copal resin. His other hand held a gilded wand with a cluster of the highly prized quetzal feathers sprouting from one end.

As the marriage train reached the temple, the brides relinquished their sedan chairs and stepped forward to join their new lord. The future husband and king censed each girl, fanning the copal smoke over them with the gilded feather wand; then they in turn sensed him in the same manner. Turning around, the three led the large tzin gathering into the temple.

The Third Reverent Speaker took the seat at the center of the hall, with a princess on either side. Laid on the floor in front of the altar was the marriage mat. It looked to be a plain mat like any other, except for the rows of sacred symbols woven around the edges.

The wedding began with several old men, in turn, coming forward to deliver lengthy eulogies on married life; they expounded on fidelity, hard work, reverence to the gods, etc. The voices droned on, as Maria stood there for what seemed like hours. No wonder a man only married his first wife like this, she thought; to have to sit through this more than once would certainly curtail you from getting married too often. She held back a laugh as she thought of all of Montezuma's wives.

Maria let her eyes discreetly scan the room to observe the faces of those present, mostly to keep herself occupied and awake. One set of eyes had already been holding their focus on her own when she found his, Montezuma's. She shifted uncomfortably but couldn't let go of his stare. The heat of his eyes seemed to bore a hole through her and her knees began to buckle in weakness. Her breathing stopped, until at last she pulled her gaze away. She forced her focus back onto the wedding party, as her heart pounded. She scolded herself, wondering why she always reacted this way. She knew he would be there; of course he would be there.

She tried to still her emotions with the words of the High Priestess, reminding her that fear was not a good thing for a priestess to entertain. Perhaps The Goddess was just testing her willpower; yes, she thought, perhaps this attraction was just an illusion and not real at all. Well she wouldn't fail this test! She pulled herself back up to her full height and took a stronger repose. Besides, he couldn't possibly be attracted to her, not with all those beautiful women in his harem.

Her thoughts returned to last night's encounter with the Cloud Maiden; she had called her a hideous, pale thing, a creature. Those words seemed to ring through her mind, even while she slept last night. It didn't matter, she tried to tell herself; after all, she wanted to be a priestess and then it really wouldn't matter, she reasoned, covering the wounds of her scarred young feelings.

Surrendering her problems, she returned her mind to the wedding which looked to be almost over. A black clad priest stepped forward and called on the gods to witness. He tied the edge of the girls' blouses to the hem of their husband's mantle, and raising his hands above the trio's heads he proclaimed the marriage sanctified. After the priest handed them all a bowl of maize cakes, the princesses fed the bridegroom, and he them. Their garments were untied and the ceremony was complete.

The brides and groom led the gathering to the banquet hall where more guests awaited. Festoons of colored ribbon and flowers decked the white marbled pillars and long, beautifully set tables were made ready for the feasting to begin. Maria was delighted to find the High Priestess in attendance; she didn't know Chimalma had been invited. The Priestess explained that the High Priest and Priestess of each temple were automatically invited to any major events within the city; not to mention that she was a third cousin to the princesses on their mother's side.

Maria was called to the main table to present the casket of bracelets to the bridegroom. The Third Reverent Speaker watched her approach with more than a keen interest. After she had presented the gifts and was returning to her seat, he drank in her curves with lust-filled eyes, that saw the pale one had a body to cause a goddess to weep.

Montezuma had been watching closely as well; however, his focus had locked in on his new son-in-law's intentions. A palace scribe stood before him holding the prepared marriage papers waiting to be stamped with his seal. Montezuma's coat of arms came down with such force and anger that the scribe fell to the floor in prostration. Not only was it a royal slight to his daughters, but he couldn't bare to think of another man thinking of Maria in that way.

The feast was most enjoyable. The High Priestess seemed to be in a very relaxed mood as many of her childhood friends came forward to acknowledge her, and she entertained Maria with a discourse on the Tzin houses of Tenochtitlan. Maria was glad Montezuma seemed to be too busy to approach her, and she was relieved when he disappeared behind his dining screen as the feasting began.

The wedding meal consisted of a clear soup with bits of mild peppers and onions, sweet potatoes covered with a rich glaze, a delicate whitefish in a tart cherry sauce, a potpourri of vegetables cooked in fragrant herbs, and corn cakes drizzled in honey. Chimalma eyed Maria's fish and reminded her that she wouldn't be allowed to eat anymore flesh after her vows, so she'd better enjoy it now.

A troop of dwarves sang, danced, and rolled around in general buffoonery until the banquet hall echoed with laughter. They were followed by warrior acrobats attempting the seemingly impossible, with no apparent respect for life or limb. The entertainment continued with a group of slender dancing girls with numerous tiny bells on their ankles, wrists, and dangling hair braids. Eventually, Teja and Meja's mother approached Maria and informed her that it was time to prepare the bridal chamber. Chimalma too, rose and announced it was time for her to return to the temple; she would send back the chair later, for Maria.

Maria giggled with the other Tzin girls as they followed in the queen's wake. She was happy and grateful. The princesses' friendship had signaled acceptance among the Tzins for her, and she knew she would be more at ease among them now. The small party of women entered the bridal chambers through a series of doors that opened out on a private garden; a fountain splashed just outside.

The night's calling birds had begun filling the room with their song; servants had already lit several braziers, lending the room a soft glow and a woodsy fragrance.

They set about their preparatory work with a light air; the mother of the twins glowed as she led the others through the details. She began by placing a stone washbasin on the bed's night table; it was filled with warm, soapy water and scented with a hint of jasmine. Then came full length, poncho-like night shirts which they draped on the large bed.

"What's that for?" asked Maria, as the older woman placed a stiffened white cloth in the middle of the bed.

"The proof cloth," said the mother, "a bride must be a virgin; this cloth will catch the proof blood."

"Oh," said Maria thoughtfully, remembering the bloodstained sheets flying on the balconies of newlyweds back in Spain. "What happens if a bride is not a virgin?" she asked carefully.

"An Aztec bride must be a virgin," she said haughtily. "It is the Aztec way and nothing else is acceptable."

"If the bride is not a virgin," one of the Tzin girls spoke up, "at the next day's feast the groom serves tortillas in baskets with no bottoms and the food falls out in all the guests' laps."

"And the groom can send the bride home in shame," added the other Tzin girl.

"That seems rather harsh," frowned Maria.

"That would not be harsh Maria," the Second Queen said, hardening her tone. "Aztec girls are raised to be virtuous; our whole culture expects it and depends on it. My daughters will not fail in this I am sure."

"What happens to the girls that fail?" she asked softly.

"Most of the time they have to marry much below their Tzin station," said one of the girls.

"If the gods are with them they can become one of the auianime, or perhaps a concubine; however many take their own lives," the Second Queen Mother said.

"Sometimes, when a man is in love with a girl and he has already taken her virtue," one of the girls giggled in Maria's ear, "the couple will cut the husband's manhood for fresh blood for the proof cloth." All their faces winced in mock pain, then they burst out in laughter; tension lifted, then they went back to the work at hand.

At last they opened a jeweled box, and from it took handfuls of precious blue feathers and brilliant pieces of jade, scattering them across the bed. "This is for the children that will come," the mother explained, as she smiled at Maria. It is our custom that bridal beds be strewn with feathers and jade to symbolize the couples fertility; the feathers represent the boy children and the jade represents the girls."

"The twins will be busy then," laughed Maria, eyeing the covered bed. "Do all couples do this?" she asked.

"Yes, all," the older woman smiled. "It is the Aztec way of honoring the new life that a marriage brings."

"But what about the poor people that can't afford feathers and jade? What do they do?" she asked, fondling one of the rare gems.

"Oh, they do the same thing," said one of the girls, "only with very few feathers and jade, and they have to rent them."

The sound of drums announced the arrival of the wedding party. The chanting crowd escorted the trio to the door, then all but a few withdrew. The princesses were led behind a carved cedar screen to change from their finery into the simple, poncho-like nightgowns. As Maria helped, she noticed Meja's hands trembling while Teja held a bright smile, but her eyes were wearing clouds of fear. She felt sorry for them. Why were they being married so soon, more than two years earlier than the normal marriage age? She shot a quick stab of anger towards Montezuma. How could he be permitting this to happen to his own daughters, she thought?

The girls were presented to the young groom and declared to be virgins; he was declared to be virile and discreet. They were laid down in the bed with the girls on either side, and ceremoniously covered with a royal purple blanket. The groom's attendant un-rolled the marriage mat under the bed and the group exited.

It had been the hottest day of the year, and he'd sat in audience nearly all day. The audience hall seemed to grow stuffier as the lines of petitioners had grown longer. The sun hung low in the sky but everything still seemed to be swimming in waves of heat, and the two cold bathes he'd taken earlier offered little relief. He watched the sun sinking lower in the sky as it turned the horizon into flames of red and orange. It reminded him of the incident two years ago when the eastern sky had turned crimson at nightfall—a crimson that held thousands of shining specks of light. Eerie voices had come from the sky, proclaiming disaster amid cries and groans of pain. The priests had cut out many hearts the next few days in hopes of appeasing the gods. The city seemed to walk on tiptoes for many weeks as if the gods would forget about them, and the calamity would be abated.

Slowly, life had returned to normal and most everybody pushed the incident to the back of their minds to mingle with the rest of the omens; but he knew the time was coming soon. He could feel it.

A sudden noise from behind his throne startled him from his reverie; he swung around in anger, ready to strike out. He stopped short at the cringing form of the Cloud Maiden.

"What are you doing here?" he bellowed out in frustration.

"You sent for me?" she asked, as she stepped back trying to keep her face in the shadows.

It had been five days since her battle with the pale one; at least her nose wasn't broken, but her eye still held traces of angry purple. The King hadn't sent for her in all those days. At first she was glad, not wanting him to see her like this; but since she had arrived, he had never let more than three days pass without sending for her. She began to fear that the pale one had told the King. The other women in the harem weren't treating her with the respect she'd been able to command before as the favorite, and it was all that witch's fault. Yes, that's what she was … a witch! No normal human could look like that, she thought vengefully. Well she had a plan, and no one would get in her way. She would use her beauty to make Montezuma name her as a wife, and she would be with him everywhere. Then everybody in the city would know who she was.

"What happened to your eye?" questioned the King.

"You mean you don't know?" she said with cunning. Seeing that she had already won, she threw herself at his feet crying, "Oh my lord, send away the foreign pale one," letting tears roll from her eyes.

"Why? What reason have you to want her gone?"

"My lord, she batters your women behind your back and no one dares to raise a hand against her because she is your guest; but see what she has done to me," she said while pointing to her eye.

"When did she do this?"

"The eve of the princesses' wedding," she whimpered.

"What did you do, that she would hit you?" he said, not believing Maria could do such a thing.

"Nothing my lord! She is jealous of us," she said, as she took his hand and began to caress it.

"Did she hit anyone else?"

"Well, no my lord; she hates me the most!"

"Why would she hate you? She's not one of my women, and your not even a wife."

She cringed at his words.

"Oh my lord, please send her away," she said with guile.

"She's in the temple; isn't that good enough?"

"I mean far away, perhaps 'Flowerland.' The gods like hideous creatures; she would make a good sacrifice."

Withdrawing his hand, Montezuma went cold. She realized she'd gone too far but in desperation she continued. "I mean lord, the gods like unusual people; you would earn their favor. Lord, she has no respect for you. Look how she despises your women!"

"I will not sacrifice her," he said, brushing the Cloud Maiden from his side. "And I've heard nothing but good reports of her conduct from both my wives and the temple. None but you have complained. And as far as being hideous, I find her anything but hideous."

"That's because she's bewitched you!" screeched the girl.

"I'm not bewitched," he said, restraining his anger. "And I don't have to explain my preferences to anyone, least of all you; especially since at this moment you're not part of those preferences. Now leave me," he said, annoyed and irritated, "and when you get back to the harem, send my wife Shasa to me. Go!" he barked at her.

The Cloud Maiden ran from the audience hall; real tears of anger and frustration clouded her eyes. Her tears turned to wrath as she plotted her revenge. I'll make myself so desirable he won't be able to resist me, she fumed. I'll make him see that I'm the most beautiful woman in the One World, her embittered heart cried. I swear to the gods on my life—she clenched her fists furiously—to destroy that hideous pale one who's ruined me. I swear!

❖

As Maria tried to meditate, her stomach was growling and complaining. She was in the middle of a fast to gain mental clarity, but so far the only clarity she'd gained was how uncomfortable her body was. Finally, focusing her willpower, she was able to drain the discomfort into the ground and return to the exercise she was attempting.

She was supposed to concentrate on being in another place with her mind, while still sitting in meditation. Chimalma had placed several objects in a particular room in the temple, and all of the girls practicing the exercise were instructed to describe them. Maria kept trying to picture the room while feeling as if she were already there. All of a sudden she felt a deepening, an expansion within her; it felt good, and she relaxed even deeper into it. She remembered she'd been told that one minute your trying to meditate, the next you're doing it; there are no in between stages. Shera had said that you just have to unlearn the belief that you can't, and that deep inside everyone already knows how to do everything.

The expansive feeling grew deeper and deeper until she felt a high-pitched hum inside her head ... then a loud pop and she found herself in the room. The expansive feeling was languid and sensuous, yet it allowed her to feel the walls, floor and furniture without even touching them. Then she saw the objects she knew had been placed there by Chimalma. Resting on a table was a small red vase with a green scroll next to it. A gold platter engraved with the Mother Goddess along with a pink-lipped conch shell lay underneath the table. Suddenly, she found herself hovering high above her body and looking down on it. Her body sat straight-backed on the meditation bench and her eyes were closed. Fear assaulted her. Was she dead? The fear seemed to suck her back into the dense body below, and she sluggishly opened her eyes.

Her heart pounded with surprise and confusion. She felt a bit drugged, as she told Shera and Chimalma what had happened. While she described herself hovering above her body, the two priestesses watched her intently.

"It's time," Chimalma said to Shera. "Let the others know to prepare for tonight's ceremony." Then she sat down with Maria and explained to her what had happened. "Maria, you've learned that the soul leaves the body after death; but sometimes, usually with training, it will leave the body for short periods. We call this astral projection, and that's what you've just experienced. You were only supposed to sense the room but since you were able to take it a step further, you're ready to participate in tonight's special ceremony in the inner sanctuary."

"But I thought I'm not allowed in the inner sanctuary," she said fearfully.

"You will be tonight. Now go rest; the ceremony will take strength."

Maria had been instructed to wait outside the room while the priestesses made all in readiness. At last she was led into the forbidden inner sanctuary. The temple walls were dressed in red jasper and green marble slabs, and several small braziers placed around the altar burned the rich copal resin. The altar itself was a large, black obsidian centerpiece to the room. On it stood a stunning statue of the Mother Goddess intricately carved from alabaster and detailed with gold. The Goddess' skirt was studded with pearls and carnelian, while two jade snakes intertwined around her waist.

The door was shut behind her, and Chimalma led a prayer to the Mother Goddess. Maria was instructed to remove her clothes and stand naked in front of the altar, as an offering to symbolize her willingness to bare her body and soul before the Goddess. She blushed with embarrassment, but relaxed when she saw that the other priestesses were disrobing. A priestess took every opportunity to express her commitment to the Goddess, she was told. Maria knelt before the altar in prayer and someone poured a rich scented oil over her; it ran down her back and chest.

A priestess started to beat a drum and another took up a small wooden flute. The praying of the priestesses turned to chanting; as the chanting grew faster and faster, so did the drumbeat and flute. Soon the women started to dance, circling the altar and beckoning Maria to join them. First it moved slowly; back and forth, left and right went the circle of The Goddess Dance. Then they danced faster and faster, on and on, past the point of fatigue.

Maria danced until her body seemed to dance of its own accord; coated with perspiration and oil she felt alive and free. Her ears rang with the steady beating of the drum as it droned out the heartbeat of the Aztec people. The naked, dancing figures glistened in the soft firelight as the mist of the copal smoke enveloped them. They danced on, nearly all night until Maria felt she was in another world. She began to feel invisible figures dancing with them, and her eyes began to see bodiless headdresses with tall feathers swaying to the drumbeat. She didn't know if her eyes were playing tricks on her. It didn't matter … she was in ecstasy. A feeling swept through her. She knew she had done this before…in a time when she had long, dark hair and the firelight had reflected off her naked, copper-toned breasts.

Barefooted, with sandals tied together and slung over their shoulders, Maria and Taka hurried across the great plaza. "Be careful," warned Taka, "too many people fall on this polished marble because they're rushing."

They'd been to the market; the High Priestess had needed extra herbs for the upcoming festival, and they both carried several small pouches of fragrant roots and flowers.

A group of wealthy pochtecas was descending one of the pyramids, followed by a black clad priest with bloodstained hands. Maria turned away with a shudder.

"Oh, those pochtecas must be going on a trip," Taka said, as she glanced their way.

"Why do you say that?" asked a bewildered Maria.

"See," she pointed, "they've been on top of the pyramid for their departure sacrifice."

"You mean they sacrifice something when they're going on a trip?" The thought of needing to sacrifice for something so simple appalled her.

"Of course," said Taka calmly. "It's also so the empire may prosper. They usually buy a slave for the purpose."

"You mean they sacrificed a person?" she asked, while holding back the nausea.

The idea of sacrificing an animal for such a purpose was preposterous enough, but a person was even worse. She'd known there were small sacrifices happening throughout the city; this was the first she'd come across. Even though she hadn't actually seen it, it repulsed her and she couldn't push it from her mind. How could the gods allow this, she thought? It wasn't right; it couldn't be.

This brought something else to mind. Why did there seem to be two priesthoods? Quetzalcoatl's priests—like the priestesses of the Mother Goddess—wore white, seemed to be celibate, and ate no flesh. However, most of the other temples wore black, seemed to do all the sacrificing, and according to what she'd been told, practiced anything but celibacy. It was also rumored that they ate some of their sacrifices.

As soon as they returned, she sought out the High Priestess. "One priesthood is of the ancient lineage following the laws that stretch back to time unknown," Chimalma began to explain. "These laws tell us to honor the Earth as a living thing; to honor all men and women as our brothers and sisters; to not eat animal flesh because they too are our lesser brothers; and to keep our bodies clean and wear white...white showing the purity of our hearts. All that the Mother Goddess dictates we prescribe to. There are many others, all of which you shall gradually learn; but these I've mentioned are the basic ones we must follow. These laws were given to us by the ancient ones of The Great Pyramid to the north. Besides us, the priests of Quetzalcoatl follow them; half of the priests of Huitzilopochtli follow them; and the temples of the Flower Goddess follow most of the old laws."

"What of the others, the ones who wear black?" Maria asked.

"Mmmmm," droned the High Priestess. "After these laws had been given, there came a time that some of the priesthood didn't want to live by these laws that the Pyramid gave. They wanted power ... not for the gods but for themselves. It started with just a few; then more and more thirsted for power until nearly all the temples fell to this darkness. Now there's only a few of us left that follow the old ways. They believe," she said sadly, "that their black vestments express piousness; to us it symbolizes the darkness that eclipses the light. Now nearly all is darkness. That is why the Aztec world may be entering its deathrows."

"Do you really believe such a thing could happen?" Maria asked, not sure what to think about all these reports of doom.

"I hope not, maybe we can learn before it's too late; but the omens have spoken and still the people do not change their ways ...

so we shall see! And now you have a baptismal tonight my friend, hadn't you better run along and get ready." She smiled and shooed the girl out the door.

The baptismal group wound its way through the alley that separated the two temples. Maria carried a torch and followed Chimalma to the small door. In silence, two priestesses waited for them inside the mud bricked entrance. They closed the door behind them, and led Chimalma and Maria into the depths of Tlazalteotl's temple. It was a small temple, only about half the size of the Mother's temple, and much of its purity still remained.

Filth Eater, what a strange name for a goddess, thought Maria. The High Priestess had explained that when someone was about to die, a priest or priestess from Tlazalteotl's temple would come to them. They would confess all the bad they'd done and the goddess would then eat all the filth in their lives, leaving them purified to pass from their bodies. Of course, you didn't have to be about to enter Flowerland to have Tlazalteotl eat your filth, she'd been told.

They were led to a pool of water in a natural rock cavern; the pool bubbled up from the only natural spring in Tenochtitlan. A rock wall was built up about the pool, and a torch flickered on the water's dark surface. A priest and priestess, both elderly, dressed in white, and wearing the black skull insignia, entered the water and motioned for Maria to join them. The water was icy dark; it caught her breath as she entered the pool, and her legs and hips rebelled at its numbing touch. The old couple stood on either side of her, as the sound of a conch bellowed from somewhere behind them.

The old priestess called on the goddess to listen to one who chose to do wrong no more ... one who was dedicating herself to the gods. The priest asked her if she came of her own free will, and if she was willing to give up her old habits and live by the law of the Mother Goddess now. As soon as she answered yes, the two of them pushed her head under the icy, waist deep water. It happened so quickly that she didn't have time to take a breath before she was pushed back down into the bitter cold. The next thing she knew she was being led from the pool; and her freezing, drenched body was following Chimalma through the courtyard and out the door. Not a single word had been spoken except those done in ritual.

"Come Maria", said the priestess, "give me a hand." Several bundles of maize stalks stood in the reception chamber.

"What are these for?" asked Maria.

"We'll put them in the inner sanctuary for the Goddess to bless," Shera said. "They're for the coming festival."

"The Corn Goddess Festival?"

"Yes," Shera said.

"But why are they here? Shouldn't they be in the Corn Goddess temple?" asked Maria.

"The Mother Goddess oversees the Corn Festival because the Corn Goddess is her daughter. So we do as much of the work for this festival as the Corn Goddess priestesses do, if not more," Shera explained. "As you know, Chimalma has instructed that you have a hand in all that transpires for the festival, since it will be your last real function before your initiation. It'll be a lot of work, but you'll have fun too," she added smiling.

As they were carrying armloads of the maize through the courtyard, she saw the High Priestess walking by the garden pool with a tall, handsome man wearing a spotless white mantle and loin cloth. As Chimalma smiled up at him, the man reached over and took her hand tenderly. Maria was so surprised, she nearly dropped the armload of stalks she was clutching. "Whose that?" she asked bewildered.

"Oh, that's just Mayatzin," Shera laughed. "He's Chimalma's brother and they're very close. He's also the High Priest of Quetzalcoatl's temple, and is well-loved by the people. Now we must hurry; there's much to do today."

"I have to sleep here?" Maria asked, as she looked around at the polished walls and hard floor of the inner sanctuary.

"Yes," said the High Priestess, handing Maria the thin mat that would serve as her only bedding.

"But why?" she said, not understanding.

"Tonight you will sleep with the Goddess. If there's anything she wants to reveal to you in preparation for your upcoming initiation, she will tonight." Chimalma turned to leave.

"How can I sleep on the hard floor?" Maria whined.

"You'll have to figure that one out for yourself," she said, as she swept from the room and latched the door behind her.

For a long time Maria sat on the floor in front of the altar, waiting and hoping the Goddess might speak. But every time she attempted meditation, something would disturb her; either the floor was too hard, her nose itched, or the maize stalks piled up around her kept shifting, causing a distracting rustling. It was always some little thing; it was worse than when she first learned to meditate. She just couldn't seem to concentrate. Finally, she gave up and laid down on the floor to sleep. But it was the same thing, nothing was comfortable; either her tailbone hurt as she lie on her back, or if she tried to turn over and curl up in the fetal position, her hip and shoulder felt bruised by the unyielding floor...and it was just too cold!

She sat up in frustration, burying her head in her arms. Suddenly, from somewhere in her mind she heard a calm voice saying, "Lie down and concentrate on the Goddess. Ignore your body; it's only giving you trouble because you're letting it. You're being tested. Overcome it." She lied back down, and with focus and determination she concentrated on the Goddess. Soon she felt a deep drowsiness coming over her.

She was standing in a dark tunnel and couldn't find her way out. Several passageways beckoned to her temptingly: one led to a room full of books of all kinds—bibles, Greek mythology, Aztec scrolls, Spanish sonnets and more; another was full of wooden ponies and handmade dolls she had played with as a child; one cave-like passage held the monster that she just knew had lived under the bed when she was a little girl. In horror she turned to retreat, but the passage behind her closed up. She saw a dim light at the opposite end of the cave, and she knew she'd have to cross the cave to get to it. She tried to run, but suddenly she found that her feet were so heavy they wouldn't budge.

A chill ran down her spine, and she began to sweat as she felt the monster closing in on her. Fear compressed her lungs until she could hardly breathe. Then she remembered a verse from the Bible...a verse that had always spoken to her. "If you call on Me, believing help will come, it surely will". So she called out loud for help...trusting...knowing...that the Divine Mother wouldn't let her down. After what seemed like an eternity, her feet began to move in slow-motion. She struggled her way across the cave, feeling the hideous monster creature breathing down her back. But as her trust and willpower grew it became easier to move, and at last she made it to the opposite side of the cave.

The dim light began to grow brighter and brighter; then it flowered into the twin figures of Mary and the Mother Goddess, who again melted into one. The Goddess ordered Maria to turn around and face her monster. The shapeless, grotesque monster transformed into a brilliant angel whose multicolored wings of light filled the whole room. He smiled lovingly at Maria...and then vanished. The soft voice of the Goddess caressed her, saying, "See, there was nothing to fear but fear itself. You stand ever safe in my hands. You didn't let your fear consume you; you've passed the test." Her smiling face hung in the air...her form gradually dissipating, as Maria awakened on the sanctuary floor. The door was opening and the early morning sun shone across her face.

11
Sacrifice

She stood on the top of Huitzilopochtli's Pyramid, leaning on her broom and shooing a loose strand of hair from her face. It was hot. Shimmering waves of heat rolled up from the ground and bathed the city in watery illusions. The women of the city bustled about everywhere, brooms in hand. All the temples and public buildings had to be thoroughly swept in preparation for the coming festival. Of course, only the priestesses were allowed to sweep the inner shrines; that was their job alone.

Looking up, Maria gauged it to be just past noon; the goddess was reigning. The Aztecs believed the gods reigned from sunrise to noon, and then at noon the goddesses took over until sunset. In the temples, all heavy work was done in the early hours and the afternoons were spent in reflection or artistic endeavors. It had been explained, the gods represented outer action, the goddesses inner action.

Maria turned to survey her progress. The gold veins in the alabaster walls seemed to reflect the golden sheath worn by the statue of the Sun God. The floor was clean. She couldn't find a single spot her broom had missed. She still had two more sanctuaries to do today and she'd better hurry, she thought. Exiting the upper temple, she lowered her head at the curious scrutiny she received by two old women who had come to sweep down the pyramid steps. She was amazed; certainly they didn't intend to sweep, all by themselves, three hundred and sixty-five steps on each of the four sides.

At the bottom of the pyramid, Maria found Taxca playing with a small baby whose mother was sweeping a nearby shrine. Taxca gathered up the child, explaining that his mother was her older sister and she missed not being able to see her family while she was still in temple school. The small boy laughed as he tried to grasp Taxca's eyelashes, then reached an inquiring hand for Maria's bright red braids.

The girls joined a group of young women resting from their sweeping duties. Several of them sat in a circle, suckling infants, gossiping and speculating on who would play the Corn Goddess. Many seemed to know Taxca and welcomed her. Most of them stared at Maria, but after they'd satisfied their curiosity, they chattered on.

"I believe it will be the girl from the province," a stocky woman declared as she fed pieces of banana to a sleepy child in her fleshy lap.

"Well it shouldn't be," another said haughtily, "after all, we don't even know if she's pure Aztec. You know how those provincials are; they'll breed with anything." They all laughed. "The girl should be from the city," she went on, "so we know what her lineage is."

"Lineage! What does that matter?" said the heavy set woman. "She looks Aztec and the girl is one of the most graceful dancers I've ever seen." Several voices rose in agreement.

"The position of the Corn Goddess is too important to give to just anyone," said the second woman, determined not to surrender. "After all, just think how many girls married into 'tzin' status after holding the role."

"Well, the temples will make the right decision, whatever it is," added a small woman nursing a child, her belly starting to swell with another.

"Well, just so she's not like the one two years ago," said a fourteen year old, munching on a mango and trying to sound grown up.

"The gods save us," declared an old woman, casting her eyes heavenward.

"What happened two years ago?" asked Maria.

The old woman glanced around, making sure no unwanted ears were listening. "A young woman petitioned for the honor of Corn Goddess, with her family assuring the temples that she was of upstanding virtue and worthy of the position. Well, the despicable young thing carried her charade all the way through to the final decision and was chosen to play the role as Corn Goddess. Then when the High Priestess examined her, she was exposed as unfit for the title. Her virginity had already been taken."

"What happened?" asked Maria.

"Well I'll tell you, the city was shocked that someone would ridicule the sacred trust!" she hissed.

"Didn't she know she would be examined?" said Maria.

"Everyone knows the girls are checked for purity," she said.

"Well that doesn't make sense," said Maria, "maybe she was raped at the last minute."

"Oh phooey," said the woman, dismissing Maria's comment with a wave of her arm. "The girl was evil or stupid, which one I don't know. Her family was shamed! I know someone who was a friend of her mother's; they hadn't known about their daughter. They were good people, yet public shame rained upon their heads. Of course the second choice girl was made ready, but the festival held a gloom and the crops that year failed."

"But what happened to the first girl?" persisted Maria.

"She disappeared into the wilderness with her lover," giggled one of the girls.

"No one really knows," said Taxca, "all kinds of rumors sprang up about her disappearance."

"I heard the temples told her parents she could be sacrificed," said the young mother, "but her father wouldn't allow it and so the girl was sold into slavery instead."

"I even heard, her mother beat her to death out of shame," said Taxca.

"Taxca!" "Don't talk of such things," scolded her older sister, who entered the circle of gossiping women and took the now sleeping baby from her lap. "You shouldn't be idly gossiping while there's still so much to do before the festival! I've just seen the Priestess Shera. You're to return to the temple; they need your help with the flower garlands. Both of you!"

"Look Maria!" They were making their way back to the temple when Taxca stopped suddenly. "It's them," she said, pointing out three exquisitely beautiful, young girls being escorted by two corn priestesses through a crowd.

"Who's them?" laughed Maria.

"Those are the candidates for the Corn Goddess," she said.

Each girl walked with her head bowed in humility, a wreath of cornflowers crowning her glossy black hair. The crowd stood back in reverence as the trio passed. A child ran forward to touch one of the girls' hands, then ran back to her mother's side.

"The tall one is the one from the countryside the women were all talking about earlier. Some don't want her to be chosen because she isn't from the city. But I want her to win," said Taxca.

Maria admired the girl. She was at least two inches taller than the other two girls, but it was her beauty and grace that set her apart. Maria secretly chose her as well.

Chimalma walked so fast that Maria had to run to keep up with her. "Where are we going?" she asked, breathing hard.

"The Corn Goddess Temple," said the High Priestess. Tonight a girl will be chosen to represent the Goddess; the heads of all the Goddess Temples must be there."

"But why are you bringing me?" she asked.

"Remember, I've told you you're to be a part of every activity, especially the sacred ones. If you want to be a priestess, you will need every opportunity to know what it's like to be Aztec."

The temple gates were wide open, corn stalk bundles standing like sentries at every wall. A row of braziers led the visitors into the temple's interior. At their appearance, the frail High Priestess of the Corn Goddess approached Chimalma with a corn stalk in hand.

"Divine Mother," she said to Chimalma, "bless your daughter."

"I gave you birth to nurture the sacred maize," said Chimalma, placing her hand on the old woman's head. "I now bless you again, that you may pass this blessing on through your maize. Daughter, I am well pleased with you."

Maria felt a chill, recalling that those very words were spoken to Jesus at his baptism and later recorded in the bible.

Chimalma's simple ritual signified the start of the festival. That night, the blessed young girl who was to play the Corn Goddess would be chosen.

Chimalma and Maria were escorted to the inner chambers and led to their seats alongside representatives of the other temples. The three girls were led into the room and presented to the gathering. A few words were spoken concerning each girl: their name, family, where they came from, how old they were and such. Maria was again taken aback by the tall one they called Chieyere. Soon they were led into a small antechamber to wait, and as they left another girl appeared. She was about Maria's age, slender with huge, dark eyes. The fire in the inner sanctuary cast a sparkle to the red highlights in her black hair and she wore a copper slave bracelet on her wrist. She too was presented to the temple heads, each nodding their heads in consent; then she was led away.

"Who was that?" asked Maria.

"The Flower One," Chimalma said. But before she had any time to elaborate the girls reemerged, flush with expectation. The High Priestess of the Corn Goddess Temple announced to the assembly that each one was acceptable and they were again ushered outside to a cell to await the decision. Chimalma asked Maria to wait out as well.

As Maria wandered about, she found herself in a courtyard much like the one at her temple, only smaller. She sat down by a moonlit pool with white lilies floating on its surface. The breeze brushed the tendrils of a willow tree across her shoulders with a soft caress. She sat in quiet reverie and waited.

Just then a door at the courtyard's edge opened and the slave girl that Chimalma called the Flower One followed a priestess from the room of merrymaking out into the courtyard. Through the door Maria could see heavily laden tables of feasting and a rich smell of roasted meat drifted from the door. Her empty stomach rumbled in response; she'd been fasting in preparation for the festival. She watched the priestess lead the pretty slave girl to another room across the courtyard, then returned her glance back to where they'd withdrawn from.

By the looks of the half-filled plates of rich food, it didn't look like a temple meal, but more like what she'd seen at the palace. The priestess closed the door to the girl's room, retraced her steps to the room of feasting, closed that door and left the courtyard. Maria was grateful, now that she didn't have to smell the forbidden delicacies.

As she settled back down, making a game of counting the stars she could see over the temple's roof, two more figures appeared in the courtyard. It was the same priestess again; this time she led a young man in priest garb, wearing not black or white, but red. He appeared handsome in the shadows and wore his hair to his shoulders. The priestess brought him to the same room off the courtyard that she had led the slave girl to and then departed, closing the door behind them. Maria instinctively knew the two would make love. Was this part of the ritual, she wondered? Before too long, someone came from the inner sanctuary and fetched the three candidates; Maria stood and followed the group back in.

❖

"Hurry Maria," called Taka and Taxca, "the dancing will start soon!" Still tying a golden ribbon at the end of her braid, she ran to catch up with her friends, quickly hugging Itza as she rushed passed her.

The plaza was full of the merrymakers, all dressed in their best clothing. Nearly everyone carried a stalk of maize, a feather, a flower, or something to honor the bounty of the earth. The girls worked their way through the dense crowd led by slender Taka, determined to find a choice spot near the Pyramid of the House of Song where the dancing would start. The excitement of the crowd was infectious. Only once did Maria shy away, when she realized a group of peasants were pointing and staring at her. As of late she'd almost forgotten how alien she looked, but Taxca's contagious laughter soon coaxed her out of it.

Then it began. The air rang with the calling of conches and drumming, announcing the start of festivities. Another fanfare of music, and the doors of the House of Song burst open as the performers began making their way down the steps of the small pyramid. Musicians dressed in maize decorated costumes headed the procession, bright feathers hanging from their neckbands. They were followed by a group of dwarfs that danced, tumbled and jostled the crowd good naturedly, stopping every so often to insult or tease some unfortunate person standing too near. Two of them stopped right in front of Maria. One began yelling "fire!," while the other went through the exaggerated motions of putting Maria's hair out. Taka ran them off with her maize stalk and the crowd roared with laughter.

The tempo of the music picked up as the warriors appeared. Their feathered headdresses were so large and elaborate that some of them needed an extra wide berth. Their loin cloths were done with feathers worked in intricate details and designs, and they wore gold bracelets and necklaces. Many of them even had gold noseplugs. By their side danced the auianime. They wore yellow painted faces with bright-red lips and cheeks, and they too displayed the high plumed feathered headdresses. Their eyes were circled with black paint and their blouses were so short, they exposed the whole of their midriffs.

The long line of warriors and their women wove in and out. Faster and faster they danced as they made their way through the central square. The warriors ran, leaped and pivoted, waging mock battle; the sweat on their skin glistened in the sun. The women shook rattles and shimmied their hips in time with the music. Gradually the tempo slowed as warriors and auianime came back together in sinuous movement, hands on shoulders and hips in a snake like motion. The warriors pulled the women's hips close to them while the auianime rubbed up against their groins and then pulled away again.

"I thought the Aztec people were usually discreet by nature," blushed Maria.

"Oh we are," laughed Taka over the din. "This is to show that the maize will grow fruitful!"

Soon the whole crowd was dancing and singing to the endless beating of drums and music, not the erotic dance done earlier, but a joyous and free-spirited one. Maria joined in happily, waving her corn stalk in the air with glee. The dancing seemed to erase the usual class conventions, as rich and poor alike mingled. Peasant women with children strapped to their backs danced with tzins, and slaves and chair-bearers could be seen everywhere, dancing with their masters. Young men and women, usually separated by Aztec customs, edged close to one another with longing.

Suddenly, in front of her she spotted a familiar face with a gold diadem and large, iridescent, blue-green plumes. Her heart leaped to her throat as their eyes met. He stopped dancing and came and stood right in front of her. Placing his hands on her shoulders, Montezuma began dancing again, gradually increasing the pace and drawing her in. Soon she was mesmerized by pounding drums, constant flowing movement and his presence. She no longer felt afraid of his touch; it was electrifying, warm and exciting. As if in a trance they danced on, stealing touches at each other's face, breasts and hips. Within the movement time stood still, and they were no longer King and visiting subject; they were simply man and woman.

They would stop only long enough to feed each other anise flavored maize cakes, followed by cooling water, and then were drawn back into the overwhelming excitement of the Dance of the Corn Goddess. The day passed on, the sun prepared for its nightly departure and still they danced, lost in a world of exhaustive bliss and transcending rhythms.

The Cloud Maiden watched Montezuma and Maria dance, her face growing dark with anger. All her efforts, and now the King was dancing with that Spanish freak the first chance he got. She had schemed and seduced, playing for endless hours with the King's favorite children. Making herself more alluring and beautiful, she practiced in front of the mirror with her deceptive charms. Finally, she had won back his favor, having stooped to begging the King's forgiveness and praising the Spanish witch. She was called to his bedside regularly and was again feared in the harem; she'd even persuaded him to keep her at his side during public ceremonies. She had used every possible persuasion to fill him with lust for her and would stop at nothing to get him to make her a wife.

The Cloud Maiden's heart raced as she watched them dance, and jealous hatred scorched her thoughts. She had heard of a witch living somewhere in the city. She could steal from the harem at night, go to this witch and have her cast a spell on the hideous Spanish one. She would make sure she died slowly and painfully; then no one would suspect her. She laughed maliciously, then turned abruptly into the stern face of the High Priestess of the

Mother Goddess. Having heard the stories of this tall one's abilities to read someone's mind, she froze with fear. How long had she been standing behind her and watching, she wondered. She forced a sweet smile and passed around the priestess, feeling the powerful gaze of the woman scrutinizing her as she went.

The sun finally slipped over the horizon and the city began to light up everywhere. Bonfires sprung up at street corners and braziers surrounded every home. The crowd showed no sign of dispersing while drums and flutes still played on in the night's air. All over the city, voices rose in song.

The dancing stopped just long enough for everyone to share the night's meal of sage turkey, tamales and sweetened corncakes. Montezuma fed a piece of the sweetened cake to Maria as they sat on the bottommost step of the Great Pyramid. They were in their own world, oblivious to the merrymakers surrounding them, and oblivious even to those who stopped to look curiously at their King and this strange foreign one. As the cool, early autumn night air replaced the warmth of the day, Maria involuntarily shivered. Montezuma removed his green feathered cape and placed it on her shoulders. She was in a daze; the long day of dancing had drained all resistance from her body, and she longed for him to wrap her in his protective arms. Maria quivered as her young muscles still did their dance. Although she'd stopped, the drumming continued to resonate throughout her body. As the night grew late, Maria noticed couples slipping off into the shadows and somehow it seemed the most natural thing to do. On this night, nearly the whole city would celebrate until dawn.

Montezuma had a litter drawn with curtains and stationed on its own pavilion so that he might rest as needed, from time to time throughout the night. He led Maria to this litter, aching to quench the fire he felt for her, but dim reasoning in the back of his mind told him no. He had many wives and, although he wanted her, she was not his. She looked so young and vulnerable and he knew her defenses were down. He realized she was hypnotized by the dance and he did not want to shame her, but she would at least be safer in the litter than on the streets.

As he held open the curtain so she could climb in the litter, she heard a warning bell in the back of her mind, but she pushed it aside, wanting nothing to spoil her whimsical state. The King handed her a goblet of cooling juice, iced with snow from the heights of the sleeping volcano peak. She knew the icy drink was a delicacy, and its coldness raced through her delighted body. Then her eyes met his and she began to melt. She was hardly aware of his taking the golden cup from her hands. He drew her near and an electrifying, wet warmth surged through her body. She moved to pull him closer and opened her lips to his mouth. At first he pulled back in surprise at the unfamiliar kiss, but then pulled her closer to savor the fire she transferred from her mouth.

"Maria! My King! It is I, Chimalma!" Just outside the pavilion, the priestess' strong voice brought them back from the edge of their passion-claiming abyss. "It's time for Maria to return to the temple."

Brought to her senses, Maria bolted from the curtains to follow the other girls back to the temple.

"I thought everyone stayed out all night this night," Maria said sullenly.

"Not the girls and priestesses of the Mother Goddess," said Chimalma, "We have to return to the temple by midnight so that we aren't tempted to do something we shouldn't."

"It looks like we came for you none too soon Maria," giggled one of the girls.

"But it was the King! I don't blame her," said little Taxca. "What was it like, Maria?" she asked, her eyes all aglow. "Shush now, girls," the priestess said, turning and picking the rest of her charges out of the crowd.

"Maria, you didn't did you?" asked Taka quietly, as she sidled up next to her. "If you're going to be initiated, you know you can't," she said with worry on her face.

"No Taka." She was touched with her friend's concern. "I don't think I did anyway; we just kissed...I think," she added, trying to remember if anything else happened.

"Kissed! What's kissed?" Taka looked puzzled.

"You know, when you kiss each other's mouths."

The blank look on Taka's face told Maria that the Aztec people didn't kiss. No wonder Montezuma acted strangely. What must he think of her now, she thought? Embarrassment kept her quiet the rest of the way back to the temple.

"Each of you girls is to return to your beds now. You may meditate or sleep, but you may not talk until the gong sounds," Chimalma instructed.

Itza was already asleep when Maria entered her room. She slipped from her dress and snuggled into bed, her thoughts filled with the day's events. She wondered at the changes in herself. No longer was she afraid of the feelings she had for Montezuma. She pondered what would have happened, had the High Priestess not come for her. She could still feel the warmth of his arms around her. Meditating appeared impossible. As she turned over, even sleep came wistfully. At last, fatigue settled in.

She awoke to the booming of the temple gong as it reached into the haze of her dreams. She began to stir, and was met with stiffness and pain. Her overextended muscles had tightened during the night and she could hardly move. She allowed Itza to herd her into one of the small steam baths for a massage and scrubbing down. The hot steam seemed to coax her body back into a state where she could at least use it again. As Maria stepped from the steam room, Itza poured basins of cold water over her body while she stood gulping in the brisk, early morning air.

The eastern sky hadn't yet dawned and a canopy of stars was overhead. A group of temple girls passed them, urging Maria to hurry, as they would be leaving soon. When she joined the others in the courtyard, she was dressed in a white dress heavily embroidered at the neck and hem with symbols of the Earth Mother's fruitfulness. Chimalma tied an ear of dried corn to the ends of Maria's yellow sash, marking her as one of the attendants for the day's ceremonies.

The sun was just coming up when the now familiar, slender form of the one portraying the Corn Goddess appeared. Her tall figure was clothed in a strapless dress of shiny golden disks. Several turquoise necklaces were wrapped about her neck. Her gold crown sported tall, green blue plumes piped in golden flakes and she wore red sandals to honor the earth. She carried a small, round shield of feathers woven in bright geometric designs, with golden yellow beads and feathers cascading from the bottom. In her other hand she held a rattle shaped like an ear of corn.

"I'm so glad they chose the provincial," Taxca said, handing Maria her own corn rattle.

"Me too," said Maria, "but what's she doing here?"

"The Corn Goddess Priestesses are allowed to remain in celebration all night, so traditionally the goddess representative spends the night in the Mother Goddess Temple in safety." Taxca explained knowingly.

The gates were then opened and the procession quickly made its way to the Corn Temple, where it was joined by the blurry eyed priestesses who had spent the night awake. Winding their way through the city streets, they beat drums, blew conches and shook rattles, alerting the crowd of the coming Goddess. Maria was fortunate enough to be walking behind her as she danced through the city. The Goddess moved like a lithe snake, then jumped like a joyful deer. Her long, dark hair swirled around her as she took on the imbibing spirit of the Corn Dance. It was true, thought Maria; all who saw her could not help but admire her graceful dancing and beauty. She was the Goddess manifest.

The procession worked its way back to the plaza, where a platform awaited. The Goddess took her place on a gilded throne of mock corn stocks, and her attendants sat around her. A fanfare of music announced the opening events as the doors of the House of Song swung wide open. Across from where she sat, Maria could see the royal platform where Montezuma and his dignitaries were sitting. Her muscles tightened when she noticed the Cloud Maiden sitting on a bright red cushion at the King's feet. She was annoyed, as she watched the girl flatter herself. How could Montezuma have her by his side, she thought? The girl was so vengeful and wicked, couldn't he see that? She couldn't watch anymore and painfully turned away.

The performers were enacting the story of the gods coming to Earth, and the gift of maize from the Corn Goddess. The play ended with The Dance of a Hundred Virgins, each one wreathed in yellow and orange flowers. The virgins paid obeisance to the Goddess, and thus the final passion play was over.

Soon they were standing, and Maria again found herself behind the Goddess. As they passed through the crowd, everyone bowed in reverence before them. Suddenly, she was face to face with the King. Their eyes locked for a moment as she passed the royal receiving area, and then he was gone from her view. Maria steadied herself as she followed the Goddess up the steep pyramid steps with the rest of the attendants.

At the apex, the girl stood before the sacred brazier that was shaped like the sun. She threw a handful of copal and corn flowers on the flames, offering herself as nourishment for the people; turning toward the sanctuary, she was gone. Then another girl, dressed exactly the same, was shoved out in her place. The girl wobbled on her feet and Maria was instructed to help hold her up. Maria recognized her as the slave girl who had also been chosen a few nights ago, the one the priest had been led to at the Corn Temple. She also saw from the girl's eyes that she was heavily drugged.

A corn priestess took the girl's other arm and guided them into the pyramid's upper-apex sanctuary. They had just stepped through the door, when abruptly Maria was pushed aside as an axe whizzed passed her. The head of the slave girl rolled to the ground, splattering blood across Maria's dress as it went.

Chimalma watched Maria's face go ashen and went to hold her up. She led her out of the sanctuary saying, "You have been honored by the Goddess, look at your dress." Chimalma relaxed when she saw that Maria wasn't going to scream or faint. She'd worried about how Maria would take the sacrifice and knew that if she was to take initiation, she would first have to witness one close up. She had actually arranged for Maria to be by the girl's side.

Maria looked down at her dress, barely registering the bright crimson splashed across it. She was in a deep state of shock. Her mind and emotions were in utter turmoil. She'd known there was to be a sacrifice but had pushed it out of her mind; it had become an unreal thing. Now she was horrified and ashamed at the part she had played in another person's death. She felt betrayed, especially by the High Priestess.

The rest of the day passed, with Maria in a fog. She did as she was told, but ignored the sweetened cakes people tried to give her in honor of the Goddess; ignored also were the people who came up to touch the blood on her dress.

As evening fell, she sat slumped by the temple pool in her bloodstained dress—alone and betrayed, or so she felt. This was how Chimalma found her. As the High Priestess neared her, she sensed the girl's anger and confusion, and placed her hand gently on Maria's shoulder. When she went stiff at her touch, Chimalma ordered Maria to stand up and follow her. Hoping the girl would soften in a more authoritative setting, she led her to the office and directed her to sit on the stretched hide stool. Chimalma then sat in the high, carved chair of the Mother Goddess and commanded her to speak.

"Why did you lie to me?" she blurted out. "You said the gods were kind and only wanted the best for man. Was it kind to kill a young girl? We don't do things like that in Spain!"

"Yes you do," Chimalma said calmly.

"We don't sacrifice people!" she cried.

"You've told me about many things in Spain, remember?" she said.

"But we don't kill people like that," she said, stubbornly scowling.

"What about your inquisition; you told me they kill many people...isn't that so?" The priestess held her ground lovingly.

"Well, only the heretics," she said.

"Who's to say what a heretic is; why does someone have to be bad just because they think or believe in a different way? Have you learned nothing in the time you've been here?" Maria tensed from the priestess's sharp tone. "The Gods don't ask for sacrifice, man does. So the gods simply let man do so, until he outgrows it."

"Well then, our priests must have already outgrown it because they don't do it," said Maria, refusing to let go.

"Is it better to offer sacrifice in the light of day, thinking you are helping? Or is it better to torture and kill just because someone is different?" Chimalma scolded softly, as shame began to spread through Maria. "Besides, you know there's no such thing as death."

"But why did you call me 'honored' today?" Maria asked, looking at her dress with distaste.

"The girl gave her life to the Goddess; she was a slave and didn't have much to offer. She gave all she had and her blood was her life's essence. She gave it to you. I wanted you to be aware of the magnitude of a soul giving up their life willingly. You may not understand now, but this very experience may help you through your initiation. Today was a test, and you did better than you know; you must trust me in that. Now go, and sleep with the Goddess.

12
The Initiation

Montezuma was on his way to audience. It was two days after the festival, but the sights and sounds of that special day still walked with him: endless hypnotic dancing to the erotic rhythms of the music; the dying rays of the sun crowning Maria's brilliant hair; feeding each other maize cakes. And when she'd put her lips on his, she transferred fire to his veins that he could still feel.

After the High Priestess claimed Maria, he lay in silent euphoria until the Cloud Maiden had entered his curtained litter and made love to him. Usually he didn't like a woman to lead, but he'd been so focused on Maria that he'd thought it was her. When he fully realized who it was, he quickly took control. He was curious if it had been the pressing of lips that had sent the electrical spark through him; he tried it with the Cloud Maiden. It had been pleasant, but not the same.

Upon entering the audience hall and seating himself on the throne, his thoughts turned reluctantly toward his sovereign responsibilities, as the chamberlain led in the first petitioner.

"Sire," said a slight man in a simple, provincial loincloth and mantel, as he bowed. "The Chimechas to the north keep raiding our outlying towns; they think their distance from the capital will protect them."

"I've always ignored them in the past," Montezuma said. "They're a starving people and they only raid fields. It's not their fault that the gods fashioned them too stupid to farm for themselves."

"This is true my Lord," the man said, "but now they grow bolder. Last month they attacked a merchant and stole all he had.

217

Another man ran out to protect his fields and they murdered him; now his wife and four small children have no one to care for them."

At this Montezuma grew angry. "The Aztec Empire shows them sympathy and this is how they show their thanks…behaving like dogs. Do you know which villages of these Chimecha dogs are doing the raiding?"

"Yes Lord, we do."

"Take two squadrons of Eagle Knights back with you and crush their villages as an example. Their leaders are to be sent back to the capital as the lowest form of sacrifice. Three of the men that live are to be given to the farmer's widow to support the farm and her children. The rest are to be given to the merchant as slaves that he may sell at will."

The thin face of the man couldn't hide his pleasure, as he left to do the King's bidding. Montezuma would have welcomed the opportunity to get off of his throne and lead a group of warriors on a mission. Fondly he thought of his days as Regent when his loving uncle had been the Chamberlain. Then he had been free to do as he pleased, trusting the older man to hold audience, but now he was burdened with full sovereign responsibility.

"Sire, a civil dispute." The Chamberlain stood in the middle of the room, his staff of office held upright.

"A civil dispute? That goes before the tribal tribunals, not me," said Montezuma.

"One of the parties is a Tzin and demands the right of the King's ear," said the Chamberlain.

"Oh, very well," said Montezuma, now irritated.

Two women entered the audience hall and approached the King. One was middle-aged, and so fat you could hardly see her eyes concealed in the flesh of her face. She was dressed in a richly embroidered poncho and skirt, and was dripping in jade and gold. She waddled vainly forward, content that amongst her peers things would go her way. When she got down to prostrate herself, so big was her bulk that it took two warriors to get her back upright, and soon the couriers present were tittering with glee.

To keep a straight face, Montezuma turned to the other woman present. She was a young girl, small in frame and wearing the plain skirt and blouse of the simple folk. When the girl stood from her prostration, he noticed a red welt under her gazelle-like eyes. She looked young and scared, but her jaw was set with determination.

"Our Lord King and First Reverent Speaker," the Tzin woman began dramatically, "I am the wife of the dear, departed Lord Pazatzin, and also the daughter of Lord Metzin. We are an honest family and of good rapport. We paid the parents of this shameless creature," she said, pointing to the girl, "for her board as a house servant. As is fitting with a house servant, our son took a little time of dalliance with her. She became pregnant, the parents bought back her contract, and then they were suddenly killed in the floods two years ago. She produced a boy child," she said, while glancing at the young girl obnoxiously. "But my son, a great Jaguar Warrior, was killed in battle. He didn't marry a good Tzin girl such as I suggested, and left no issue. I claim this girl's child as my rightful grandson and will raise him Tzin, not some stupid peasant. But this creature refuses to give him to me!"

"And you?" the King asked, turning towards the girl.

"It's true my Lord. My parents sold me into bondage even though we have been good farmers. This lady's son and I found much to like in each other."

"You lie!" shrieked the Tzin.

"Silence!" bellowed Montezuma.

"We wanted to be together, but his mother refused to allow him to marry me. Please believe me Lord; I am a good girl," she pleaded, with tears welling up.

"Continue."

"I had two older brothers; one became a warrior and gave his life for the One World, and the other died from the bite of the snake with a gourd at the end of its tail. My parents bought back my contract, so they would at least have one child. At my son's birth they rejoiced, knowing there would be a male issue to pass the farm to. But my son is all I have now," she cried. "Please don't let him be taken from me. I promise you I can support him. My cousin lives with us now; with his help our farm not only feeds us, but there's enough left over to sell at market. Please Sire, I loved my son's father, and our son is all I have left of him."

"You slut!" the Tzin roared, as she lunged at the girl. The Chamberlain stepped between them, forcing the woman back with his staff.

"Lord, may I speak?" a handsome Jaguar Knight asked, as he stepped forward from the back of the room.

"What do you have to do with this?" asked Montezuma.

"I am Teratzin, the best friend of the child's father. We grew together as children and then became warriors. He truly cared for this girl. Many times he talked of the pain in his heart, from not being able to marry the one he loved; that was why he refused to marry any other. His mother was a domineering sort, and threatened to disown him if he married the girl. He was waiting to reach his year of inheritance transfer, to go ahead and marry her anyway. His heart was heavy that his son was born out of 'covenant of the mat'."

"Is this true?" An angry Montezuma turned on the woman whose face had gone ashen. "Since you recognize the boy as your grandson, I decree that half of all your holdings be turned over to this girl for the boy, and that Tzin be added to the boy's name with all the rights and privileges it includes. The boy is to remain with his mother, and she is to be respected as the widow of a Jaguar Knight. And you," he said, glaring at the fat woman, "because you dare to call yourself a mother, yet resort to such profanity, you disgrace the Tzin class and the Aztec people. From this day forward you are not welcome at court. Now remove your disgusting person from my sight."

As the women were ushered from the hall the Chamberlain spoke out. "Sire, Chimalma, High Priestess of the Mother Goddess is present and wishes audience."

"Of course, send her in." Montezuma relaxed gratefully.

Graceful and stately, Chimalma came forward and bowed. All present in the hall went still with respect.

"My Lord, this matter is both secular and civil," she began straight away. "The Spanish girl, Maria de Velaquez, has requested to take initiation at the Old Pyramid to the north, but since she is a hostage of the state your permission is required."

"How can she take initiation? She isn't Aztec and she hasn't trained in the temple," he said with haste.

"She's been training for some time; the Goddess requested it. And may I remind you Sire, the pyramid was not built by Aztecs so it's not exclusively ours."

Montezuma leaned back in his throne to think as emotions began to stir. He didn't want Maria dedicated to the temples in absolute—his body shivered as he relived the warmth of her lips— nor did he want to go against the Goddess' wish.

"Since the Goddess wishes it, I cannot stand in the way. But since she is still a hostage and may have future use as such, I forbid her to take the final vows until I deem fit."

At least I've bought more time, he thought to himself. The High Priestess smiled knowingly, bowed before him, and took her leave.

As Montezuma called end of audience a message arrived from Texcoco. "Sire," the messenger spoke with remorse, and head lowered respectfully, "the Second Reverent Speaker, Lord of Texcoco, has died."

"How?" Montezuma froze in shock, not ready to accept it.

"He was walking in his gardens this morning and suddenly fell dead. The conclave has already gathered to name the next Lord and Reverent Speaker."

Montezuma fell back onto his throne, as the painful truth stabbed at his heart and his breath fell short. He had been a loving mentor, at times even more like a father than his real father had been. He must go and find his first wife, and tell her that her father had entered Flowerland. Raids, Maria taking initiation, and now the death of his father-in-law…not a morning he wanted to repeat.

The shrine they now stood in front of was six feet high. It was a simple rock structure, with an alcove holding a sun disk and an offering platform. Maize, fruits of the earth, prayer petitions, and small fetishes covered the altar. The offerings came from the simple farming folk of the area. The group of small children who'd followed curiously, had grown quiet when they reached the small shrine…the third such shrine they'd stopped at today. Chimalma and her brother Mayatzin placed some copal on the altar and asked the gods for protection. Then the small group that was accompanying Maria, the six priests and priestesses of the Quetzalcoatl temple along with Mayatzin and Chimalma, blessed the delighted children. Living this distance from the Mother City they rarely saw high priests or priestesses, only when one passed through on their way to the Great Toltec Pyramid.

Maria stood alone. A sheer, white veil separated her from the world; she was to talk to no one, and no one talked to her. Walking a few paces behind the others, she was supposed to remain in inner communion with the Goddess; however, she couldn't seem to get a hold of her thoughts. She kept seeing Itza's tearstained face begging her not to go. "Many die at big pyramid during initiation. Maria too young to die," she had said, as she wrung her hands. "How old Itza live, with daughter gone?" she kept saying. Itza's haunting face and mumblings about death kept filling her mind. Was she making a mistake, she wondered? Perhaps she wasn't trained enough yet. Suppose something did go wrong? It's not that she was afraid to die; she was more afraid to fail, she kept telling herself. Calling on the Goddess to bring her clarity, calm, and peace of mind was all she could do.

As the group made its way north, it passed many small villages hugging the shore of Lake Texcoco. The children would run out to join the pilgrimage for a while, receive their blessing, then run back, only to be replaced by another group from the next village. They stopped at a place along the lake where the water was fresh and a portion of the water had been partitioned off; a rich green substance grew luxuriously through it. One of the priests strained some of the water through a mesh-like bag which left some of the green vegetation in the bottom of the bag. Several dippings and strainings later they left the banks of the lake, with the priest wringing the bags carefully so as not to lose any of the green substance. They skirted by the city of Texcoco and headed away from the lake, moving ever northward.

That night Maria was fed some of the green substance. She was told it was an algae cultivated in the fresh part of the lake; it cleansed the body from the inside out, and lent a special power of clarity to the mind.

The evening of the second day they arrived at Teotihuacan. The ancient city rose from the dusty plain, a mute testimony to an earlier

Golden Age. Many pyramids lined broad avenues. At the end of the avenue the Aztecs called the Street of the Dead, rose a huge pyramid four tiers high. The Pyramid of the Sun looked like a small mountain to Maria; it was hard to believe that human beings had built it. The base covered a far broader area than did the Great Pyramid in Tenochtitlan.

After a long, arduous climb to the top of the huge pyramid, they reached the apex where a temple stood. The temple had been constructed at a later date by the Aztecs and was quite simple. Stone pillars held a roof protecting an altar and a stone chair. The priests cleaned the altar, placed a brazier upon it and gave Maria several pieces of charcoal to keep it going. A chunk of resin was placed on the fire, and the priests and priestesses placed their hands on Maria's head to bless her, telling her they would return in the morning. They then gave her a thin blanket, and turned to descend the pyramid as the rays of the sun withdrew from the western sky. Utterly alone now, Maria shivered as she prepared to face the first part of the initiation—the vigil they called the dark night of fears.

It had grown completely dark now. Maria placed another chunk of copal on the fire and walked to the edge of the pyramid's apex. Her escort party had withdrawn to a small, flat topped pyramid below. Two cooking fires illuminated the cluster of tents, and she could just make out the tiny figures moving about cleaning up the evening's meal and preparing for the night. Although she could hardly see them, she took great comfort in their presence. She knew…they in turn had all been in the same place she was that night.

The moon was cresting the distant mountains as she allowed her line of vision to run up the broad avenue they called the Street of the Dead. At its end loomed another huge pyramid, the sister pyramid to the one she now stood on, called the pyramid of the moon. Its name sake bathed a silvery glow across the building, deepening the shadows that played around the pyramid and it's apex. For a moment she thought she saw movement on the apex, a fleeting shadow running to join the other shadows. For a moment she thought maybe one of the priest's was visiting the other pyramid, but no priest's shadow could be that large, she thought. Besides, it moved too fast, it had to have been her imagination.

Thoughts of Itza came flirting through her mind. The dear one had cried mercilessly, pleading to be brought along, but Chimalma had refused saying Itza would distract her from her contemplations and purpose. She remembered how she could still hear Itza wailing in the distance, as if Maria was already dead from the initiation, as they had slipped down the streets away from the temple gates two mornings ago. Why did some people not live through initiation, she thought as she returned to sit on the cold stone chair. As she pulled the thin blanket around her she shivered suddenly, a shiver not caused by the cold but by something unseen.

I wonder if this temple is haunted, she thought as she recalled the huge shadow on the other pyramid. Just then, a cloud passing over the face of the full moon plunged the temple into darkness. Maria started in fear, taking several deep breaths to calm her racing heart as she thought of specter fingers closing in around her throat to cut off her life. A rustling from behind startled her and she jerked round to peer into the darkness at her possible abductor. Are there snakes here, she wondered. She still couldn't get used to snakes, pretending she wasn't bothered when she saw one, but her stomach always went queasy. Even the small harmless ones with their cold beady eyes.

Again came the rustling from behind. Maria jumped up to search the tiny sanctuary, if there was a snake, or something else for that matter, she wanted to know about it. Glancing up she saw the face of the moon again revealing itself. She could just see the apex of the moon pyramid, a huge shadow clung where no shadow should've been. She caught her breath, straightened up and looked to the sky to see of it could be the shadow of a cloud passing the moon. A small cloud did pass by, but the huge shadow didn't move. A chill ran down her back as she felt a piercing stare coming from the huge shadow as if it was alive. She closed her eyes shutting it out, hoping it was her imagination. When she reopened them, it was gone. Sighing with relief, she returned to her chair chuckling at herself for allowing her imagination to run away with her.

Another cloud drifted over the moon and in the distance she heard a whoosh, like something traveling at a high speed. The hair on the nape of her neck rose into the air as something whizzed passed her, just inches from her shoulders; and suddenly she was surrounded by a cold clammy presence. The air stunk of rotten eggs and threatened to gag her. She couldn't move, it felt like the unseen presence had glued her to the chair and was pricking her with sharp needles. She opened her mouth to scream but nothing came out. Two flaring red eyes without a body suddenly hung in the air before her, the stench became unbearable and she felt a putrid burning running across her skin.

She sat bolt upright, something was wrong. Chimalma gathered a blanket around herself and stepped into the night air. The fire had burned to embers and a cloud covered the bright face of the moon. She looked up to the pyramid and her heart froze. A dark mist covered the temple, it pulsated and formed dark tendrils moving in the air. She could feel the evil from where she stood. Was this part of the red-haired one's fate, she wondered? Something deep inside of her told her no, this was an interference.

She was about to wake her brother and the other priests so they could go to the pyramid and exorcise the evil thing, when she heard the voice of the goddess telling her that the evil one would kill Maria the second they set foot on the pyramid. The demon would need to be rooted from its source; but what was its source? She tried to think quickly but calmly of who wouldn't want the foreign one on the sacred pyramid.

As she began to think, she felt the goddesses' presence merge into her thoughts as she began to unfold a series of pictures before Chimalma's searching eyes. She saw the cloud maiden, the kings' favorite harem girl, then she saw a replay of the corn festival and the venom in the cloud maiden's eyes for Maria. Now she saw the cloud maiden visiting the witch by the waterfront, and the witch handing the cloud maiden a doll she had constructed of Maria. The goddess slipped from her mind and she was fully herself again, she would have to act fast or Maria would die, and to die in the hands of a demon wasn't something she would wish on anyone.

She sat down and tried to send her mind to the cloud maiden, but there was a barrier about the harem, a barrier she couldn't penetrate. The witch had done her job well. She began praying to the goddess to destroy the barrier when she saw the face of the sleeping king. She ingrained his face deeply in her mind and began calling his name over and over again. She called to him telling him of Maria's grave danger, and that the danger came from within his harem.

His eyes flew open to the darkness of his room and his heart beat in alarm. He'd dreamt the Cloud Maiden was choking Maria; he lay back down knowing it had to be just a dream. He tried to fall back asleep but a current of urgency rang through his body. In his mind he could see the face of the high priestess but he couldn't hear what she was saying. Suddenly, he knew something was very wrong in the harem.

The silver pin gleamed between the cloud maidens' slender fingers as she held it to the light, savoring its sharpness. Slowly, she stuck the pin in the belly of the doll, smiling wickedly as she pushed, wiggled, and jabbed it, and then laughed as she pictured Maria crying out in pain. Using the force of her hatred she kept the image alive. I just know it's working, she thought to herself. Soon I'll be rid of the hideous pale creature and no one will be the wiser, than I'll have what is my due.

She picked up another pin and was about to push it into the doll's head when the door burst open and there stood Montezuma dressed only in a loin cloth. She gasped in shock and threw the doll under the bed. The King retrieved the doll and held it up to the light. It had a black cord tied tight around its neck and silver pins covered the mangled body; and there was no mistaking the fiery colored hair. The desperate girl tried to grab the doll and throw it into the flames of the brazier but Montezuma held it out of her clawing reach. Clamping a hand around her wrist, he bellowed at the group of shocked female faces gathered at the door to get the guards. But in the same moment, two eagle knights entered the room followed by his first wife.

"I thought you might want some help," she said quietly eyeing the spell doll.

"Take this woman out and execute her. Now...tonight!" He shoved her towards the guards. She screamed, throwing herself at his feet.

"My lord, you can't mean this! You love me, you want me," her face went flush with terror.

"I want no black witch under my roof," he said with disgust.

Shrieking, the warriors hauled her to her feet and pulled her from the room.

Telling his first wife to send the women back to their rooms, he shut the door behind him. His heart was in his throat as he examined the numerous pins. Was this what Maria was going through right now, he wondered. Was it too late, was she already dead from this black art? Gently, he removed the pins as fast as he could. The screams of the cloud maiden reached him from the courtyard, one long cry, then silence. At the same moment, the black cord around the doll's neck came undone and fell to the floor just before he could touch it.

❖

Her stomach burnt with a fire of nausea and a cold invisible band kept tightening around her neck. She could hardly breathe now and her head erupted in white flashes of pain. She knew she was dying, and her last thoughts were of her parents in Spain and of the man she loved. Suddenly, the pressure eased from her neck, the clawing smell of stench left her nostrils and the clammy cold air was replaced by the natural cool of the night. She opened her eyes just as the dark clouds were lifting from the face of the moon. The moonlight now filling the temple felt clean and the last traces of stench were wicked away by the nights' breeze.

The stinging pain left her body and she tried to stand, but her muscles felt weak from the battle and she was forced to sit back down. Her blood went cold as she heard a heavy thud on the temple roof above her head. It must be the creature again she panicked, what else could fall on a roof hundreds of feet in the air! All of a sudden a feeling washed over her, a clean feeling calming her frazzled nerves. Somehow she knew it wasn't the evil thing. A sliding sound made its way to the edge of the temple roof and a head appeared followed by a body. Maria's heart nearly burst as she watched a serpent as big around as her body slither down the pillar in front of her. Its body was a silver blue that glowed in the moonlight, and it wore a red and blue band around its neck. As it got closer to her she could see the band was actually red and blue feathers growing right out of its skin.

Bile rushed to her throat as she watched the gigantic creature approaching her. She wanted to jump from her chair and race down the side of the pyramid, but something told her this was what she'd come for, she was being tested for courage and this was all part of the initiation. If she got up and ran away she would have to face Chimalma with her failure; pride kept her rooted to her chair. She gasped and nearly fainted as the huge snake began to crawl up her leg, across her lap, over her arm, across the back of her chair and back down her front again. The bulk of the serpent was so great she felt she was being crushed, yet she was aware it seemed to be keeping the greatest portion of its weight off her. As it moved, its feathers scratched her skin in contrast to the slippery texture of the rest of its body.

Finally, after what seemed like an eternity, it slithered off her and coiled itself up about five feet in front of her chair. She realized she'd been holding her breath, aware that the serpent could've squeezed the life from her body or swallowed her alive. The head of the snake began to rise in the air until it reached the height of a man; it stayed erect and still, regarding Maria with unblinking eyes. Its form began to waver and fade as if she was watching him through a moving liquid veil. It completely faded into watery illusion than began to reappear, gradually, into a more distinct form, until a man stood where the snake had been.

His luminous skin was a pale silver and his golden hair hung to his shoulders. His eyes seemed to be deep pools of quick silver, and his nose and mouth still held the slightest vestiges of the serpent. A heavy crease ran from his thin lips to his small nose, yet it was the face of a handsome man; a god. A golden sundisk glowed on his chest in the form of a medallion that seemed to be lit from within. A short blue tunic covered his body but it kept changing, almost as if he were clothed by light rather than cloth.

"I am Quetzacoatl," he hissed, his voice sounding like soft music. "You have done well my child."

Awe and fear pulled Maria off her seat and to her knees, never in a million years did she expect this peculiar blessing and honor. She stumbled and moved like someone asleep when he told her to seat herself again.

"I will tell you a story of prophesy," he said, "which you are destined to witness."

Maria slipped into a rhythmic like trance as she listened to his voice.

"Thousands of years ago a race of people arrived from the stars and they brought the secrets of their home. Many mingled and married with the people already here. At that time a huge city was here, one that predates the ruined one you now sit in. A huge temple once stood where this pyramid now is, and inside this temple was a black obsidian block. A block composed of volcanic fire and tiny gold flecks, this block was the doorway to the infinite beyond, the stars and their home."

His presence was so loving, it was hard for Maria to focus on the story.

"This city went the way of time, and her people spread to many lands. When the temple fell to ruin, the block was hidden in safety until another race arrived in this land. This race also quested for the stars, the ones called the Toltecs. They built their city and great pyramid directly over the old temple. I appeared among them to teach the old arts that would one day lead them back to the stars. For it was also I who brought the volcanic block from our home in the stars to this land. In their misunderstanding, they forced me to leave, and I vowed to return when they were ready to be taught. As you can see I never really left, it was they who left me. They fell to sacrificing their brothers," he bowed his head, "and their city too went the way of time."

"Then the Aztecs arrived, also questing. Those among them who were pure were shown how to use this shrine and the star-gate block. They've been given a great civilization, but that too is now doomed."

"Not by my people," begged Maria.

"They are only a part of it," he hissed, seeming to touch her heart and feelings with the sound of his voice. "The Spanish race is simply acting out a drama that began long ago."

"I don't understand."

"Some of your legends of Atlantis are not just legends," he

smiled deeply and Maria wanted to laugh. "Once there were two great civilizations on the earth, both of these great nations sunk beneath the waves and their people came to these lands to live. Inhabiting the lands to the far north and south of here as well, the people at first lived as brothers, equal and in peace. One was a fair race, the other, a copper colored race."

Maria knew he must somehow be speaking of the Spanish and Aztec's ancestors.

"But soon they forgot their kinship and they fought among each other. The copper children soon grew in number and the fair ones grew weaker and smaller in number. They were forced to flee, taking to ships and crossing the great eastern sea to new lands. The rest of these golden skinned children were either killed or forced into submission."

Maria seemed to know what he was going to say next.

"All actions demand an equal reaction, and now the time has come when the descendants of the fair skinned ones are returning back to these lands, and the earth lords are ready to help in their return action."

Maria watched as he seemed to shimmer back to his snake form for an instant as he spoke these last words.

"Here in these lands, and to the north and south, these reactions will take place. There will be an exchanging of power and the drama will repeat itself again and again until these two groups learn to live as brothers."

"But how will it end?" she asked.

"Far in the future there will be a great nation of these fair skinned ones residing to the north. The copper children will go to this nation hoping to be accepted and risking everything they have. The fair skinned nation will scorn them, but it will be to no avail and they will enter in masses. The people of this great nation will not understand that the lords of the earth have deemed it so to equalize their hatred and to see if the two races have yet learned to live in peace."

"But how am I involved and will I see this happen?"

"Not as you are now," he said as he began to waver again.

"What do you mean?"

"You know you've served the goddess in the past and you will again, but differently."

"How will I be different and who are the lords of the earth?" she asked just as the sun made its appearance over the eastern horizon. It startled Maria, she had lost track of time and she blinked at the sunrise. When she returned her glance to him, he was gone.

She was sitting quietly in the chair when the priests arrived a few minutes later. She knew she was not allowed to speak of her experiences during initiation so she contained her excitement, got up, and followed the priests back down. The group descended down the pyramid's north face, stopping about half way. They stepped to the side of one of the tiers while Mayazan and two of the other priests counted off a sequence of stones. While the three pressed on the selected stones at exactly the same time, the center stone began to pivot inward. It revealed a passage made of rough hewn limestone blocks lit by a single torch in a wall bracket.

Entering the cool, damp passageway single file, Mayazan took the torch from its bracket and they started inward. What's next, thought Maria as they entered a torchlit oblong room of highly polished stone. A carved altar stood at the center of the room, decorated with intertwining snakes at each side. Passages led off from either side and in front of the left passage stood the three priestesses. But Maria's attention was captured by a huge block of obsidian suspended over the altar at a forty-five degree angle. The torchlight reflected off the tiny flecks of gold spattered across its surface.

"The star-gate! It's real!" she breathed.

"Lie down on the altar," instructed Chimalma as she placed a mask of terra cotta over Maria's face. "I want you to begin to think of all the times you've said or done something bad in your life, and then follow the essence of those things to where they rest in your body."

Maria began to fidget, but then relaxed when Chimalma placed her hand on her arm. "Then you're to run the essence through your body and into the mask."

Almost immediately, thoughts and visions began to flow by her. She remembered the time she glued one of the sisters habits to a chair. And the time she put a litter of kittens in a box and hid them in a bell tower to see how they would react to the sound. When she came back they were all dead from the gonging. Both of these incidences were lodged in her hands. She pushed the thoughts and feelings into the mask. When she stole into the jungle against Cortez' orders and then lied to him seemed to be in her throat, that too she pushed into the mask. On and on they seem to come. All the times she stole, cheated, and lied, they were all over her body like a map. She was amazed at how much she'd done, when all along she'd thought she'd been such a good Christian.

Soon the mask felt alive, it seemed to squirm and crawl like a nest of vipers. Chimalma stepped over, sensing Maria was finished, she and her brother lifted the now stifling mask from Maria's face and dashed it to the ground proclaiming Maria cleansed. A few of the priests began to leave, the braziers were brought close to the altar, she was instructed to concentrate on the gold flecks in the star-gate, the rest began to leave and suddenly she was alone again.

The longer she watched the gold flecks the more they began to look like stars in the night sky. The buzzing in her head was ringing louder and louder now, then something snapped. She observed herself magically moving through the star-gate, she was moving freely and effortlessly into the nights' sky with stars passing by her on all sides.

In a flash she was inside a strange, round, silver object that was speeding through the sky. Seven other people were with her, and she was dressed in a silver suit that covered her whole body like a second skin. The handsome people around her all had blue skin and white hair, with large, luminous dark eyes. She too had blue skin, she observed as she looked down at her own hand guiding some control knob on a cabinet of bright flashing lights. The people seemed to be very upset, then she saw the craft was out of control and heading fast towards an unfamiliar planet. She tried staying calm by putting her hand on the shoulder of the man sitting next to her. Suddenly, she knows that he is her beloved and he stills her trembling fear. He stands and holds her close in his arms as they crash into a huge body of water on the planet.

She sees some people with strange pink colored skin fish them from the waters and they go to live with these people in a crystal city filled with lakes that have boats like graceful swans drifting over their surface. As she dies, she feels the sorrow of not being able to return to her home planet again.

Now she is a woman with long dark hair standing on the balcony of a huge building that is shaking violently. Tremendous sheets of water are washing up from the sea and volcanoes are belching black smoke in the distance. She knows her civilization is doomed.

She is standing in the desert feeding grass to a strange huge animal with humps on its back. In the distance she can see smooth sided, glowing white pyramids. Her mother joins her telling her they must hurry, the festival will be starting soon. It's Itza! Her Mother is Itza. Although she doesn't look like Itza now, she can tell it's her. She is much older now and is wearing a long white dress with many pleats and standing next to the huge pyramid. She's shaking some kind of strange rattle as the sun is coming up in the distance. She glances over to a tall man standing beside her, a stripped cloth covers his head and fans out to both sides. The warmth in his familiar dark eyes gladdens her soul.

She looks down and is surprised to see white bandages around her tiny feet, she sits in a chair in front of a beautiful half moon bridge. The air is filled with the fragrance of sweet smelling blossoms. An old woman approaches to tell her that her father as arrange her marriage. Fondly looking into the old nurses eyes she sees that it's Itza again. A young man joins them, his robes are richly embroidered, his eyes have a strange slant, and his long black hair is in a pigtail down his back. She loves him on sight.

She is a young girl running in the forest gathering berries, a thatched roof cottage is in the distance. Her tall, elegant sister is with her; Chimalma is her sister.

She's wearing strange pants that are cut off at her knees and expose her legs, a wide brimmed hat is on her head. She's looking at the Pyramid of the Sun through a small box, pressing a button on the box, she hears a click! A man with short blonde hair is with her, he is dressed much like her. He's taking measurements of the pyramid, and she feels they're searching for the very same hidden room that her body now rests in. She opens a book and writes in it. At the top of the page is the date October 12, 1992. Gasping, she realizes she's seeing the future. Suddenly, she is being pulled backwards until she finds herself over the same pyramid. She can see the last vestiges of Quetzacoatl, and from the apex temple one of the temple attendants is folding up her blanket she'd left in the chair.

Now she was being pulled through the stone pyramid and was standing on the other side of the star-gate looking down at her own resting body through a veil of golden stars. Then, for just an instant, she could see the lovely green planet in space she had come from. She could see the Great Ones, the Earth Lords, men and women who were once just like her. Men and women who'd mastered life and overcome, who now directed the affairs of man, seeing that each person got the lessons necessary to also overcome.

Becoming aware of a presence next to her, the familiar white headdress of the mother goddess began to manifest. Touching Maria in the middle of her forehead she said, "Remember my child." Maria saw herself as a tall elegant Indian woman crossing the desert with a large tribe; the same ring she'd gotten at the market appeared on her finger and she carried a medicine pouch. She saw an eagle sitting in a tree with a snake in it's beak and a village springing up around the tree. Then she saw herself much older, making a journey to a huge pyramid to the north. A vision tells her how to open the secret door and to lay on the very same altar. She is named the first High Priestess of the mother goddess; her name then was Chimalma!

Standing before the goddess again, she quickly reminded Maria of the man on the falling spacecraft, the man with the stripped headdress, the man with the black pigtail and finally the man from the future. An exhilarating warmth rushed through her body as she realized they were all Montezuma.

"He is your eternal love," the goddess melodiously whispered. "The two of you are two parts of the same flame." Placing her hand on Maria's head she said, "You see, you were Aztec then, just as you are now. You can best serve me and the Aztec people by returning to serve at Montezuma's side in the trying times to come."

Suddenly, Maria again found herself laying on the altar and gazing up at the star-gate, dazed and overwhelmed, yet complete and whole.

13
Wars and Weddings

The early evening air was quickly turning cold; it was going to be a cool autumn. Montezuma adjusted his mantle to give himself more warmth. He could call an attendant for a brazier, but he wanted to be left alone with his thoughts. He watched the fish darting around in the water, as they played tag below the leaves. This particular garden pool always seemed to give him special consolation...maybe because it was so far from the palace, and in its own little niche.

His heart was heavy today; he'd received another report. The pale ones were very close. Soon they would arrive in Cholan and be right at his doorstep. Everywhere they marched, they overcame, and thousands of tribes—all enemies of the 'One World'—rushed to join the one called Cortez. He could yet destroy the Spanish, but the old doubts continued to fester and haunt him. Yes, he knew Maria had said they were not gods, but what of the forces of nature that seemed to accompany them...the thundersticks, the huge beasts that did their bidding! Maria said they were just machines, but didn't it take gods to turn the forces of nature into machines?

The thought of Maria opened the ache in his heart. He had brought her here to this spot a number of times, and the place seemed haunted with her delicate laugh. He remembered how the summer sun would turn her hair to fire. He hoped no harm had come to her at the Toltec pyramid. It had been two days since he caught the Cloud Maiden practicing the black art. Funny, he had lain with her many times, desiring her golden body, but when she'd threatened Maria's life he had executed her without question.

He had never shared pleasure with Maria, but she affected his heart and mind like no other. Was this love, he thought, such as the poets speak of? Strange that he would find it with a foreign one. And now his love had been taken to the sacred pyramid, where so many had gone attempting mastery, but had died in the process. Even if she did live, she would be a priestess, and forever out of his grasp. He wondered if she was already dead...by the will of the gods or by the hand of the Cloud Maiden.

As he brooded into the reflections of the water—with the last dying rays of sunlight twinkling on its surface—he saw a figure appear behind him. He looked up to see Maria standing there, dressed in the simple temple dress with a blanket wrapped around her. She dropped to her knees beside him, and taking his hands in hers, she said, "I love you...and if you will have me, I am yours." Montezuma's heart leapt with joy with her words. "Have you? Of course I'll have you, I've always wanted you."

She looked more lovely than ever; she carried a new strength from within. The girl had been left behind at the pyramid...this was a woman. She blushed as he answered her, and beamed like a new found puppy dog.

"I was worried for you," he said, taking her in his arms.

"I know, I felt you; that is why I came directly here first. But Itza has worried much also, I must go now and see to her."

He walked her back through the gardens, each in their own thoughts. There was no question of whether or not she would be made a wife, but what bothered Montezuma was that he knew the Spanish kept only one wife. Would they try to interfere, and say it was invalid since he had so many? He couldn't give up his other wives; many of them came as unconditional treaties. He had to do something to guarantee the marriage. He wasn't going to let Maria go, now that she was his. Then it dawned on him what he could do. Of course it was completely against tradition and it would shake the Tzin court, but he didn't care. The first condition could be handled at the marriage, the second would come later.

The barge slid slowly up to the palace landing. Maliche was weary; the ordeal in Texcoco had been trying for her. She still couldn't believe he was gone...she had loved him so. She felt like a tree that had been transplanted in the desert. Her father was her strength, her shoulder to lean on. Now where would she turn?.... certainly not to her mother, or her brother for that matter. She didn't even think him equipped to take over as Second Reverent Speaker. Montezuma? He was just a husband in name now.

As she was led through the gardens to the harem, she noticed the strange way the servants kept regarding her. What's going on, she thought? When she reached her quarters, one of her personal maids threw herself at Maliche's feet and wailed.

"Miala, why are you crying?" She stroked the girl's hair. "It's been ten days since the Second Reverent Speaker died."

"Oh my Lady, you haven't heard?" she gasped.

"Heard what?" Maliche felt suddenly chilled. "Tell me!"

"The King is going to marry the pale one," whimpered the girl, afraid of the consequences.

"The foreign one? But I thought she was going to be a priestess. Well she's not a Tzin, but even if he does marry her I hear she's of nobility in her own land. But that's hardly reason enough to be so upset."

"But my queen, he's going to marry her as first wife in the sacred mat ceremony," she said, burying her head at Maliche's feet.

Maliche went pale and her head started to spin. How can that be? It's not possible to have more than one first wife unless the chosen ones are twins. And Maria's obviously...she became nauseous.

"Leave me. I want to be alone."

The servants all scurried out with heads lowered. What should she do, she thought? Did this mean her children would no longer hold their claim to royal standing? But I'm the First Princess of Texcoco, she cried softly. How could he do such a thing? Who could she turn to defend her station? Who would speak against the First Reverent Speaker on her behalf? Only her father would have dared to speak for her sake, and now he was gone. She threw herself on her bed, buried her head and muffled the sobs of anguish, so that no one would hear a proud first wife in despair.

❖

The cold morning air greeted the girls as they exited the steam baths. Everyone was filled with excitement...today Maria would marry. The temple had never played host to a bride on a wedding day before, and all the girls wanted to know what had happened at the pyramid that Maria would come back a bride to be instead of a priestess. They especially wanted to know why the High Priestess seemed to be so friendly with Maria all of a sudden, treating her practically like a sister. Everyone had shared in the excitement the day before, when messengers arrived almost hourly bearing perfumes, oils, feathers, dresses, jewels and much more...all for the bride to be.

The sacred bridal bath—with perfumes, oils and lotions—had been completed that morning, and now Maria was seated with Itza, applying her makeup. Itza had been running around like a proud mother hen, and had practically been more hindrance than help.

"Oh, no," cried Maria, "I look like a freak!" She put the obsidian mirror down, and was about to wash her face against the objection of the old woman.

"What wrong? All brides do makeup like that on wedding day!"

"I won't look like this," declared Maria, just as Chimalma appeared at the door smiling.

"What's going on here?" she laughed.

"Itza been painting wedding faces all her life," she said, defending herself.

"Look at me!"

Her face was an ochre yellow with red patches covering her cheeks and lips; thick black soot dwarfed her pretty eyes. Maria was right, thought Chimalma...what looked beautiful on an Aztec girl, overpowered Maria's delicate coloring. Itza bowed out grudgingly, as Chimalma wiped Maria's face clean and began to reapply everything with a light touch. When she was done, Maria's face glowed naturally; only her lips were a rosy red and her eyes gently defined, letting her green eyes stand out even more.

Maria finished dressing just as Itza returned to announce the arrival of Montezuma's family and the palace chair. As the door opened, many of the curious girls stuck their heads in to see Maria in her finished state. They oohed and aahed as she stepped from the room in her splendor. Her brilliant hair hung long and full down her back, and she wore a golden headdress with long, white peacock plumes. More peacock feathers decorated her skirt and blouse, with large pearls lining the edges. A heavy pearl belt girdled her, and lapis strands decorated her neck, wrists, and ankles. She looked exquisite.

She was led to her chair where she was met by some of the King's family. Montezuma's sisters adorned her with flowers and anointed her with rare perfumes, while his two younger brothers led the bridal procession through the streets. At the palace gates his eldest son met Maria sullenly, but determined to do his father's will, he escorted her to the King. When their eyes met, love and warmth passed between them; they hadn't seen each other since the evening of Maria's return.

Montezuma was dressed in royal splendor. He wore a gold-trimmed mantle and loincloth that hung to the ground and was adorned with pale blue peacock feathers and jade beads. His sandals were set with jade and lapis, lacing fully to his knees, and a gold amulet hung from his neck. His diadem was made of lapis and gold, and long, full peacock feathers hung down his back to his ankles.

The royal censer he held in his right hand was magnificent …two golden swans intertwining over a large, clear quartz crystal before a mother of pearl pond, where copal resin sat smoking. He fanned the burning copal smoke across her body with the royal fan of iridescent white feathers; it was set on a solid quartz crystal handle that was shaped like a lotus. When he was finished, she in turn did the same to him; then taking her by the hand, he led her to his private chapel.

The chapel was teeming with people; everyone wanted to witness this unethical wedding that broke their sacred laws. Maria couldn't help noticing that some of them looked upon her with cold, unexcepting eyes. They sat on the sacred mat and listened to the elders' seemingly unending lectures on marriage; this was lasting even longer than the twins' ceremony had. Finally, the presiding High Priest came forward and tied Montezuma's mantle to Maria's blouse. As they fed each other the small corn cakes, the union became sanctified. Maria's one regret was that her mother wasn't there to witness her wedding day, but when she looked into Itza's proud beaming face...she knew that she had.

After the couple led the crowd back to the palace banquet hall, Montezuma and Maria went behind the royal screen to eat in private. Their table was set with pure gold dishes and plates, and a centerpiece of a rare breed of exquisite red flowers imported from a jungle far to the south. The feast started with a clear soup made with amaranth and the flesh of clams, followed by pheasant cooked with an orange sauce, venison with sage and tomatoes baked in little clay pots to extract the wild taste, sweet potatoes with honey, and the ever present tortillas. Between each course Montezuma's other wives provided them with towels and finger bowls of hot soapy water. For dessert a sweet maize cake appeared; it was adorned with apricots dripping with honey, and was served with a golden cup of cocoa and a tiny golden whisk to whip their cocoa to a frothy brew. This was one of Maria's favorites, and she knew the Aztecs adored their cocoa, even valuing it so much as to use it as currency sometimes.

For Maria the day was perfect. Everything around her seemed to serenade her. The flowers were more fragrant than seemed possible; the food tasted like food had never tasted before; and Montezuma...Montezuma, her love, was never more handsome. They had finished their meal and she was cuddling up in the soft rabbit fur rug draped on her chair, when the Chamberlain discreetly poked his head around the screen and announced that the entertainment would be starting shortly. Montezuma escorted Maria back out in front of the screen, and the guests became hushed.

As they sat down at the bridal table, Montezuma motioned for a steward with a large cedar casket; he came forward and placed the chest before Maria. Upon opening the lid, Maria went pale. In it she found a jade ring set with coral so large that it covered her entire knuckle, a necklace of jade and gold, a comb carved from mother of pearl, a set of silver perfume bottles with turquoise stoppers, an exquisite belt of pearls and coral with the palest green jade, and finally...she withdrew a two foot, pure jade statue of the Mother Goddess. The Goddess' dress was made of gold, and set with turquoise snakes; a necklace of tiny pearls adorned her neck. The crowd was dumbfounded; the statue's value was inestimable, and worthy of a temple. How was it that the King was giving it to a mere woman?

As Maria shed tears of gratitude, she motioned for Chimalma to come forward. She carried a wooden box which contained Maria's gift to Montezuma...a golden statue of a fabulous mythological beast, like the one on the King's personal crest. It had jade eyes and mother of pearl wings, and had come from the secret treasure chamber beneath the pyramid at Teotihuacan. The crowd relaxed. She too had given a priceless treasure. Toltec art was considered rare and highly prized; collecting it was a passion amongst the Tzin class. To have an exquisite piece such as this was enviable indeed.

Maliche sat nearby, stricken with melancholy. She'd waited these last few days to see if there would be any change in her status, but nothing had happened. She'd run into Montezuma in the palace corridors and he'd spoken to her like he always did, but he refused to meet her eyes. Could it be that he intended to keep her as a first wife, along with Maria? At first she had been relieved, taking up her duties in the harem with caution, but a deep resentment quickly set in. She was unsure of how she was to treat Maria once she moved into the harem; but then word came that she wouldn't be moving in at all. Maria would be occupying chambers right next to the King's.

Tonight she had worn all of the jewelry that marked her as first wife, but the gifts the King had given Maria so belittled her jewels, that her statement was all but lost. It was quite obvious Maria was going to be different than his other wives. Just yesterday she had noticed several of the harem girls were experimenting with the strong smelling substance the Auianime use to turn their hair a red orange, and they were using lemons to bleach out their complexions. Overnight, Maria had turned from the pale, hideous one to someone to be copied if you wanted to stay in the King's favor...not that Montezuma noticed; he hadn't called anyone to his bed in days.

A deep voice from behind stirred Maliche from her thoughts. "May I sit with you my Queen?" It was Cualpopaca, the revered Eagle Knight. This was quite unusual, she thought; what does he want with me? Then she saw something in his dark gaze that warmed and awakened her womanhood. "Pardon my directness my

Lady," he said, "but are you not the Princess of Texcoco, and the real first wife of our King?" His question so shocked Maliche that she couldn't find her tongue. No one had expressed her predicament so bluntly before her; most were so afraid of Montezuma that they kept their council to themselves. "Are you not irritated that a foreigner would usurp your place...you a royal princess of Aztec blood? You don't find that unusual?"

Cualpopaca glared toward the dais at Maria with distrust, but found his manhood aroused by her strange beauty instead. He'd had another dream about her. Naked, she had entered his room and the flames of the brazier flickered on the luscious curves of her body. Roughly, he'd grabbed her, wanting to force her into submission, but everywhere he had touched her his hand had been burned by fire. A cold resentment crept into his eyes, and he forced his attention back to Maliche whose beauty was natural and safe, not evil. Perhaps he could make an ally of Maliche. A high placed palace official would be very beneficial, he thought, as he turned on his charm while counseling her in the injustice of her treatment. Then he changed tactics.

"The foreign woman is most unusual," he said. "I sense she is not natural; look at her effect upon the King, and even the High Priestess of the Mother Goddess rallies to her cause. I wonder if she has made an unholy alliance with the dark ones!"

Maliche went stiff. "Are you accusing the High Priestess of witchcraft?" she said angrily!

"No of course not, but I believe the power of the foreign one is unnatural," he said with guile.

"But surely the High Priestess would know if she was an evil thing; she even went through the great initiation and survived," said Maliche.

"Who's to know what happens at that far citadel? Maybe she's woven her power over the priestess too," he suggested.

Maliche looked at Maria in a new light. She had thought this whole thing was Montezuma's doing; but suppose he was under a spell. That would certainly explain his rash behavior. It's true her son had gone to his father and tried to talk some propriety into him. The King wouldn't even listen to him. It was as though this woman had become more important than all of his family.

"It's known that soon her people will arrive here, and the King has done nothing to stop them," he went on.

"The King isn't sure that they're not with the returning Quetzalcoatl," she said, defending her husband.

"Baaah...gods don't come as these Spanish ones do," he scoffed, "and what of the signs? I think the omens have come to warn us of these people. What I see is...they conquer the outside while she corrupts and conquers from the inside. They're in alliance."

"But she has told Montezuma not to let them come," Maliche said, becoming confused.

"A ploy," he said. "She says one thing and does another."

"She looks so young," Maliche said.

"Looks can be deceiving. There's no one here who could swear as to when she was born. The dark arts are said to preserve beauty, as long as one stays in alignment with the evil ones. I'm not sure of this," he said shrewdly, "but wouldn't it be better to be safe? If you love your people, you could perhaps keep an eye on this woman's activities."

"And report back to Montezuma? What good would that do?"

"No, if he's under her spell that will just alert her to the fact that we're on to her. Report to me; we together can just perhaps save our people." He touched Maliche's hand, and looked into her eyes with a warmth and intensity that unnerved her.

Maria looked up to see the warrior regarding her with cold eyes. It was the same man from the earlier banquet, who had made her feel so uncomfortable. He was sitting next to Montezuma's first wife, and now they were both watching her with such animosity. She could understand it with Maliche. She would need to make friends with the woman, so she would know that Maria only wished the best for her.... but she had done nothing to the cold eyed warrior. Turning back toward her beloved, she quickly allowed the wonder of this special day to wash all else from her mind.

At last Montezuma stood, took Maria's hand, and led her from the banquet hall. They were quickly swarmed by members of the court and old Tzin women, again lecturing on the demands of marriage and reminding them of their responsibilities. When they reached Montezuma's chambers they were whisked behind their separate unveiling screens. Itza, Chimalma, and Taka were all waiting to act as Maria's family. Removing her clothing and jewelry, they slipped the traditional long, white poncho over her head; then they led her around to stand opposite Montezuma.

The leopard skin covered bed separated them, and she could see the edge of the marriage mat under the bed. She wondered if the women had laughed and played, as she had when preparing the chamber for the princesses. She was sure that the bed was readied with the special proof sheet to catch the blood of her virginity…and with that thought, the particular fears of maidenhood rushed forward to distract her. The voice of Montezuma's brother rang out to announce his virtues. He was answered by the High Priestess who affirmed Maria's as well, and she finished by declaring Maria to be a virgin.

The High Chamberlain swept back the blankets, so each could crawl in from their own side. Suddenly, Maria broke out in laughter. Soon Montezuma was laughing too, and one by one, everyone in the room had joined them. Itza had prepared the bed. Instead of the usual handful of feathers and pieces of jade that were used to represent the children to come, in her zeal she had filled the bed with dozens of feathers and jewels. Finally, Chimalma declared that they need not follow Itza's idea, so she cleared away the stones and feathers, and helped Maria into the bed. Soon they all exited, the doors were closed, and they were alone.

They lay there looking at each other for quite some time, each afraid to touch the other…Maria because she wasn't sure how to begin, and Montezuma because for the first time in his life he was in love. He wanted it to be perfect for Maria. In the past he had just taken his pleasure, not regarding his women; but now his emotions warned him to be gentle, and he wasn't really sure just how to do that. The tension was too much for him; he climbed out of bed, took Maria's hand, and led her to the terrace.

The moon hung in a crescent and the garden below reflected its pale radiance. As Maria looked down at the fountain, she caught sight of movement in the bushes. A small figure emerged from the foliage and turned his face to the moon; then like a fugitive, he glanced around. Not spotting anyone, he made a dash for the fountain. The little blue faced monkey was nicknamed 'the bandit'. He had an uncanny ability to get out of his cage and raid the palace gardens. Even now he sat by the fountain peeling bananas he'd stolen from somewhere in the gardens. He perched on the pool's edge delicately munching his contraband, then dipping his paws in the water just like a country squire using a finger bowl. His actions were so adorable that Maria broke out in laughter. At the sound of her voice 'the bandit' scurried back to the bushes with an expression of outraged indignation.

This broke the tension, as they laughed at the monkey and then looked into to each other's eyes. Of its own accord, Montezuma's hand went to Maria's hair. He'd been right; it did feel different. It was soft...soft as the pelt of a rabbit. He ran his fingers through it, and a smile came to his face. He'd never felt curly hair before; its texture fascinated him.

He bent down slowly—so as to not scare her—and rested his lips upon her mouth, as she'd done to him. She met him equally...her tongue probing deep into Montezuma's mouth, lighting a fire within them that sent a weakness to their knees.

He scooped Maria up in his strong arms and carried her back to the bed; all the while he smothered her neck, face, and head with the delicate things she called kisses. A voice in the back of his head warned him to slow down. With great difficulty, he slowed his breathing and allowed his passion-filled eyes to focus. The brazier light gave Maria's skin an alluring warmth and glow, as he flicked his tongue across her red, swollen lips and then along the inside of her tiny, delicate ear. She gasped and pulled him close to her. Gently he pushed her down on the bed, telling her he wanted this to be a gift to her...his gift.

She sighed, while his warm, strong hands played over her body...stroking and caressing her. The warm glow inside her body was becoming a raging fire, and she closed her eyes to concentrate on the pleasure he was rendering her. Then, after removing his own garments, he pulled Maria to a sitting position to remove hers. As she opened her eyes she went weak at the sight of his smooth, well muscled torso, and strong arms. She hadn't really noticed it before, but his body looked like paintings of statues she'd seen...statues of Greek gods. He was a god with burnished skin, high cheekbones, and streams of jet black hair. She liked how his eyes sparkled gold when he looked at her, as he was looking at her now.

Many times he'd fantasized what Maria's body would be like, but nothing could have prepared him for this. Her skin was alabaster, as if the sun had never touched it. Her breasts were round and full, and tipped not with dark brown nipples—as he was used to—but by a delicate pink, like the inside of a shell. He cupped his hands over their fullness, and then lowered his mouth to feel the nipple swell under the ministration of his tongue. A groan escaped her lips as he ran his tongue down her flesh to her navel. He caressed her slender waist, and ran his hands over the swells of her hips. As he traced down her legs, he flung the blankets back and ran his hands up the inside of her thigh, to be greeted by the second surprise. Where there was usually only a few strands of hair, Maria had a full, lush complement; it was a bright, fiery red...even redder than the hair on her head.

Maria looked down at Montezuma as he fingered her pubic hair with one finger, and teased her now brightly swollen nipple with the other. A sudden fear ran through her...did he think her too different, too outlandish? His dark eyes swept up her body to meet her emerald ones. His voice was thick, "You are beautiful, more beautiful than I ever thought a woman could be."

She sighed and lay back, opening herself totally to him. He gently separated her legs, and with fingers and tongue she felt him start a fire that began to consume her. Her legs started to quiver and her breath came in short gasps. Suddenly, the fire broke loose, and waves of flame washed through her body and blotted out her mind. When her breathing had slowed and she could again focus her eyes, he was poised over her. She felt his swollen manhood brush between her legs, then she involuntarily tensed as he entered her.

As she tensed, he stopped his movement and stroked her face and hair lovingly, inwardly begging the gods to help him go slowly. The passion raging through his body made him want to consume and devour her. He had to push to the deepest part of her womanhood...now! His breath was ragged in his struggle for self-control. He whispered in her ear, "It will only hurt once, only once."

Feeling her body relax, he pushed through the barrier of her maidenhood. She gasped first at the sharp pain, and then again with the all-consuming pleasure that followed. She let her hips move of their own accord, reaching up to meet his deep thrusts. They rode wave after wave of ecstasy until fleshed demanded its due. A double cry of communion, and they were bathed in the pool of eternal bliss... two souls sealed together forever.

The Spanish stood in long lines, awed at the beauty of the city in front of them. A group of officials had come from the city to greet them. The Head Chief was carried on a magnificent gold litter, and the runners now stood to the side and reverently allowed the leader to speak. "Welcome to our city; our homes are your homes. May our peoples know each other as friends, and may you find joy amongst us." Then the Spanish were led into the city and entrusted into several palaces.

Once settled, Cortez poured himself a liberal goblet of the strong native brew, octili. He'd acquired a palate for the smoky tasting drink. Of course it would never match a good Castilian wine, but now and then it kept him from breaking into his own precious stock. He kicked back and rested among the cushions of the divan; one black boot was propped on a delicate blue cushion, leaving a permanent dark stain.

As he drank deeply from his cup, he sighed with satisfaction. It had been a long and bloody road. Some tribes had rushed to join his banner, as if they sensed his mission was holy; but just as many of the heathens had stubbornly fought his army, and he had been forced to destroy them. At first he'd had twinges of guilt about wiping out whole tribes to make examples of them, but the good fathers had eased his heart by telling him it was God's will...that the heathens either submit to the Holy Catholic Church and the Empire of Spain, or die.

A quiet knock came at the door.

"Enter!" bellowed Cortez.

The young girl let herself in. Her white skirt and blouse were decorated with red flowers that matched the bright red, silk, Spanish shawl…a gift from Cortez.

"Ah ha, Dona Marina, what do you say now?" Cortez sat up with the bright look of triumph on his face. "You said the Tlaxcalans would be our strongest foe, next to the Aztecs. Well here we are in the Tlaxcalan capital of Chochulan, and they've welcomed us as friends. They ran to our banner!"

"Beware!" she said quietly. "They are cousins to the Aztecs."

"Cousins! Baah, I believe they're soft, and don't want to see their pretty city destroyed; besides, they obviously see we're the greater power. Perhaps they too, no longer wish to be under the Aztec yoke!"

"Perhaps, but…"

"Do you think me lax?" He laughed at her. "I left our native allies just outside the city with their spies, even now amongst the Chochulans. My officers have been ordered to enjoy themselves, but to stay alert. Of course I don't trust these people yet, but I'll not destroy this city if I don't have to. I'll not follow your advice and make it an example. Now come here woman and fulfill your duties to pleasure me, and leave the war plans to the men."

An hour later a young woman slipped from the Spanish stronghold. Her red silk shawl and richly embroidered dress were replaced by a white smock and the plain grey shawl of a simple townsperson. Dona Marina had braided her hair neatly over her head, like a matron; a heavy earthen jar was balanced atop her head. Something bothered her. She felt that this city held secrets…secrets that could be dangerous to the Spanish cause, and she felt a part of that cause. She always had a hidden understanding concerning the part she was playing with the Spanish. She often knew things before they happened. She knew her lot was best with Cortez, and she'd been able to make him dependent on her. Now she was protecting her interests. There was a place in any city where a woman could find out just what was going on; she headed for that place now.

The sound of soft footsteps woke him. The room was suspended in the flinty gray of twilight, as the servants removed the food trays and lit the braziers. The soft firelight stole through the room, as he sat up. It had been three days since the wedding; in the past he'd always returned to his duties before the four day wedding period was over. But now he found himself regretting that there was only one day left. He wanted to stay here forever…sleeping, eating, bathing, making love, playing silly little games with each other, and again making love. He couldn't get enough of Maria. When he thought he'd been given enough pleasure to last a man a lifetime, he surprised himself by wanting her firm, warm body again an hour later.

She sighed in her sleep and turned over. Montezuma pushed a strand of the beautiful hair from her face. He never ceased to marvel at how the light set it afire, or of its softness. He studied her face as she slept; she looked so young, so innocent. A feeling of protective tenderness moved so strongly in his heart that it almost hurt. This morning—thinking to make her happy— he had told her any son she conceived, he was sure could be the next Reverent Speaker. But instead of being happy a tear came to her eye, and she said that in order for her son to be King, he would have to be dead. She wanted him to stay with her forever. If she knew that not having a son would guarantee that Montezuma would always be with her, she would hope to never conceive, even if it meant being thrown back to the harem for being barren.

Was it possible she could love him so? What had he done to be so blessed? He quietly slipped out of bed and pulled a heavy blue mantle around himself. He would prepare a surprise for her…something that would show Maria forever, how deeply she had touched him.

She hurried through the darkening street; she wasn't used to carrying a heavy water jug anymore, but it was part of her disguise. What she'd heard at the communal well made her want to drop the jug and run, but she couldn't afford to draw any attention to herself. If anyone recognized her, she was sure she'd never make it back to Spanish headquarters.

Finally, she rounded the last corner. Two Spanish guards stood against the tall, mud brick wall. The relaxed way they held their lances told Dona Marina that they hadn't heard a thing yet. She dropped her jug and started to run toward them. When at first they spotted an Indian woman running at them, the guards snapped into a defensive stance; but upon recognizing the now distinctive features of Cortez' native interpreter, they relaxed and held open the door to the garden wall for her.

Cortez lie napping on the divan when she burst into the chamber; his innate soldier senses snapped him to alert. In haste, Dona Marina explained that she had gone to one of the Chochulan public wells. Throngs of women were gathering water and leaving the city with the children; the men were laying in wait, intent on ambushing the Spanish this very night as they slept. Cortez was furious as he sprang into action, sending dispatches to his Indian allies waiting outside the city, and gathering his officers together for an immediate war council. This ignoble deceit the Chochulans were planning would cost them their lives, thought Cortez...and their precious city too. He slapped Dona Marina on the behind and kissed her tenderly; again she'd proved her worth in gold, and he was pleased.

Maria lie asleep as he slipped back into the room. She was lying on her side, and the light from the braziers touched her hair and spilled over the soft curves of her body. Montezuma quietly slid into bed beside her, and began to trace his fingertips along her cheekbones and eyelids. Suddenly, he felt time slipping through his hands and he wanted her awake to share this moment, as though every moment counted. His caresses became more persistent, and she responded with soft moans and caresses of her own. As she traced the contours of his muscular back, it seemed her fingers left a trail of liquid fire. He intertwined his fingers in her hair and gently, but persistently, pulled her lips closer to his. He then slid his other hand down her smooth backside, and grasping her firm roundness he pulled her warmth into him.

What started as a gentle rhythm together, built to a crescendo of raw need...a driving force. When she whispered, "Take me," into his ear, it was as though an animal was let loose within him...an animal he couldn't control. He took her with a frenzy that went beyond need, beyond mind, beyond body.

❖

Chaos reigned throughout the city streets of Chochulan, and raging fires reflected off the shiny Spanish armor everywhere. Don Diego worked his way toward the plaza; his sword was bloodied and his right arm fatigued from the work he'd already done that night. The sound of battle cries sent his squadron down a burning street where a pocket of Chochulan warriors valiantly held their ground. Two shots rang out, and two of the warriors fell dead. Diego and several of his comrades charged into the fray, as the cry "for Spain" rose up. Again the wooden war clubs were no match for the toledo steel and armor. The last warrior fell, but not before he left a gaping wound in the thigh of one of the conquistadors.

The Spanish attack had been a total surprise. Everywhere, the Chochulan warriors had been preparing for battle, but they had not expected the attack to be on them. Groups of Indian allies had been steadily entering the city, and were now ransacking the houses or setting fire to anything that would burn. Several of them carried around jars of the native brew, as they staggered and whooped down the debris-strewn streets.

Cortez had ordered that the city be taught a lesson; and Don Diego felt a little sick to his stomach as he watched an Indian ally brutally slaughter a small frightened dog...just for being there. Gunfire roared out nearby, and he watched a screaming woman and her two young children being dragged off by a crowd of drunken, laughing men. He liked war—squaring oneself off against an adversary—and victory always tasted sweet, but this he didn't like. This wasn't manhood or honor; it was the lowest sort of animalism, and he refused to have anything more to do with it.

The far off sound of conches woke Maria from her troubled dreams. She slipped out of bed, throwing a rabbit fur blanket around her shoulders to ward off the early morning chill. It was late autumn and many of the garden's trees were half-stripped of their leaves, and in the dim morning light they had a foreboding effect. Again the conches wailed from the palace grounds, this time accompanied by drumbeats. She turned in the direction of the pyramid plaza to give her own homage to the rising sun.

Maria shivered as she remembered her dreams; she had seen war everywhere, and the whole city was ablaze. A Spaniard and an Indian were locked in a death grip, each refusing to yield. The dream brought back the vision she'd had at the pyramid...of the ending of the Aztec Empire. She rejected the feeling that the vision might now become a reality. She wanted it to be far in the future, and to never threaten the ones she loved.

The sun began to creep over the horizon, as she returned to their chambers. A ray of sunshine stole across the bed and illuminated Montezuma's handsome face. The love that stirred in her heart felt as pure and golden as the ray of sun upon his face. She reached out her finger and traced his full, sensuous lower lip. His eyes opened and slowly he captured her hand, kissing each of her fingers and drawing her body close to him. Tenderly she kissed him on the lips, and slipped her tongue into his warm mouth. Then she began a string of kisses down his neck, over his shoulders, across his chest, and ending at one of his nipples. Slowly, she straddled his hips and carried him gently to the mountain peak of pleasure. Only later as they lie in each others arms, a thin sheath of moisture bathing their bodies, did Maria's mind return to her dreams.

It was midmorning and Cortez sat in the partially-wrecked Chochulan palace. During the night's battle several of the Indian allies had stolen in and ravaged it as well. Braziers were overturned, tapestries had been ripped from the wall, and the once beautiful, gray marble walls were scarred with scorch marks everywhere. Not much was remaining; only his private quarters had been left untouched.

The same cacique who'd so politely invited the Spanish into the city—in an attempt to trick them—now sat at Cortez' feet. His old face held the horror of his ravaged city. He wondered in distress, how they knew and who had warned them. The Spanish had fought like demons, trapping and killing his best warriors while the city burned most of the night. The allies of these pale ones—the primitive jungle savages—had looted and destroyed the beauty of his city without conscience. Several women had not gotten out of the city in time, and had been brutally raped and even gutted by these savage beasts; even small children had been used as sport.

King Montezuma's message to the Chochulans had been to hold the city at all costs; but now he was a broken man, having nothing to hold the city with. He knew that the Indian allies were now combing the surrounding hills, searching for the hiding places of the Chochulan women and children. He had to do something fast...his daughters and grandchildren were out there somewhere. Perhaps he could persuade some sort of peace proposal.

He touched his forehead to the ground in the lowest form of servitude, and found himself telling Cortez it was the fault of the Aztec tax collectors. He had just wanted to be friends, but the tax collectors wouldn't hear of it, and forced him to take the course of action...action that had ended in disaster. He watched the Aztec girl Cortez called Dona Marina, as she translated for him. Suddenly, waves of anger rushed over him. It was her; somehow he knew she'd been responsible for his betrayal. He would rush a report to Montezuma, a report that would include this young Aztec girl. Meanwhile he would bide his time and watch, hoping the gods would handle this injustice.

Garlands of fall flowers gaily decorated the banquet hall. Many of the Tzin class were present, but the crowd was subdued; word of the Chochulans' fate had reached the capital. Most had never expected Chochulan to fall, and were in a bit of shock. The warriors, however, were furious; they wanted Montezuma to send an army at once to completely surround Chochulan, and put an end to these pale ones...once and for all.

This was the first time the King had appeared since his marriage to the foreign one, and now that the four-day honeymoon period was over, many hoped he would take action immediately. Again he disturbed the crowd, by arriving with the Spanish girl walking by his side instead of following him, as was proper.

Maliche sat with several high ranking Tzin ladies, all discussing the events at Chochulan. She seemed to have retained her status, and still governed the harem. She hadn't been ordered out of the first wife's apartments, and word had been confirmed that a suite of rooms for Maria was already in planning...right next to Montezuma's. The new wife had refused to live in the harem.

Maliche shook her head and rubbed her temples; times were so strange now, nothing seemed sacred anymore. At least she still had free run of the palace, she thought tentatively.

The dispatch from Chochulan had said an Aztec girl was translator for the one called Cortez. Maliche had heard the rumors. Could it be possible this Aztec girl was really her own half-sister? She thought of the last time she'd seen her.

Maliche had been a teenager when the harem conspiracy had taken place. She could remember all too well when five of her father's wives, one of her older half-brothers, and several servants were all strangled that day in the palace courtyard. The entire household had been forced to watch as a warning, and her poor father had looked on, saddened and disturbed by the whole affair. She remembered the sullen child who didn't even cry through the whole ordeal, and when her mother was strangled by the flower disguised cord the expression on her face had become flat and hardened. She'd been led away into slavery, remembered Maliche. Her mother had said that the children were fortunate to have been born to the compassionate Second Reverent Speaker; any other Aztec leader would have had them strangled, right along with their mothers.

She inwardly thanked her father for insisting his daughters become educated along with his sons. She'd never been interested in state business before, but since her talk with Cualpopoca, she'd been keeping a close eye on everything for the sake of her people. Thank goodness she'd been able to read the dispatch, even if it was disturbing.

Montezuma entered the room, and all present became still to pay homage to their King. Both Maria and Montezuma were dressed in white, their clothing trimmed with turquoise gems and white feathers. She wore her hair loose and full; by Aztec custom this would be the last time she could wear her hair loose in public, as the young girls did. Maria spotted the warrior a few tables away, and as usual he wore a disapproving scowl. She'd come to expect it of him and sadly turned away.

Montezuma led Maria to the edge of the banquet platform and lifted his hand for silence. "I wish to honor my new wife in the fashion that is customary in her own country," he said. Then he signaled the High Chamberlain forward, and removed from a small cedar chest a gold diadem studded with turquoise, jade, and pearls. It was a small replica of his own crown. Lifting it with both hands, he ceremoniously placed it on her head and proclaimed her his Queen.

Maliche was shocked. Aztecs did not crown women, she thought...and if they did the first wife would be crowned Queen. Slowly she became conscious of several people staring at her; they were stunned, and sympathetic. With pride intact, she got up from the table and left the banquet hall; her face was marked with composure. Only when she got to the empty hallway, did the tears blur her vision and her knees buckle beneath her. She leaned against the wall in misery, and after she'd openly cried for a time she noticed a figure watching her. Cualpopoca stepped forward, and wiping a tear from her eye he examined it as if it were alien.

"Do you still doubt me?" he said. "Can't you see what this witch has done to your husband, and will now try to do to the Aztec Empire? You must help me now, for the sake of the people."

The Tlaxcalan warriors moved stealthily through the battered streets of Chochulan, disguised in the simple garb of farmers carrying produce on their backs. They made their way past random Spanish patrols and headed for the steam room of the public palace, now being used to hold the Aztec tax collectors as prisoners. Afraid of Montezuma's wrath, it was the Chochulan cacique who'd organized the Tlaxcalan warriors to free the tax collectors from their imprisonment. The warriors worked their way into the rear palace courtyard, prepared for a confrontation at any moment. That night the gods were with them; the courtyard was empty, and the two sleeping Spanish guards were easily overtaken. They dressed the tax collectors as farmers and set out on their way back to the capital. This small escape would later prove to provoke Cortez into unwarranted actions.

14
A Meeting of Fate

Cortez held his breath; nothing in his life could have prepared him for such a sight. The city rose like a jewel from the surrounding lake, and even from where he stood he could see that the streets were broad and straight...unlike anything Spain could challenge, both in size and beauty. As he admired the view, again the feeling of destiny rose up from within him.

They began their descent down the mountain, and soon the Spanish columns were passing Aztec farmlands. Peasants peered out their doors, in wonder of these strange men. In the distance, Cortez could see people working on floating islands that were lashed to the shore; being a technically inclined man, he marveled at their ingenuity. As he arrived at the outskirts of the city he noticed that many of the streets were waterways, and his attention was captured by the bridge he was now crossing. He could see that it had been designed to be removable, and his mind went to work on the logistics of capturing and holding a city with such a clever form of defense.

Upon entering the city limits they noticed that several officials, accompanied by long rows of elite warriors, were waiting to greet them. At Cortez' approach, a thin, bird-like man was carried forward; rising high above his chair flew a feathered standard, depicting a green serpent.

"It's Snake Woman, the second most powerful man in Tenochtitlan," whispered Dona Marina to Cortez. Cortez smiled at the thought of this little old man being called Snake Woman, but the solemn dignity he carried soon had Cortez acknowledging him respectfully. As Snake Woman's greeting was read to the Spanish,

Cortez noticed the looks of animosity coming from several of the Aztec warriors. An uneasy feeling settled in, and he knew he would have to remain alert. These people were not short, he noticed warily, unlike so many of the other Indian natives they'd come across thus far. The Aztec race appeared as tall—if not taller—than his own, and their lofty headdresses made them tower over the Spanish.

As the newcomers were led through the streets the citizens came out to curiously examine them. Small children ran behind their mothers' skirts as the huge horses passed in parade. Cortez could see there were warriors everywhere; he couldn't even begin to guess how many. By the looks of them he began to appreciate how they'd become the rulers of the surrounding territories. Suddenly, for the first time, he had an eerie feeling that he might've made a mistake by entering the city, and that it could easily swallow him up. He squared his shoulders and called for Colorado to be brought forward. High atop his war horse he could recapture his vision; regaining his esteem he rode the rest of the way into the city.

Eventually they arrived at an immense plaza paved with a white marble so slippery that he was forced to dismount. Pyramids bordered it on all sides, and one huge one had red smoke rising from its apex. Groups of men—some in black and some in white—stood on its many stairs. Cortez was led to a smaller pyramid on the north face of the plaza, where he was invited to ascend the pyramid with Snake Woman. Cortez was amazed how fast the little, aged man climbed the steep, narrow stairs.

Once they got to the top he was led into a small building at the apex of the pyramid, and through a cloud of incense he saw a handsome man with a gold diadem atop his head. He had shiny, shoulder length, black hair; several gold necklaces hung around his neck and his mantle was made from a beautiful jaguar skin.

"Tlataoani Montezuma, First Reverent Speaker of the One World," announced the Chamberlain. Dona Marina prostrated herself, as did Sandoval; even Snake Woman fell to his face; finally Cortez relented and sunk to his knees.

Montezuma studied the one called Cortez for a moment, then ordered the group to rise.

"Welcome to my city," the King said in Spanish, before

returning to Nahuatl. Cortez knew immediately he could have only learned Spanish from Maria Velaquez. She must be held hostage here, he thought to himself. He wondered how he would be able to get her back without giving up any concessions of his own. Montezuma stood down from his throne and presented Cortez with several golden necklaces; one of them held a huge jade eagle with a carved emerald snake in its talons. Cortez in turn presented Montezuma with a necklace of red and blue glass beads.

"I understand how important the worship of your god is, so I will give you the use of this temple while you are here in our city," said the King solemnly....and the fateful first meeting of Montezuma and Cortez was over.

It had been three days since the Spanish had entered through the south gates of Tenochtitlan; reports were coming in that they were busy exploring the city, and were amusingly trying every public flush toilet, like small children with a new toy. Cortez had spent two full days in the great market trading his little glass beads, and one day studying the layout of the city. Montezuma had graciously turned over his father's old palace to the Spanish to use as their headquarters, and Cortez had settled in quickly.

The pale, late November sun shone through the audience hall as Maria sat down on the small stool concealed by the gilded teakwood screen that stood behind Montezuma's throne. Even though she'd seen him only an hour ago, her heart leaped as the King's arrival was announced. Last night she had tried to explain to him about living many lives and that they'd been together before, but he had a hard time understanding. Part of him accepted it because being with her felt so right, and then he had argued that if he'd lived before, why didn't he remember?

She snapped to attention when the High Chamberlain announced the arrival of Cortez; shivering, she pulled her shawl closer around her. He was dressed much like he'd dressed for the Easter Festival, and was accompanied by Dona Marina who was wearing a Spanish shawl and skirt. It was an interesting twist of fate, thought Maria...the two of them had virtually exchanged clothes and cultures. Also with him were two of his captains, and of course, Sandoval. Maria leaned forward at the appearance of the titan-haired man. Many nights she had gone to bed dreaming of Sandoval, now he didn't elicit a response at all. Thank goodness, she thought; it just reconfirmed there could never be anybody but Montezuma. She sat still as they began to speak.

"King Montezuma," said Cortez, "I wish to thank you for this audience and the graciousness shown to us thus far."

"What is it you wish of us?" Montezuma said.

"I, Hernan Cortez, represent the Great Emperor and King, Don Carlos of Spain, and as the King's ambassador it is my wish and responsibility to seal a bond of friendship between our two great empires and their monarchs. I feel," he went on arrogantly, "the best way to seal this friendship is for me to be your guest and to be shown the city of Tenochtitlan in royal fashion."

"I welcome a friendship with the Spanish King," Montezuma said, politely amused with Cortez' presumption.

"A friendship is based on trust," proclaimed Cortez. "My troops entered your city unarmed; on that basis, I would like a small token of trust from you."

Montezuma had expected Cortez to be shrewd and began to play along with him.

"And what would you have in mind!" he said carefully, "since you seem to have already given thought to this subject."

"I heard that the niece of the Governor of Cuba, Maria de Velaquez, resides here as a hostage." As Cortez spoke, Maria went stiff. "I would appreciate her safe return to me. Spain would smile greatly upon this action."

Montezuma's jaw tightened as he measured his words carefully, then replied. "It's true that Maria is a resident here now, but she is my wife and Queen and not a hostage."

"Of course I would like to hear this from the young lady herself," he quickly said, after the initial shock of the news.

"So be it!" Montezuma glared angrily at Cortez for challenging his word, threw up his hand to signal end of audience, and walked out.

❖

"My lady, there is a visitor to see you." The young servant stood respectfully at Maliche's door.

"Show them in," Maliche said, as she worked her gold and silver threads into the blouse she was making for her daughter as a surprise. She wondered who would come at this hour—the time most people were resting after the midday meal.

Dona Marina swept into the room, carrying herself as if she were the Queen. She wore heavy gold earrings and numerous gold and jade rings, while proudly displaying her red silk Spanish shawl. "Hello!" she said suavely.

"It's true," breathed Maliche, as her needlework slipped to the floor.

"What's the matter my dear sister, surprised to see me? Perhaps you were hoping I died in slavery and would bring no more shame to the family name?" Marina taunted.

"Mexitla, I didn't rejoice in your misfortune." replied Maliche.

"Don't call me that! Mexitla is dead, I'm Dona Marina now," she snapped.

"Is that why you can betray your own people?" Maliche asked sharply.

"Betray? I'm not betraying my own kind. My people are the Spanish now!"

It was then that Maliche realized the girl had used the herb that turned one's hair red brown.

"I seek to punish those who would ruin a young girl's life when she had done nothing."

"So you've come to destroy me? I too was young; how could I do anything to harm you?" Maliche said, trying to reason with her.

"Not you, but what you stand for. I will take my rightful place; the gods have ordained it."

"You see yourself in my place?" she laughed. "You're too late someone else already has it!"

"The gods have entered the city now," said Dona Marina ceremoniously, "and perhaps they will rule now."

"If they are gods and intend to rule," Maliche smarted back, "how do you know they will not toss you out for one of their own kind, the Spanish one who is already here?"

"Who?" said Dona Marina angrily.

"Why, Maria of course," Maliche said.

Dona Marina quickly remembered when she was first with Cortez. One of those two women who'd been kidnapped had been named Maria.

"She's just an old woman!" scoffed Dona Marina.

"Well," Maliche said, sitting back in her chair, "obviously they don't tell you everything or else you'd know she's a young, attractive girl. Now leave me. As you can see, I'm busy."

She picked up her needlework and ignored her visitor. Confused, Dona Marina finally left the room; Maliche stood and began pacing the floor. She knew she'd won a slight victory from her half-sister, but what Dona Marina had said deeply disturbed her. Did they really intend to take over and rule Tenochtitlan? She'd been living with the Spanish and seemed to imply they were gods. Could it be so? Well, she obviously didn't know about Maria; that was quite evident.

❖

"Itza, you wait here. I'll only be a few minutes." They were in the entrance foyer of the old palace. The woman promptly sat down on a low wooden stool; she had no desire to see Senor Cortez again. Maria continued down the hall, where two Spanish guards looked surprised at the approach of a young Spanish girl dressed like an Aztec. As she was ushered into Cortez' rooms she almost gagged on the stench of body odor coming from the two men. Had she stunk like that, she wondered?

Cortez sat writing in his journal, and a tallow candle burnt by his elbow. He stood in surprise, as Maria entered. She'd matured into a woman; her Aztec attire set him back as well.

"Well if it isn't our Maria De Velequez. I'm glad you're here. When we are ready to leave, I'm sure you can return with us to Cuba and your family. I believe I can arrange it with very little difficulty."

She knew Montezuma had told him that they were married, and that she wasn't a prisoner. Now, what was he up to?

"Senor Cortez," she began warily, the old tongue seeming a bit alien now. "You don't understand, I'm not a prisoner here. I'm Montezuma's wife and am quite happy here; this is my home and I have no intention of leaving. However," she went on, "as I don't wish my parents in Spain to worry any longer, I'd be grateful if you would take a message to them when you go."

Cortez sat back down in his chair regarding Maria with cold eyes.

"Young lady, it's my opinion you're neither old enough or experienced enough to make such a decision for yourself. And as far as this heathen marriage is concerned, it was not sanctified by the Holy Catholic Church, therefore it is null and void...which amounts to you living in sin with this savage. And if you think I intend to leave you here like this, to shame your family name, you'd better think again."

"How dare you have the nerve to speak to me of shame! You're married and you sleep with that Indian interpreter; and don't tell me you don't because I saw you together," she said furiously without discretion. "And I know you're not the Spanish Ambassador. You disobeyed my uncle and you're here illegally, so don't play games with me!"

Cortez' face hardened with anger. "You've been separated from us a long time now and you don't know what's happened. I'm the representative of the Spanish crown."

"I don't believe you," blurted Maria.

"My dear, I don't care whether you believe me or not. It doesn't change anything, and I have no intention of sitting here arguing with a child parading as an adult."

Maria turned on her heels and stormed from the room without saying another word. But inside she seethed...vowing somehow she would put a kink in Cortez' plan. She slowed her pace when she realized she'd lost her temper. What was it about that man that always caused such discord within her?

Maliche had pulled the black shawl close around her face, so she wouldn't be recognized slipping out of the palace. She'd spent the day thinking about what her half-sister had told her, and she knew she had to speak with her again. Entering the old palace had been easy; the guards weren't challenging any women that looked busy. She didn't know how she'd find Dona Marina, but at the sight of a familiar figure she withdrew down a darkened corridor. It was Maria! What was she doing here? Maliche dreaded the possibilities. Maria looked angry and seemed in a hurry; then Maliche noticed the door she had exited from. She could just see through the open door…a smug Cortez lounging in what used to be the old King's chambers. Had he and Maria been secretly meeting? This could only mean no good. Then it was true…she was in league with the hairy foreign ones! She knew she couldn't tell Montezuma; he'd never believe her. She would seek out Cuolpopoca immediately. Her womanhood was aroused as she thought of him.

Warriors gathered from all over the city. Some crept in stealthily—not sure of the honor of this meeting—and others came boldly and defiantly. They were at a merchant's house on the far side of the market. Approximately forty warriors sat in the reception chambers with more arriving every minute.

Cuolpopoca paced back and forth. He wasn't unloyal to the King, and he hated to do things secretly like this. But he couldn't wait any longer; the information Maliche had given him a few days ago confirmed his suspicions.

As they entered the reception chambers, several of the rash young men were angrily discussing the Spanish in their city; these he knew he already had on his side. It was the older, more experienced warriors—the Eagle and Jaguar Knights—who sat back making no opinion, these were the ones he would need to sway. Cuolpopoca boldly walked to the center of the room.

"My brothers! A great disgrace lies heavy upon our heads. The foreign ones have entered our city and we've welcomed them with open arms. They've proven they are enemies to the One World Empire, yet there are some who believe they are gods!"

Hoots and catcalls rose up from the younger men, and Cuolpopoca raised his hand for silence. "I do not believe they are gods. They do not act as gods would; and could you imagine a god smelling like a cesspool? If they are gods they will understand if we behave as our divine guidance dictates. They will understand if we challenge them, but will they understand if we behave like a bunch of old women?"

"We're not old women!" shouted some of the men, not enjoying the insult. There was a mulling in the room, and Cuolpopoca turned to notice some pochteca merchants watching at the doorway. This meeting concerned them too; even now some areas of trade had been affected by the Spanish.

One older, well-respected warrior stepped forward. "What you are suggesting is treason! The King has welcomed these men as his guests. Montezuma has always been a good ruler and a worthy warrior. I for one will not do anything disgraceful to dishonor him."

Several of the older knights gave their hearty approval.

"I hold much honor for my brother, Montezuma," said Cuolpopoca, "but now he is bewitched and is not responsible for his actions."

"You have proof of this?" asked an Eagle Knight.

"My eyes are my proof! First he dishonors an Aztec princess by taking the foreign one as first wife, engaging in unseemly behavior such as that embarrassing crowning of a woman; then he invites her people into the gates of our city, after what they did to our brothers in Chochulan. The so called new Queen," he said with contempt, "is obviously a witch!"

At this, the room erupted in chaos; it was some time before order was restored.

Tetertzin, the Captain of the Eagle Knights, who up until now had sat quietly saying nothing, spoke out. "This Spanish woman, Maria, isn't it true she resided in the temple of the Mother Goddess, and was befriended by the High Priestess? I think our High Priestess has the ability to discern evil. And isn't it true she was honored at the Great Pyramid as a priestess? I do not believe she is a witch, and I'll take no part in any action that will dishonor Montezuma."

With this he got up and walked out; several of the other knights followed suit. Cuolpopoca watched in dismay as they left. He'd been afraid this might happen.

Turning to address those remaining he said, "I assume the rest of you agree with me; our empire is in danger and it's up to us to protect it!" The men shouted in support. "We'll watch and be ready; we'll be the guards of our people. I promise you this...the time will come to act, and when our brothers see we are right, they too will join us. This place will be our headquarters; now go in this trust."

❖

The day was cold, and she was wrapped in a fur cape. Maria was filled with a special excitement; she still loved this day in spite of everything she'd been through. It had been Sandoval who delivered the invitation for she and the King to attend the Christmas festivities, and she in turn had invited Chimalma to join them. She'd been apprehensive about Cortez, but when Sandoval assured her that he meant no harm, she succumbed. Of course she really didn't believe him, but she would lay her mistrust aside for the birthday of her beloved Jesus.

The old temple of Huitzilopochtli, which had been given to the Spanish for their use, had been transformed into a Christian shrine. A wooden cross had been erected over the roof of its apex, the statue of Madonna and Child was erected inside, and the scent of copal had been replaced by frankincense. Dozens of tallow candles created a smoky haze, as the rough conquistadors kneeled in front of the altar.

As the priest announced, "He is born! Joy to the world!" the whole chapel rang out in song with peace on Earth goodwill to men. Even Montezuma seemed impressed. After the mass he told Maria that he wished to learn more of this Jesus Christ. Once Montezuma heard the story, he decided Jesus really did resemble their god, Huitzilopochtli.

A cold north wind blew off of Lake Texcoco on this gray Christmas morning, as Cortez and Sandoval escorted the King and his party down the pyramid. It seemed to blow right through Maria's rabbit fur mantle and chill her bones. Even though there had been peace in the city since the arrival of the Spanish, a growing sense of foreboding was bothering Maria. Life went on in Tenochtitlan as it always had; even now, a jovial Cortez was explaining to Montezuma that all he would like to do is to arrange trade agreements, and a friendship between Spain and the Aztec Empire, before he left.

Cortez kept his distance from Maria, and gave no more signs of intending to drag her back to Spain against her will. Sandoval made several conversational contacts with her and was polite. At one point he quietly asked her with an urgent look in his eyes, "Are you sure of what you're doing?"

"Of course," she responded coldly. He turned away to join Cortez, and then she was sorry for having been so sharp with him. He was her only buffer with Cortez; she would make an effort to be more cordial.

The small group began forming at the bottom steps of the pyramid. Her beloved Montezuma cut a magnificent image against the steel gray sky. The white fur mantle he wore, along with his thick black hair, was offset by his gold diadem that was set with pearls as big as a thumb. Maria admired his classic profile as he stood casually conversing with the smaller, somberly dressed Cortez.

Dona Marina stood calmly while translating, but she was quite aware of the smoldering looks Cortez kept giving the cool High Priestess. An anger began to burn in her. Cortez always had a wandering eye, although invariably he'd return to her. But this was different; the looks he was giving Chimalma filled Dona Marina with painful jealousy. She knew the High Priestess was known to be celibate, but still she remained uneasy and alert. She pulled herself to her full height and carried her most haughty expression, hoping to appear equal to the stately priestess. She felt greatly relieved when the King withdrew and returned to his palace, taking the priestess and the red haired one with him. She would be glad when they returned to Vera Cruz. She didn't like this city. It held the presence of death, but whose she couldn't tell.

"Gold!" The cry rang up and down the halls of the old palace. Men ran from their rooms in all directions shouting the news, until the palace resembled a frenzied beehive. Soon men were rushing into Cortez' outer chambers with axes, bronze brazier stands, and anything handy to disassemble a wall. The jasper stones were yanked from the wall, and the ragged gap grew until the light revealed gold everywhere the eye looked. Chests were brimming over with thousands of tiny gold currency hatchets, necklaces, bracelets, rings, and the heavy gold earrings favored by the Aztec noblemen.

Cortez entered the alcove with a look of disbelief on his face; the room held a king's ransom. In some places the chests were piled as high as a man, and in addition to the gold there were baskets of pearls and emeralds, some as big as a man's fist. Silver vases held jade jewelry, and baskets of brilliant feathers were in excess. The gold was covered with a thin patina of dust; it obviously had lain undisturbed for quite a long time. Cortez thought to himself, could it be that these people have so much gold, they can just store it away and not even care?

It was he who had noticed that one wall in his reception chamber seemed to be constructed a bit differently than the rest. He knew he was staying in the rooms that had belonged to the old King, and he figured perhaps the reception chamber wall concealed a secret passage. For several days he had searched for a secret door; then finally he had ordered two of his men to tear out one of the blocks in the wall. Now he stood numbed by the shock of his find.

He doubted that even His Majesty, King Don Carlos, had this much gold in his treasury; and yet the Aztecs could afford to just throw it away as they did. A plan began to form in his mind, as a madness took over him. Already, all over the old palace one could hear the smashing of rock and the thuds of the blocks as they were pulled from the walls. The insanity of the Spanish had taken hold. It had begun.

❖

The young apprentice held the copper bowl as she shifted from one foot to another in the youthful dance of impatience. Chimalma took a deep breath to calm herself before she placed the last delicate blossom in the altar arrangement; then she took the bowl from the young girl and sent her on her way. These days everyone seems on edge, she thought. The old temple attendant stood just outside the door, waiting to catch the high priestess' eye.

"Yes, what is it Quenta?" she said.

"Visitors," she replied, "the Spanish one called Cortez." Then she dropped her voice and whispered, "And the Aztec girl who serves him."

Chimalma quenched the irritation that began to rise up inside of her. What was he doing here, she thought? He was the cause of the current unrest in the city; ever since he'd knocked down the wall concealing the palace treasury, the pale ones were reportedly attempting more and more outlandish things. She'd actually heard they'd been questioning many of the palace attendants as to the size and whereabouts of other treasure vaults belonging to the King. Her brother had told her yesterday that one of them had been caught trying to pry a golden disc from the walls of Quetzalcoatl's temple, and she sensed that these pales ones were about to become even more rash. Chimalma straightened herself, pushed back a loose strand of her ebony hair, and went out to see what Cortez wanted from her.

The heels of his tall Spanish boots clicked on the creamy yellow, stone floor as he paced back and forth. He pulled the heavy, dark cloak around him against the chill of the winter day, as he waited. The winters were colder here than in Cuba, but at least they weren't as cold as they could get at his childhood home back in Spain. He remembered how the howling winds would beat against the bare branches of the trees in the courtyard of their home. He would wrap himself in blankets, shivering constantly in the big, old, drafty house that could never get warm enough. He would sit and dream of riches and conquest that would make the Cortez name honored and known throughout Spain. Now he stood poised to capture the glory and riches he'd dreamt of. They were just within his grasp, and he wanted it...he wanted it all!

Soft footfalls stirred him around as Chimalma entered the audience room. The afternoon light made her flawless skin appear golden and warm; her legs were long and sleek, and she was at least as tall as he was. Dona Marina sullenly got to her feet to translate for Cortez. He greeted her formally and watched her full mouth and perfect, white teeth as she replied.

He began to pace again—this time out of need—for how could he tell the High Priestess he wanted her? He tried to put into words that the reason for his visit was out of goodwill for her people, as well as his. He found himself proposing a special alliance on behalf of both Aztecs and Spanish...an alliance that would have the two of them working closely together. Cortez became irritated with Dona Marina; her voice was sounding angry and hostile as she translated. He hoped she would translate correctly, perhaps he'd made a mistake in bringing her. Maybe he should've depended on De Aguilar's rapidly improving Nahuatl, but it was too late now.

"Why are you approaching me with a matter better meant for the King?" She responded with her cool, throaty voice, but he had hardly noticed. He was busily studying her full breasts, and imagining what her nipples would look like. When he looked up, both women were staring at him in cold contempt. He wished he knew more of the language, so he could dispense with the girl all together. If he could explain his feeling and his concern for her people, he was sure he could drive home his point. After all, she was just a woman, and he'd always had his way with women. It wasn't like she was a nun; he'd heard the priestesses in the city did it in the name of whatever idol they worshipped. So why shouldn't it be with him?

But for now, it appeared the situation wasn't in his favor. He should've known he couldn't get a proper response with another woman present; now all he could do was make a graceful exit. So he offered his friendship, and promised her that if she ever needed him, he would be there. He bowed with a flourish, and departed with an angry Dona Marina in his wake.

Trying not to use the blade of his sword, Alvarado fought his way into the tight knit group of fighting men. Three of his comrades were trapped at its center…a screaming, tugging, cursing knot of bodies. This was the third time he had to lead a patrol on rescue of his comrades. These sneaky heathens attacked when least expected; already six Spanish men had been murdered by the savages, and no one ever seemed to know who was responsible.

Suddenly, an angry face loomed in front of him. As his attacker prepared to strike, Alvarado's instant reflex brought the flat of his sword down on the man's head, and he slipped to the ground unconscious. When he reached the besieged men, two were severely wounded and the other lie still on the ground, with streams of blood running across his head and face. Alvarado stooped down and raised his eyelids; the glazed over look told him he'd been too late. He let out a roar of anger, and almost without thinking, he ran his sword through two of the nearest Aztecs. Several of his men followed suit, and a scramble ensued as half-naked warriors rushed to escape Spanish steel.

The riot spread as Alvarado's patrol chased the Aztec men into the great market. The one Alvarado was after purposely knocked over a display of glazed pots, forcing him to dance and weave through the rolling pottery. The two men ran through a poultry stall, sending dozens of gobbling turkeys and frantic, quacking ducks every which way, adding to the surrounding pandemonium. A small boy ran in front of Alvarado and he swept him out of the way, ignoring the boy's cry of pain as he connected with the hard stone of the market fountain. The fleeing man ran over blankets spread with fresh chilies, and was suddenly tripped by a low rack of drying spiced meat. As his adversary tried to disengage himself from the wooden slats, Alvarado drove his sword up under the back side of his rib cage where it found its mark. The Aztec man staggered two more steps, and then collapsed in a heap at the feet of a middle aged woman, carrying a basket of dried, ornamental corn. She dropped her basket, and screamed a blood-curdling scream that carried over the already noisy din of the market. Alvarado wiped his sword on a discarded shawl that was nearby, and walked from the market; he was pleased to have gotten his mark, regardless of whether or not his victim had been the man who'd killed his friend.

Court was somber this morning; news had reached them of the deaths of several more civilians at the hands of the Spanish madmen. Montezuma sat with his usual impassively masked face, but his thoughts were in turmoil. How could he get these pale ones from his city without causing the death of anymore of his people? True, he could strike in force with his warriors, but he'd prefer using tact before slaughter. He would risk no more Aztec lives. Just this morning a heartbroken, young husband had stood before him sobbing; his bride of only several months had been caught in one of the riots spawned by the insane greed of the Spanish. She had fallen, and her pelvis was crushed by the hoofs of the beasts the pale men rode. She—never to walk again or bear children for her young husband—had taken her life during the night.

Pleas were coming in from all over the city. He knew that some of the riots were being instigated by a group of outlaw warriors within the city; he also knew they were attempting to force his hand to fight. But sadly, they couldn't see what a battle within the city would be like for the innocent. If he could only get the Spanish away from the city itself, he would turn his forces on them and wipe them out for good! He was quite sure now that they weren't gods; he wasn't even sure if they were human! They desecrated temples, stole from the market, killed nobles at night for their jewels…and no one ever knew who did it.

"Hernan Cortez," the High Chamberlain's voice rang out. Cortez wore his breastplate, armor, and helmet; he also had high, thick, leather boots to protect his legs. With Dona Marina by his side to translate, he strode forward. Barely stopping long enough for a short, quick bow, he began addressing the King straight away. All those present gasped at his audacity, and his insult to the throne. He may have been the Foreign Ambassador, but no one behaved that way before the King when he was in audience. Montezuma held his temper, took a deep breath, and allowed Cortez to continue.

"King Montezuma," he said, "it is my duty to inform you that there are warriors within your city that are traitors to you. They attack my soldiers, who they know are your guests; this is a personal insult to you and to the Spanish Crown, which we represent."

Montezuma let him run on, amazed at his ability to twist the truth.

"My good King," he continued, "we have heard that these same warriors intend to assassinate you. We can't let this happen. We've sworn our friendship to you, so we propose that you become our honored guest in the old palace, where we may protect you. After all, we can't be sure if any of your guards are involved in this treasonous plot. May I add, this would show the people your friendship with the Spanish Crown, and perhaps they would see that you don't support these traitors. I don't want anymore of your people being hurt; you see I love and honor your people as my own," he embellished. "But we must put down these insults to you and the Spanish Crown with as heavy a hand as possible…. and so you see to avoid anymore injury, this plan is the most suitable solution."

Some of the courtiers held their breath in amazement; these pale ones were crazy and intended to get crazier.

"Of course you should bring your servants and wives," he went on. "And we'd be honored if you would consider holding court in the old palace; naturally you still need to run your empire. I will await your answer." He bowed unceremoniously, and then exited without a single word coming from Montezuma.

Montezuma dismissed the court and returned to his personal chambers. His warriors' blood burned hot for revenge. His heart ached for the misery of his people, yet his head remained cool. He knew this invitation was nothing less than his imprisonment.

Maria lit the brazier, threw on pieces of copal to thank the Goddess for the day, and then walked out onto Montezuma's balcony. The night's sounds rose in a symphony to serenade her, but Maria could not hear. She had heard of Cortez' visit that afternoon, and she felt anger at the very Spanish blood that ran through her veins. After audience Montezuma had entered his private chapel, refusing to see anyone. Now Maria had come to her husband's rooms to stand vigil until he returned.

When the half-moon was at its zenith in the night's sky Montezuma reappeared. If he was surprised to see Maria sitting and waiting in a dark corner, he didn't say it. He looked tired and his face was pale under its copper coloring. She offered him a cool drink of water and he thankfully drank it, as his sad eyes glanced up and down her frame. Then inviting her into the warm, strong circle of his arms, he stood holding her for a long time before he spoke.

"You've heard of Cortez' visit?" he asked her solemnly.

"Yes my love, it makes my heart so angry!" she said. "When will you crush him?"

He stood back away from her, and held her face between his hands.

"I can't attack him while he's in the city."

"But why?" she said, not understanding.

"He would kill rashly; he's not an honorable man. He strikes down children and women, as well as warriors. He's placed several of the city's orphans within the old palace, and if they are attacked at night he'll use them as human shields."

He stood quietly studying Maria's face. "I'm going to take him up on his offer."

"What?" Maria stepped back away from him. "Are you mad? It's not an invitation; it's a trap." She began to rage, and paced her fear and pain into the floor. "He's using you.... can't you see that?" she cried.

"Be still!" He grabbed her by the shoulders to silence her. "I can't attack them in the city, and I can't let this go on. Too many innocent lives are being taken. They must be stopped; I fear for my people. If I go into their custody, I can buy time until I figure out how to get them out of the city. And in the meantime, the warriors will stop fighting if they see I've gone in good faith."

Maria began to sob uncontrollably and her tears fell freely. Montezuma picked her up and carried her to the bed. He lay holding her until she'd sobbed herself out. Gently he kissed her tears away; soon his kisses ran down her neck and played across her breast. Maria relaxed and her breathing came full and easy.

"Well at least I'll be with you in the old palace," she said.

Montezuma tensed, and then raised himself to meet her eyes.

"You can't," he said softly.

"But he invited you to bring your wives!" she said. He placed a finger on her lips to gently quiet her.

"I want you to go live at the temple during this time."

"But why? Don't you want me to be with you?" she moaned softly.

"Of course, my heart aches at the thought of your absence. But I need to remain clear-headed, and if you're under the same roof with Cortez I won't be able to, for fear of what he might try and do with you. I cannot bear to think of loosing you. Please my love, I'll feel best if you're safe at the temple. Now come my flame haired Jaguar Woman, let your eyes glow with the fire of passion, that I may be warmed for my imprisonment."

Silently she cried tears of sorrow, as she pulled her body close to him. She kept hearing the voice of the Mother Goddess saying she was to serve by Montezuma's side, yet now she was being ripped away. At last she relented to his passion and warmth, and let him drink her up. The soft light of the brazier wove purple highlights into his hair and burnished his skin. She knew she would recall this moment forever. Shivering as he slipped his fullness into her, he drove all the thoughts from her mind. A cry of unison...and deep within the moist depths of her body she felt a light fuse.

❖

She paced the courtyard; she was furious with Cortez, with herself, with the world. How could he treat her like that? No matter what, she was still an Aztec princess. Even if she despised the Aztecs, she deserved better treatment; he wouldn't even be here if it wasn't for her. Dona Marina pulled her heavy shawl up over her head. The night wind quickened and the first silvery stars were making their evening appearance. She had to get away and think. She wasn't going to let any woman upset her place...priestess or not.

Yesterday, when they were returning from visiting the High Priestess, he'd told her that her jealousy had gotten in the way of a important alliance. She'd blown up, accusing him of trying to seduce the priestess, and having no loyalty to her. He'd just looked at her with cold eyes and told her that she wasn't his wife, and that he wasn't going to let a whore tell him how to run his affairs.

A panic had blended with her anger. If he dropped her, she'd have no place of honor with either the Spanish or Aztecs. She knew he had a Spanish wife in Cuba, but he'd told her that he didn't love her. He'd told Marina that he loved her instead, and she figured that he would eventually put his wife aside for her. But now he was calling her a whore! What was she going to do? She had to get away and think...figure out a way to get him back by her side. She slipped out of the garden and through the gate, dressed to blend in with the women of the city. The night was still early, and she would come up with a plan.

The cacique had sat watching from the doorway all day; just waiting...waiting for something he could use against the pale monsters. Having personal interest in seeing the destruction of the Spanish, he'd come from Chochulan to see what he could do to help the besieged capital. They had destroyed his beautiful city; his people were starving; many of them had no permanent homes; and the cries of his people were in his head, even while he slept at night.

He spotted a young, plainly dressed servant woman exiting the gates of the old palace where the Spanish were headquartered. He decided to follow her; perhaps she could be made to spy for him. The woman made her way toward one of the public city parks and paused by a platform at the edge of a pool. Families out for an evening stroll were lolling by the braziers to warm themselves from the winter chill. She moved in close to warm her hands at a brazier that a young couple had just left, while he blended into the crowd nearby.

As she stepped up to the flame, he caught sight of her face. It was the traitor! Hatred had burned her image into his mind permanently. He could recognize her anywhere! Fingering the bone handle of the dagger strapped under his mantle, he withdrew into the shadows and waited for her to retrace her steps, so he could take his revenge.

It was time for her to be getting back to the old palace, she thought. At least she'd had no problem mixing in with people. She would come here regularly and gain valuable information for Cortez; that would increase her worth to him. The street leading back to the old palace narrowed and became dark. She was so lost in thought that she didn't even hear the sound of footsteps from behind. She was just in sight of the gate...when a hand clamped onto her arm and whirled her around. An older, hate twisted man stared into her eyes.

"Traitor!" he hissed. Just in time, she saw the shiny blade coming down to meet her flesh. She screamed and twisted, as the blade sliced into her shoulder with white hot pain. She struck out with her good hand, raking his face with her fingernails and leaving him momentarily blinded. She twisted loose and screamed for Cortez. The garden gate burst open, and out ran a Spanish patrol. She ran crying toward their welcome presence. Clutching her shoulder, she glanced around to see how close her assailant was. He turned and ran from the approaching Spanish patrol, but not before Dona Marina recognized the face of the ruler of Chochulan.

It was late the following afternoon, when the Captain of the Guard at the old palace ran from the gate and yelled, "Get Commander Cortez." As he began to open the gates wider, several other guards materialized to help him. The procession was led by many of Montezuma's palace guards; servants followed loaded down with boxes and baskets, while several women and courtiers were carried through in sedan chairs. Bringing up the rear was a magnificent, golden sedan chair; peacock feathers adorned the high rising back canopy. On it sat a somber faced Montezuma, looking neither left nor right. Then the gate swung shut behind him, sealing the fate of the Great Lord of the mighty Aztec Empire.

15
Dark Secrets

"Sandoval!" roared Cortez. "Come here now!"

Sandoval was sitting at a green marble table that had legs carved to represent coiling serpents. He'd been working on the tallies of what had already been obtained, and setting aside the King's one-fifth. He was well aware that the King's treasure was their protection against disobeying the governor's order; if the King made enough, all would be forgotten. He also intended to reserve a portion for Velaquez, enough to salve his wounded pride.

At the note of pain in his friend's angry voice Sandoval got up quickly, followed Cortez into his reception chamber, and shut the door to guard against eavesdropping ears.

"Read this." Cortez swept a parchment from his desk and pushed it into Sandoval's hand. "It came with a runner from Vera Cruz this morning."

Commander Cortez
February 20th, 1520

Your Excellency, two days have past since an envoy sent by Governor Velaquez arrived here in Vera Cruz. Its leader, Captain De Narvaez, has orders to capture you and take you back to Cuba to stand trial for treason and kidnapping. My Lord, many of your ship captains and crews are siding with Narvaez. They fear they've been stranded here and will never see their gold.

Sir, I would advise that you return at once, for I fear all will be lost. Senor Narvaez intends to march all the way to

*the capital and inform the Aztec King you are an outlaw
bandit. I will try and detain them as long as possible, but
even now they are preparing to depart. Godspeed.*
                                        Your Captain,
                                        Pedro De Gomez

"Velaquez probably sent that viper Narvaez, hoping that the
snake would find an excuse to execute me on route," Cortez raged,
"then he won't have to get his own hands dirty."

"He must know about Maria if he's charged you with kidnapping," Sandoval said, after reading the parchment.

"Of course he does. And I'm sure he knows it was the Aztecs
and not us who did the kidnapping. It's just another excuse for him
to get his hands on all our gold; after all, he never made the charge
until word reached Cuba about the gold I'd found."

"He may not have formally charged you," said Sandoval, "but
a man must protect his family's honor."

"Well, what do you expect from me? I can't help it if she stowed
away on my ship! And I sure can't let that bastard come here and ruin
all I've built. Alert our allies. Half our forces will leave with me for
the coast immediately."

"Do you wish for me to remain here?" Sandoval asked, as he
stood preparing to leave the room.

"No, I need you with me at Vera Cruz. Alvarado can hold the
city." he said, without looking at him.

"Are you sure? Alvarado can be quite rash at times."

"Custody of the city will be calm enough."

Cortez, who'd been anxiously pacing, stopped to look at
Sandoval, and a smile spread across his face.

"Gather most of the gold. We'll use it to turn Narvaez's forces
against him; then we'll use one of his own corracks, and send it
straight to Spain loaded with the King's fifth. I know Captain Delez
can be trusted with such a mission."

"What about Narvaez?"

"After I teach the bastard a lesson he'll never forget, we'll send
him back to Cuba along with that brat, Maria. That should soften
Velequez's family pride," Cortez said sarcastically.

"I don't think the King will just let you take Maria," said Sandoval.

"How's he going to know?" smiled Cortez. "He's here at the palace, and she's at that heathen temple. They don't even communicate; I've had them watched."

Cortez walked to his desk and picked up a gold Aztec bracelet studded with cream colored pearls.

As he traced its workmanship he said, "It won't be hard. I'll get her out of the temple on some pretense, and she'll be whisked from the city before she knows what happened."

"I hope you're sure of what you're doing. Montezuma might become outraged," Sandoval warned.

"He'll get over it," Cortez exclaimed with a wave of his hand. "He's got at least a thousand women in his harem, he's not going to miss one...and certainly not that troublemaker."

After watching them together on Christmas Day Sandoval wasn't so sure, but he held his council.

The warm spring sun felt good on her back, as Maria sat embroidering to calm her mind. She chuckled as she slipped a stitch. How she'd changed, she thought...resorting to needlework for relaxation was not the old Maria.

A door to the courtyard opened and several chattering young girls exited. She didn't recognize any of them. The temple was full of new girls now; so many of the girls she'd studied with had gone home. Toxca was still here, but she was usually tongue tied around Maria since she'd married the King. Yesterday she had spoken with Taka, who had moved back home. She planned to be married next moon, and Maria would attend. But now Maria felt lonely; she was a priestess with no priestess duties, and the temple routine had no place for married women. Now that all the girls were in awe of her, she knew how Chimalma must always be feeling...everyone afraid to approach her. She'd grown even closer to the High Priestess these last few weeks, but she missed Montezuma terribly.

Looking up with the approaching sound of laughter, she spotted Itza slipping around the corner and chattering with her other attendants. How she loved the woman so. She had explained to Itza that she needn't act like a servant anymore, but she wouldn't have anything to do with the idea. She took care of Maria and that was that.

The old woman had been beside herself with joy ever since Maria's wedding. All she talked of was Maria's children and how she would help raise them. Itza had said she was sure they'd be in the temple only a short time before Cortez left; then they could return to the palace, and life would go on as usual. Maria wasn't so sure. She couldn't shake the vision of destruction that was shown to her in the Great Pyramid. Another sense of urgency seemed to be warning her, but what could she do?

A gentle breeze bathed her in a shower of loose cherry blossoms falling from the tree above her. She was brushing the blossoms from her lap when a temple messenger approached her.

"There's a visitor to see you. He waits in the reception chamber my Lady." The messenger bowed and waited for Maria to rise. Maybe Montezuma has sent a message from the guest palace, she hoped. The anticipation of seeing him again carried her with a light step.

With excitement Maria hurried into the reception chamber, but when she saw who it was she stopped short. Cortez nervously fingered the edge of his ruffled cuff as he paced the reception chamber. When he forced a smile a warning bell went off in her head. Stepping forward, he reached for her hand and placed a kiss on its back side. Turning on his charm, he explained that Montezuma desired to see Maria at the guest palace. Noting the cautious look on her face, he rushed to explain that since Montezuma had been his guest, his admiration for the King had grown deeply. In fact, he now considered himself a good friend of the august ruler, and he felt it was his duty to make amends with his wife. He expressed sorrow at all the unfriendly encounters they'd had in the past, and to prove his change of attitude he'd offered to bring the message himself. He would even come this evening to personally escort her; this way it would be obvious to all concerned that she was free to come and go at will. Then he hastily left, adding that he would return before the meal hour.

A mounting feeling of unease carried her back to the courtyard bench. She wanted to believe that he really had made friends with

Montezuma; then he might just leave without causing anymore trouble. But her priestess intuition told her otherwise...and she would act accordingly.

Later when Cortez returned to get Maria, he was informed that she had disappeared. The surprised look on the face of the temple guard, as well as the genuine concern of a young girl who was looking for Maria, convinced Cortez she wasn't in the temple. He returned to the guest palace to see if she had come there, but she hadn't. The little witch, he thought...why did she seem to be such a source of constant unrest for him? He would have to leave without her; his forces were assembling just outside the gates of the city waiting for him. Command had already been transferred to Alvarado, and Cortez needed to leave under the cover of night. After all, he couldn't allow the Aztecs to see how much of their gold he'd taken with him. He would have to send Maria to Velaquez later.

Two figures witnessed Cortez' departure that night. The first pulled his mantle over his head, so no one would recognize his face; Cualpopoca had quit leading raids on the Spanish since they held his King prisoner, but he never stopped watching and waiting. The second figure sat in the shadows and observed the men pass on the opposite side of the temple gates. As she pulled herself up to her full, stately height, she looked skyward to examine the positions of the stars overhead. She quickly retraced her steps to the temple's inner sanctuary, observing that the stars had marked a victory, but whose...it was unclear.

"Maria, you can come out now." The throaty voice drifted to the girl sitting in the alcove behind the sanctuary altar.

"Are they gone?"

"Yes," Chimalma assured.

Maria breathed a sigh of relief and leaned momentarily against the door lintel. "I've made Cortez an enemy tonight, but when the voice of the Goddess came warning me not to go, I knew I must hide."

Chimalma watched the young girl as she spoke...her eyes wide, the slight quiver of her chin; she was still very young to be playing such an adult role. She gently smoothed Maria's hair, knowing that for Maria it was not nearly over.

"You must find Toxca and tell her you are well; I'm sure she is quite frantic by now. I didn't tell her you were hiding. I didn't want her to have to tell an untruth to the Spanish Commander. Besides, he's astute enough to have noticed if she had. Now goodnight." Chimalma returned to study her star charts. She wanted to be ready. There were many powers lying dormant within the inner priesthood, maybe now was the time to activate them.

The man stopped brushing the chestnut mare. She would deliver soon, he noted, as he smoothed her swollen belly. Cortez was wise not to take her with him, he thought. Alvarado brushed the sweat from his face; the sun was hot today. He looked up as the sun glinted off the breastplate of the approaching guard.

"Captain Alvarado," the man said, standing at attention, "there are some Aztec Lords who want to see you, they sent you this sir."

The guard opened his fist, revealing a handsome golden chain with alternating links that held bright emeralds.

Alavarado held up the necklace, admiring the craftsmanship. "Admit them," he said.

The three old men approached respectfully. They stopped a few feet away and apologized for disturbing the Captain's afternoon, but they had a request to make. An Aztec festival was approaching; it was important to the well being of the city. They had tried to speak with the King about it, but he had canceled all audiences for a time. They were hoping the Captain would approach the King or give his permission for the festival to take place. After they skillfully played to the vanity of Captain Alvarado, he gave his permission. Fortifying him with several gold trinkets, they took their leave.

He thought he had outsmarted Montezuma, assuming that the King didn't want the festival to take place so his subjects would stay in discontent. He would give them what they wanted and thwart the King's intent by assuring goodwill between the Spanish and Aztecs, but just to be safe he would mount the two big cannons on the wall overlooking the plaza; he would have his men on alert ready to act if anything happened. He wouldn't tell Montezuma what he'd done, that way the King wouldn't have time to circumvent his decision. Arrogantly pleased with his plan, he returned to his quarters with his gifts of gold.

The day was stifling. May had struck with a vengeance... no gentle spring warning, but right into the tempest of summer. Maria sat by the garden pool, her bare toes playing with the spongy stem of a water plant. She scooped up handfuls of the cooling liquid and splashed it on her legs and shoulders, allowing it to run deliciously down the inside of her blouse. She had finally fallen back into temple routine, and today her heart was full of joy. Montezuma had sent a message; this night she was to have dinner with him...a banquet at the old palace. She hadn't seen him in several weeks.

She was walking in to plan her attire, when she saw the High Priestess motioning to her from an open doorway.

Chimalma's brother, Mayatzin, was with her and Maria hugged him close. She had come to care for the gentle High Priest of Quetzalcoatl.

"We have an idea, come look," Chimalma said, unrolling a sheet of heavy bark paper, so old its edges were starting to flake and crumble. The outlines of several buildings were clearly visible, interspersed with what looked like dark paths connecting through them.

"This," she said, pointing with her long, slender finger, "is the temple here, and there is the old palace." Pointing to the paths she said, "These are underground passages that were created when our forefathers built Tenochtitlan. Wherever they could, they connected the palaces and temples to these underground passages that lead out of the city. Being at war much of the time, they needed ways to get the reverent speakers and priests out of the city secretly if necessary."

"Now our plan," Mayatzin said, taking over, "is to get the King out of the old palace through this passage," he explained, as he began to trace his fingers along one of the lines, "then along this route and out into the countryside to regroup. Then the warriors can free the city while Cortez is away."

"But these passages are in the lake," Maria said, squinting at the map.

"Under the lake," Chimalma corrected her.

"I had no idea they even existed. Are they used often?"

"They haven't been used in many generations," Mayatzin said solemnly. "They've been forgotten for the most part. It was these maps that I found in the recesses of our temple that reminded me of the existence of the tunnels."

"But it's quite possible that many of them are flooded or destroyed," said Chimalma, "that's why we'll have to explore them first and find out. We don't want to alert anyone else of our plans until we are sure. But we'll need you to inform the King tonight when you're with him."

"Agreed! I'd like to help you explore the tunnels too."

Mayatzin and Chimalma looked at each other with concern.

"It could be dangerous," Mayatzin said. And we don't know what might be there after all this time."

"Well I can't stand waiting around anymore. I've got to help do something!" Noting their hesitancy, she said sternly, "He's my husband."

"Yes, you're right," said Mayatzin. "You're part of this too. We're just concerned for your safety; after all, you are the Queen."

"Good," she said. "Now if you'll excuse me, I must go prepare for this evening."

As she entered the banquet hall that night she saw many of the nobles cramped around their tables, and some of the Spanish were present in the back of the hall. The old palace banquet hall wasn't nearly as large as Montezuma's. As she was escorted behind the royal dining screen her heart seemed to explode when she saw her beloved. He was dressed all in white, from the top of his peacock-feathered headdress to his white and gold sandals. Tiny opal beads sparkled over his mantle and loincloth, and to Maria he looked like a god.

He gathered Maria into his arms and drank deeply from her eyes. As usual, when he kissed her she melted, but she perceived a dark countenance about him. When he released her and she took her seat beside him, she could see a tired look in his face. He remained silent and stared off at the screen. Her heart began to sink...what was wrong with him? Then she realized that many of the girls from his harem had been with him all along. The astounding beauty of the young women was unnerving, she thought, as she watched them serving him scented napkins and offering him dishes of food. Could it be he no longer loved her? Something was definitely amiss; he had never stayed so quiet and within himself. She couldn't stand the silence.

"What's wrong?" she asked.

At first he didn't stir, but then he pulled himself together.

"Alvarado has given my people permission to hold the Sacred Warriors Festival in a few days," he said warily.

"This is bad?" she asked, relieved that it didn't have anything to do with her or any other women.

"I had made myself unavailable for the purpose of preventing the festival from taking place," he said, beginning to let his anger move. "But now it's too late to stop it, too many arrangements have been made. It would dishearten the people too much to forbid it now."

"But why would you want to stop it?" she asked, leaning forward in puzzlement.

"The event honors Huitzilopochtli. Sometimes it can turn violent, and even out of control during the best of times. Many new warriors are given honor during this time, and they've been fasting and preparing for days now. The city is tense enough as it is, anything could happen. I sense the Spanish will not understand, and there seems to be nothing I can do to stop it. It's in the hands of the gods."

He looked forlorn. Hoping to lift his mood Maria moved her chair closer to him, and lowering her voice against eavesdropping ears, she shared with him her news. "Chimalma and her brother have a plan. They've uncovered some maps that reveal tunnels running underneath the city. They believe we can slip you from this palace into these tunnels, and out on the other side of the lake. There you could lead the warriors on a attack to free the city before Cortez returns."

His mood seemed to lift, but "perhaps" was all he said.

The day dawned bright and warm. Big yellow pennants honoring the Sun and War God were displayed all over the city. The streets were filled with merrymakers, all anxious to put the depression lurking in the city out of their minds. High above the crowd the black robed priests of Huitzilopochtli offered the golden gilded sun dagger to the sky, and then plunged it into the chest of a captured sacrificial warrior. The heart was expertly cut from its protective shield of ribs, and still wildly pumping, thrown into the sacred fire. The torn body of the sacrifice was pushed down the stairs of the pyramid to the cheering crowd below...thus began the festival.

Several of the Spanish soldiers watched from the high walls of the old palace. Some of them turned away in disgust while the rest remained to watch the morbid festivities. Soon a procession began at the base of the pyramid. Singing children carried sun colored streamers; they were followed by musicians and singers from the House of Song. Lithe young dancers in short yellow dresses stomped and gyrated down the street. Then came scores of young men hoping to become future elite warriors; they were the pride of Tenochtitlan. Dressed simply in loincloths and browbands with a bow strung over one shoulder, their eyes glowed bright from the excitement and the days of fasting in preparation for this day.

Manuel Jemez shifted his weight to lean on the long pike handle; his armor and helmet gleamed in the sun. Regardless of the heat—which was rapidly becoming intense—Captain Alvarado had ordered all guards to be fully armored. Secretly he wished to be as coolly dressed as the throng below him. Stepping to the edge of the wall, he watched with interest the scantily clad young women dancing and gyrating their hips in the streets below. Lifting his gaze to the pyramid summit before him, he watched a column of smoke rising from its apex. It verified that the heathens were still at work with their disgusting activities. He'd watched body after body tumble down the side of the pyramid this morning, with the crowd rushing forward to dip their clothes in the gaping holes of each sacrificial victim. He was sick with their behavior, yet somehow he found himself being caught up in the crowd's exciting frenzy.

He could just make out Captain Alvarado's form in the garden behind him. A grim look masked his face. He's probably worried that Cortez will have his hide for allowing this heathen festival, he thought. One of the padres was yelling and pointing to the pyramid. Good, he thought...he didn't mind watching Alvarado squirm; he didn't like the son of a bitch. He may be a good captain, but

Alvarado was just plain vicious, thought Manuel. He didn't trust him; the man would sacrifice anything or anyone to achieve his goals. Turning back to the crowd, he caught the painted face of an alluring young woman looking up at him. A smile spread across his face, as the whore winked and rolled her shoulders to better display her crimson covered breasts. Regretfully, he pulled his eyes from the inviting encounter. Alvarado would shoot him if he caught him dallying with a whore on guard duty.

Now the flanks of the new warriors were approaching his post. A peculiar admiration stirred within him. The pride shining on their young faces reminded him of himself as a young Spanish soldier. The first time he put on his armor, helmet, and high boots, he was on his way to wealth and honors in the new colonies discovered by Columbus. The voyage over had rung out his guts, and the pox carried by a moor slave had left its life mark upon his face. Since then he'd seen jungles, wars, and a hard life, and still hadn't seen his wealth and honors. Eyeing the abundance of gold on the people below, he thought that was all about to change.

Shrill cries stirred him from his daydream. Far across the plaza throngs of warriors rushed the fringes of the crowd. The people shrieked and scrambled to clear the way for the fierce, painted-faced men in their three foot, feathered headdresses. Confused, Manuel glanced to the young warriors below for a clue.

They remained still a moment longer before answering with war whoops and shrieks of their own. The crowd near the wall became a mass of running, screaming humanity. Behind him he heard Alvarado yelling to make himself heard over the din. "They're attacking! Fire the canons!" he ordered.

The wall trembled as the first of the loaded canons roared. Only too late did Manuel realize that the cries of the crowd and the war whoops were all in jest for the festival. But as the canons exploded, they were soon replaced by earnest ones. Manuel tried to prevent the slaughter by running along the wall screaming for them to stop. He futile watched one old woman crumble in a pool of blood; a young mother screaming, her arm a mass of lacerations as she tried to protect her already dead infant; a farmer valiantly attempting to protect his two small children against the panicked stampede, but he too went down with the roar of the next canon. It was complete mayhem.

At last Alvarado realized his mistake. Even after he hurried to stop the canons, it was too late. When the smoke began to clear they saw broken bodies of warriors, men, women, and children all heaped together. People were slipping on the blood glazed streets; screaming women were crying for their babies; and young husbands and wives were frantically searching for their loved ones. Even the hardened Spanish war veterans were sickened by the slaughter.

Manuel seemed dazed by it all; the shouting and crying deafened his ears. Aztec faces registered shock, disbelief, pain, and sorrow at the wreckage around them. Nearly a thousand lie dead or dying. The crowd had been so tightly packed together, there'd been nowhere to run. Most of the older Aztec warriors had been out of canon range, and as they made their way through the crowd, he could see their faces go from disbelief to anger with this latest of Spanish atrocities. Manuel's stomach knotted; he knew this mistake would cost the Spanish dearly. From the corner of his eye he saw one of his comrades pitch forward, clutching his neck. The thin, feathered shaft of an Aztec arrow had found its mark, and the retribution had begun.

❖

Maria gingerly stepped over the bodies. She could see Itza in the distance cradling a child with heavily bandaged limbs; her graying head lowered as she reached for the cup of herbs to quiet the child's pain. Maria's arms felt like lead, as she pushed back a curl from her tired forehead. The herbs were almost gone; Chimalma had sent several of the young girls into the countryside to try and find more. The temple courtyard itself looked like a battle zone, with injured lying everywhere. She had not slept more than twelve hours in the last five days.

Her heart seemed ready to break as she reached down to close the eyes of a small boy, no more than five years of age, who'd finally given up. She had to get away for a moment or two; all this senseless death was taking its toll on her, and soon she'd be no good to do the healing work. She walked near the front gate, allowing the refreshing twilight air to calm her. She knew the High Priestess would be calling for her soon. She stopped to get a drink of cool water, hoping to quench the nausea in the pit of her stomach.

A group of shouting warriors carrying torches and spears ran past the temple gates. Instinctively she knew they were after some Spanish soldier who'd foolishly left his guard down. The warriors had been rioting nonstop since the outbreak five days ago. And except for all the death, she was glad; perhaps now there'd be an end to the Spanish manipulation over the Aztecs. She yearned for Montezuma, and was afraid for his life. Knowing that he was locked inside the old palace with the Spanish made her furious, and there was nothing she could do. Just then, she saw Chimalma calling her to council at the inner sanctuary.

No matter how he worded it, his report sounded dismal. Alvarado sat at Cortez' desk, attempting to scrawl a message to be smuggled out to Cortez. For five days now they'd been besieged. The Aztecs wouldn't let up day or night. The canons continued to rest upon the walls, but his men couldn't get up to them; Aztec bowmen waited outside the walls for a sniper chance. His men were tired and hungry, provisions were low, and the palace servants kept disappearing and taking food with them. The only servants left were those taking care of the King.

A banging on the door heralded the arrival of one of the Spanish cooks, who unceremoniously dumped his dinner on the table and left. The dark, stringy meat looked about as appetizing as a slosh pot. Lately, they'd been killing the zoo animals within the palace walls for a source of meat. He didn't want to think about what his dinner once was.

He knew that everyone considered him to blame for the mishap. These stupid heathens wouldn't listen to reason, it had only been a mistake. He offered Spanish soldiers to bury the unfortunate...what else did they want? By God, he would show them! Somehow he would capture some of the savages and make an example of them.

Maria joined Chimalma in the sanctuary, and she perked up with interest as the priestess closed and locked the door behind her. Just then Mayatzin stepped from the shadows, his dark traveling cape effectively hiding his priestly garments. Chimalma produced two more capes for Maria and herself. Mayatzin used the tall brazier to ignite two pitch-covered torches, while Chimalma reached under the altar cloth. A quiet click, and the massive altar of the Mother Goddess rolled backward revealing a square opening. Stone steps led down into the inky blackness. First Chimalma entered, then Maria, and Mayatzin brought up the rear.

The steps ended in a small chamber. Stone shelves holding scrolls, gold statues, jade incense burners, and other ritual objects covered three walls. But the fourth wall was what caught her attention…it was a full length mural of the Mother Goddess. The Mother stood with a tree branch in one hand and a human heart in the other; the sun—with the face of her son within it—enfolded her from behind; a snake was her headband, and an eagle stood adoringly at her feet; below her, the faces of the Aztec people looked up to her and her sun/son for guidance. The mural was magnificent…and she gasped in awe.

Chimalma lit another torch that hung in its place on the wall. After she tore her eyes from the mural, Maria noticed all was clean and orderly. "I don't understand. I thought you said these tunnels and rooms were forgotten!"

Motioning for her brother, Chimalma took the map from her waistband and spread it out on a small stone table in front of them. "We're not in the old tunnels yet Maria; this is a chamber under the sanctuary. All the temples have one, but only the High Priest or Priestess knows its secrets."

"In the secret chamber under the altar of Quetzalcoatl is where I found the map," explained Mayatzin. Mayatzin studied the map, and then went to a shelf that was level with the Mother's head, just to the right of the mural. Raising his hand, he began to probe the shelf's edge. Maria noticed the large obsidian dagger tucked in his waistband.

"Yes!" he exclaimed triumphantly, as his handsome face broke into a big smile, and a seemingly solid piece of the shelf slid out noisily. He then pushed on a section of the mural, and Maria watched in delight as the solid stonework began to pivot inward. Mayatzin and Chimalma—each carrying torches—entered with Maria walking in between them.

She could see right away that for the most part, the tunnels were made from a pre-existing cavern system. Cream-colored walls held striated mineral deposits of all sizes. Symbols were carved in the walls, but their meaning was virtually obliterated by the ceaseless dripping of water across them. As their eyes continued to adjust to the lighting they saw three tunnels, all heading in different directions. Mayatzin studied the walls—running his fingers over the carvings—before picking the right hand tunnel. Ducking low, he led the women into the maze.

The floor was uneven and several times Maria stubbed her toes on loose stones. A bone chilling cold pervaded the air and she pulled her cape close around her light temple smock. Dripping water echoed everywhere. She shivered as they stopped for Mayatzin to study the map. Several more tunnels branched in different directions, and as they moved on it became quite apparent that they could become lost at any moment if they weren't careful.

All of a sudden Mayatzin stopped so abruptly that Maria ran into his back. Before them loomed a huge chasm in the earth…a sheer drop with the sound of rushing water far below. Chimalma pointed to a narrow ledge to the left. As Maria inched along the wall, her eyes tried to pierce the darkness below; she couldn't even guess how far of a drop it might be.

Now the ceiling was right above their heads and Maria thought of the citizens of the capital going about their business, entirely unaware of these amazing caverns below their city. Just then, movement all around her feet frightened her. She let out a scream…something seemed to be climbing on her ankles. Mayatzin laughed as he lowered his torch to see mice scurrying away from her feet.

Chimalma put her hands on Maria's shoulder and said, "Remember you're a priestess now. A priestess must use her inner strength at all times."

Finding more of the symbols to follow, Mayatzin led them down a passage that ended at a masonry wall, much like the one in the temple's secret chamber below the altar. He slid his hand along a stone ledge, and again a quiet click gave way to hidden handholds for pulling the stone door open. A narrow corridor with passages to each side opened in front of them. As Mayatzin was about to start down the passage, Chimalma, who'd been studying the map, grabbed his arm. They noticed several raised stones in the floor; reaching his torch out in front of him, he gave the stones a shove and a piece of the floor fell away. The tremendous crashing of rocks below had them all covering their ears. At the same time, the ceiling overhead rang out with the muffled sounds of running feet.

Someone was speaking Spanish just above them...they were right below the old palace! Maria signaled for silence so she could listen to them. The Spanish began testing the floor with heavy thumping, and her heart rose to her throat. If they were discovered it would end all hopes of rescuing Montezuma, and most likely the three of them would be imprisoned as spies. Maria began praying to the Goddess, as the pounding got louder and chunks of dirt started dropping from the ceiling onto their heads.

They could hear more people running into the room above them. Then she heard, "Captain Alvarado! There's been a breach in the wall and there's fighting in the courtyard."

"You idiot," she heard Alvarado say. "The crash came from outside the wall, not here!"

Maria went weak with relief as the footsteps above them retreated. She translated what had been said, thanked the Goddess for intervention, and they were on their way again.

Choosing another side passage, Mayatzin guided them to a set of stone stairs covered with lichen. A huge spider as large as a fist darted from the torchlight. Mayatzin pushed the webs out of the way as he ascended the slippery steps. Taking the dagger from his waistband, he probed a dusty ledge until he found a latch, and the same faint click was heard. Maria joyfully started up the stairs, assuming this entrance joined the room that Montezuma was lodged in. Mayatzin grabbed her arm and pointed to a spot over the doorway. Sometime in the past the door had been battered down, then hastily repaired. The mortar was cracked and flaking; already several small stones had tumbled from their mountings. Mayatzin whispered, "The door should only be used once. We'll try it when we're actually rescuing the King." He led a disappointed Maria down the steps, clearing away the rest of the webs as he went.

Further on, Chimalma spotted an old discarded torch lying in a forgotten niche. The wood of the handle was pitted, but the heavy coating of pitch still looked good. She picked it up, touched her flame to it, and it roared to life. She handed the spare torch to Maria. Mayatzin also saw a discarded torch, and stuck it in his waistband for any possible emergency.

Maria moved on ahead, and as she entered into what looked like the main passageway she noticed what seemed to now be a well finished wall. Spotting a side entrance to a room, she reached her torch out in front of her to get a peek inside. She gasped with disbelief! Chimalma found her standing against the wall, looking ashen and faint. When Maria pointed to the room, she too glanced inside.

The room's contents cast a warm glow that reflected from the torchlight. It was gold! gold everywhere…golden nuggets, gold plates, bracelets, rings, noseplugs. Gold headdresses held disintegrated traces of white feathers…gold cups filled with pearls, emeralds, and jade. A larger than life size statue of a god wearing a sunburst headdress dominated the center of the room. But what caught her attention was a line of human skeletons slumped against the far wall; they were dressed in crumbling swatches of dusty, faded cloth…some still clutching the slender, feathered shafts of their demise.

Looking back at the statue, Chimalma gasped as she recognized who it was. "It's Tan, the Father of the Sun!" she said. "Legends say he was the one who taught the Toltecs how to build the Sacred Pyramid to the north. He was the secret husband of the Mother Goddess."

"Tan!" Mayatzin's deep voice whispered, as he joined them. "So it's true, the statue does exist. I wonder if it still has the power to speak."

"What do you mean?" asked Maria. "Who was this Tan?"

"He was the father of the Sun God, Huitzilopochtli. When the Sacred Pyramid was opened, this statue was found in the stargate chamber. A great many miracles were attributed to it, then it disappeared. I always thought it was a legend," Mayatzin said reverently.

"Well, now you know where it disappeared to," Maria smiled.

"Come," she said, not fully understanding their awe of the statue, "it's time to move on. We still need to find an open tunnel leading out of the city."

They went single file down a passageway for what seemed like hours…sometimes going downhill, sometimes up. Sometimes the walls were stonework, and much of the time the walls were natural caverns. After a long downward stretch it began to get damp. A thin trickle of water was now accompanying them downhill, splashing over tiny pebbles that littered the floor and making the footing slippery. They reached a fork in the tunnel, but the incessant water had long ago washed away the wall symbols that guided the way. Even the map was unclear about which fork to take. Sensing at this point that both ways led out of the city, it was decided that Mayatzin would take one fork, and Chimalma and Maria would take the other.

No more than thirty paces down their tunnel, they discovered a huge boulder blocking nearly the whole passageway. The two of them had to press themselves against the damp, moldy walls of the cavern to get by. On the other side of the boulder, several more tunnel openings greeted them.

"We'll have to try each one of them systematically," sighed Chimalma.

The first passage was blocked with rubble after just a few feet. The second one had a puddle of water that became deeper and deeper until they were walking in knee-high brine water before finally turning back. At the junction, Maria wrung out her cape and dress as Chimalma chose a third tunnel.

The wet garments clung to her legs, and her drenched sandals sloshed and squeaked as she walked. The cold seemed to penetrate to the marrow of her bones, and the nausea was back in the pit of her stomach. She wished she could be like Chimalma…poised and assured no matter what was happening. Looking around, she noticed the tunnel they were now in seemed to be getting dryer. She wondered if they'd made a wrong turn, and were actually heading back toward the city instead of under the lake.

"It's getting lighter!" she heard Chimalma voice out. And sure enough, a faint grayness lie just ahead propelling them onward. Almost before they knew it they had reached a small cave with a pebble-strewn floor, just high enough to stand in while bending over. "We made it!" they cried together. They did what hadn't been done in hundreds of years.

The cave was on a small hill overlooking miles of farming milpas, with the thatched roof huts of peasants clustered together in the distance. The smoke from the evening's cooking fires drifted up through the gathering twilight; they'd been in the tunnels all afternoon. Chimalma stopped Maria, as she started to pull away some of the vines and tall grasses covering the mouth of the cave. "No, leave them," she said. We don't want the tunnel noticed from the outside." Then, after pausing a few moments to catch their breath of fresh air and to familiarize themselves with the landmarks outside, they started back down the maze of tunnels to join up with Mayatzin.

As they traveled back up the tunnel, Maria noticed a mark in the wall that she hadn't seen on their way through the first time. It was a handprint carved in the wall. Something about it caused her to stop. Her hand seemed to move of its own accord, fitting perfectly into the impression. The moonstone and amethyst ring on her finger seemed to pulsate at the contact. "Look Chimalma," Maria cried out excitedly. "The print fits my hand! Chimalma?"

That's when she realized she was standing in the tunnel alone. Chimalma hadn't noticed that she'd stopped. Maria turned from the wall, and was hurrying down the passage to catch up with Chimalma when she noticed the fork. Which one had she taken?

"Chimalma! Chimalma, where are you?" she cried out. She called out several times, and then listened; but all she heard was her own voice echoing back to her. She started to worry, and an unsettling feeling began to come over her. At last she chose a tunnel, hoping it was the right one. Hurrying down it, she found it was blocked. Turning on her heels she fled back up and turned right, but that led to a dead end as well.

Now she'd done it, she thought. She was lost and she couldn't even find the way back from where she'd come. She stopped several times to call for Chimalma and Mayatzin, but only the echo of her own voice came back to haunt her ears. Maybe she could try and find the exit again. It wasn't too far away, and once she was out she could always walk back to the city. She kept her eyes wide open for the hand print in the wall that would tell her she was at least in the right tunnel.

As she rounded a corner, a huge underground cavern spread out before her. Delicately hued stalactites hung from the cavern ceiling, and answering stalagmites formed fantasy shapes on the cavern floor. Maria's heart plunged all the way to her feet. They hadn't come this way or passed anything like this. Now she knew she was truly lost.

She couldn't seem to quench the rising panic in her, as she turned to run back up the tunnel she had just come through. She spotted a fork ahead and hoped it was the right one. It didn't look familiar, but then nothing did at this point. As she ran down the right hand tunnel, a still damp sandal strap caught on a stone below her feet and suddenly she found herself pitching headlong in the air.

Somersaulting forward, she caught her hands on a rough ridge while her torch was flung from her grasp and continued falling. In spite of her best intentions she let out a bloodcurdling scream, as she realized she hung over an abyss and was suspended by her finger-tips. She watched her torch falling faster and faster away from her, until it disappeared into the inky darkness. Tears of fear filled her eyes as a piece of the ledge gave way. Her fingers were screaming in pain from her body weight, and as she kicked to get a toehold, her body was assaulted by the pain of her knee hitting a jagged outcropping. The warm blood began dripping down her leg and her fingers began to slip from the strain.

A cold, numbing fear was pulling the strength from her young body. Her mind was telling her it was now useless, and she should just let go. Out of nowhere the face of Montezuma appeared, and seemed to be giving her the strength to hold on. She rejected the siren call of indifference, and summoning the last bit of her strength she swung her leg up over the ledge. She blocked out the pain when the outcropping slashed and grazed her legs as she rolled back from the ledge.

She began to cry helplessly; she didn't want to die here all alone in the pitch cold darkness. Then a warm feeling started to fill her, and suddenly she wasn't alone…it was the Mother Goddess. Maria thought she heard her say it would be all right. As she started to calm, the voice grew clearer and louder. She could hear the Mother Goddess calling Chimalma's name. Then she heard voices...not in her head, but far away. Maria held her breath and sat up to listen better. It wasn't her imagination; a faint glow brought a rush of relief, and the dear voice of Chimalma calling out her name.

Maliche slipped into the doorway and let the armored men pass. The torchlight caught the golden hair of one of the men, and she gasped. She stepped back and pulled the shawl closer around her face. It was Alvarado..."the crazy one," as they were now calling him. She had a right to be in these halls, but if he saw her, he would drag her back to her husband's quarters or to the harem; then she would surely not get back out of the palace this night.

She had important information for those who fought in the city. She waited for the men to pass, and then slipped out a door and into a side garden. A clump of pyracantha bushes gave coverage when a Spanish patrol passed in the gardens. There were now so many of these awful men out on patrol since the siege began, that she wasn't sure whether she'd be able to make it to the hidden door in the garden wall, or not. When the men rounded the corner she stood to dart away, but as she broke out in a run, her dress snagged one of the sharp thorns and ripped. Hidden by the darkness of the new moon, she hurried across the lawn. Maliche didn't want him seeing her in torn clothes, but it was too late to go back. Besides, this was the only dress that she had that resembled what the peasants wore.

She jumped behind some rose bushes and listened to the women singing in the room above her. She wondered if Montezuma would notice her absence. Would he even care? She decided the answer to both those questions was no...if the answer had been yes, she wouldn't have been out there in the first place. He only cared that she kept his household running smoothly. The darkness hid her tears, as she slipped through the garden wall.

The streets were in chaos...warriors ran everywhere, and fire burned in small clusters. She could hear the sound of battle raging in the distance. She stopped one of the young apprentice Eagle Knights and questioned him. "Where is the headquarters of the

Eagle Knight, Cuolpopoca?" she asked.

The tired face of the young man took in the simple, torn dress of the woman in front of him, and noted her regal bearing. Could it be the First Wife, he wondered? He decided it was none of his business if a Tzin was dressed as a peasant; he'd seen stranger things in the streets as of late, and he pointed the way.

Numerous braziers were burning at the home of a wealthy pochteca who'd given up his house to serve as battle headquarters. The place was swarming with the elite warriors of Tenochtitlan, and Maliche's heart swelled with pride as she was ushered past the strong, capable men. Surely they would save the city, she thought. She was given a seat in the back of a room filled with warriors, and allowed to listen to the meeting going on there.

She was warmed by the sight of Cuolpopoca as he paced the meeting room. She watched the play of muscles under his bronzed skin. He wore only a simple loincloth against the warm, late spring night, and a set of gold armbands encircled his muscular upper arms. He was as beautiful as Montezuma, she thought. Before Cuolpopoca took command of the room he allowed the others to report their news, and then he spoke.

"The siege is near success! The pale ones are tired and trapped behind their walls. Their food is gone and the allies are pinned down outside the city limits and can't help. Now all we have to do is attack and wear them down...all day and all night if we need to. There are many of us and few of them. We will attack until we win!" His words brought cheers from the men.

"But what about the King trapped inside under their guard?" a man in the back of the room asked. "Won't we put the First Reverent Speaker in danger?"

"That is why I've called this meeting," Cuolpopoca said. "New information has come to me concerning exactly that. This morning the High Priest of the Quetzalcoatl Temple came to me with a plan. He knows a way to get Montezuma out of the city through secret means."

Cuolpopoca had no intention of letting the tunnels become common knowledge before he had a chance to explore them for himself.

"In the country, we can again regroup and the King can personally lead an attack to liberate the city. And before Cortez returns, we can then march to the sea and destroy the rest of the pale ones."

"Why not lead the raid yourself? Isn't it true you no longer have honor for the King?" one of the young, brash warriors called out.

"Who said that?" The room grew silent. "I honor and love our King. I'm not a traitor," he said angrily. "I just desire to see him set free of the Spanish witch's spell."

Maliche gave a great sigh. She too wanted Montezuma free of Maria's charm. Ever since she'd returned to the temple, the King had been finding constant flaws with his other women; he hadn't even called another to his bed since he'd married her. His other wives—now angry with his indifference—fought and bickered amongst themselves, making Maliche's job twice as difficult.

When she heard Cualpopoca call an end to the meeting she lowered her shawl from her head. His eyes met hers…first registering surprise, and then what appeared to Maliche to be a lustful warmth. Would he make her feel wanted again, she wondered? Would he make her copper colored skin acceptable, and bring her womanhood alive again? Her breathing came in short breaths, as he motioned her to join him outside the meeting room.

"You shouldn't be here," he said. "Too many know the face of the King's First Wife."

"I had to, I bring you important information." The tone in her voice softened him. He could feel the woman's heat from where he stood. He sensed her need, her hurt. "Cortez has started back," she said.

"What? I'd hoped for more time."

"The word in the palace is that he is finished at the great water and is already on his way." It now warmed her heart to play the part of informer. Cualpopoca swiftly turned back to the meeting room, and called back one of his fellow knights to give him new orders.

"We'll have to get the King out now; send word to the High Priest of Quetzalcoatl." Turning back to Maliche, he said, "It's late, let me find you a guard to take you back to the palace. You're too valuable to the cause to have harm come to you."

"I won't be missed now," she found herself saying with mixed emotions, as she reached out for his warm arms. She hated to act like an Auianime, but she couldn't control the longing that raced through her. His eyes widened with caution, and then took on a second quality of calculation. Looking around to make sure no one was watching, he led Maliche down the white plastered hallway to his chambers.

The soft light of the brazier cast shadows on them as they embraced. Cualpopoca pulled off Maliche's dress and buried his head in her neck. She took the pins from her hair, allowing it to tumble down her back. He hastily yanked off his loincloth and plied his hands over the curves of her body. Grabbing a handful of her thick hair, he forced her backward as a rage took over. She was part of Montezuma, but he now possessed her and no one could stop him.

Maliche sighed as he took control of her; she liked his roughness, his virile way. He buried his hand in her hair and tried to push her mouth to his swollen manhood, but she resisted him, knowing what every good Tzin lady knew not to do. Then he jerked her around and pushed her legs open...she knew he'd be a strong lover. She gave a small cry as he entered her. She pushed a warning bell to the back of her mind to make way for the fires too long banked.

He whispered in her ear his love of all things Aztec, his distrust of the pale ones. The fire started in her groin and spread to her whole neglected body. His movements became more and more frenzied, carrying her to new heights never shown to her by Montezuma. Suddenly, as they reached the peak of their lust, with ecstasy and agony he cried out the name, "Maria".

Maliche's pleasure turned to ashes. No, no...how could it be? He hated the pale ones. The cry of a tortured heart erupted from her lips, and she pushed the heaving man to the side. Stinging tears made it hard to see, as she stumbled pulling on her torn dress. Draping her shawl over her head, she fled headlong into the unforgiving night. Sobbing, she ran back toward the palace. Small stones cut into her unfeeling bare feet as she ran. Why had she ever come out this night? Her heart threatened to burst with exertion and pain. She'd thought like a warrior...now she felt less than the dust on the street.

Suddenly, she was surrounded by shoving, yelling men, as a torch flashed across her field of vision. Without realizing it, she'd ran into the thick of the raging street battle. Turning, she met a line of yelling, painted faces…their midnight dark obsidian war clubs raised and threatening in the air. A panicked scream erupted from her. As she turned to flee, a slashing pain ripped through her stomach. Looking up the long metal pole, she met the dark, surprised eyes of the young Spanish soldier, whose pike she had impaled herself on…as the dark curtain of death claimed her.

Cortez sat high atop his horse as the men filed past. His eyes turned to the water one more time; the ship was far out to sea, a black dot on the horizon. The other ship left for Spain yesterday, laden with the King's gold and a promise for more. He knew Captain Deinda would wait near the coast until the evening brought a favorable wind to Cuba. He wasn't sorry for what he'd done to Narvaez. He glanced to the group of padres wiping dirt from their hands as they descended from the hill, which held a group of new wooden crossed graves.

Cortez watched as the last group of horsemen—led by Sandoval—arrived from the still smoking little hamlet of Vera Cruz. The quiet man saluted and reported all was ready, as he shaded his eyes to see the corrack sitting on the horizon.

Will it be enough, thought Cortez? With the promise of more to come, De Velaquez will forget he ever heard of Narvaez…let alone that he sent him to imprison me. It's too bad his niece couldn't have been on that ship with the treasure, that would have appeased him; the little minx will be on the next one.

"Come friend," Cortez said, "we have a long journey ahead of us. News has just arrived, they're still under siege at the capital. It's good Narvaez' men like gold more than they like him."

"But will they be loyal to you?"

"Put them in a city with a bunch of screaming Aztecs who are after their hides, and the promise of more gold than they ever dreamed of, and their loyalty will be assured. Come!" He laughed as he pounded the other man on the back, "I feel lucky today."

❖

Maria ran to the pottery basin retching; her stomach was a raging inferno. Suddenly, she heaved last night's meal. Itza found her there, dejectedly clutched in her own arms. "What's wrong little one?"

"Itza, I'm sick."

Worried, the chubby woman waddled over to feel her brow, and eyeing the remains of last night's dinner, she broke into a delighted laugh. "You not sick, you making baby." She chuckled while patting Maria's tummy.

"Oh Itza, I'm not pregnant," Maria said sullenly, still miserable. "It's been months since Montezuma and I ..." Then she remembered there'd been no moon cycle for close to two months now. She'd been so occupied that she hadn't noticed. "Itza, I think you're right."

She found herself lifted off the stool by a delirious Itza babbling about being a grandmother. Itza then shot out of the door, intent on informing the rest of the temple...the rest of the city if possible.

Maria stood placing her hands over the previously unnoticed, slight swell of her stomach. Montezuma's baby...she a mother? A wonder came over her. A mother! She was now seventeen, and she realized it was early June; she'd turned seventeen five months ago, in January. She had forgotten all about it. Then a darkness passed over her...the Spanish were still in the city, and Cortez was on his way back. In two days they were to get Montezuma out of the city. If they failed what would happen to this child? They couldn't fail!

❖

Mayatzin pushed the door open slowly, as he watched the unstable masonry overhead...the masonry held. Maria and Mayatzin breathed easier. They had waited for another battle outside, so its noise would perhaps cover theirs. By luck, a heavy tapestry hung over the wall and concealed the door; a large overhang gave them about a three foot gap to hide in. Peaking around the tapestry, Maria was delighted to see several of Montezuma's personal things. The gods were with them...this was his chamber. Maria motioned that she would wait, while Mayatzin went on ahead to mark the passages.

While she waited she toyed with how she would tell Montezuma of the child. She didn't have to wait long; voices and the sound of sandaled feet announced the King's arrival. Peering around the corner she watched the wives—who had obviously just served him dinner—light the brazier for the coming twilight and remove his sandals. One went to prepare his evening bath, while the other started to undress him. They moved as seductively as possible, hoping to catch his eye. The slight movement of the tapestry brought his warrior senses to the surface. Spying Maria's pale face, he dismissed everyone from his chambers. He closed the door, and thought his heart would melt as her lovely form appeared around the tapestry.

They flew into each others arms...their lips a torrent seeking relief in the other's flame. His need for her was so great, he wanted only to carry her to his leopard skin covered bed and never let her out again. But sadly, she stopped him, "They will be here soon, this is the night you will leave this palace, my beloved."

As they waited, she told him of the tunnels. He held her closer when he heard of her narrow escape from death. She ended with informing him that she carried his baby. She watched his face as she made this last statement. The joy...the love...the longing in his dark eyes was almost too painful to look at. Tears glittered there as he kissed her hair, her chin, and rested his head on her breast. His gentle hand warmed her tummy.

They started at the sudden, loud noises of running feet in the hallway. Montezuma pushed Maria behind the tapestry just as the door burst open. The torches in the hall reflected off the Spanish warriors' armor. One stepped forward, and removing his helmet with a flourish and bowing low, he said, "Forgive me Sire. I was worried for your safety."

Cortez! Maria slumped against the wall. How did he get here so fast?...they were too late. She wanted to scream out her frustration. All was lost, her arms flew protectively over her stomach.

16
Death of a King

The gates swung open and the tired patrol bolted for safety. The din outside built to a crescendo at the sign of an opening. Just before the gates were bolted shut again, two Aztec arrows whizzed through the air...one finding its mark in a young soldiers arm, the other buried deep in the thick wooden gate door. The feathers of the shaft hummed its anger.

"Sir," a tired captain said, as he approached Cortez, "we couldn't get any farther than the edge of the plaza. The heathens are everywhere...they're crazy. This is the third reconnaissance I've sent out and none have gotten any farther than the plaza. Just when it looks quiet, the savages appear out of nowhere."

Cortez needed a rest...a chance to plan a retreat out of the city. He needed to obtain more supplies; those he'd brought from the coast wouldn't last much longer. Most of his Indian allies had either escaped back to their villages, or were pinned down outside the city. If he'd known they were pinned to the south, he would have taken that route back into the city and used his cannons—if necessary— to free them. He'd thought the siege was over, judging by the way the Aztecs had let him enter Tenochtitlan with no opposition, then they'd closed in on them once his men had passed through the palace walls. He could kick himself. He should have been expecting something like this. For a second, he wondered if fortune had turned on him. Was this the end?

No, by God!...he thought, as he reminded himself of his vision. He'd get out of this, and he'd win. He had to! Besides, he still had Montezuma. He'd have him speak to his people; after all, the King wanted peace too. He'd speak all right. If he didn't, Cortez would turn the cannons back on the city...starting with that precious pyramid of theirs! If he set the cannons for long range, they could easily hit the pyramid from the palace walls.

"My love, go now," Maria begged. She spoke low so the Aztec girl, Cortez' interpreter, couldn't hear her. She glanced at the partially open hall door where Cortez and the others waited. "Tell him you need a few hours; you can sneak out the secret passage. We'll go back to the temple. If you wait in the chamber below this room, we'll find you and lead you to safety. Cortez won't even know until it's too late."

Maria couldn't squelch the rising tide of panic that had started as soon as she heard that Montezuma was going to speak to the city. Something felt very wrong. She'd come to the palace demanding to see Montezuma. As Cortez was leading her to the King's chambers she recognized desperation in Cortez, and had sensed the need for urgency. Montezuma would have to sneak out the secret exit now, even if Cortez was waiting just outside the door. Tears of frustration filled her eyes and she began to cry.

"Shhh, they will hear you." He laid his fingers on her lips, a supplication for silence. "You are the most precious thing in my life, but I have my responsibilities as the First Reverent Speaker." He turned to pace, and as he spoke the dying sun shone through the terrace doors, igniting crimson sparks in his dark hair and glinting off his golden armbands. "I will not be used against my people any longer!"

The intensity in his eyes frightened Maria. "What are you going to do?" she whispered. The uneasiness in her stomach turned to stone.

He studied every detail of her face and hair, gathered her in his arms, then abruptly turned on his heels and headed for the door, where an impatient Cortez waited. She watched Montezuma's departing back through tear filtered eyes; she knew suddenly she had to follow. Jumping up, she bolted for the doors that were swung shut, barring her passage by Montezuma's orders. She ran to the terrace door, but could see nothing over the high inner garden walls. She could leave through the secret passage, but Cortez knew she was here. If she disappeared, he would tear the very walls apart until he found the passage. She stepped behind the tapestry to make sure no visible evidence of the door remained. Returning to Montezuma's bed and gathering the familiar leopard fur throw around her for security, she said a small prayer to the Goddess to protect him...and to give her strength as she waited.

Montezuma followed Cortez up the broad wooden steps leading to the western roof. He thought of what he was about to do, and his mind went back to a time of early adolescence. He'd proudly entered warrior training—days on end of practicing with club, shield, and bow. His young body had been covered with bruises and nicks, for once he was treated like everyone else. It was wonderful to sleep on the cold stone floor and eat out of a simple wooden bowl, just like any other boy. He wondered what happened to that boy...lost in the trappings of thrones, palaces, rich food, endless wars, and women. He thought of his old teacher, Huizal; he had gone to bed cursing that man nearly every night. No one was tougher or less forgiving, but in the end he realized that tough, arduous training had saved his life again and again. He found himself trying to remember the secret hand signals he knew when he was young. All Aztec warriors knew a whole language that could be transmitted across a battlefield.

The face of his mother came up. She'd died when he was a small child, and he'd forgotten what she looked like.

As they reached the roof he glanced at Cortez' mistress, his old friend and father-in-law's errant daughter, Dona Marina. When she caught the King's eye on her, she raised her chin to a more arrogant tilt. Yes, she was an Aztec princess through and through, perhaps even more than her older sister, his first wife, whom had been found dead in front of the palace several weeks ago. He'd wondered what she'd been doing outside the palace; he was sure it had something to do with him. Guilt rushed through him. He'd not been a good husband to her. Finally, Maria's face floated through...her fiery hair, her alabaster skin, the sound of small silver bells when she laughed. He remembered how her emerald eyes darkened when they made love. For a second he almost changed his mind from what he was going to do. Then the scene of the plaza slaughter reared its head. The screams of the women and children still echoed in his mind. He was responsible. He should have protected his people.

The heart of Montezuma constricted. His noble face took on a new resolve as he stepped to the roof edge to address his people. His words parroted Cortez. He spoke of throwing down their weapons and returning to a peaceful state, while his hands subtly signaled to his warriors that he was being used against them. His last orders were to kill him and set themselves free. His eyes found the eyes of Cualpopoca and a communication passed between them, a slight nod of his head. A volley of rocks pelted the roof…and the dying sun outlined the fallen forms of Montezuma and two Spanish guards on the darkened roof.

Cortez was furious as they carried the King's body down the stairs. What had happened? His own people had turned on him.

The door to the chamber burst open and several men came in carrying a prone body. Maria gave a startled cry when she saw Montezuma's ashen face and the dark, thick blood running from his head. The old ship's surgeon listened to the King's chest and raised one eyelid. Then looking at Maria, he said, "I'm sorry." Straightening to face Cortez, he added, "He won't live."

Cortez glanced at Maria, who looked accusingly at him. "His own people did this, not I." He turned and hurried from the room.

"Let me go! How dare you!" Maria yelled, as she pushed at the restraining arm. The two Spanish guards had crossed pikes to bar her exit. When she'd tried to dodge out, one arm had flashed upward, to restrain her. An outraged Maria had been struggling with the guards, when Cortez arrived. "How dare you hold me against my will!" cursed Maria.

Cortez looked at her coldly and said, "You are my responsibility. Your husband is dead."

"No, he's not!" yelled Maria, hating how Cortez could still reduce her to a child.

"For all purposes he is, so you will stay with me until I can deliver you to your uncle."

"I need to go to the temple. My things are there," said Maria, pushing back a lock of her hair, and changing tactics.

"Your Indian maid and your things have already been sent for, they should be here any minute," he said coldly, with a pretentious bow. Refusing to let Cortez see her cry, she stalked back to Montezuma's room.

The doctor was just leaving, and he held the door for her as she entered. Montezuma's face looked marble grey. She took her chair by his side, where she had sat since last night. Her heart seemed to be growing heavier by the minute, until she felt it too might stop beating. And now as she watched him, his spirit seemed to be gradually leaving his body, bit by bit. She had tried to use the Mother Goddess' healing techniques on him several times, but her own pain and fear had kept her from being able to connect with the healing force.

She decided to fetch either Chimalma or a healing priestess from the temple, but then remembered that now she too was a prisoner. She had called out to the High Priestess and the Goddess during the night, but it seemed her plea was falling on deaf ears. Why didn't Chimalma come? She needed her now more than ever before. She reached out and clasped one of Montezuma's waxy hands, and buried her tears there.

The tall form raised its arms in supplication...listening, hoping...still the same answer. A shudder rocked her form as she lowered her arms. She could hear Maria's plea from across the city, but she could do nothing. The Goddess had shown her what must be. All she could do was wait.

The room was getting dark, as a brazier burned in the corner. Maria stretched and yawned, while her muscles protested from having slept in a chair. She'd dreamt of running in an open field with Montezuma. They were together and free, and he was alive and healthy. She would've preferred to not have awakened from the dream at all, but she had, and her aching muscles wrenched her out of it.

As she rubbed the gritty feeling from her eyes, she noticed a woman tenderly stroking Montezuma's hair. At first she was angry and was about to order the girl from the room. With the death of Maliche, the harem now gave her the respect of First Wife, but the look of sad supplication in the girl's eyes stopped her. The wistful way she had touched Montezuma struck a cord of sympathy in

Maria. Before now, she had mostly ignored Montezuma's other wives, never having lived in the harem. He had never called them when she was there, and for the most part she saw them only during mealtime when they served the food.

In Maria's mind, they had been more like servants. Suddenly, she saw them as other women, like herself, loving the King. She realized that their hearts must be as heavy as hers. All of them had been his wife much longer than she.

Maria asked the other wife to sit down. She found out that the girl was of nobility; she'd been married to Montezuma for three years; she had a little girl a year old; and she loved the King. She looked wistfully at Maria, as she explained that Montezuma had called no other since his marriage to Maria. Only wives were here to serve; all concubines were left at the other palace. Maria watched Montezuma as the girl spoke. All the while, conflicting emotions raced through her. She felt waves of love for this man who would forsake all others for her, yet compassion for his wives who loved him dearly. The two women spoke softly for a time, then watched each other closely until Maria took the other's hand. A bond of sisterhood was forged.

The morning's light had just started to filter through the terrace door. Maria wrapped herself in a light blanket, and moved to blow out the candles the doctor had given her. It seemed so quiet in the mornings now...no drums and conches to welcome the dawn, not since that fateful festival day. Maria stood on the terrace watching an inquisitive blue jay hop across the lawn, searching for a late worm. It was June 27th...about a year ago she'd seen Montezuma for the first time. So much had happened since then. She smiled as she thought how her heart had leaped to her throat when she saw him sitting on his throne. She'd half been expecting to lose her head...she lost her heart instead.

Stepping back inside she again sat by her love's bed, waiting for Itza to bring her breakfast. Well, at least her morning sickness was over. She turned her attention to the child, who probably would never see his father. She felt it was a boy. He would certainly know of his father, she would make sure of that! Just then, she noticed

Montezuma's eyelids flutter and open.

Maria grabbed his hand, caressing his face with her other hand. His face softened, as his eyes focused on her. "You're here," he whispered. "I dreamt I was in a tunnel with a great light, but I had to see you first." He looked around the room. "It's true," he said to himself. "Listen to me. Maria you must leave for your sake, and for our child's sake." His fingers moved as though he was trying to squeeze her hand. "This city is not safe for you."

"Beloved, I won't go. I won't leave you," she cried.

"My love, I'm leaving now."

"No!" Tears rolled down her cheeks.

"No, my flame. Don't let my last memory of you be one of tears. Smile for me."

As Maria wiped away her tears, she allowed her lips to curl into a trembling smile.

"That's better. Now promise me you will leave and return to your family in Spain. I can go in peace, knowing you are safe. Promise me."

"I promise."

"Don't grieve for me. I have seen the light…and it's beautiful. I will wait for you." His last words were almost a sigh, as the Last Reverent Speaker closed his eyes, and Maria was alone in the room.

17
Night of Sorrows

Fires burned everywhere. The waterways into the palace had been smashed from the outside. Word had spread throughout the city...Montezuma was dead. An endless supply of warriors harangued without quarter, while the tired Spanish cried for relief. Their nerves at an end, they had even taken to fighting amongst themselves.

Dona Marina angrily stomped along the smoke filled corridor, kicking the hungry, slat ribbed dog that was lying across the hallway, and sending him yipping into the smoky night. Throwing open the door and ignoring all courtesies, she entered Cortez' chambers unannounced. "How could you?" she screamed, pacing the tile floor. "I should be in those rooms, not her."

Cortez, who had been speaking with an aid, sent the man away and turned to face the girl. "What can I do for you?" he said smiling, pleased to have an aversion from the siege.

"You put her in the King's chambers; they were promised to me. She lives in a rich set of rooms, while I suffer in one small room." In actuality, Dona Marina's room had tapestries on the walls, onyx tables, and fur rugs on the floor.

"I need to keep her in a safe, secure spot. The dead King's chambers are perfect. Besides, she was the King's wife."

"Baah, the King had many wives, all more important than her. Put her in the harem! I am a king's daughter, they should be mine." Dona Marina claimed her parentage when it suited her.

Growing tired of her jealous tampering, Cortez said, "I have put her where I see fit. She will stay there."

"No, put her in the harem! I demand my rights," the girl

stormed.

"I'll decide what your rights are," Cortez barked angrily.

Undaunted, Dona Marina continued, "How dare you put that upstart ahead of me!"

"She's important to my plans. She may be a pain and a nuisance, but she's the niece of the Governor of Cuba, and I intend to deliver her back to him."

"Important! That hideous red haired freak...I'll tear her eyes out, then we will see how important she is to you. She is nothing!"

"Touch her and you'll be given to the ugliest, meanest man I have," warned Cortez.

Her eyes widened at his cold threat. Once again she had gone too far. Thinking quickly she stepped closer, cooing while she ran her fingers suggestively along Cortez' shoulder. "Forgive me lord. I just want to love you so much, I am jealous. I bow to your wishes of course. The Governor's niece is important to you, as such I will gladly do as you wish."

"Good...now run along, I'm busy," Cortez admonished.

Dona Marina left the room with a new resolve. She had to get rid of the Spanish whore somehow. She couldn't chance Cortez turning to one of his own women now, not after all she had done. She was determined to be Queen over those who had betrayed her. Maria was in the way and she would do whatever was needed to be rid of her, but Cortez must never know the action was hers; there was no doubt he would be true to his threat. Since De Aguilar had become proficient in Nahuatl, she was now replaceable and would never be missed. Shuddering, she remembered the look in his eyes. She couldn't push him; she would have to get her way through other means. Cortez had to retreat from the city soon, but would return to take over the Aztec capital. No other woman but she, would be at his side then. Of his Spanish wife she gave no thought at all. Hurrying away, she plotted Maria's demise.

"Look sharp you," Cortez bellowed. The men were loading the gold in sacks—some to be tied to the horses, the rest to be carried by the men. It had been calmer the last two days, so Cortez chose this particular night to leave. Some of his men were in better spirits now, believing the Aztecs were tired, or all fought out. But Cortez knew they were regrouping and probably planning a new strategy, and he didn't want to be around when they implemented it. His plan was to use this calm to escape.

The men were taking as much gold as they could stuff in their pouches, pockets, and saddlebags…even draping gold ornaments and statues across their mounts. The amount was foolishly in excess, but they were being happily carried by the wings of greed. Hastily they packed the exorbitant goods that would prove to be the death of many on that night. Cortez carried only what could be tied to Colorado without weighing down the horse, plus a small bag of perfect emeralds tucked inside his shirt. He'd seen Sandoval take only a bag of gold dust, and now he was trying to get the rest of the soldiers to quit loading themselves down, but his warnings were falling on deaf ears. Finally, Sandoval gave up and walked away shrugging his shoulders.

In the hallway a group of women huddled together, with black shawls pulled over their heads in mourning. The small children with them were wide eyed at all the activity. Itza was sitting in the corner with a small child cradled in her arms when Maria joined the group. She stroked the little girl's glossy black hair, realizing it was the little girl with the jade bracelet at the picnic long ago. Her heart broke when the child raised sad, employing eyes to her. Her young life had been shattered…she'd been taken from her home, her father murdered, and now she was about to start a long journey into an angry night.

Maria looked at the sad group of women and children. Cortez was forcing them to come with him, thinking that having Montezuma's wives and royal children would protect him from the Aztec wrath. She met the eyes of her new friend Shasa, and the two wives exchanged a knowing glance.

Suddenly, weary, Maria sat down leaning her head against Itza's knees. The last year seemed like a lifetime, now she felt numb. Itza's warm hand rested on Maria's head and she looked up at her face, noting the new strands of silver painted in the woman's hair. Itza's eyes told her to be strong for the baby's sake. She felt a flood of love for this Indian woman who'd become her foster mother.

She turned her thoughts to her other mother in Spain. Maria

knew she would be seeing her soon, and wondered how she would react to her marriage and this new life she carried within her. There would be a quarrel for sure, her mother was a proud woman. She'd be angry at what Maria had done to her marriage prospects at court. She knew her mother loved her under that haughty facade, but what about her child? What of Montezuma's son? How would she—and the rest of Spain for that matter—react to this half-Aztec prince? Itza would be with her; the woman had promised her. She would help Maria take care of the child, and she would hold her head proudly. She knew there'd be those who'd scorn her, but she'd let no one make her feel shame...after all, she was a Dowager Queen.

She thought of the orchards behind her father's house. She would take her son to play there, just as she had once done. Perhaps not everything will be that bad, she thought. Perhaps it would be good to go home.

She stared at the brightly painted ceiling in the hallway, as if seeing it for the first time. It reminded her of the throne room, where she had waited with such fear the time she first saw Montezuma. Montezuma's face stole through her mind. A smile played across his lips—the kind he had when he teased her just before they made love. His face was replaced...first by Chimalma's, then Taka's, Shera's, and Taxca's. In her mind she could see the city as it looked when she first entered it, and then she saw the Temple of the Goddess...and again Montezuma's face passed before her.

She had tasted love—a taste she would live on the rest of her life. No matter what her mother said, she'd never marry again...she couldn't. But she would do everything in her power to teach the Spanish about the Aztec people. She would talk of her friends. Somehow she would make the Spanish understand, so they would leave this great civilization alone.

The sacred pyramid suddenly loomed before her, the face of Quetzalcoatl; he seemed to be trying to tell her something. He was joined by the Mother Goddess. She strained trying to hear the inner message, but it faded. She opened her eyes. It must have been a validation, she thought! It was her next mission from the Mother Goddess to serve as a gobetween for the two races. Her heart began to open, and she knew she could go on. Suddenly, they were jostled to their feet.

"Wait little one." Maria smiled at Itza still calling her little one. The woman stood on her tiptoes to pull the shawl more securely over Maria's head; she tucked the fiery wisps in, and pulled it to shade her face. "I don't want you to get a chill," Itza said sweetly. Maria squeezed the woman's hand. It was a warm summer night and she knew Itza had only done it to conceal her identity.

Leading Colorado, Cortez signaled the gate to open. It was decided that the horses would be walked from the city, since a mounted rider would make too easy of a target. Sandoval sidled in close by Maria, using his body and his horse as a shield for the women. As they passed through the gate Maria held her breath, half-expecting to be greeted by war whoops, but the plaza was quiet. Sadly, Maria directed her attention to the darkened pyramid. In the distance, she could vaguely see the familiar gates of the Mother Goddess Temple, and in her heart she said her farewells to Chimalma and the city she loved. She'd been told that the High Priestess, herself, had come to the palace requesting the body of the King. Surprisingly, Cortez had given it to her. A distant dog's bark rang through the night, but no other sound greeted the silent retreat.

Just ahead of her, one of the royal children broke into a wail, quickly stifled by her worried mother. Maria stroked the withers of Sandoval's horse, as it plodded silently along on padded and wrapped hoofs. She'd had a strange dream last night. It was similar to the scene the Mother had shown her at the pyramid…Montezuma wearing another face and body. He was wearing pants that left his legs bare, and a bright, close fitting shirt. He smiled, and pointed a little black box at her that suddenly flashed. Up in the sky a monstrous silver bird glided by with a great rumble. What could it mean? Was Montezuma trying to communicate with her? What a strange way to do so! Suddenly, a woman's cry rang through the night. They'd been spotted.

The refugees began to run. Soon an arrow whizzed overhead, then another bounced off the helmet of one of the conquistadors. As angry cries erupted all around them, an Aztec warrior swooped in and attacked a heavily gold laden man, his burdened movement bringing him to his death.

Sandoval parried a war club, and ran the warrior through with his sword. Pushing Maria and Itza back, he yelled for the soldiers to get rid of the extra gold. Maria watched in horror as a volley of arrows caught one of Montezuma's wives, and she fell clutching the vibrating shaft. All along the column the greedily weighted down men began falling to the Aztecs as they refused to relinquish their booty...thus they fought their way through the streets.

When at last they reached one of the canals they found that the bridge had been removed, leaving them stranded. All at once warriors crowded into the street behind them, effectively cutting off their retreat. Thinking quickly, Cortez formed two lines of artillery, firing in rotation to keep the main body of warriors at bay. Meanwhile, Sandoval arranged to have the horses pull down a nearby stone roof and maneuver it across the canal. Cortez, yelling to make himself heard above the roaring guns, directed the women and children against the wall. A young prince of about nine bolted from the group, and reaching the canal's edge he leaped into the inky water below. Maria smiled when she heard the sound of swimming...he'd made good his escape.

At last the makeshift bridge was ready. Cortez slowly made his way across with two horses to test its strength. Satisfied he motioned for the rest to follow. Maria was halfway across when the war canoes turned the corner. The way was now jammed, and not being able to go forward a panicked horse balked and reared in confusion. Maria and Itza turned to go back, but the press of bodies made that way impossible too. The canoes were directly under the bridge now, and she screamed as an arrow whizzed past her—inches from her face. As the packed bodies behind her pushed relentlessly forward, she slipped on a pool of blood and fell to her knees. Almost being knocked off the side and into the canal, she was suddenly lifted upright, with Itza and Sandoval on either side of her.

Just ahead a warrior leaped to the bridge, intent on killing Alvarado...who ducked. The war club buried itself in Shasa's shoulder. Maria cried out and ran toward her new friend just as she toppled backward into the canal, carrying her small daughter with her. Maria leaned over the edge and reached for her, but was horrified as the dark water closed over the child's face.

Sandoval pushed her forward. Reaching the other side, she turned once more to the spot where Shasa had disappeared. Maria hoped that a warrior had perhaps fished her from the canal, but there was no sight of her. She turned back and pushed on, as another gold laden soldier fell to his death at her feet.

Suddenly, Itza cried out behind her. Maria turned as the old woman fell to her knees. She rushed to her side, looking around for a now vanished Sandoval. A feathered shaft stuck out from Itza's back, and Maria cried out as she tried to raise her...to no avail. Spying a fallen roof piece, Maria pulled her foster mother under it.

Dona Marina cringed against the wall, as she hid behind Colorado. She too wore a black mourning shawl, so as to not stand out from the other women. Finally, the arquebuses cleared the way ahead, and the desperate column started to move forward. She had seen the Spanish girl's maid fall and the girl pull her under a broken roof section. She was about to call Cortez' attention to it, when she remembered her plan...and said nothing. If the Spanish one gets separated she will surely die, she thought; no one would need to accuse me of anything.

Tears filled her eyes, as Maria pulled her shawl off and made a pillow for Itza's head. She debated whether or not to pull the arrow out. Finally, breaking its shaft she pulled Itza into her arms to comfort her. She racked her mind trying to figure out a plan to get her back to the temple. Tansa would know what to do! She held Itza for a long time, as tears streamed down her cheeks and chin. "God...oh why? First my love, now Itza...please don't take her," she cried.

When she felt Itza's hand grip hers, she looked down. Itza's eyes were open, and they studied her with a sad expression. "No, no little one...don't cry for Itza. I live good full life, but you just begin. Only sad I won't see your baby."

"Yes you will. I won't let you die," cried Maria.

"You are the daughter I lost. I love you but ..." A coughing spasm caused a little trickle of blood to run from the corner of her mouth. "Itza can't stay with you. The gods make these decisions, not us. If there is another place after this, Itza will find your beloved and we wait for you. Now leave me, let an old woman die."

"No! I won't go!" Maria held her closer.

"You are stubborn, little one," she said, mildly rebuking. Her eyes got a faraway look; her voice was faint, her face pale. "I told you this place held my death," she breathed.

Maria held her body for a long time. She stroked her silvered hair, imprinting her dear, wrinkled face on her mind forever. With a start, she realized Itza had spoken perfect Nahuatl. Had she been fooling around about her broken speech all along? Or was she manifesting the gifts of spirit at the end? Her final words haunted Maria, as she covered Itza's face and climbed out from under the roof piece.

The street was deserted. A gentle rain started to fall, washing blood from the fallen bodies, and trickling along the pavement stones. For a moment she thought about following the Spanish out of the city. She had promised Montezuma she'd leave Tenochtitlan, but judging by the amount of fallen conquistadors, Cortez might not even make it out. Besides, there would be many wounded Aztecs after this; maybe they would want her help as a healing priestess. In a daze of mourning, she began to wander back toward the temple, where she might find someone left that she loved.

As she turned the corner, she spotted a Jaguar Knight standing over one of the fallen Spanish. With disdain, he rolled the man over with his foot. Spotting a sacred jade necklace he pulled it from the man's shirt, intending on returning it to the temple. At Maria's approach his eyes widened, then went hard. Maria was surprised at the look of hatred the warrior shot her, and then she realized her shawl had been left behind with Itza...her identity was revealed. She took a few more tentative steps toward him. Cualpopoca's eyes roamed Maria's body, and shortly took on another quality before settling back to rage.

"Witch!" he hissed.

"Leave me alone," Maria said calmly.

"What? Did you come back to gloat at your evil deeds, witch?" he asked, pointing to the fallen body of one of Montezuma's children.

"I didn't do this. I never wanted this to happen, I tried to prevent it. I told Montezuma not to let Cortez come here."

"You lie, witch!!"

"Why do you call me witch?" Maria noted her own calm as she faced the angry man.

"Because you bewitched me, just as you bewitched the King. You'll not work your evil here anymore," he said, as he raised his war club in menace and swung. Surprised by her resolve, he stayed his hand in midswing...and what was meant to be a killing blow, just injured her. Maria fell to her knees, clutching her head and coughing blood. "Thank you," she uttered.

Cualpopoca stood back, bewildered. "Why didn't you run?" he demanded.

"I have no desire to live without Montezuma, my love."

"You love Montezuma," he said, the truth coming to him. You're not a witch then?"

She gasped and raised her eyebrows, as if to say no. Cualpopoca felt his shame reflected in her glassy emerald eyes. Quickly his senses called to him to put her out of her misery. This was, at least, the only befitting thing to offer his young Queen...now in such pain.

"Forgive me, my lady," he said, as he struck a killing blow to her skull. As the darkness became a tunnel of light Maria saw Montezuma standing in front of her, wearing a white loincloth and mantle; a tall headdress of iridescent plumes graced his head. He smiled, held his arms out to her, and beckoned her home.

Later that night, when the gentle rain had washed much of the blood from the streets, a tall, cloaked figure accompanied by several Eagle Warriors searched the streets. Chimalma let out a sad sigh upon sighting Maria's crumbled form...right where the Goddess had shown her. She motioned for one of the warriors to pick up Maria's body. Tenderly she pushed a shorn lock back from the girl's face, noting the peaceful look. She ordered the warrior to carry Maria back to the temple, where she would be buried alongside Montezuma in the secret tunnels, as the Goddess had ordered. Now, she had to hurry...the night was late and she had much to do.

Meanwhile, somewhere in the city a proud Jaguar Knight carried a lock of fiery red hair. His personal code of honor demanded he carry the hair as the spirit of the one he had wronged...that she might live on in the memories of the gods.

Epilogue

June 30, 1520, Cortez fought his way from Tenochtitlan on what became known as "The Night of Sorrows." On this night, he lost a good portion of his men and most of the gold. Of the six wives and eighteen of Montezuma's children he'd forced to leave with him, not one survived. Cortez, however, made his way to the coast, and gathered a larger force and many more cannons. He returned to Tenochtitlan, mounted his cannons on boats, and continuously bombed the once beautiful city until it was near rubble; then, the water supply into the city was cut by smashing the viaducts. Bombarded, starved, thirsty, and riddled with another gift from the Spanish—smallpox—the proud Aztecs finally fell.

Cortez entered the city, intent on recovering the gold…but it was nowhere to be found. He tortured and burned several people until he found one old temple attendant. The old man told him that on The Night of Sorrows the priests and priestesses of the temples had gathered the gold together, and taken it to their ancestral sacred mountain far to the north, where the Spanish would never find it.

Many Spanish expeditions in search of this gold were mounted in the area now known as the southwestern United States, but the Aztec gods triumphed…for it was never found.

Linguistic experts tie Aztecs and Apaches together, and some legends have it that the very same gold carried from Tenochtitlan is buried in the Superstition Mountains in Arizona, sacred to the Apache.

One thing is for sure…the two great races—carried through the bloodlines of the European whites and the red Native Americans—still battle for supremacy. Perhaps soon…once again…Quetzalcoatl will come and set the dance in balance. Yes, Quetzalcoatl shall come and set the dance in balance.